"A gritty, realistic look at the dangers of meth, *Full Tilt* takes readers on one serious roller-coaster ride. Hang on."

BILL MYERS
BESTSELLING AUTHOR OF *THE PRESENCE*

"With a cast of captivating characters and a plotline as taut as one of Everett Lester's guitar strings, Creston Mapes has delivered a riveting tale of intrigue, the rock and roll subculture—and divine destiny. *Full Tilt* is a superb story from a gifted storyteller."

MARK MYNHEIR
AUTHOR OF *FROM THE BELLY OF THE DRAGON*

"Fast-paced, intriguing, and compelling—and yet this page-turner pauses to display grace, too. I appreciate the author's willingness to tackle a subject that many shy away from—the devastating consequences of this country's growing methamphetamine problem. Well, done, Creston! My husband and I both enjoyed it."

MELODY CARLSON
AWARD-WINNING AUTHOR OF *CRYSTAL LIES*
AND THE DIARY OF A TEENAGE GIRL SERIES

"Creston Mapes has scored another knockout with this tale of addiction, darkness, and redemption. *Full Tilt* is an emotional, psychological thrill ride that will leave you breathless."

BRIAN PALMER
STAFF REVIEWER FOR *INFUZE* MAGAZINE
AND AUTHOR OF *THE LAST PAGE*

"My son dove into Crestion's first novel, *Dark Star,* and devoured it. This, from a young man who doesn't read much! I know what book I'm getting for him next—*Full Tilt!*"

BESTSELLING AUT ... NN
... ES

"*Full Tilt* rocks! With compelling characters and intriguing plot, Creston Mapes delivers a compulsive novel that will leave you in eager anticipation for the next Rock Star Chronicles installment."

VENESSA NG
ASSISTANT EDITOR, FOCUS ON FICTION

"Creston Mapes keeps this *Dark Star* sequel going *Full Tilt* to the very last page. Another real page-turner, Creston weaves a story as compelling as it is powerful. I've been waiting impatiently for this follow-up to *Dark Star*, and it truly delivers! Well worth the wait…and well worth the read. I plan on reading anything this author writes."

WANDA DYSON
CRITICALLY ACCLAIMED AUTHOR OF POLICE THRILLERS
ABDUCTION, *OBSESSION*, AND *INTIMIDATION*

"*Full Tilt is* good old-fashioned evangelism wrapped in a modern, street-smart novel. For those about to rock, Mapes salutes you…with fast-paced stories full of memorable characters."

ERIC WILSON
AUTHOR OF *EXPIRATION DATE*
AND *DARK TO MORTAL EYES*

"A fine blend of character and plot. Creston Mapes reconciles apparent contradictions of life with integrity and imagination."

BARBARA MCINTYRE
AKRON BEACON JOURNAL

"Creston Mapes draws a compelling portrait of an uncertain Christian trying to escape his sordid past—and demonstrates a gift of building an almost unbearable level of suspense in every situation."

CHRIS WELL
AUTHOR OF *DELIVER US FROM EVELYN*

THE ROCK STAR CHRONICLES
BOOK TWO

FULL TILT

A NOVEL

c r e s t o n
m a p e s

Multnomah® Publishers *Sisters, Oregon*

FULL TILT
published by Multnomah Publishers, Inc.

Published in association with the literary agency of Mark Sweeney & Associates,
28540 Altessa Way, Bonita Springs, Florida 34135
© 2006 by Creston Mapes, Inc.
International Standard Book Number: 1-59052-506-X

Cover image by Daly & Newton/Getty Images

Unless otherwise indicated, Scripture quotations are from:
New American Standard Bible ©1960, 1977, 1995
by the Lockman Foundation. Used by permission.
Other Scripture quotations are from:
The Living Bible (TLB) © 1971. Used by permission of Tyndale House Publishers, Inc.
All rights reserved.

Multnomah is a trademark of Multnomah Publishers, Inc., and is registered in the U.S. Patent and Trademark Office. The colophon is a trademark of Multnomah Publishers, Inc.

Printed in the United States of America

For information:
MULTNOMAH PUBLISHERS, INC. • 601 N. LARCH STREET • SISTERS, OREGON 97759

Library of Congress Cataloging-in-Publication Data
Mapes, Creston, 1961-
Full tilt : a novel / Creston Mapes.
p. cm.
ISBN 1-59052-506-X
1. Rock musicians—Fiction. I. Title.
PS3613.A63F85 2006
813'.6—dc22

2005031140

06 07 08 09 10—10 9 8 7 6 5 4 3 2 1 0

For Patty,
Since we were children, I knew you were the one.
I'm ever indebted for your love and faith during this journey.

ACKNOWLEDGMENTS

When we're in the book-writing mode, my family has endless patience and understanding. To Patty, Abigail, Hannah, Esther, and Creston—thanks for your love, joy, hope, and prayers. I treasure our family!

The team at Multnomah is fantastic. Julee Schwarzburg is a magnificent editor—creative and what an eye for detail! Thanks for teaching me, Julee. There's a family hard at work behind the scenes at Multnomah to whom I'm grateful, including Chris Sundquist, Penny Whipps, Sharon Znachko, Nancy Childers, Lesley Warr, Angela Jones, Tiffany Lauer, Renee Akaka, Kevin Marks, Doug Gabbert, Don Jacobson, Chris Crosby, Darren Henry, Chad Hicks, Cheryl Reinertson, Jason Myhre, Dave Sheets, Cliff Boersma, Brian Flagler, and many others.

Several people helped with insights and details about various aspects of this story. My heartfelt thanks to Randy Powell, Rick Estes, Craig Smith, Mary Young, and Sergeant James Russo, NYPD.

We've enjoyed incomparable support from some very kind folks in the industry. My gratitude to Dianne Burnett, Ellie Schroder, Rick Stevens, Tony Hines, Dee Stewert, Brian Palmer, Vennessa Ng, Sheila Zbosnik, Gregg Hart, and Building 429.

Several fine writers have taken time to coach me in the business and spiritual aspects of the game. Thanks for your encouragement Robin Jones Gunn, Bill Myers, Mark Mynheir, James Scott Bell, Melanie Wells, Wanda Dyson, Kathy Herman, and Melody Carlson.

A very special thanks to all of our readers! And, for those who encourage me just by being there, thank you Steve Vibert, Bern Mapes, the Buechlers, Frank Donchess, Paul Ryden, Bill Hayden, Mindy and Bill Root, friends at CCSM and CCG, the Byrds, Bernie and Anita Mapes, Gary LaFerla, and the gang at Stein.

Full Tilt and *Dark Star* wouldn't be in print if it were not for my agent, Mark Sweeney, who is one of the finest gentlemen I know. And his wife's quite special, too. Thanks, Janet.

Praise be to Jesus Christ, who's given me the delight of my heart and deserves all the credit for these novels. May they glorify You, Lord.

*"If you search for good you will find God's favor;
if you search for evil you will find his curse."*

PROVERBS 11:27, TLB

Black night. Familiar backstreets. Windows down. Cold air. Cruisin' free.

Top of the world.

This was what it was about, baby. Lit on meth and movin' at what seemed like the speed of light.

Lords of the night.

Over to Fender's Body Shop on autopilot. Hands drumming on the dash and seats to the beat of the night and the pulse of the blood pounding through their veins.

Down the slope.

Whoa.

Past the dimly lit customer entrance and around back of the shop the Yukon swung and jerked to a stop. One, two, three of them exited the SUV and glided through the gate that was cracked open.

Wesley Lester was last to pass through the high chain-link fence. He slowed to peer at the snow-covered wreckage way out back of the shop, much of which had sat unchanged, like an eerie sculpture, for months beneath a haze of dim yellow lights. Dozens of mangled cars and pickups, SUVs, a hearse, vans, and an old school bus sat like jagged headstones in a haunted cemetery, some piled one on top of the other.

Several hundred yards away, in the vicinity of the far lamppost, David Lester's black Camaro lay still and sinister. Wesley's little brother and two teenage friends had perished in that car with David at the wheel. Seventeen years old. Too dang young to die.

After having rushed to the surreal scene of the wreck in nearby White Plains a year ago, Wesley had never ventured back to reexamine the remnants of his little brother's car—or the totaled Chrysler that carried an elderly couple from Scarsdale, also pronounced dead at the scene.

On the way toward the huge body shop, Wesley shivered at the chill of the New York winter—a feeling his little brother would never experience again. Grinding his teeth, Wesley ran several yards, bashing the already dented door of a white Beamer. Spinning away, he welcomed the sense of release, thrust his dead brother out of his jumpy mind, and followed the others.

Brubaker led the way through the employee entrance, slamming open the heavy steel door against the outside of the fabricated beige metal building. "Ah, smell that?" he said, not looking back. "Good ol' Bondo. Be high all day if you worked in here."

Wesley cruised in last, leaving the door wide open and purposefully taking a giant whiff of the pungent air that reeked of metal and plastic dust.

Like mice, the three figures zigzagged through a maze of half-repaired vehicles toward an area that glowed white, back in the far corner of the building.

As they drew closer to the dancing light and long shadows, hard-driving music mixed with the static sound of a welder. A dark blue '65 Mustang sat up on a hydraulic lift, and beneath it—behind a welding hood—stood Tony Badino.

Brubaker and Wesley came to a standstill, fascinated by the sparks that rained down on Tony's dirty, charcoal coveralls and scuffed brown work boots; the kid stopped between them, equally entranced.

Tony must have seen them but went on welding like a macho man, his brawny legs braced apart, tool belt hanging low around his lean waist, broad shoulders and triceps locked in place as he hoisted the blazing welder.

Brubaker was like a four-year-old. Constant motion. Bobbing his head, singing unintelligibly, rubbing his face and arms, and repeatedly peering back toward the door and out the dirty windows. His paranoia was enough to make anybody start seeing things. The kid in the middle watched spellbound as Tony melded metal to metal.

In the scalding flame, Wesley remembered his brother, curly haired and anxious, slapping a twenty-dollar bill into his hand for a teener—one-sixteenth of an ounce of some of the best crank Wesley had ever come across. Then he flashed back to David's demolished Camaro hours later—what was left of the engine, parts of the car scattered along Post Road, still smoking.

Once again Wesley was slapped in the face by the fact that he was the one who had poisoned his brother's bloodstream the day he drove to his death.

No. No. No!

It wasn't the meth that killed his brother. It was the years of Everett Lester's tainted music that had contaminated David's mind. It was Everett's empty promises and repeated letdowns that had sent David longing for the grave and a so-called better life on the Other Side. And Everett would burn for it; uncle or no uncle, he would pay. Because Wesley was hearing the voice again.

Wesley actually jerked when Tony snapped back the flame, lowered the welder in his right hand, and flipped the dark visor up with the other.

"Boys." He eyed the dazed kid in the middle.

"This is the dude we told you about, from Yonkers," Brubaker yelled proudly above the music, rubbing at the insides of his elbows with his wrists. "Needs an ounce."

Tony extinguished the pilot on the welder, lowered it to the concrete floor by its cord, then walked over to the stereo and turned it off.

"Slow down, Brubaker." Tony shook off his big, stiff gloves and removed the hood to reveal a tough face with small, pronounced features and a glistening scalp covered only by what looked like about two weeks' worth of brown hair.

Reaching inside the front waist pocket of his coveralls, Tony pulled out a silver Zippo and a pack of Marlboros. Tapping one out, he stuffed it in the side of his little mouth and lit it with a grimy hand. As he took a long drag and snatched the cigarette away with his left hand, Wesley noticed a small tattoo of an upside-down cross on the inside of his wrist.

Tony was one creepy dude. Knew what he wanted. Had kind of a fiendish aura about him. People were naturally scared of the guy. Maybe that's why Wesley liked running with Tony, because it was risky and unpredictable. That gave him a rush. And it didn't hurt that Tony always had the best jenny crank on the street.

Grabbing a hanger light from the frame of the Mustang, Tony walked beneath his work, inspecting the length of the exhaust system.

"How do you know Lester and Brubaker?" He tapped the muffler, cig in hand.

"Uh…a friend introduced me to Wesley at a party," the middle kid said.

"When?"

"Last week."

"And Brubaker?"

"Met him a couple nights later."

"Been tweekin'?"

"Uh…when do you mean?" The kid's eyes darted to Bru then Wesley.

"Tonight." Tony stopped and stared at him.

"Earlier today," Wesley interrupted. "Couple teeners."

Tony went back to inspecting his work. "That same stuff from the other day?"

"Yeah. Finished it off." Wesley coughed, feeling somewhat like a raw recruit reporting for duty before some high-ranking officer.

"This new cristy blows that stuff away." Tony glanced at the three visitors, his right eye twitching. "Just in from Pennsylvania. Keep you amped for days. I've been workin' nonstop since yesterday—goin' on, what? Thirty-five hours?"

Brubaker and the stranger nodded, swayed, and laughed. Wesley simply stared, promising himself he wouldn't bow down to the grease monkey like everybody else.

"So you need an ounce." Tony held the light up close to the tailpipe.

"Yep," piped up the kid in the middle.

"Good old Wesley Lester. I can always count on him to bring me the finest clientele." Tony nodded toward Wesley. "Do you know who this guy is? Who brought you here tonight?"

The kid stared at Tony with hollowed eyes and shrugged.

"This is the great Everett Lester's nephew. Bet you didn't know that."

What the heck?

The kid turned to Wesley. "No way."

"Straight," said Tony. "You're in the presence of the bloodline of one of rock 'n' roll's greatest legends."

"Dude," the kid exclaimed, "I saw one of their *very last* shows—at The Meadowlands. They played three and a half hours, at least."

"With Aerosmith," Tony chimed in. "I was there. Wesley was supposed to be there backstage, but Uncle Everett stood him up."

"That's cold," Brubaker mumbled.

Silently, expressionlessly, Wesley agreed.

Tony smirked at Bru, but it went right over the head of the kid in the middle.

"I lived and breathed DeathStroke," the kid said. "Lester was so stoned out of his mind that last show, he could barely stand by the end. But they jammed their *hearts* out."

"And now he's a Jesus freak." Tony's eyes shifted to meet Wesley's, but his head didn't move.

Wesley met his glance without flinching. His nostrils flared and his temper cranked up like the flame on the welder. He searched Tony's face for the reason he would be trying to push Wesley's buttons.

The kid in the middle picked up on the friction.

Tony smirked, knelt down, and began banging his tools into the drawers of a tall red metal toolbox on wheels.

"What's he like, anyway?" the kid barged ahead. "Everett Lester, I mean…"

Brubaker looked uneasy, twisting and bouncing slightly on his toes.

"He's a loser, okay?" Wesley snapped, walking over to a workbench cluttered with jars of nuts and bolts and old tools. "Dude's a lyin' hypocrite. Dang *waste of breath*!"

"Where does he live?" the kid asked. "Does he still have a place in Manhattan?"

Wesley's back was to the others. He fingered the tools without a word. *I wonder if he'd shut up if I heaved this jar of bolts at his head.*

Brubaker ran interference. "He has a farm near Bedford and a place in Kansas—where his wife's from."

"Oh yeah, that chick who converted him," the kid said.

Tony slammed the middle drawer closed.

"That was some story. I heard she wrote to him ever since she was like a teenager—Jesus this and Jesus that. And finally it stuck…can you believe that? The guy went off the deep end!"

Tony stood, banging another drawer shut. "Some people hit you over the head again and again with that Jesus hype till you're brainwashed. Seen it happen."

"Well, look at the guy," the kid said. "I mean…he's changed! I saw him and his wife on *Larry King Live* and he, I mean, it's like he's a different person—"

"Let's do this deal!" With three long strides and a commanding kick, Wesley booted a large piece of scrap metal twenty feet across the dusty white floor.

The corners of Tony's mouth curved up into a quick smile as he raised an eyebrow at the kid in the middle, stomped out his cigarette, and walked over to an old white sink. Pushing up his sleeves, he rinsed his hands and squeezed a glob of gray goop into his palm from a bright orange bottle.

"You got the cash?" he asked the kid above the running water.

"Yeah, yeah." The kid dug almost frantically into his front pocket and pulled out a clump of folded bills.

"Count it, Wes," Tony ordered, still washing.

Wesley hesitated before snatching the wad and rifling quickly through the bills. "Fifteen hundred. It's here."

Tony dried his hands with a dirty towel, wiped his face with it, and looked at himself in the smudged mirror above the sink. Then he found the kid's reflection in the mirror. "You don't know where this devil dust came from."

"Oh…d-definitely n-not." He smiled anxiously. "I don't even know you. We never met, as far as I'm concerned. Nope. Never met."

Tony dropped the towel on the edge of the sink and walked to the tool chest. Lifting the top, he pulled out a Tech .22 assault pistol with his right hand and a good-sized bag of off-white, crystal-like powder with the other. Turning, he tossed the bag to the kid, who fumbled it awkwardly but mangled it at the last second before it escaped his hands. Embarrassing.

"You hear about the body that turned up in Canarsie other day? In the scrap yard?" Tony approached the kid, whose forehead was glistening with sweat.

Here we go. Wesley wished Tony hadn't picked up the gun but, at the same time, found it strangely exciting.

"Uh...no." The kid eyed the piece. "No, I missed that."

"Well, don't *miss* what I'm telling you." Tony's voice grew vicious as he neared the kid's face. "That guy had it comin', okay? I know that for a *fact.*"

The kid's mouth was wide open, big eyes flashing, cheeks red as radishes.

"He was blabbin' about *where* he got his rocket fuel."

"Listen, I..."

But before the kid could eke out another word, Tony lifted the modified Tech .22 sideways, shoulder-high, squinted, and blasted six rounds across the base of the metal wall beneath the workbench with one squeeze of the trigger.

Brubaker floundered back four feet as the smell of gunpowder hung in the air and the rattle of gunfire echoed in their ears.

The kid's red face went ash white, and he looked as if he might lose his dinner.

Wesley kept a stone face, not wanting to show a trace of the fear that was making his hands shake.

"You know how many twenty-twos this mag carries?" Tony grabbed the fat magazine with his free hand.

The kid jerked his head in one rapid no.

"Twenty. And I got it rigged so I pull the trigger once and the thing can unload. You understand?"

The kid opened his mouth, but nothing came out.

"Word on the street is, the dude in Canarsie was a rat-squealing tell-all." Tony lightly tossed the Tech .22 in his right hand. "He got himself *whacked* for blabbing."

"Oh...don't worry—"

"And *the same* will happen to you if you tell one soul where you got that cristy, you read?"

"Oh, hey, I read, I read. I'm not about to—"

"Now beat it!" Tony hoisted the weapon up to his shoulder and the kid scrambled an about-face, practically sprinting for the door with a blubbering Brubaker right on his heels.

Badino's dark eyes locked in on Wesley, followed by the cock of his head and a smirk. "He ain't gonna do no talkin', now is he, Wes?"

Wesley watched the two figures scurry into the darkness. "No, I don't believe so."

As Tony banged the Tech .22 back into the toolbox, two things occurred to Wesley: 1) He would love to see the bullets from that weapon rip through Everett Lester's sickening, superspiritual flesh, and 2) if you ever wanted to commit a murder, Tony Badino was probably a very good person to know.

2

"I'm about to go on." Everett Lester sat hunched over a wooden bench in a carpeted locker room, his head almost buried between his knees, speaking into a tiny cell phone.

"I'm so excited for you," his sister said. "It's been a long time coming. Are you psyched?"

Chanting and foot stomping from the thundering crowd one floor above reverberated around him in Queens Arena.

He stood. "I'm feeling weird."

"What's wrong?"

He found a row of sinks and looked at himself in the big mirror. "I feel like bailing."

"What are you saying? You were made to perform!"

He got close, examining his intense brown eyes. Somehow, looking beyond them into his restless soul. "I guess I'm worried about what people are expecting…"

"What people?"

"Everybody. Fans. Reporters. Former DeathStrokers. The whole world. Everybody's watching."

"Since when have you cared what other people think?"

"I've got to set a good example, Mary."

"I know, but—"

"I had a guy chew me out at the Pro-Am in Pebble Beach." Everett hoisted himself onto the countertop. "He told me his fifteen-year-old, who'd heard I was saved, got there at seven in the morning to follow me around for eighteen holes. But he followed me for four and went back to the clubhouse. You know why?"

She waited in silence.

"I was complaining about the pin placements…"

"And?"

"I must've said something raunchy; it was an accident. I didn't know anyone was listening. I'm not perfect!"

"Nobody is—"

"He gave up on me! Told his dad I couldn't be a Christian."

"Ev, God knows your heart—"

"Yeah, but I'm under a microscope!"

"So what? Most people are gonna like what they see."

"I just feel like I need to be this…saint." He hopped off the ledge.

"Who else is making you feel that way? Not Karen?"

"Sometimes I feel like I'm supposed to know the Bible as well as her dad," Everett said. "Like I'm supposed to lead her in spiritual things. Heck, she knows the Bible better than I do. But it's like she's waiting for me to step up and be this mature leader—overnight."

"And you're—"

"I'm not there!" He swung around and peered at the "new" Everett Lester in the mirror. All tidied up. Short hair. Tattoos gone from his wrists and the back of his neck. "I'm trying. I love the Word. I love what God's done in my life, and what He's doing—"

"That's enough, Ev!"

"No, it's not! It doesn't *feel* like enough. You can't imagine the expectations. I'm telling you right now, I can't carry the load. People are just waiting for me to blow it."

"You don't have to be someone you're not!"

"That's exactly what I feel like." A mixture of regret and frustration stirred as he ran a hand through his two-inch-long brown hair and examined the long-sleeved sweater he wouldn't have been caught dead in two years ago. "Why do you think I cut my hair and had those tattoos removed? Why am I livin' on a farm in Bedford, New York?"

"What are you saying? You feel some guilt complex about 'looking' the way society says a Christian's supposed to look?"

"That's part of it."

"What else?"

"I wanna be what Karen and her folks want me to be."

"You don't need to change for Karen or Sarah and Jacob. I know them. They don't think about that stuff."

He turned away from his image, knowing she was right.

"Let me ask you something. Are you feeling pressure from God to be this overnight spiritual sensation?"

"I don't know." Everett meandered back to the bench, positioned between two rows of beige lockers. "All I know is, I'm not perfect. Never will be. Can't live up to it."

"You may not like this, Ev, but I think you're doing this to yourself. You're letting the enemy get to you. This is a guilt trip Jesus doesn't want you to go on! Satan's the one who wants you cowering. He wants you all inward-focused, so you won't have the impact he knows you can have."

He hoisted a foot onto the bench and leaned over, pushing up a sleeve and stroking one of the black serpents he hadn't had removed.

"I've been where you are," she insisted. "I've done the legalism thing. You know that. I did the works. I did the performance grid thing, for God and for other people. It'll burn you out! And it may even lead you away from Christ."

"Well, what do I do?"

"Just know you're His child. Love Him with your life. Don't worry about what anyone else thinks. That's between them and God. If you've got that vertical relationship, nothing's gonna stop you."

"I just want to reach these people…" His sentence was cut short by a surge of emotion. He cupped his mouth and dropped his head backward to relieve the stiffness in his neck.

"You be yourself, Everett Lester! God made you *precisely* the person you are, for *His* purpose—for this concert today. He had your life all planned out way before you were born. And you're on the right track."

He took a deep breath and exhaled. "I want to reach the ones on the fringe, Mary, the ones like me. The ones with ratty hair and nose rings, and tattoos and drug problems. The ones who are so confused; they're all just searchin'…"

"That's right." Her voice quivered. "You meet them where they are."

He dropped his head in his hand, so thankful for his older sister.

"You're different, Ev." She got her wind back. "You're creative and caring and charismatic. You've lived in the depths of hell. Remember what God's done. He's given you a platform. Explain what's happened. Be transparent. They'll respond, Ev. I promise—"

"There'll be opposition."

"Absolutely. Praise the Lord! He's gonna stir the pot today. You're gonna go out there and be the fragrance of Christ to those who are perishing and to those who are being saved."

Dropping to the bench, he found himself laughing and crying at the same time. As usual, Mary's exuberance was contagious.

"I'm so excited for you," she said. "Jerry and I are gonna pray for you the whole time! God's gonna move."

"Thanks, Mar."

"Is Karen there?"

"She's got a doctor's appointment, but she'll be here later."

"Why'd she make an appointment for today?"

"OB-GYN. She's had it scheduled a long time."

"Routine checkup?"

"Kind of. She wants to make sure all her equipment's running right, you know, for the dozens of kids we're going to have."

"Gee whiz." Mary laughed. "You haven't even been married a year yet."

"You know Karen. She's been ready to have babies since day one. And if *she* checks out okay, guess who's next in line for the doctor?"

"Uh-oh. Now there's where we may run into a problem."

"Ha, ha." He glanced at the wall clock. "Hey, I gotta run. Thanks for talking."

"Call me anytime, brother. When will we see you?"

"We're playing Cincinnati, remember?"

"That's right. I'll check your website for the dates. We wouldn't miss it. Neither would the boys!"

"Can't wait to see those big guys," he said. "We'll set you up with passes. Love you. Thanks again."

"Love you, too. Break a leg, Godspeed, and all that good stuff."

Everett closed the phone in his hand and leaned on his knees. He was where he was supposed to be, where God wanted him. But was his mind strong enough to stay the course, to be a godly example, not only for the day's gig, but for life?

It would be a long road. He was well aware that he had blind spots and weaknesses. The serpent on his arm served as a daily reminder of the man he used to be. He wanted never to forget the Everett of old, how he would have gotten high or bolted right about then.

But he wasn't the same.

He stood and made for the door.

It was time to rock.

Karen was so excited. She'd met two expecting mothers in the plush waiting room at her ob-gyn's office. One, a petite brunette, was seven months along and let Karen feel her baby kicking and rolling within her hard, round tummy. Karen treasured the notion of someday seeing her and Everett's baby on the ultrasound monitor. Could she possibly muster the patience to wait for that day?

She smiled as she recalled the last time she and Everett had discussed baby names. It had been fall. They were parked in his convertible at an old-fashioned drive-in hamburger stand. With his penetrating brown eyes and contagious smile, Everett surprised her by bringing up the topic and even introducing several names he'd come up with. The one he suggested for a girl was Joanna, which meant "God's been gracious." For a boy, he dug the name Cole, which meant "people of victory." Karen adored them both. One of her top picks was Vivien—"full of life."

The brunette said good-bye and Karen was left by herself in the tranquil waiting room, trying to picture her body at seven months pregnant and vowing to purchase the coolest maternity clothes.

She needed to speak to her doctor once more to go over all her results, then get on the road. She checked her watch. Everett's concert had started, and she desperately wanted to make it, at least for several songs.

Admiring a subtly lit painting of a cabin by a stream, Karen prayed that thousands of people would come to Everett's show, and that many would begin a relationship with Christ because of it. That had become the passion of Everett's heart.

When Dr. Margaret Jannell opened the door to the waiting room, Karen was bewildered. Usually an attendant slid open the tinted window that blocked off the reception desk and asked patients to come back.

"Let's go into my office, Karen." Dr. Jannell held a blue folder across her chest in one hand, gold-rimmed glasses in the other, and propped the door open for Karen with her tall, slender body. "We'll have more privacy in there."

Privacy. What do we need privacy for? Why is she so serious?

The rest unfolded like a bad dream, like a slide show. Passing the enormous crystal-clear aquarium in Dr. Jannell's office and its colorful assortment of stones and tropical fish. Being escorted to the soft, maroon leather chair next to the tinted windows that overlooked the busy parking lot. And the doctor's words, the cursed conversation Karen feared only in the recesses of her mind.

"I'm sorry, Karen." The blond, middle-aged doctor spoke softly, making direct eye contact. "The infection you had in the womb and Fallopian tubes, back when you had the abortion, has caused tubal infertility—"

"He said it was nothing!" Karen bolted to the edge of her seat. "The doctor said it would heal and I'd be fine. I am fine!"

This was a nightmare, right? It had to be.

Wake me...please.

"Karen, you're right. Pelvic inflammatory disease, when treated properly, almost always goes away, especially in young ladies like you were—"

"He assured me!" She gasped. "The doctor promised me I could have babies."

"No one should make that kind of promise. There are adhesions in your Fallopian tubes. The tubes are shut, Karen, as if they were mended together. I'm sorry about this. I know how much—"

"We've got to do surgery! Can we do that? I don't care about risk."

The doctor's mouth had become a small, horizontal slit.

She shook her head.

And the room spun out of control.

The first placard Everett made out amid the frenzied crowd when he jogged onto the scuffed, black stage at the free concert at Queens Arena read: "Go to hell, Lester."

A quick pan of the packed thirty-six-hundred-seat auditorium revealed more of the same. A skull and crossbones. Clenched fists.

Beer cans flying. Angry faces screaming obscenities. Nazi swastikas. And dozens of revelers pushing with all their might to bulldoze the gate in front of the stage.

"Hey!" Everett's booming voice pierced the room like a fog horn blaring on a battleship. If there was one thing this Cleveland boy knew how to do, it was take command of an audience.

"I don't know why you came here tonight. *You* may not know." His own words were all he could hear as they rolled off the stage with the mist from the dry ice machine. "But I'll tell you what—we're glad you're here. *Let's rock!*"

Drumsticks clashed, flash-pods exploded, purple and yellow lights flooded the stage, electric guitars blazed, and Everett whirled the microphone stand as if it were a stick on the playground.

Five adrenaline-filled minutes later, Everett flew off the drum kit with his legs curled behind him, perfectly timing the end of the first song with his landing. The second he hit the stage, more explosives detonated, the stage went black, and Everett heard people cheering. A lot of people.

3

Wesley's throat was nuked and his nostrils burned raw. But it didn't matter. He'd take a little pain in exchange for the buzz any day.

Flyin', baby.

Forgettin' the messed-up past.

Enjoyin' the moment, the very *millisecond* he was livin' in.

No worries about tomorrow, 'cause tomorrow he could be dead—like his brother.

Not goin' there.

He and Tony Badino had met Brubaker at a flophouse in Fairview earlier in the day, where they smoked some of the new cristy just in from Pennsylvania. Now they were geeking in the Super Wal-Mart.

Tony was probably spellbound somewhere in the automotive department while Wesley was lusting over the Winchesters, Rugers, Weatherbys, and Brownings in sports and recreation. There were bolt-actions and pumps, lever-actions and semiautomatics—and all that lovely ammunition. Wesley had developed an affection for guns since hooking up with Tony—who was constantly buying and selling used firearms.

"Excuse me," came an unconfident voice from behind, then three taps on the shoulder. Wesley turned and looked up at a tall, shiny-faced man wearing a bright blue vest—one of Wal-Mart's finest. "Can I help you in some way?"

The guy looked concerned. Or was he annoyed? Curious? Honestly trying to help? *Wait a second—he knows I'm lit!*

"I don't need anything." Wesley turned back to the glass case.

Scopes and choke tubes, magazines and barrels—

"It's just that…you've been here a long time," came the voice again.

Wesley faced him once more. The man wore a half smile and was tentative, examining Wesley all the way up and all the way down.

"Yeah. No. I just…" Wesley rubbed hard at his blazing nose. "I'm just lookin'. Okay? Is that a crime? There's not a time limit for browsing, is there?"

Who am I foolin'? This dude knows the symptoms. Everybody knows. I'm a rail. He's scoping the purple ring under my eye.

"No, that's fine. You've just been standing in this area for, well, it's been hours now."

He thinks I lifted something. He's called security. He's stalling!

Walk. Just walk.

Walk fast!

Find Badino. Get out.

Wesley began to march, looking back at the man, who was staring, staring, staring.

BAM.

He crashed into a huge crate in the middle of the aisle, full of winter hats and scarves, and a sign that read Three Dollars Each. He peered back at old Blue Vest meandering toward him.

Move. Keep moving. To automotive.

That dude's gonna call the cops!

Baby stuff. Music. Electronics. Photo department. Shoes and more shoes. Fabrics. Automotive. *Yes.* We got gas treatment and power steering fluid—car mats, wax, accessories—even those cool little air fresheners that hook to the air vents in your car.

There. Badino. By the stereos, speakers, and fuzz-busters.

"Let's go, let's go, let's go!" Wesley yanked Badino's arm. "The guy by the guns made me. I think he called the cops!"

Tony fumed at Wesley with his meanest scowl. "You idiot, Lester." He shook his arm free, turned down the volume to the sample speakers, and scanned the area. "Chill out! What'd you do?"

"Nothin'!" Wesley's whole body jerked. "Dude said I'd been geekin' over there for *hours.*"

Tony looked at his watch, one of those mod ones on a thick, black leather band.

"What time you got?" Wesley murmured, his head doing a one-eighty one way, then the other.

"We've been here awhile." Tony looked back at the car stereo display. "I had my heart set on one of these bad boys…"

"I'm not kiddin', Tony, we gotta blow. The whole store's probably been alerted by now. Listen for an announcement like Code Red or something secret like that, you know what I mean? Where they use code words to alert the employees. Have you heard anything like that? Over the PA?"

"You're losin' it, Lester," Tony puffed, examining Wesley up and down and giving the stereos one final touch. "We better scram, just in case you're not hallucinating for once."

Tony led the way by several paces, heading toward the front of the store. Wesley peered back toward sporting goods as he tagged along, but old Blue Vest was out of sight.

"You're so paranoid. I can't take you out in public."

"Not quite." Wesley's heart drum-drum-drummed like a rabbit's inside his baggy green army jacket. "We'll be lucky to make it to the car. Keep your eyes peeled. You don't have anything on you, do you?"

"Just the usual." Tony sneered, buttoning the top of his coat.

"Are you crazy? How'd you get it?"

"Dude went to help a lady find somethin'. Left the pharmacy door wide open. No one else around."

Wesley shook his head. "They're gonna bust us for sure."

"They ain't gonna bust *nobody*, Lester."

They trucked past the paint, past the hardware, then past the toys, toys, toys. Past the pet stuff, beauty supplies, and pharmacy.

"I guarantee this place is going to be crawling with heat when we hit the doors," Wesley whined. "You watch."

"You watch me walk straight to the car, you wimp."

A cold wind ripped through the giant entryway, where all the candy and pop machines, shopping carts, and arcade games were situated. The thin, orange-haired lady whose job was stamping returns shot them a crooked-toothed smile.

As they hit the huge parking lot, Wesley shoved his hands in his coat pockets and wrapped the army coat tight around his waist. Passing a homely Santa wearing headphones and ringing a bell by a red kettle, Wesley gnawed at the inside of his bottom lip again. Chewing, chewing, chewing. But there wasn't any pain now—wouldn't be for a few days.

Tony was four feet ahead of him, gray stocking cap tight over his head, hands cupped at his mouth, lighting a Marlboro. He took a lungful of smoke and waved his arm through the air in a big circle.

"I told you you were freakin' out over nothin'. That's 'cause that stuff we smoked was *la glass*, baby. One hundred percent pure *meth-am-phet-a-mine*!"

Wesley was relieved to be out of the store and breathing fresh air again. He even allowed a smile to break out as they hustled in the direction of the SUV.

Just get to the Yukon, get to the Yukon, get to the Yukon.

"I stepped all over that package we sold your buddy last night," Tony boasted from his own little world. "That stuff was half baking soda and vitamin B12." He cackled as a pang of sorrow unsettled Wesley then disappeared.

Footsteps. Coming quickly.

You're just paranoid.

A stocky white guy in jeans, a tan coat, and a Mets stocking cap locked a big arm around Tony's shoulder.

Wesley heard the words *in-store detective* and beat it for the SUV, the pavement feeling like it was a mile away from each step.

Keys out of pocket, dancing with each stride, he looked down frantically and hit "unlock."

The Yukon's lights flashed and horn beeped at the same moment Tony exploded, ripping the detective's arm from his shoulder and whirling the dude around with all his might. In the fray, four yellow boxes of cold medicine tumbled to the pavement from beneath Tony's overcoat.

As the detective's eyes flashed toward the ground, Tony squinted and sent his legs into the air like a windmill. His right boot bashed the detective's Adam's apple, sending him crunching into the side of a maroon Toyota Tundra then to the hard ground.

Wesley brought the Yukon to life, and Tony found the passenger handle as it was darting backward. The detective gasped for air and clutched his neck as onlookers gathered at the store entrance some forty feet away.

As soon as Tony's left boot touched the floor of the passenger side, Wesley mashed the accelerator. The force of the Yukon lurching forward almost threw Tony back onto the blacktop, but he pulled himself in, laughing hysterically as his door slammed shut and the Yukon sailed through the Wal-Mart parking lot.

4

M ist sprinkling her tearstained face, Karen walked the barren hillside in silence. She'd forgone the concert in
Queens and returned to Twin Streams, Everett's and her farm estate in
Bedford. The leafless trees on the ridge in the distance were black and
spindly against the bleak sky, resembling black ink spills, like the
stains that threatened to blot out the vibrancy that once filled her
heart.

As usual for December in New York, the late afternoon sky was
pale gray, almost matching the color of the melting two-day-old snow
on the rolling hills. The only sound Karen noticed was the soft squash
of snow beneath her boots. The collies, Rosey and Millie, tagged along
out of breath, their pink tongues dangling, their fluffy tails wagging,
with no clue Karen's world had forever changed.

She struggled to put one numb foot in front of the other. Her
insides ached for her home and church in Topeka, her roots and family
and things familiar.

Unreal, wasn't it?

Married less than a year to the handsome rock idol whose salvation she'd prayed for since she was a teenager. Wealthy beyond measure. Yet, she'd be lying if she didn't admit how often she contemplated the drastic changes her life had taken. Everything used to be so easy, so carefree. Now, it seemed, there were new trials to bear each day, new crosses to carry at every turn.

But she couldn't say she hadn't been warned.

Stopping in the snow, eyes closed, her mind drifted back to the slimy, lukewarm waters of South Florida, the slinking alligators, the rope cutting into her wrists. Back to the filthy green camper—and her accoster, Zane Bender, laughing hideously during those endless days, crying out in torment at night as he swore to stop Everett and her from leading their followers to God. And if Zane didn't, he promised others would come against them—evil spirits, vessels of dishonor, antichrists…

In an attempt to banish the lurid memory with motion, she forged her way up the hill once again, taking in the 218-acre farm with an utter sense of nothingness, recalling how she and Everett had envisioned rearing children here, lots of them. There were woods and open spaces, two fast-running streams, a large two-story barn and silo, and seventy acres of tillable farmland, which Everett decided would become his hobby and, perhaps one day, that of their children.

Not to be.

She trudged toward the stately, white, two-story house, which they had bought to be closer to Everett's brother Eddie, his wife, Sheila, and their children, Wesley and Madison. They'd lost their youngest son, seventeen-year-old David, in a tragic car accident, and Everett made it a mission to reach out to them. Although his aim was admirable and compassionate, it was one Karen questioned in the secret parts, and prayed about often.

Everett had come from such a different world than hers—a tough, nasty, troubled, rebellious world. He was a new Christian, still a little jagged around the edges, and greatly in need of her encouragement, energy, and support.

How's he going to react when he hears the news?

Would he determine Karen's infertility to be *his* fault? Some kind of cruel payback for his past sins? He was still prone to guilt at times, and she didn't know if she had the strength to deal with his reaction.

The headlights of Everett's Audi popped over the hill about a half-mile away. The sky was darkening fast.

Give me strength.

Karen climbed the slope approaching their home at the top of the plateau and prepared herself for the scene that was about to unfold. Everett would be anxious to talk about the concert. She would let him share first—determined to listen and encourage.

The sickening news that churned like acid in her stomach would wait until later in the evening. If she could hold out that long.

Before Karen could eke out a greeting, Everett marched into the kitchen, hoisted her into the air, and spun her in a half-dozen circles.

"Where've you been?" He swallowed her up in his muscular arms. "I didn't see you at the show. I've been calling—"

"The appointment lasted longer than I thought." She rested her arms across his broad shoulders. "I just came home. I've been outside—I didn't have the phone."

He lowered her feet back to the floor, grabbed her hands, and held her at arm's length. "How did it go?"

She was thankful he asked. But after the momentum with which he'd sprung into the house, his question was like asking the First Lady about her new dress when the President was about to announce a cure for cancer.

"I want to know what you're so fired up about first." She assured him with a half smile. "Talk to me."

"Babe, it was so incredible. Come here." He led her by the hand into the den, turned on a lamp, and brought her down next to him on the couch. "The crowd was insane. There were nasty signs, people throwing stuff, drugs, mosh pits—"

"Oh my gosh. What'd you do?"

"We just got out there and jammed. It was amazing. Honey, there must have been two hundred people who came forward near the end."

"Praise God, Ev."

"People were screamin' in their faces, but they just kept coming." His voice succumbed to the sentiment, and he buried his head against her shoulder. "This is what I'm supposed to be doing," came his muffled voice. "I just know it. This is why I'm here."

Karen held him, stroked the back of his short wavy hair—and waited. Dusk had passed, and the antique lamp cast a warm golden glow over their favorite room. Rosey and Millie moseyed in and curled up on the floor.

Everett pulled back from her and wiped his face with the back of his hands. "These people are so desperate, hon. I could so relate to them…"

"You've been there."

He nodded and laughed. "I was so emotional sharing my story, by the end, they were fighting their way down front, praying."

Karen reached her arms around him and latched on tightly, celebrating with him, seeking the comfort she so desperately needed.

"I know it wasn't any Billy Graham crusade—"

"But it was good," she whispered.

"Oh, it felt so right, babe. Think about it. We're gonna see those people in heaven!"

Karen nodded. With their faces nestled close, they rocked silently in each other's arms.

Souls were saved today. Isn't that all that matters?

Could it be that God didn't want them to have children because of what lay ahead? Concerts much of the year? Worldwide travel? Menacing crowds? Danger? They'd had their share of that already.

Everything in Karen wanted to spill over, but she made herself stop.

Wait.

She didn't want to ruin this for him. "Did Gray show up?"

"He sure did. He was nervous, 'cause people were shoulder to shoulder. The place was a firetrap. But by the time it was over, he was diggin' it."

"How is he?"

"Great. He's on some kind of health kick. Lost weight. Feels super. And get this, he's going to church."

"For real?"

"Yep." Everett leaned forward and reached into his back pocket. "He brought this." Everett sat back and unfolded a page from a magazine. "From *Billboard.* Just out yesterday. Read it with me. I haven't had a chance."

As he read, Karen closed her eyes and forced herself not to be angry. There was no one to be upset with but herself. She'd made the call to hold off about her news, and he wasn't a mind reader.

She glanced down at the headlines, the photographs of Everett, and was sucked into the story.

BILLBOARD
DAILY MUSIC NEWS
Former DeathStroker Inks Dates for
Free World Tour

The once beloved bad boy of rock, Everett Lester, is gearing up for his upcoming Living Water tour, which will send the former DeathStroke lead man to venues in thirty-six cities worldwide. And get this, each concert will be offered *free* to all who choose to come to the well.

"Everett's desire is to take his new music—and new message—to as many people as possible," says former

DeathStroke manager Gray Harris, who will quarterback the tour that derives its name from Lester's latest solo project, *Living Water*. "Obviously, some dramatic things have happened in Everett's life, and he wants to share those experiences personally with his new fans and hopefully the old."

However, the recent album and news of the tour have not been music to the ears of some former DeathStroke fans, who are still distraught over Lester's departure from the group and, ultimately, the band's demise. Although original DeathStrokers John Scoogs, David Dibbs, and Ricky Crazee attempted to keep the band flying after Lester's exit, going through several lead singers, it seemed destined for failure without its flamboyant front man.

Ever since Lester, thirty-five, left DeathStroke and was acquitted for the murder of LA psychic Endora Crystal last winter, his newfound faith has hit a nerve among diehard fans and with some of the public in general. Lester has reportedly been stalked at times and has received hate mail and even death threats.

"Although many people in the Christian community have embraced Everett's new direction, we've received a great deal of disturbing correspondence from former fans, and others," says Jeff Hall, former president of the DeathStroke fan club, whose services have been retained by Lester to help transition as many fans as possible toward his new music.

"DeathStroke meant the world to literally millions of people," says Hall. "While the majority of those folks have let the band rest in peace, some refuse to accept its end and even seem determined to impair Everett's new mission, which is to share what the love and power of Jesus Christ have done in his life."

Lester comments, "The anger and hatred definitely hurt, because my intent is to build relationships with our old fans. But frankly, the threats are nothing new. I received similar hate-filled thoughts from people who were opposed to DeathStroke, long before I became a Christian. However, in my eyes, at least now I'm being persecuted for something worthwhile—my Christian faith."

Tour manager Gray Harris says security will be extra tight throughout the Living Water tour, which will kick off January 7 in New York City and conclude February 27 in Lester's hometown of Cleveland, Ohio. (While in Cleveland, Lester is expected to be inducted into the Rock and Roll Hall of Fame and Museum.)

The band has been practicing for the tour on and off for several months in New York with a warm-up concert scheduled for Queens at this writing. Rumor has it that Lester's new wife of less than one year, Karen Lester (formerly Karen Bayliss), twenty-nine, has quit her job as a business manager for a Topeka software company and will join her husband on tour. Likewise, her father, Jacob, will join the Living Water entourage while taking a brief sabbatical from his independent insurance work in Topeka.

"I wish they'd leave you out of this—and your dad." Everett left the article in Karen's hands and stood.

She continued looking at the story, which featured an old photograph of Everett and bandmate John Scoogs yelling into the same microphone, the huge DeathStroke logo glowing in the background. Adjacent was a recent picture of Everett seated on the steps of the porch at Twin Streams, playing his acoustic guitar. The shot was used as cover art for the recently released *Living Water* album.

"I mean it." He peered down at her, hands on his waist. "You've been through enough. Why does the press have to keep mentioning you?"

"We've had this discussion, Ev. We knew this would happen."

He shook his head. "It just bugs me."

She was drained. "Mom and Dad are going to be there, and Gray, and security."

"I know. I'm just not gonna let you be harassed again—no matter how minor it may seem."

"I'm gonna be fine." Nothing could hurt her now, not as much as she'd been wounded that afternoon.

"You promise you'll come home if there's *any* problem, any threat—to me or you or anyone else?"

"I promise."

He reached out and she took his hands. He pulled her up from the couch and wrapped his arms around her waist, resting his head on top of hers.

"I'm responsible for you now, Karen Lester."

"I need you," she whispered. "You're my best friend."

"So, tell me when all these babies are gonna start showing up."

As his words took hold, her breathing quickened.

This was it.

In a flash, she tried out two, maybe three opening lines in her head but wasn't satisfied with any of them.

The land line rang.

"Hold on." He left her to grab the phone. "Hello, Karen's nursery." He shot her a grin, but she couldn't hold his gaze. Her eyes found the window—until he began speaking again.

"Eddie?" His smile disappeared, and he covered his free ear. "I can barely hear you."

Karen stopped rehearsing her lines and stared at her husband, wary of what was about to come.

"I'm sorry, bro…you're breaking up. Where *are* you?"

Everett crossed to the window and peered into the darkness.

Karen noticed his concern in the reflection.

"Who? Who is it?" He grasped the windowsill. "Calm down, Eddie."

On autopilot, she went to the desk, got a small pad of yellow paper and a pen, and walked them to Everett. He shot her a look of concern and walked to the desk himself, setting the pad down and leaning over it.

"How–much–do–you–need?" He pronounced each word slowly, loudly. It didn't take much to rattle Everett, but the tension in his body said something was going down. She approached him with her arms crossed, trying desperately to batten down the emotions that raged within.

After a pause and a quick shake of the head, he jotted down $24,000.

You've got to be kidding me. Eddie was prone to danger, and Karen was growing weary of Everett's repeated efforts to prop him up—especially now.

"Who do you owe this to? Who's after you?"

He pulled the phone away from his ear and increased the volume. Karen stepped toward him, her heart picking up its pace. She was concerned for Eddie's safety. But he'd been in and out of so many needy situations, she just wanted to scream for a time-out. Freeze everything. Let her be with her husband for two minutes to tell him they will never in their entire lives be able to have babies!

"You're still breaking up...*tell me where you are.*"

Everett's dark eyes searched the den. Then he repeated his brother's words and scribbled them on the pad at the same time. "*Bronx...Mars Hill Racetrack...Pelham Parkway.* I'll be there as fast as I can."

Please don't leave me, Ev...

"Sit tight!" He hung up and handed the phone to Karen as he headed out of the room.

"What's wrong?" She followed him, her mind reeling.

"Eddie's in trouble... He's been gambling."

"He owes *that much* right now? At the track?"

Everett opened the hall closet, grabbed his wool coat, and hurried for the kitchen. "He's *at* the track, but he was out of breath. Something's wrong."

She handed him the cell phone and his keys. "I'll go with you." That was all she wanted, to be near him. Couldn't he see it?

"No way, Karen. This is Lester business."

"I'm a Lester, too!" She was fed up with their different worlds. "Let me come."

"No! Please, just stay here."

"Is Eddie hurt?"

"Not yet...but it sounds like someone's after him. He owes money. I need the checkbook—money market account."

She hurried toward the desk in the den, feeling as if she were racing through a minefield. When was Everett going to stop babysitting his big brother? *Why is this happening now, Lord?*

"Why doesn't he call 911?" She returned with the checkbook and stood there as Everett bundled up.

"He may be into something illegal."

"Oh, great. Everett, this sounds dangerous! You need to call the police."

"He told me not to."

"So that means you don't?" She'd had it! How dare Eddie pull Ev into his dangerous world?

"I'll call them when I get there, if I have to, honey. Trust me."

"Everett Lester, you be careful!"

"I will." He headed through the kitchen door to the garage. "I'll call you when I know more."

"It better be soon." *I can't believe this is happening.*

He jogged to the Audi TT Roadster, ducked in, turned it over, and revved it back out of the garage into what was left of the now crunchy snow. Karen crept down the steps into the cold garage, arms folded in front of her, her hands covered by the sleeves of her big red sweatshirt. The collies followed.

She wanted to motion for Everett to roll down the window so she could tell him they needed to talk. Instead, she gave a quick little wave and watched her new husband blow a kiss and race into the frigid New York night.

It wasn't until the dogs trotted out of the garage to do their business and Karen crept out too that the danger of the situation gripped her. Something about being outside—perhaps the cold air or the vastness of the black sky—sobered her, and she wished she'd hugged Everett before he left. But it was too late now.

She followed the Audi's shrinking taillights with her sore eyes.

"I'm sorry for being so selfish, Father." She began to cry again. "Forgive me, please…"

The taillights disappeared.

"Please protect them, Lord. I'm sorry for judging Eddie. I'm just so…tired."

The sound of Everett's car faded over the hills, and Karen inwardly screamed to the heavens.

At least let me keep Ev, Lord, please! Let me keep my husband.

5

Wesley and Tony celebrated their close-call escape from
Wal-Mart back at Wesley's basement apartment, which
wasn't really even a basement. It was more like a massive terrace-level
apartment. For an hour, Tony had been entranced by Wesley's Harley
Davidson pinball machine, smoking cigarette after cigarette while
cursing the ringing, blinking, roaring piece of equipment.

When he'd had enough, Tony breezed between the oversize
couches and chairs, and plopped down on the floor. Wesley grabbed
them each another Miller in the kitchen and joined him. The carpet
reeked of spilled beer, but Wesley was proud of his pad, his fifty-inch
plasma HDTV, his Bose home theater speaker system, and his indepen-
dence.

Tony sat Indian-style with the Miller and a Marlboro in one hand,
keeping the other busy either rubbing his dark skin or doing
hand motions as he yakked a mile a minute. Wesley sipped his beer
and noticed the black soot beneath Tony's fingernails.

"How much do your parents know?" Wesley asked.

"'Bout what?"

"What do you think?"

Tony smirked and stared at the bottle in his lap. "They know everything. Put it this way." His eye twitched. "My old man knows for sure; more than you can imagine. My mom, she probably knows but ignores it."

Wesley understood, closing his eyes and nodding.

"What about you?"

"They know," Wesley moaned, "but they don't have the *guts* to do anything."

"What do you want 'em to do? Narc on you?"

"No."

"What're you mad at, then? Huh?"

Wesley didn't answer.

"Spit it out," Tony urged.

"They're supposed to be my parents!"

"Right." Tony wagged his head in disgust. "Loving, understanding parents—"

"I just don't trust anyone anymore—okay? I'll never trust anyone again."

Tony eyed him with a sinister grin. "Even me?"

Wesley paused, choosing to dodge the question. "They *knew* my brother was messed up, but they didn't do anything."

"How'd they know?"

"There were a ton of signs. David got nailed with a bag of pot at a football game. One night, he and his buddies got arrested on the roof of the school, drunk as skunks. He was awake days on end after tweaking. He had two speeding tickets—"

"What'd your folks do?"

"Ha! He had to miss *one* football game. Couldn't go to a party one night. *Ridiculous.* They were afraid of him, just like they're afraid of me."

"But that's good, right? That's what we want, isn't it?"

Tony was digging now, prying into Wesley's mind, and asking questions people don't ask when they're not amped. That's why meth was such an indescribable trip—at least, before you came plummeting back to reality.

Where had that come from? Wesley focused hard on the conversation, trying to forget about the worst part, the dark part, the part that made you want to crawl into a closet and become a shoe. The part that always came.

He floundered for an answer.

"You want them to fear you." Tony swigged his beer. "That way, you get what you want. Am I right? Tell me I'm right."

"I guess so. Part of me wants to know another way, though. That's all. Part of me wishes David had known another way. Something better…"

Looking down at his beer, Tony shook his head and sneered. "Lester, you just broke your own rule."

"What do you mean?"

"You trusted me."

Wesley picked at the label on the Miller. "Just like my brother trusted my uncle."

"Everett Lester." Tony sneered.

"Yeah."

"And Everett Lester let him down, didn't he?"

"Yeah, he did." Wesley grunted, getting to his feet. "I'll show you."

He made for the kitchen, reached on his tiptoes into a cupboard, and brought down a digest-size black book. He walked back over and dropped to the floor.

"This was my brother's." He flipped through the pages. "I found it in his room after he died." After a bit of searching, Wesley read: "'December 2. The entire Lester family met in Cleveland for Christmas. Uncle Everett promised to be there. I was stoked. But he was a no-show. Again. He said he'd take me skiing to make up for it. Something to look forward to…'"

Wesley turned the pages as he'd done a hundred times. "Then this, 'February 3. Total bummer. Uncle Everett backed out of the ski trip to Lake Placid. Dad, Wesley, and I went, but it wasn't the same without E. L. I had told all my friends. Now I'm going to look like a liar and a fool. So what else is new?'"

Without a word, Wesley flipped to a later entry while Tony got near the bottom of his Miller. "'My parents show their affection by giving me things—almost anything I want—but the feelings I get from them are superficial. They're busy chasing their dreams. I can relate so much to Uncle Everett. To heck with relationships and rules and rigidity. He knows how to live for the moment! He's daring. He jams his fist in the face of authority and says, "I'll do it my way." I want to be closer to him, but he doesn't have time. He's a world famous rock 'n' roll superstar.'

"Now listen to this." Wesley turned the page. "This is the next day: 'I've been tweeking. My senses are so keen.

I got ten lives, ten lives.
Just watch me fly.
Ain't never gonna die,
Never gonna die,
'Cause I got ten lives.
—DeathStroke, "Ten Lives"

"'Uncle Everett says there's no heaven or hell, that everyone who dies has an afterlife on the Other Side. Sometimes I feel like I want to go there—soon.'

"This is right at the end of DeathStroke," Wesley said, finding his place and draining the Miller. "'I am coming down from being geeked for something like ten days. My parents either didn't know or pretend not to. Same old story. Wesley and I were supposed to see DeathStroke at the Meadowlands this past weekend and go backstage with Uncle Everett. So much for that. He was either too blown out of his mind to remember or doesn't care. I guess he's proven that. Nobody cares enough to step into my dark world and free me from myself.'"

Tony rose to his feet, took Wesley's empty, and got them each another brew from the fridge. "Keep goin'." He sat back down.

"This is just before the wreck." Wesley smoothed the pages of the journal, stopping to drink savagely from the new bottle before beginning to read. "'I'm a meth junkie. They call me "Skelly"—that's short for skeleton. My body DEMANDS crank. I have scabs everywhere from picking at myself. I'm never hungry and seldom go to the bathroom. My face is breaking out. I'm losing hair. A miserable, depressing existence. I think I'm crazy. I know I need help, but I don't know where to get it. The simple route would be making a jump for the Other Side. I'm afraid. I cry out for a different life than this.'"

Wesley closed the journal and squeezed it between his fingers, knowing this was the most substantial thing he had left of his little brother.

"New life." He seethed. "That's what he thought he was getting when he slammed his Camaro into that oncoming car."

"How do you know that's not what he got?" Tony raised an eyebrow above his twitching right eye.

"I just know."

"I do too." Tony's eyes were like circles of fire. "There are no heavens, or 'other sides,' or spiritual fantasy worlds," he growled. "We got *one shot* at this existence, then we die. Blackout…oblivion."

Was this the voice of truth?

Wesley stared at Tony's small, sour face, which was distorted—like a melting wax mask. "Our lives are about *indulgence*, Wesley—that's it. That's all that matters. I know! I've explored Christianity. I've done the homework. I *know* it's a lie. I saw what it did…"

Tony's eyes seemed twice their normal size. "Let me just tell you something. David was on the right track." His voice became low and nasty, yet he seemed to gurgle with laughter at the same time. "He was drinking in every last ounce of gratification he could find in this existence. But in the end, he listened to the wrong voices. That's all. He listened to Everett Lester and his lies about the Other Side. He listened to his own demons, trying to find more to this life than there really is. You and I aren't gonna make the same mistake, are we?"

"No." Wesley stared straight ahead. "No, we're not."

"We ain't gonna live for anything but the here and now. Am I right?"

Wesley's eyes shifted to meet Tony's, and he nodded.

"But your Uncle Everett, dude, he's peddling this Christian nonsense, big-time. Got a new CD. New tour. It's gonna take its toll on a heck of a lot of people, just like your brother."

"Yeah, I know."

"Well, what do you suggest we do about that, *nephew* Wesley?"

Their eyes locked.

Tony groaned as he stood. "Why don't we go for a drive." He motioned toward the door with his head. "Get some fresh air."

"Good." Wesley stared.

"I thought we'd take a spin over to Uncle Everett's farm. Just cruise by, you know? See how the other half lives. Whaddya say?" Tony threw on his long black coat.

"Fine with me." Wesley got to his feet. "The way I'm feelin' right now, I may want to do more than just cruise by."

"Ooooh." Tony headed for the door. "Sounds like we got some vengeance in the air tonight." He pushed the door open and pivoted to wait for Wesley. "Come on, bad boy, let's do it."

6

There was no answer on Eddie's cell phone, so all Everett could do was continue to frantically cruise the wet crater-filled parking lot at Mars Hill Racetrack, searching for his brother's silver Kia Amanti.

The place was a dump. Everett could see the bright lights from the horse track and, with windows cracked, heard the cheers from the crowd.

A dude in a wide-brimmed hat and full-length fur coat walked boisterously beside an Asian woman, who wore a short skirt, a leather jacket, and shiny knee-high boots. She was shivering and tripping through asphalt chunks and puddles as they argued their way across the parking lot.

The windows of a parked Buick were fogged with condensation, but the glow from the pipe being passed about illuminated the silhouettes of the people inside. For a moment, he was there in the car with them, ignoring the rancid tang of the pot in his mouth and the harshness of it hitting the base of his throat—and reliving the euphoria of the buzz.

Was there a bottle of scotch or gin being swigged and passed about in that car? Was there a torn cardboard case of beer on the floor, or maybe a fresh stash of coke? Everett couldn't ignore how dangerously seductive the drugs and drink still were to him.

His old self had been crucified with Christ. The Holy Spirit lived in him now. Yet, there seemed to be an ugly, bitter, deadly force lurking in the shadows of his mind, haunting him, trying to trick him into thinking that his old self still lived and would make an encore appearance someday, on a day when Everett was at his weakest.

He rolled on through the puddles, vowing—as he had since he'd been born again—to live hour by hour, step by step. God had given the Israelites enough food for one day at a time, no more. Similarly, God's grace would carry him day by day. He needn't look beyond that.

On the very last row, in the darkest part of the lot, Everett's breathing was interrupted by a wave of panic. Beneath a flickering lamppost, next to a sagging chain-link fence, he spotted something—or someone.

Jerking up on the parking brake, he hurried out of the Audi and dashed through the headlights' beam to the mound that lay still between a beat-up conversion van and an old Mazda. It had to be garbage. Maybe a homeless person. Certainly not his brother, not out here like this.

Everett made out a shiny black wingtip, and all the air left him.

"Eddie?" He raced toward the shape on the ground. "Eddie Lester?"

No movement. A gray trench coat. It was a person, dressed nicely.

Everett's knees wobbled. He told himself to stay calm and asked Jesus to help.

The rest of the puzzle became clear: an arm oddly twisted, a necktie half submerged in a puddle. *Lord, no!* And his brother's head, lying awkwardly on the cold ground, blood clotted in his graying hair and smeared on the side of his face.

"Eddie!"

The cold rainwater soaked into his knees as Everett knelt over his brother, gently lifting his head in trembling hands

Eddie coughed, blinked, and gasped for air. His cheekbone was cut deep and still bleeding, just beneath the right eye. There were several bruises and another slice high on his forehead.

Has he been shot? Stabbed? Unable to work the buttons, Everett ripped open Eddie's overcoat, searching for bullet holes or blood or—who knew what else? Nothing wrong underneath.

"Eddie, it's Everett!" He yanked the lapels of the overcoat, wanted to make his brother's eyes open. "Can you hear me?"

With shaking fingers, Everett wiped the blood from his brother's nose and mouth.

Eddie's eyes opened. He was dazed and limp.

Jesus, let him hang on!

Everett laid his head back down, fumbled for his phone, and dialed 911.

"No." Eddie grunted, turning his head sideways to look at Everett out of half-closed eyes. "No cops."

"Eddie, we need an ambulance!"

"They'll kill me," he gurgled, still laid out flat. "Don't…"

"I'm callin' an ambulance!"

"No!" he groaned, shifting to his side and trying to sit up. "I'm okay. Wait. Just wait." He reached for Everett's glowing phone. Everett pulled it away.

Drooling and moaning, Eddie forced himself up. "Knicks were…on the take last night." He smiled, eyes closed. "Had to be. Favored by eight over Atlanta. Only won by one in overtime… Turn off the phone, brother."

"Is that what this is about?" Everett closed the phone, slid it into his pocket, and examined his brother's mouth and facial cuts.

"Hawks. Worst team in the league. And they come within one of the Knicks. Had to be fixed."

Everett scanned the parking lot. "You lost twenty-four grand on one game?"

"It was double or nothin'." Eddie groaned, licking a small cut at the corner of his mouth. "I owed twelve. Couldn't believe they gave me eight points and the Knicks. It was a no-brainer."

"Are you on anything? You been drinking?"

"Nothin'." He grimaced. "This is who I am, brother."

"Who'd you bet?"

"Let's go, can we? I'm soaked. Think I cracked a couple ribs."

"You need a doctor."

"No." Eddie looked around for the first time, getting his bearings. "I've had worse. Just get me to a hotel. I don't want Sheila to see me like this, or the kids."

"Where's your car?"

"A lot near my office."

"How'd you get here?"

"Cab."

"I'm not takin' you to a hotel. I'll take you to a hospital, your house, or my house. You make the call."

Eddie closed his eyes and could only shake his head, wincing.

"Never mind," Everett said. "I'll decide."

Slowly, Everett helped his brother make it from the car to his house. Karen rushed to meet them at the door, gaping at Eddie's bloodied body and shooting Everett a look of distress.

As they entered the toasty kitchen, Eddie barely made eye contact with Karen, insisting that his injuries were not substantial. But his body language said otherwise.

After taking a pair of blue sweatpants and an old white sweatshirt of Everett's that Karen had retrieved, Eddie insisted he didn't need his brother's help changing. Thirty minutes later, he gingerly emerged from his room carrying his dirty suit and overcoat in a white laundry sack Karen had given him.

In the light of the family room, Everett was taken aback by how much his brother had aged—mostly in the past year, ever since David had perished. Long, wavy cracks creased his forehead, and myriad lines trailed from the outsides of his eyes like streamers. He looked beaten and resembled their deceased father, Vince, more each time Everett saw him.

The abrasions on Eddie's thin face had been cleaned, but his normally shining brown eyes looked tired and sunken above his puffy cheeks. He had combed and spiked his hair, which was more gray than black now.

Eddie seated himself in a soft chair by a standing lamp, with Karen at his side. She used a washcloth and warm water from a silver bowl to clean the wounds on his face again, as well as several they discovered on the back of his head. From the opposite side of the chair Everett followed with peroxide, Neosporin, and several butterfly bandages.

"What'd they use, bro? A lead pipe?"

"One of 'em pistol-whipped me." Eddie stared straight ahead. Everett could tell he was embarrassed, especially with Karen there.

Everett shook his head. "How many were there?"

"Three. They liked to kick. I'm pretty bruised up."

His older brother had always been tough, seldom shedding a tear, even when their father had beaten his bottom raw with his thick leather belt. "Who are they, Eddie?"

His weary brown eyes flicked to Karen, who tried to look busy putting away the first-aid supplies.

"You know I've been strugglin' with betting at the casinos, and whenever I travel—"

"Yeah, but I thought you had it under control."

"Not quite." Eddie chuckled. "Couple months ago I made the mistake of getting a bookie." He looked at Everett, who peered back at him, waiting. "A friend told me it would be more convenient than going all the way to the casinos or the track. Plus, I wouldn't be taxed on the winnings."

"And…" Everett prompted.

"And pretty soon I was betting every day."

"On what? What could you possibly bet on every day?"

The tilt of Karen's head and her slow blink told Everett to cool it. He felt the strain in his face, his neck, his whole body. *Be patient.* He made himself relax.

"You name it. Between the horses, the pros, college—there's always something. My bookie gives me the spreads, and I make my picks. Or he gives me total points, and I say over or under. You remember how dad used to do it—"

"Five bucks, Eddie. He bet *five bucks* once in a while on the Browns."

"I got no excuses." He turned away.

Everett felt like shaking him, screaming at him to grow up and straighten out his life. He was embarrassed by his brother in front of Karen. But just as quickly, he remembered his own pitiful life. He, too, was but dirt. He, too, had been trapped in the mire and blinded by Satan. "Who did this to you? The bookie? His cronies?"

Eddie exhaled and his shoulders slumped. "I thought the bookie was just some empty suit." He looked at the floor where Rosey and Millie had curled up. "Apparently, he has connections."

"With who, the mob?"

"I dunno, Ev. Maybe. Possibly." Eddie stood and walked away from them. "These guys tonight were definitely somebody's hired guns. All business."

"What'd they say?"

"That I needed to pay what I owed by Friday." Eddie found a mirror and touched several of the wounds on his face.

"Did they mention your bookie or anyone else?"

"Nope, just pay what you owe by Friday."

"Or what?"

Eddie turned to face Everett. "If these are wiseguys, you don't want to know 'or what.'"

"I thought the mob was dead," Karen chimed in.

Eddie looked at her one of the first times all evening. "There are still pockets. And they don't mess around."

"Well, we need to pay 'em their money and be done with it," Everett said. "And we need to get you some help."

Eddie closed his eyes, looking like a teenager who'd been told what to do once too often. "I've tried to get help."

"Where?" Everett challenged.

"Gamblers Anonymous…my psychiatrist. None of it's worked."

"Maybe there's a treatment center that could help you," Karen said. "There must be places around here that deal with gambling addiction, maybe even from a Christian perspective, if you'd be interested…"

Eddie pursed his lips, stuck his jaw out, and nodded. "This thing tonight sobered me up. If you can help me pay the $24K, Ev, I'll pay you back, a little each month."

Everett patted his older brother on the back and kept his hand there, rubbing gently. "Let's not worry about your paying us back. The first thing we need to do is get the bookmaker his money and tell him this'll be your last transaction. How 'bout we do that tomorrow?"

With his mouth sealed, Eddie closed his eyes and nodded slightly.

"And after that, we'll see," Everett said.

"Honey," Karen peered at Everett, "can we pray?"

"Yeah." Everett glanced at his brother, feeling a bit awkward. "Okay with you, bro?"

Eddie shrugged.

Keeping his hand on Eddie's back, Everett closed his eyes. "Thank you for sparing Eddie's life tonight, Lord, for protecting him from worse. We pray You'll help end this relationship with the bookie and whoever he's hooked up with. And that You'll free Eddie of this problem."

During a brief pause, Everett raised his head slightly to find Eddie staring wide-eyed at the dogs, mouth closed tight. They made eye contact for a fleeting second, and Everett dropped his head again.

"Lord, please also heal Eddie's marriage to Sheila and his relationships with Wesley and Madison. Help them to be a loving family."

Everett heard Eddie stand and cross the room. He opened his eyes and watched his brother tilt open the top slats of the plantation shutters and look out at the darkness. "I'm sorry, but you don't know how bad I *don't* want to hear that right now."

Everett shot a helpless glance at Karen and got the same in return.

"Eddie—"

"When you've lost your seventeen-year-old son," Eddie's voice overtook his brother's, "*lost* your marriage of twenty-three years, *lost* your children's hearts—and *lost everything* you've worked all your life to build…" The emotion rose up and choked him midsentence.

"I'm sorry, Eddie. I've just seen God do so much in my life—"

"Don't get me wrong. I believe there's…something bigger out there." His laugh was strained and crazy as he seemed to fight for breath. "But I also believe you play the cards you're dealt. And it looks like you just got a better hand than I did, little brother."

7

By the time the white Yukon crept down Old Peninsula Road, past the driveway and well-lit house at Twin Streams, it was approaching 11:50 p.m. Tony sat tight-lipped and beady-eyed in the passenger seat, glaring back at the Lester estate while Wesley's heart thundered beneath his old green army jacket.

The white lines on the narrow weathered street were barely visible, and there were no streetlights, nothing but New York night. The darkness didn't faze Wesley. The meth they'd smoked made him feel like a Navy SEAL on a midnight operation, wearing infrared night goggles, with caffeine coursing through his veins.

"Turn around," Tony mumbled.

Wesley swung the Yukon into the next driveway, nearly bashing into a shiny black gate he hadn't seen until it was two feet in front of the SUV. Heading back up the sloping road toward Twin Streams, Wesley slowed the vehicle to a crawl as they approached the house again.

"Old Uncle Everett's up late." Tony peered through Wesley's window toward the cozy house. "Aw, ain't that purty. They got the Christmas lights goin'. Tree all lit up. And the manger scene. Stop and turn out the lights, Wes."

"Here?"

"Yeah, here. Just for a minute. Ain't no cars out here. This is Boonesville."

The Yukon crunched to a stop on the frigid street. Wesley glanced over at Tony, who was opening his door.

"Shhh." Tony held a gloved index finger to his lips. "Come on."

Nudging his door shut just enough to douse the dome light, Tony crossed in front of the SUV. His shadow expanded several hundred feet as he passed one headlight, then the next. He scampered down through the ditch toward the house, waving for Wesley to follow.

Wesley looked in all directions and cursed Tony under his breath. He was stoked about spooking his uncle but didn't exactly plan on getting caught, either. He put the Yukon in drive and pulled into the dirty snow at the side of the road. Clicking the lights off, he quietly opened the door, endured the shock of the cold night, and closed the door behind him.

"What're you doin'?" he yelled to Tony, who was walking casually through the brittle grass, still covered in great part by large patches of snow.

Tony swiveled his head back toward Wesley, scowled, and gave him a regimental "c'mon!" with the jerk of his arm. *Uh-oh.* Tony was mad because Wesley didn't leave the car smack-dab in the middle of the street.

Weirdo. Wesley hated it when Tony got angry, because when he did, he got crazy angry.

The manger scene, still about fifty feet in front of Tony, was lit by a single floodlight. Joseph, Mary, and baby Jesus appeared to be made of wood. The figures cast long shadows onto the snowy lawn and up against the stately white house.

Hands in the pockets of his army jacket, Wesley trotted toward Tony with his eyes glued to the lit rooms in the house. This was getting close—too close. Although he was amped with a ten-million-watt buzz, the people inside the house were not.

"What're you doin'?" Wesley caught up with Tony, attempting to defuse the time bomb.

"Why'd you move it, Lester?"

"I'm not gonna leave a truck in the middle of the road."

"You're gonna need to learn to do what I say, or we ain't gonna have a future." With both hands on one of the manger figures, Tony rocked it, front to back, then side to side.

Wesley kept his eyes on the house.

"Here." Tony grunted, finally loosening the figure from the frigid terrain and hoisting it at Wesley. "Run this to the car. We're takin' it."

Wesley checked the house, then the street, and made a run for the Yukon, banging the heavy figure against his legs and cursing as he ran. Stealing a religious figure—especially Jesus—spooked him. The more he dwelled on it, he nearly convinced himself he'd be cursed by God for the crime.

Once it was in the rear hatch, he stood there a moment, actually contemplating dumping the figure and taking off in the SUV. But he didn't dare. Badino was such a mental case, who knew how he would retaliate? Wesley dashed back toward the house.

"Good job." With the gray ski cap pulled well below his ears, Tony bent over and started running toward the big house, black trench coat flapping behind him.

Nutcase.

Wesley darted behind Tony all the way to a clearing at the side of the house where they glided to a stop, side by side, backs to the wall, puffing steam into the night.

"The shutters are open at that window." Tony nodded. "Let's take a look-see."

Without waiting for a response, Tony quick-stepped it along the side of the house, then slid to his knees, crawling beneath the glowing window, then stood. Wesley took the same path, stopping on the opposite side of the window.

Easing his head about an inch in front of the window, Tony stared at the interior of the house. Following Tony's lead, Wesley did the same.

It looked like a Hallmark card—warm and cozy. Like make-believe. There was a large family room with shimmering wood floors, big rugs, expensive furniture, a baby grand piano, and a Christmas tree with colored lights—and gifts beneath. In the distance were a carpeted dining room and several cabinets with glass doors, filled with silver and china.

Wesley would always be an outsider to such an idealistic world, a world where family members interacted in harmony and love flowed from the foundation. He strained to hear but couldn't make out any voices—just the snow crunching beneath his feet.

Ducking underneath the window, Tony patted Wesley on the back as he walked past him. "Follow me," he whispered and dashed along the side of the house.

Wesley glanced back at the street and was startled to notice how clearly he could see the upper half of the Yukon from his vantage point. He could actually hear his heart: *th-thump, th-thump, th-thump, th-thump*. The chill disappeared, and he found himself almost sweating.

He looked back and forth, listening intently for anything—anyone.

SMAAAAACK!

His head snapped forward. The back of his neck stung from the impact of Tony's ice ball then went numb as snow trickled beneath his shirt and ran down his skinny back. Along the side of the house, Tony motioned for Wesley to get over there.

Wesley got his bearings and made a dash for him.

"What the heck are you thinkin'?" Tony grabbed Wesley by the lapels of his baggy coat. "Are you with me or not, you moron? What are you, scared?"

"I can see the SUV clear as day!" Wesley squealed, looking back at it again. "I'm ready to get outta here. Why'd you hit me?"

"No you're not!" Tony bent him to the ground. "Get down on all fours. I'm gonna hop on your back and look inside."

"This is it." The icy wetness seeped through the knees of Wesley's baggy cargo pants, and he wanted to be back in his apartment. "We're going after this. Hurry up."

"I'll tell you when we're going." Tony hiked up onto Wesley's back with his left foot, then the rest of his weight with the right.

Wesley groaned and bowed, letting his shaved head rest on the surface of the snow. Tony continued to reposition his boots on Wesley's back, but he became indifferent to the weight. *This is about what I'm good for.* He shivered again, anguish creeping up on him. What was it, guilt for being here? Condemnation about taking the Jesus figure?

"We need to do some more of that cristy." Wesley turned his head sideways. "You hear me?"

When no reply came, Wesley craned his neck just enough to see the light from inside the house reflecting in Tony's little black eyes as they invaded the privacy of his uncle's home.

"No way… You ain't gonna believe this."

"What?"

"Your old man's in there with Lester and the wife. Looks like he got the crap beat out of him."

"Who?"

"Your old man."

"Lemme see." Wesley squirmed and Tony jumped down, landing with a thud on both feet. He hit the ground and squared his back so Wesley could hop up.

Everett and Karen were seated next to each other, holding hands on a flowered loveseat. His dad was on the edge of a chair next to them, elbows on his knees, head in his hands.

Although he tried, Wesley couldn't make out a word of what looked like an intense conversation.

Suddenly, Karen rose and leaned over to say something to Everett, her long, shiny blond hair brushing against his shoulder. Then she left the room and the collies eased up from the floor to follow her.

When Karen was gone, his dad raised his head toward Everett. There were bandages on Dad's forehead and cheek. His eyes were bloodshot. He squinted and pleaded urgently with his hands.

What's he doing here?

Both Tony and Wesley's heads spun as a bolt lock clicked and a door opened on the front porch just around the corner. Then a bunch of light footsteps. Claws clicking on wood. And jingling.

Tony began to rise from the ground, Wesley jumped from his back into the snow, and they froze like plastic soldiers.

"Brrr. Go on, go potty, girls," Karen yelled from what must have been just forty feet from them. *Can she see the Yukon?*

After shooting a worried glance at Tony, Wesley's eyes became transfixed on the dogs, whose name tags clinked at their collars as they moseyed and sniffed a little ways out from the house.

"C'mon, girls, hurry up, do your business! It's freezing out here. Let's go!"

Everything appeared as if it was going to be okay until, virtually at the same time, the dogs picked up their scent and started barking.

Taking off like trained security hounds, the collies darted through the snow, as they seemed to fly five feet with each stride. Coming to within a few feet of Wesley and Tony, the dogs ducked, jumped, barked, and growled—baring big white teeth and severely testing Wesley's bladder.

The knocker from the front door rattled. Karen must have gone inside. Then, floodlights bathed the yard with light.

Wesley looked frantically at the lit-up ground then at himself. He and Tony were still in the dark, where they stood frozen, pressed against the house.

The door burst open again, and footsteps could be heard up on the porch.

This is it… Uncle Everett and I are finally gonna have our show-down.

Karen leaned out around the corner of the house and peered down into the yard.

In the white of the floodlights near the side of the house, the dogs barked and growled at something in the shadow. It was probably just a rabbit or stray cat the girls had cornered.

To be on the safe side, Karen hurried back into the house, glancing behind her as she did, and bolt-locked the door once inside.

"Ev…Everett."

Her husband was just starting to stand when she got to the door-way of the family room. "The dogs are barking at something right outside there." She pointed to the window near Eddie.

"I heard 'em." Everett went to the window and cupped both hands around his eyes to cut the glare as he peered outside.

"It's probably just some critter." He turned to Eddie. "You wouldn't believe the animals we see out here."

"Would you take a look?"

"Yeah, hon. I'll go." Everett squeezed Karen's arm, smiled at his brother, and moved toward the door. "You guys sit tight."

"I'll come, too." Eddie began to follow.

"Oh, no you don't," Everett called as he reached the side porch door. "The last thing you need is to fall on some ice. I'll be right back. Why don't you guys make us some cocoa or decaf or something."

"Sounds good." Karen thanked God she was preparing coffee for Eddie rather than helping plan his funeral. She tried to rest in the moment, doing her best to mask the mounting frustration of having to postpone her discussion with Everett.

"Eddie, have a seat in the kitchen. I'm going to make sure you have everything you need for bed. I'll be right back."

Eddie limped slightly as he made his way to the kitchen.

Karen focused on putting one foot in front of the other on her way to the guest bedroom. "Just keep going. You'll get through this," she mumbled. "Get your eyes off yourself."

She smoothed the bedspread and puffed up the pillows on the guest bed, reminding herself that God's timing had brought Eddie to Twin Streams that night. Turning out the lamp and going to the window, Karen peered outside and gradually took in the dreamlike scene that unfolded before her.

The dogs were no longer beneath the window, but something dark stained the snow. And something shone in the distance. Bright red taillights—in the yard.

No. Not right. That shouldn't be there…

Blood in the snow!

The dogs had cornered *people.* But who? DeathStroke freaks?

Frantic yelping sounded in the distance, by the road. *Rosey…Millie!*

Now, headlights swerving.

In the yard!

Smashing through the manger scene. Spinning…taillights.

"Oh my…nooooo!" Karen screamed. "Everett!"

Eddie was by her side in an instant as she fought with the heavy porch door, yanking it open into the frigid night.

"Everett!" She dashed down the steps, into the snow.

"Here," he yelled to the backdrop of a car engine roaring into the night. "It's okay. I'm okay, honey. We need to get Millie to a vet. Don't come out here, babe."

Karen's heart came up to her throat with a squeal as she ran toward his voice, through air that became saturated with the smell of gasoline.

Rosey trotted, puffed, and limped into the light to meet Karen, who began to spring toward Everett when her eyes finally spotted him in the indigo night, cradling a heavy, lifeless Millie in his lap.

"Ahh!" Karen fell to the ground next to Everett and the collie. "What's wrong?"

The air vacuumed out of her when she saw the thick, shiny band of blood covering the dog's head, ears, and neck. "What happened?" Karen moaned. "Did that car hit her?"

"She's been cut—bad." Everett hoisted Millie up into his arms as he got to his knees, but her head dangled there, odd and grotesque. "She's alive, but we need to get her help—fast."

Everett balanced on one knee then grunted as he stood, lifting Millie.

Karen took in the surreal scene as Eddie put an arm around her shoulder. The spotlight that illuminated the manger scene was gone. Pieces of the wood figures lay in splinters on the snow and half-buried in the muddy tire tracks that circled the yard and trailed off in the distance toward Old Peninsula Road.

Everett trotted toward the garage with Millie in his arms. "Karen! Get the keys to the Honda, and some rags. Do you know a vet open this time of night?"

She made a beeline for the porch. "Animal emergency in Chappaqua! I'll drive."

"I'll go with you." Eddie followed as fast as he could into the kitchen.

"Eddie, no." She searched for her keys. "You're hurt. You need to rest.

"I can probably—"

"Please. We'll be fine." She finally retrieved the keys from a black leather purse in the pantry and looked around the room, asking herself what else she needed to do or take. "I'd feel better if you stayed here anyway. Just make sure Rosey's okay."

"Isn't there anything else I can do?" He met her at the door to the garage and held it for her.

Karen hit the lighted green button to open the garage.

"I feel bad just sitting around here," Eddie said.

Everett yelled for Karen to hurry.

"Eddie," she locked eyes with him one last time, "if the higher power you mentioned earlier is God, you can pray for Millie." She raced down the steps. "And get the door for Everett!"

Eddie made his way down into the garage and opened the back door for his brother while Karen got in to drive. With his chest and hands covered in Millie's blood, Everett ducked into the backseat holding their beloved collie. "Let's roll!"

Karen fired up the white Honda and zoomed back out of the garage. *Get us there in time, Jesus. Please…*

Cutting the wheel, she took one last glimpse at Eddie, who looked so helpless yet whose life seemed so dangerous. She stepped on the gas and whirled the car down the driveway, pleading with God to forgive her for the judgment she'd allowed to fester in her heart toward the dark brother who'd found his way to Twin Streams that night.

8

A ribbon of orange sunlight brushed across the gray canvas of the eastern horizon the morning after Millie died. It was cold and brittle, and Everett prayed for Karen as he watched her tiny silhouette far out on the ridge. Arms crossed, head down, she kicked up one slow step after another. It seemed to him she was trying to reach the warmth of the sun, maybe to disappear into that painting.

Everett stood in the frozen yard amid what remained of the broken pieces of the wooden manger scene and Millie's splattered blood. As he searched for Millie's missing dog tag amid the debris, Everett noticed Eddie staring out the guest room window.

The Bedford police had come and gone fifteen minutes earlier, filing a report about the white Yukon and promising to patrol the area more frequently. It wasn't until Everett looked more closely at the manger remnants that he made a peculiar discovery. One figure was missing completely: the baby Jesus.

After scanning the property, the police pointed out to Everett and Eddie that footprints were in the snow adjacent to the house, beneath several windows. Two people who'd been wearing boots.

Looking out at Karen, Everett's spirit became as gray as the morning. A depression he used to know so well fought to resurrect itself. Once again, guilt climbed onto his shoulders and camped there. Millie's death, his brother's troubles, strangers meddling in their lives—it all brought Karen grief. A grief she'd seldom known before she hooked up with the black sheep rocker.

Everett's bloodline, his past, was nothing but sin and darkness. Sometimes he couldn't shake the lie that God was punishing him for his rebellious years. He knew it wasn't true, but in his weaker moments, he entertained such thoughts.

"Sorry about all this." Eddie sauntered up in the snow wearing sweats and an old winter jacket of Everett's.

"It's not your fault." Everett had one hand in his coat pocket and the other clutching a mug of lukewarm coffee.

"I hope not. I don't know why they would have followed me here, after they just beat the tar out of me."

"Who knows. I'll go with you today to pay what you owe."

"Do you know who may have done this?" Eddie asked.

"No. I just feel bad for Karen. I've brought so much baggage into her life."

"She's a wonderful woman."

"Way beyond anything I deserve. Every once in a while I feel like if I truly loved her, I would have let her go."

"That's crazy, man."

"I'm serious. Ever since she and I hooked up, there's been trouble. Her house burning down in Kansas, her kidnapping—"

"But that's all behind you guys. Zane Bender's gonna spend the rest of his life in the big house."

"I'm sure he has friends."

"His friends would have done worse harm than this." He kicked a piece of the broken manger scene. "Maybe this was some freaks on a joyride. They had one too many—"

"They sliced Millie's neck! And why were they looking in our windows?"

"Who knows, man. Maybe they used to be fans."

These were fans? These barbarians?

Everett walked a few steps toward Karen and stared out at her. "She doesn't deserve this…nastiness. You and I are used to this kind of stuff, but not her."

Eddie walked toward his brother. "Why is life so hard, Ev?"

The question surprised Everett like the ring of a hotel wake-up call. Here was a desperate man—his own brother—plumbing the depths of life and eternity itself, and all Everett could do was wallow in his own self-pity.

"I think it's hard because God wants us to rely on Him." He examined Eddie's bandaged face. "He doesn't care about a lot of the stuff we think is important, like big houses and cars and money. He doesn't think like we do. What's important to Him is that we understand how much He loves us. He lost a Son, too, you know? He knows your grief."

Eddie motioned toward Karen. "Oh, so He causes us trouble and pain to force us onto His team? He kills our sons in car wrecks and makes our kids rebellious? He ruins our marriages and hooks us on gambling? That *stinks!*"

Everett frowned, shook his head, and forced himself to keep his cool. "Dude, I know where you're coming from. But listen to me: God didn't cause that stuff to happen—"

"I know what you're gonna say," Eddie interrupted. "He allowed it. Isn't that right? Isn't that what you Christians believe? Everything goes through His fingers first. Why? That's all I wanna know—why have we suffered so much…loss?"

"Bro, just hear me, okay? I understand your anger and doubts. But I want to ask you something. Could it be those are the wrong questions?"

Eddie stuck an immovable finger into Everett's chest. "If you don't ask those questions, then you're just plain ignorant! Christians talk about this loving God, but they have no explanation whatsoever for all the carnage and heartache in this world." Eddie turned his back and stomped off.

"Look at me," Everett said.

When he jerked around, Eddie's bandaged face was scrunched up in a scowl, his mouth sealed shut.

"Could it be that when calamity happens in this world, in our lives, that maybe God wants us to ask ourselves, are we ready to meet our Maker—the God who holds everything together?"

Eddie huffed away, kicking the snow, reminding Everett of their father's temper.

"He *is* a loving God. Look at the patience He had with me. All my addictions and rebellion. All the women I used. All the people I led astray. But He waited for me, dude. He drew me to Himself. And God's being patient with you, too, Eddie—"

"Oh, I'm loving every minute of it, believe me."

"But you're here, aren't you? You're alive. I know your world's been shaken to the core. I know David's gone. But you're here with me, today—right now. Are you ready to meet Him—face-to-face?"

Eddie charged back, squaring off with Everett. "Let me ask *you* a question. Is my son in hell?"

The wind left Everett. "Eddie—"

"You see, brother, if I believe the way you do, I lose, any way you slice it."

"I feel responsible for David—"

"Nothin' you can do about it now."

"I can still help you and Sheila, and Madison and Wesley."

"Look, Ev, I love you." Their eyes connected. "But frankly, our family—what's left of it—has no interest in God, at least not the one you so blindly insist on serving. That doesn't mean we can't be friends and stay close. I want that. And I appreciate your help last night and with the money I owe. But—"

"He's also a God of judgment, Eddie." Everett splashed what was left of his cold coffee onto the snow and stared down at it. "Did you ever think your family might be in the condition it's in because you've made bad choices?"

"Who do you think you are!"

"Just someone who's found a better way."

"Yeah. The *only* way, according to you."

"It's true, Eddie. We're each going somewhere when we die—heaven or hell. I just want you to understand that the only way to heaven—to the Father—is through the Son."

"Look, I told you I believe in a higher power. Can't that be good enough for you? Geez."

"Not if that higher power isn't Christ."

"Well it's not, okay! You're so narrow-minded, Everett. I'll serve my god, my way!"

"That is such a cop-out, Eddie. I know, because all my life I was the king of cop-outs. Who are you to make up your own god and your own truth?"

Eddie exhaled heavily. "Thanks for the Sunday school lesson, brother." He set his face to the wind and headed for the house. "If you need help burying Millie, let me know."

The ground out on the ridge was almost frozen. Everett and Karen had dug Millie's grave for thirty minutes, mostly in silence.

"Would you please let me finish this myself?" he asked.

"I need to do it." Karen continued digging, red-cheeked, runny-nosed, and resolute on finishing the task.

"I can't find the baby Jesus figure from the manger scene." He pounced on his shovel with all his weight. "I guess they took it."

Karen sniffed and continued breaking up the softer dirt that he had already loosened below the hard surface.

After several more minutes of working, Everett rested both hands on his shovel handle and looked back at the house, perhaps a half mile away. It was tiny in the distance, and something he never thought he would share with such a precious partner.

After all, he was a renegade. He'd grown up neglected by his mother and in utter fear of his abusive father. His soul had once been a bastion of bile and transgression, pride and rebellion. Clearly, he did not deserve a woman of grace like Karen, nor was he worthy of God's forgiveness. Yet he had them—both. And he found himself breathing thanks to God with every fiber of his unworthy being.

Other than the slight whistle of the breeze, it was winter quiet, muffled, as if they were in their own secluded little piece of world.

Everett stared back at the spot where he'd had the awkward conversation with Eddie. Millie was still in the trunk of the Honda. It was going to be a long walk to get her out to the ridge. Rosey lay nearby, with her pretty head between her paws on the ground in front of her, raising a dark eyebrow every now and then. It grieved Everett to think about how much she and Karen were going to miss their friend.

"We can get another partner for Rosey if you want, honey," Everett said. "Maybe a puppy—or an adult who needs a home."

"Why would they take the baby Jesus?" Karen attacked the dark soil.

"I don't know."

She squinted up at him. "Are the murderers connected with your brother?"

"I doubt it. So does Eddie."

"Well…do you have any other explanation? Who did this!" she yelled. "*Why?*" She went back at the dirt with a vengeance—a side of her Everett had never seen.

"I just don't know, honey. Maybe it was some drugged-out DeathStroke fans." That haunting feeling crept up on him. *You're paying for your past. And now, so is she.* "I'm sorry."

The craving for booze came so strong and sudden, it actually took his breath away. *You should have let her go.*

Karen was down in the hole now, sweating and out of breath, throwing shovelful after shovelful onto the growing mound of earth beside the grave.

"Is this deep enough?" The sound of her voice snapped him out of it.

"Yeah." He nodded. "That'll be fine."

"I want to get a gravestone for her." Her angry front melted, and Karen dropped to the edge of the hole, her shovel falling, her anguish bursting forth in a flood of tears.

Everett jumped into the twenty-five-inch hole and nestled next to her. "I'm sorry, babe."

He got only a glimpse of her pink cheeks and wet upper lip before she buried her face in his chest.

"We can't have children, Ev," came her muffled cry.

"Now, darlin', this isn't gonna stop us from having little Lesters. I know it's been—"

"I can't have babies!" She shook her head against his chest as she clung to him. "Because of the abortion. I found out yesterday."

The silence pounded in his ears. *She must be wrong. We'll fix it…*

"What are you saying?" He pried her away so he could look her in the eyes. "Tell me! What's going on?"

"I wanted to—ever since the appointment." She moaned. "There hasn't been time! I wanted you to tell me about the concert, then Eddie called—"

"Oh, honey, I'm sorry." He stroked her cheek, backtracking to the day before and counting the hours she'd held in the news. "What'd the doctor say?"

"When I had the abortion." She had to catch her breath. "I had an infection in my womb and Fallopian tubes. The doctor said it was nothing—"

"So, what's the problem?"

"Let me finish!" she cried. "I was young enough, he said, there'd be plenty of time to heal. That's why I never mentioned it. It was nothing…"

"But the doctor—"

"Yesterday, the ob-gyn said there are adhesions on my Fallopian tubes; she thinks they're shut for good. I'm infertile!"

"We'll get a second opinion." But the discussion with Eddie flooded back to him. And somehow he knew this was God's plan. It was cold and dreadful. But it was the hand they were being dealt. Now, he would be forced once again to walk further and deeper in the blind faith he'd just tried to explain to his brother.

Karen lurched out of the hole and ran from Everett. Ten yards out, her body went limp with the siege of emotion, folding to the ground like a wilting flower. "Millie's dead. My womb is dead. My dream is *dead*! I'm not going to be able to have your children."

Everett rushed to her side as she pounded the dirt with her fists. "What did I do to deserve this?"

He couldn't help but think, *You married me.*

Rosey approached her, whimpering and nudging her wet nose against Karen's coat.

"I'm sorry, honey," Everett said. "I'm so sorry. I should have asked more about the appointment. I'm so dang selfish."

Karen shuddered at his words, the tears streaming down her anguished face. "I wanted to tell you. I wanted you there with me…"

Everett squeezed her tightly, pressing his cheek against the top of her head. *How long is this angel of a woman going to put up with a loser like me?*

Karen insisted on accompanying Everett to bury Millie. The dog was still wet, heavy, and stiffening. Although Everett had contemplated driving the tractor with Millie in the trailer, he decided not to mention the idea to Karen; she would want it to be more personal.

Karen covered the dog in a navy blanket and helped guide Everett as he carried the body all the way down and up the rolling hills that led to the ridge. Once Everett, out of breath and on his knees, gently laid the collie in the oval-shaped hole, Karen used one of the shovels to chop and jab the dirt that would cover the dog—making sure it was fine, like powder—no stones. Everett helped.

They covered their beloved collie with the soft dirt until there was a small mound slightly above ground level. Karen marked the grave with three large rocks they'd found nearby.

"I want to read something." She reached for the inside pocket of her beige barn coat and pulled out a small black Bible. Everett rested an arm around her back.

She leafed through the thin pages, her tapered fingers and thin hands pink from the cold. A line of geese honked overhead. "'Hear my cry, O God; Give heed to my prayer. From the end of the earth I call to You when my heart is faint; Lead me to the rock that is higher than I.'"

A tear slipped from the outside corner of her eye and hit the shoulder of her coat. "'For You have been a refuge for me…a tower of strength against the enemy. Let me dwell in Your tent forever; Let me take refuge in the shelter of Your wings.'"

The Scripture was about more than Millie and the wicked ones who killed her; this was about her infertility, the death of a dream, and their very future—which was going to be radically different than Karen had ever envisioned.

With the whipping wind, Everett was rocked by an overwhelming sense of inadequacy, as if he wasn't all Karen needed.

It was a lie.

Why do I listen, then?

"One more," she muttered, rolling the pages beneath her thumb. "I'll have to work on this one." She paused. "'You have heard that it was said, "You shall love your neighbor, and hate your enemy." But I say to you, love your enemies, and pray for those who persecute you…'"

She slipped the Bible back into her coat pocket and knelt, her knees soaking in the wet dirt. Then she looked up, toward the house, finishing the rest from memory. "'For He causes His sun to rise on the evil and the good…'"

9

On the gloomy trek back to the house, Everett was surprised to learn that Karen hadn't yet shared the news of her infertility with her parents.

"I wanted you to know first," she insisted.

"Okay. But it's time to call them."

"I know," she mumbled.

"Your dad's gonna feel responsible." He carried both shovels in one hand and held her close with the other. "And your mom's going to want to be with you—they both are."

Karen was subdued and didn't argue as they marched through the wet snow toward the house. Everett, meanwhile, recalled the first time he'd met Jacob and Sarah Bayliss at their home in Topeka a little more than a year ago. It was then that Jacob explained the nightmare that had changed their lives.

Some thirteen years ago, Karen's father had been the pastor of a large legalistic church. In her own way, Karen rebelled against Jacob's hypocrisy, pride, and lack of love—she became pregnant at the age of fifteen. To save himself and his man-made ministry, Jacob drove Karen to get an abortion.

Mind-blowing.

The night after the operation, in his study, Jacob had an encounter with God—for the first time. On his face, behind locked doors, Jacob cried for hours as God showed him, through that tragic experience, what kind of person he'd been.

"By His mercy, that's when everything began to change," Jacob had explained to Everett. "I asked Karen's forgiveness, and Sarah's, and God's. They were each merciful. I repented and prayed for God to change me, and He began to, that very night. And when I changed, there was a glorious change in Karen and in Sarah."

After stepping down from the pulpit of that seven-hundred-member church, Jacob had never gotten back into formal church leadership. Yet, Everett looked up to him as a spiritual mentor and one of the godliest men he knew. That's why he was so excited about having Jacob along on the upcoming Living Water tour.

After insisting on setting out lunch fixings, Karen retreated to the master bedroom on the main floor to call her parents. Everett and his brother, both red-cheeked and sock-footed, made ham sandwiches at the large island in the kitchen.

"I'd rather you just give me the money and take me to my car." Eddie put a handful of pretzels on his plate. "There's no reason for you to go with me to meet the bookie."

"No reason—after last night?" Everett said.

"There's not gonna be any more trouble, as long as I've got the dough."

"Look, I'm going." Everett poured himself a Diet Coke out of the two-liter bottle. "I just wanna make sure it goes off without a hitch."

"I don't want you to get involved, okay?"

"Well, that's tough. It's my money. And I'll go if I wanna go."

They each took a seat at a bar stool against the island. Before

Everett could suggest a prayer, Eddie had already taken a big bite of the dark rye sandwich and swung his bandaged face toward the bay window, staring outside.

Everett bowed his head and closed his eyes but found it difficult to concentrate on prayer with Eddie right there. He managed a quick thanks, a request for protection, and comfort for Karen.

He looked up, into his brother's waiting eyes.

"I'm gonna need to change before we do this errand," Eddie mumbled.

"That's better." Everett smiled. "Hey, Karen and I were talking, and we thought maybe she could come—"

"Not to do the deed…"

"No. I was going to say, we could take you to your house and get you changed. Karen's wanted to see your place and the family. If she's up to it, maybe she could hang out while you and I meet the bookie. It's not gonna take too long, is it?"

"Well, I'm not sure anybody's gonna be at my house."

"Okay. Well, where do we go to pay the debt?"

"Restaurant on East Fifty-second. Then I gotta get the Amanti—near my office."

"East Fifty-second. Near the Art Museum?"

"Close, yeah."

"'Cause Karen's been wanting me to take her to an exhibit down there, some photography show. We could drop her there, if she can't stay at your place, and I can pick her up later."

"Okay by me. I can't promise what kind of reception she's gonna get at my place, if anybody's home."

"She's a big girl." Everett wiped his mouth with a paper napkin. "You'd be surprised the kind of tigers she can tame."

It took several seconds, but when Eddie realized Everett had been talking about himself, he snickered. Everett joined in, and for a moment, they were brothers again—waxing silly over ham sandwiches at the kitchen counter.

★ ★ ★

Eddie's upscale neighborhood in White Plains reminded Karen of some of the elite areas of Topeka, only ritzier—*much* ritzier. Towering trees hung over quiet streets, sidewalks, and precise landscapes.

Eddie looked out the passenger window of Karen's white Accord and shook his head. "Look at that. Even in December, they got toys everywhere. I've told the neighborhood association about that."

Karen followed his gaze to a brown Tudor-style house on a hill. Three sleds littered the front yard, as well as a yellow Tonka truck, a leaning snowman, and a ton of footprints, mashed snow, and trampled grass. It looked lived-in to her, with traces of children everywhere. Karen squeezed her purse. It was something she and Everett would never know.

As Everett swung the Honda down the blacktop driveway, it was like pulling into a private cul-de-sac. Straight ahead—just past where the driveway widened—was a sprawling white home with a four-car garage and an arched entryway leading to elegant, double front doors.

Hands in pockets, Karen wrapped her coat tight around her. "Everett's told me about this place, but I had no idea how beautiful…" *Or how expensive it was.*

"Thank you." Eddie keyed his way into the front door and stepped in. "I can't believe it's taken this long to get you over here."

"Madison?" a female voice called.

"No, not Madison," Eddie yelled back, a tinge of pink filling his cheeks. He looked down and wiped his feet on the thick beige rug in the foyer. "Let me take your coats." He laid them over a chair in the adjoining living room and stepped back into the foyer, which smelled of cigarettes.

"Well, do you have the guts to face me?" snarled the voice from the other room.

Eddie shot Karen and Everett a bogus smile and led them around the corner into an enormous family room with glossy wooden floors, two huge Oriental rugs, a thirty-foot ceiling, and a stairway whose white banister went all the way around the perimeter of the second floor.

Karen couldn't decide what to look at first, the incredible space she had just entered or Eddie's wife, Sheila, curled up on a long, curved white leather couch. She chose Sheila, whose posture straightened noticeably as the group entered the room.

"Eddie? What happened to your face?" Her brief expression of shock was quickly replaced by a scowl. "Why didn't you tell me they were coming? This is just like you."

"I didn't want to try and explain over the phone."

Everett and Karen said hello, but Sheila maintained her rigid position. "Where've you been?"

Eddie glanced at them and back at her. "I had a little problem at the track last night. I called Ev, 'cause I didn't want to bother you. It was late."

Sheila reached for her cigarettes and lighter on the glass coffee table, lit one, sat back, and exhaled. Her thick dark brown hair was cut mod, above the shoulders, and accented in auburn. She crossed her arms defensively. Her once unique face had changed dramatically from plastic surgery, looking almost like a mask when she spoke—the words coming out, but the facial muscles barely moving.

"Those hoodlums finally get hold of you? Serves you right, you—"

"Yeah, they did," Eddie purposefully drowned her out before she cursed. "Everett's here to bail me out. Karen just came along to say hi. Madison's not home yet?"

"No."

"What about Wesley?"

Sheila's mouth dropped open. "Oh, come on, Eddie. We're not gonna play all-American family, are we? Since when would I know when Wesley's home and when he's not?"

Karen was weak from the verbal barrage. Poor Eddie. When had their relationship spiraled so out of control? What a mess. If there was ever a family that needed the power of God's intervention, this was the address.

"Look," Eddie said, "let's not argue. Everett and I have got to run into town and Karen thought she'd stick here till we get back, spend some time with you and whoever shows up. Is that gonna work or not?"

"If not, I've got other plans," Karen spoke up.

Sheila rose, agitated, from the couch and crossed to a thirty-foot wall of windows, where there were two white swivel chairs and a sitting table. She looked out, her back to them. Karen made note of the small white Christmas tree on the corner table and approached, admiring the view of the valley and woodlands beyond. "What a marvelous setting."

Wearing a soft blue V-neck sweater, powder blue jeans, and furry black mules, Sheila picked up a silver ashtray from the table. "This place cost a million a couple years ago. It's probably worth double that by now. With Madison and Wesley getting older, we'll probably sell. I want to move to Manhattan."

Karen squelched the negative reminders about Eddie's debt, which shot off in her mind like flares. But she couldn't ignore the sweet, offensive smell of alcohol, which Sheila wore like perfume.

"I'm gonna run up and change," Eddie announced, "then Everett and I are gonna take off. Karen, you can stay or go to the museum— either way." He dashed up the steps and disappeared beyond the banister.

Everett strolled over by the caramel-colored marble fireplace. "I'm sure Karen would like the grand tour, if you're up to it, Sheila."

They heard the front door open, keys jingle, and movement in the foyer. After about thirty seconds, Madison leaned around the corner. "Is Dad okay?"

"Hello, darling," Sheila snuffed out her cigarette, set the ashtray on the table, and began the trek across the large room. "Your father's fine. He's upstairs. Look who's here!"

Madison blushed and whispered a shy hello to "Uncle Everett" and "Aunt Karen," who approached, shook hands, and gave awkward pats while commenting how much their niece had blossomed.

Indeed, Madison had become an attractive, healthy-looking seventeen-year-old, with long brown frizzy hair. Karen couldn't stop staring at her, marveling at how much she'd matured and amazed at God's handiwork—how much she resembled both her mother and father. Her light green eye shadow matched her dangly earrings and Abercrombie top, while her sparkling brown eyes looked exactly like Eddie's.

"I was just going to give Karen a tour," Sheila said, as Madison hung her coat up in the hall closet. "You want to come?"

"I want to see Dad and get changed." She headed for the steps. "But I might catch up with you."

"Good seeing you, Madison." Everett waved.

"Join us, Madison." Karen watched her go up the steps. "I'd love to spend a little time…"

Madison smiled. She seemed so reserved. Did she know about her mother's drinking or her father's gambling? How had she coped with her brother's death?

Everett walked out on the spacious back deck while Sheila showed Karen around. The main living area was stark white, spacious, and contemporary, with a minimal amount of furniture. Live plants and flowers dotted its many nooks and crannies. From room to room, the home was clean, simple, and elegant; not an ounce of clutter.

Eddie returned downstairs wearing a black long-sleeve golf sweater, brown dress slacks, and polished black shoes. Sheila excused herself to get a Kleenex.

"We'll wash the clothes you loaned me and get them back to you," Eddie told Karen and Everett as he headed for the foyer. "You ready to roll?"

"Yeah." Everett turned to Karen. "What are you gonna do, babe? Stay?"

"Sure. If it's okay…" She heard a creak at the top of the stairs and assumed Madison was hovering above the conversation.

"Haven't you left yet?" Sheila barged back into the room. "Come on, Karen, there's a lot more to see. Good-bye, Everett. Don't let that blind brother of yours lead you into his sinister world."

Karen tried to make eye contact with Everett to second Sheila's notion, but he was following Eddie, who had already rounded the corner.

Sheila approached Everett, gave him a brief hug, and held the lapels of his jacket. "I mean it. Be careful. He's a liar, Ev—"

Eddie sauntered back around the corner. "What's the holdup?"

"Ready." Everett pulled away from Sheila, hugged Karen, and gave her a gentle kiss. "We'll see you ladies in a little while."

"Be careful, babe." Karen squeezed his arm, made him look into her eyes, and didn't care if the others heard her whisper, "I'll be praying."

10

After Sheila and Karen had toured most of the upstairs, they came to a door that was ajar. "And this is the magnificent Madison's room." Sheila tapped on the door and led the way in.

It was lavender, with similar hues in the bedspread, pillows, and lamps. Madison had changed into sweats and thick socks and was lying on the bed writing in a journal. She rolled over and forced a smile.

"I love the colors," Karen said. "And look at this dollhouse. My word, it's wonderful. With working lights. I had one for years. I think it's still in my folks' basement."

"She's never wanted to part with it." Sheila swiped a hand across its black roof.

"Who did these sketches, and the watercolors?" Karen examined the matted works hanging at various spots on the wall.

"I did."

"These are incredible, Madison! What did you go by to create these?"

"Some from pictures in magazines or photos. Others, I was there—like the waterfall. That was from a family trip to Oregon—Coquille River Falls—"

"In the Siskiyou National Forest," Sheila said. "Eddie insisted that we go. And he was right; it was beautiful."

"You have talent, Madison. The watercolors are so loose and free. I love paintings like that. I took some classes once…"

"Watercolor?" Madison asked. "Really?"

"Yeah, but I'm horrible. I do everything in—"

"I keep telling Madison that her father knows a bigwig at the Savannah College of Art and Design." Sheila eyed her daughter. "But she's not sure she wants to go to college. I just don't want her to end up like her older brother—"

"Mom, please."

"He just hasn't been able to keep a job. Hops around a lot. And his father still pays him an allowance—"

"*Mom.*"

"What's wrong? I'm just—"

"Aunt Karen doesn't need to hear this." Madison's eyes rolled up to the ceiling, and Karen's cheeks warmed.

"She may as well hear it. She's part of the family."

There was an uncomfortable silence. After admiring each painting, Karen spoke. "Why don't you let Madison finish showing me the upstairs, Sheila? That'll give us a few minutes to get better acquainted. How about we come down in a few minutes?"

Sheila raised her eyebrows at her daughter. "Fine." She waved her hand and exited, her voice echoing down the hall. "You two spend some time together. It'll be good for you."

Madison pursed her lips and shook her head. "Sorry about that."

"It's okay." Karen smiled.

"She takes medication. Sometimes it puts her on edge."

"Oh…for what?"

"Depression." Madison stood. "Where haven't you been?"

"Let's see. I think we covered it, except that room down there." Karen leaned into the hall and pointed.

Madison set her journal on the bed and meandered into the hallway. The room was set apart from the others, near the banister overlooking the family room. She stopped in the doorway and motioned Karen inside. "This was David's room. They've kept it just like it was, before the accident."

From carpet to walls, the room was dark blue. The focal point was a glass NBA backboard attached to the wall with a red, white, and blue basketball suspended in midair as it swished through the hoop; the basketball itself was a globe lamp, which lit up when Madison flipped the wall switch.

Karen's mind flushed blank when she saw the huge DeathStroke poster. She shot a glance at Madison, but the girl wasn't paying attention—or at least, pretended not to be. Karen walked over to the double windows and looked out over the blacktop driveway and peaceful street.

"David loved it here." Madison joined her. "He had a motorcycle. Used to spend hours riding around the neighborhood. Some of the neighbors complained about the noise, but Mom and Dad never did do anything about it." She chuckled.

"I never got to meet David."

"He was a wild thing." She picked up a photograph of him and several of his buddies. "He was searching."

"For what?"

"I don't know," Madison said. "Answers."

"Answers to what?"

"Life, I suppose. He was an emotional person. He had a good heart."

"I want you to know that Everett feels terrible about letting David down—and you and Wesley."

"David was the one who was so crazy about him."

"Everett was a different person back then." Karen couldn't help but look back at the DeathStroke poster. "He was lost. Selfish. The fame went to his head. All the drugs and alcohol, he was just unreliable. Not to mention miserable. He had a rough upbringing."

"David wrote about him a lot in his journal."

"Really?"

"Yeah." Madison opened the top drawer of his dresser and searched around.

"Oh no, that's private."

"I can't find it anyway. It's usually right here. Mom's probably got it again." She shut the drawer and moved toward the door.

"What about Wesley, how is he?" Karen followed her.

Madison stopped just before leaving the room and faced Karen. "He's bitter. Reckless. He drives my mom and my dad insane."

"Why do you think he's that way? David's death?"

"He was like that before David died. My folks have spoiled him. They spoiled each of us."

"Hmm." Karen had determined that she would never spoil her children, but now... Well, there was no use dwelling on such things.

"But material things can only go so far—you know?" Madison turned away, her shoulders back as she drew in a deep breath.

Karen put a hand on her shoulder. "You want to go back in your room for a minute? Get a Kleenex?"

Madison nodded and walked toward her room. Karen retrieved a tissue from the small bathroom and handed it to her as they both plopped down on the bed.

"I'm sorry." Madison rubbed her nose with the Kleenex. "I don't know why I'm so emotional—why I'm telling you all this. I barely know you."

"We all need someone to talk to now and then."

"My parents provide well for us, but they're so busy. My dad's always working or off—somewhere. And Mom works down at the Fashion Mart. She's in all kinds of clubs." Madison gave a half smile. "And she loves to shop."

"When I was young," Karen said, "my dad put his work above everything. Even above my mom and me. I know how that feels. It hurts. And it makes you look for that attention in other places."

Madison stood. "I don't know…" The girl looked like she needed to vent.

"What is it, sweetie? What else?"

"I just don't want him to hurt my parents anymore. They love us, I know. They've just never known how to express it. All our lives they've tried to be our friends, but they never established any…boundaries."

"You're so mature, Madison. What you're saying makes sense. You'll make a good mother someday."

"I don't know about that…"

Karen ignored the ache inside. "If what you say is true about your mom and dad wanting to be your friends and not knowing how to set up guidelines or discipline, that's probably a very stressful way for them to live, too."

"It is. My dad's a wreck. Trying to work and make deals and pay all our bills. Do you know what happened to him—the cuts?"

Karen was somewhat stunned by the directness of the question. She couldn't lie and found herself frustrated by Eddie's immaturity. "Did you ask him?"

"Yeah. He said someone tried to take his wallet on the subway."

Karen looked down at her hands, twisting her platinum wedding ring, admiring the diamonds, and letting the silence speak.

"Is that what happened?"

Karen sighed. "Your father just needs some good friends right now. That's why Everett and I are here. I can't tell you any more than that."

Madison spun away and leaned on the tall dresser with both

elbows. "This whole situation is so messed up. Sometimes I just want out."

"Why don't you go then? What about that art college in Savannah, after you finish high school? You're so talented—"

"You don't understand." She faced Karen with outstretched arms. "I can't leave."

"Why on earth not?"

Madison crossed her arms and, with a furrowed brow, took several steps toward Karen. "Wesley, okay? I don't feel comfortable leaving my folks alone with him. He's unpredictable. So are his friends. You wouldn't understand."

Karen stood, checked the door, then approached Madison. "What's he into that's making you so scared?"

Madison paced. "We better go back downstairs."

"Madison, when David was in the hospital, your father told Everett that Wesley was probably doing drugs—maybe even selling…"

She stopped and glared at Karen.

"That's not all," Karen continued. "The kid who survived David's wreck told Everett that Wesley was into methamphetamines."

"Did he tell you David was high on meth when he wrecked the Camaro?" Madison finally let go. "And that he probably got it from Wesley?"

The pacing started again, but Karen stopped Madison by gently gripping her shoulders. "It's okay. I understand—"

"Do you?" Madison pulled away from Karen. "I don't think so. I don't think you've seen some of the things I've seen, right from this very window."

"You need to talk about it, Madison. I'll be your friend."

The girl went to the window, rested one knee on her bed, and looked outside, expressionless. "Cars come in the night. All different kinds. All hours. Wesley runs out to meet them. I think he's selling meth or buying it. I don't know."

"When you see—"

"One day I was at the neighborhood pool. Wes and a friend came flying into the parking lot." She spoke as if she were staring at a TV, watching it again on video. "A car was chasing them. Wesley and his buddy ran into the pool area. Children were everywhere. They didn't care, 'cause they were so high. A man and a woman followed them in. He threatened to kill Wesley. Said Wes had put a knife to his son's throat at a party the night before."

"What happened?"

"Some of the dads at the pool had to get between them. Broke it up. Threatened to call the police."

Karen walked up behind Madison and rested her hands on the girl's shoulders.

This time, Madison didn't move away but continued talking as she gazed outside.

"I've seen low-life thugs carrying guns, waiting in their junk cars for Wesley to get home. When he gets stoned, he doesn't know what he's doing. I've heard him firing guns out back. He's nuts. And he thinks he's untouchable."

"Where are your parents when this stuff happens?"

"If it's during the day, they're gone. If it's at night, they're asleep. Their bedroom's at the back of the house. In the summer they go up to the lake on weekends, so we're here alone."

Someone was coming.

Karen grabbed Madison's hands and whispered quickly, "I want to help you. I'm here for you. Okay? You can call me anytime."

Madison squeezed Karen's hands and nodded, a minor gesture, but one that sent a healing breath of life into Karen's suffocated soul.

"Where have you girls been?" Sheila burst into the room, reeking of liquor. Madison's eyes darted to meet Karen's. "Come on, come on. Would you two quit gabbing? I want to show Karen the rest of the house."

As they were about to leave, Madison must have heard something. She crossed to the window, looked out, and immediately turned back into the room. "Speak of the devil."

"What?" Karen walked to the window.

Madison's gaze fell back to the driveway.

Karen's eyes followed to the muddy white Yukon below.

11

Even though it was Saturday, traffic was heavy as Everett drove Eddie into Manhattan under gray skies, taking FDR Drive along the East River. By the time they stopped at First Federal Bank and reached East Fifty-second, it was midafternoon, and Christmas shoppers and sightseers had converged on the Big Apple in full force.

Everett finally found a parking spot in the shadow of the towering Citicorp building. As the brothers set out for the restaurant, an arctic wind swirled amid the lofty buildings, whipping through the shaded streets, rattling holiday decorations, and making it feel fifteen degrees colder than it had in the suburbs.

"Don't forget, you've got to take me to my car after this." Eddie's teeth clacked.

"Why's it down here? I thought you were taking the subway?"

"I usually do, but I had errands. Wanted to have my car."

"I can't believe all the people down here."

"It's always like this." Eddie nodded toward the crosswalk. "That's Pappano's over there."

The Italian eatery was small and informal looking from the outside, with a dark wood facade. Red and white checkered curtains hung on gold rods in the lower half of the large window. Above it, "Pappano's" was lit up in red script.

Bells on the heavy front door jingled as Eddie entered first. The place smelled like oregano and freshly-baked bread, and Everett let the warmth soak in. A short, gray-haired woman hustled toward them, wearing a white blouse and black pants. Her olive skin was wrinkled, and she had a hooked nose.

"Two of you." She grabbed several large plastic-coated menus.

"Actually," Eddie said, "we need to see Mike. Is he around?"

Her eyes shifted from Eddie to Everett and back to Eddie. She examined the bandages on his face. "Wait here." Returning the menus to their holder, she headed to the back of the room and through a set of red curtains.

So much for his nerves calming.

"Is Mike the bookie?" Everett whispered.

"Yeah."

As Everett's eyes adjusted to the restaurant, he noticed that four tables around the room were occupied by patrons, who didn't pay much attention as the Lester brothers stood by the old-fashioned cash register.

"You won't need to say anything," Eddie said.

We'll see about that. Everett had been in his share of nasty situations before, but he hadn't fought sober since he was a boy. And he'd never had to deal with the mob. So he was gearing up for anything, taking deep breaths, getting psyched to be tough, if necessary.

The little Italian waitress exited the curtained room and headed for a four-top she was serving in the far corner of the dining room. Before Eddie could get her attention, a hand parted the curtains. A large, clean-shaven white man wearing a gray suit and white shirt peered out at them. Then the curtains closed.

It wasn't the first time Everett chastised himself for getting involved. *Lord, protect us.*

The curtains parted again and the same man stepped through, waved them back, and disappeared into the mystery room.

"That's Paulie," Eddie whispered, putting his shoulders back and leading the way. When they got to the curtains, he stuck his head in. "Mike?" He entered and Everett followed.

It was dark and smoky. A TV glowed with college football from the upper corner of the room. Below it sat four suited men with stone faces, playing poker amid ashtrays, drinks, and several dirty entrée dishes. Beyond them was a sink and a black Formica countertop, stocked with ten or twelve bottles of liquor.

The tension ratcheted up several notches. The place looked like a mob hangout from *The Godfather,* where someone could get whacked while eating a bowl of spaghetti.

At the far end of the room was an old wooden desk. On it sat a hunched man. His face was badly pockmarked, and he had thick black eyebrows and a curved scar on his forehead. "Hello, Eddie." He dangled his legs and glossy wingtips. "Glad you could make it."

"Sal." Eddie nodded toward him.

Next to the desk sat Paulie. Adjacent to him—leaning back on two legs of a chair—was a skinny, balding man with a long thin nose and dark, sunken eyes. "Eddie," he said, his voice low and thick. "Come over here. You brought a friend, how nice."

Eddie approached the men, and Everett followed several steps behind.

"This is a buddy, Mike. He helped me with this." Eddie reached inside his heavy coat and produced a thick white envelope. He handed it to the skinny man, who opened it, removed the stack of bills, and fanned them with his thumbs.

Mike smiled. "Must be nice having such generous friends."

Everett noticed the poker game had stopped momentarily as the four men at the table watched the transaction.

"Aren't you going to introduce us?" Mike motioned to Everett.

"I don't believe…" Eddie stammered. "I don't think it's necessary,"

"Oh, come on, Eddie!" Mike banged his chair to the floor. "Who do you think we are? Give your brother a proper introduction."

Eddie sighed and shot a worried glance at Everett. "Gentlemen, this is Everett Lester."

Everett nodded once. The men stared.

"If that takes care of everything," Eddie turned toward the curtains, "we need to get going."

"Hold on. Hold on." Mike laughed and stood. "Let's make sure we got this right before you go runnin' off." He smacked the envelope of bills against the palm of his hand. "We got twenty-four grand in all here, correct?"

Eddie nodded while Mike counted some of the money, then handed it to Scarface sitting on the desk. "Here's four thousand to Shy Sal. That right, Sal?"

"One thousand for the vig he missed last week," Sal said, counting the money as he spoke, "one thousand for this week's vig, and we doubled it because of the miss. That's right. Glad we could get all caught up, with everybody still in one piece." He chuckled. "Unfortunately, Eddie, you found out what happens when you miss your vig payment. Not good."

Sal hopped off the desk, approached Eddie, and examined his body, head to toe. "Although, it looks like you got off easy. At least you still got all your extremities. Next time, you won't be so lucky."

Everett's face flushed hot with rage. Not only had Eddie lied to him, but these goons were threatening to chop his brother into pieces. Everett knew what it was like to be sick with addiction, and he loathed the predators who preyed on his brother. But he had to keep his cool;

this was not the time for discord. These dudes meant business.

"Okay, that leaves twenty grand for the Knicks loss." Mike rolled up the remaining bills and held them toward Eddie. "Whaddya say, big spender? You want we let it ride—go double or nuttin' again? Villanova plays Notre Dame tonight. Irish are favored by six, and it's in South Bend."

Eddie managed a smile and shook his head.

"That's all right." Mike waved. "I understand you can't talk business around your saintly brother. You call me later and let me know what you wanna do. Personally, I like the Bears at home tomorrow versus Philly. You get eight points and the Soldier Field advantage. Let me know."

"He won't be bettin' anymore," Everett blurted.

Several of the men chuckled, and Eddie glared at his brother. Then he took several steps in the direction of the exit and stopped next to Everett.

"Will that do it then?" Eddie said.

One of the men from the card game—a short, young guy with messy black hair and deranged eyes—rose from the table and walked toward the curtained door. As he did, he reached beneath his suit coat to tuck in his shirt, revealing a gun nestled in the waist of his pants. Once at the curtains, he turned, locked his feet shoulder width apart, and stood like a statue—glaring straight ahead with his arms crossed in front of him.

"There's one more matter of business we need to address." Mike got right up in Eddie's face. "We've known each other a long time now, Eddie, and it dawned on us that you've never met the captain."

Mike looked at his watch. "It's almost time. You guys get dem plates and trash outta here before Mr. B gets here," he barked at the three card players. "Move it!"

As the men scrambled to their feet, Everett's stomach churned. These guys were all packing heat. He and Eddie were sitting ducks.

"Paulie, help clean this place up," Mike said. "And make sure there's plenty of good cigars and gin—Miller's or Bombay. And bring tonic and fresh limes. We'll need clean glasses and ice."

Shy Sal brushed some crumbs off his wrinkled suit and straightened his tie. Walking behind the desk, he tidied up the pens, papers, and ledgers, and pushed the leather chair into place. "It's not every day you get to meet the captain. You and your brother should feel honored."

Eddie leaned toward Everett, not looking at him. "Sorry about this."

Everett made himself take a deep breath and exhale. "We'll talk about it later. Let's just get out of here first chance we get."

Paulie's cell phone rang. Its bluish glow reflected off his wide face momentarily. Then he slipped it back into his pants pocket. "Mr. B's arrived. They're on their way in."

"Places, everybody." Mike motioned Eddie and Everett toward two chairs near the big desk. They crossed to them and sat down. "Stand up!" Mike shot a glance at the door. "What are you, crazy?" The card players, now stationed around the perimeter of the room, took several steps toward Everett and Eddie—who immediately stood.

The bells at the front door jingled. The door slammed shut. And Everett's heart drummed. *Lord, I give myself to You right now. I'm in Your hands...*

First through the curtains ducked a towering dude with dark green sunglasses, short brown hair, and thin sideburns and mustache. Without acknowledging anyone, he marched sternly across the room to the rear of the desk, where he assumed the posture of a Secret Service agent. "Black Bear, in position," he spoke toward a tiny mike on his lapel, then tilted his head and adjusted a clear device in his ear. "Affirmative."

Seconds later another bodyguard—this one short, old, and wiry—came through the red curtain and, in a gravelly voice, announced, "Gentlemen, Mr. B."

Dividing the curtains with black leather gloves, Mr. B glided into the room. His black camel hair coat—with its wide shoulder pads—swished behind him like a cape. He strutted for the main seat at the desk as if he owned New York City. Paulie awaited him with outstretched arms, taking his gloves, scarf, and coat, then disappearing into another room.

"Mike. Sal." Mr. B nodded as the two men stood anxiously in front of the chairs next to the desk. "Boys," he acknowledged the men dotting the perimeter of the room. "Sit."

As everyone except the border police eased into their chairs, Everett turned to Eddie for reassurance but got none. Eddie's attention was fixed on the mesmerizing mob captain, who was running one of the Honduran cigars he'd found in the wooden box on the desk under his short nose.

"Light, sir?" Paulie asked, dashing back into the dark room with a fresh gin and tonic, which he set on a coaster in front of the captain.

"Thank you, Paulie."

The flame in Paulie's shaking fist illuminated Mr. B's tanned face and what Everett assumed were expensive porcelain veneers. The mobster had short, tightly curled hair that was way too jet-black for his age; must have been dyed. Mr. B's weighty rings flashed in the dim light as he toked the cigar, rolling it in his mouth with manicured fingers.

Out of the corner of his eye, Everett detected movement from Mike. The man's eyes darted frantically toward Paulie, whom he was gesturing toward with a tapping finger, trying to signal him to fetch an ashtray—but the plea was too late.

"Ashtray." Mr. B flared, then relished a swig of his drink.

Mike's head and eyes rolled, as Paulie raced from behind the desk, grabbed one of the ashtrays from the clean poker table, and hurried it back to the captain.

"Eddie," Mr. B tapped the oily-looking cigar above the glass ashtray, "we appreciate your business. You've been a good customer for some time. I think you would agree that these fellas—Mike, Sal,

Paulie, and the boys—have been fair to you. They've taken good care of you."

The captain's wide cheeks collapsed as he took a deep drag on the fat cigar, exhaling the thick smoke in a strong, steady stream. "Are you gonna say nothing?"

"No. I mean, yes. It's been okay." Eddie inched forward in his chair.

"Have we been fair to you?"

"Yeah." Eddie squirmed.

"You need to understand the severity of missing a vig payment." Mr. B's small black eyes fixed on Eddie. "Do you? Understand?"

"Yeah, I do."

"Yeah, you do." He ran a finger around the rim of his wet glass. "You understand this is a family business? A proud, honest business? That when you borrow money from us, just like a bank, we expect to get that money back—on time, with interest?"

"Yeah." Eddie shrugged and smiled like a smart aleck.

Everett braced himself for the captain's response.

Sure enough, Mr. B dropped his head. "I don't like your attitude, Eddie. Never have. That's why, when I heard your brother was here—" his eyes came up to meet Everett's for the first time—"I came in. I've seen this scenario a million times. I know guys like you, Eddie. Good clients, until you reach a point. A point when you're runnin' full tilt. That's when you become a risk."

Eddie shifted uneasily while an antsy Everett told himself to keep filling his lungs with air.

"Come on, Mr. B," Eddie said, looking away. "I've always been good for any money I've owed you."

The captain put both elbows on the desk, leaned forward, and stared at Everett. "Look, Mr. Lester. We appreciate you keeping your brother honest. What I want you to know, right up front, is this: No one crosses the Mendazzo family. Okay? No one. When you owe this family money, you pay. If your brother here misses another vig payment, there's gonna be consequences."

"He won't be betting anymore," Everett declared.

Mr. B worked the cigar and exhaled straight toward Eddie.

"You've both been warned."

"Look, I'm just here to help my brother." Everett's temper boiled at these creeps for attempting to take advantage of Eddie. "We don't plan on seeing you again."

"And I'm here to tell you I've seen dozens of scumbags just like your brother, Mr. Lester. I know the symptoms. And lyin's at the top of the list. I'm willing to bet you all the money he owes us that he's been lyin' to *you*—and would continue to do so—unless we set the record straight. Now, Sal, I want you to explain to Mr. Lester here exactly what his brother is into us for. Don't make it long and drawn out or nuttin,' just sum it up."

"It's like this." Shy Sal licked the fingers on both hands, like a quarterback. "Eddie's been bettin' a whole lot with Mikey here. Doin' fine. Winnin' some, losin' some. Payin' his bills. But as the bets got more frequent and larger in sum, Eddie hit a bad beat. Found himself needin' to borrow funds to pay his debts."

Eddie dropped back in his chair and undid the top few buttons of his sweater.

"That's when Mikey informed him that our family does loans," Sal continued. "In order to pay some of the bets he lost, Eddie borrowed twenty grand from me. Now granted, our interest rates are higher than most," he snickered, "but Eddie got the loan he needed on the spot, to pay his debt—and save his neck."

The captain rolled his cigar in the ashtray. "Sal here is what you call a shylock, Mr. Lester. That's basically a loan manager. Tell him about the vig, Sal."

Sal seemed to enjoy having the floor. "Vig. Vigorish. It's interest Eddie has to pay us. In this case, he borrowed twenty grand. The vig is ten points and each point is a bean, sorry, a hundred bucks—"

"Come on!" Mr. B fumed. "I haven't got all day."

"Sorry, cap'n. Okay. What it boils down to is—Eddie owes a vig payment of one thousand dollars a week," Sal said. "As long as he pays that grand a week, everybody keeps breathing."

Everett glared at Eddie, but his brothers' eyes evaded him. Looking for any way out of this bad dream, Everett raised his hand halfway and spoke after Mr. B nodded. "So, my brother's supposed to pay a thousand a week, until he can pay you the full twenty thousand he originally borrowed?"

"Right," Sal said.

"Is any of the thousand he pays each week going toward the loan amount of twenty thousand?"

Beginning with Mr. B, thunderous laughter broke out around the room. "This ain't no savings and loan." Sal clapped. "Your brother has two options—keep payin' the weekly vig or pay off the entire loan. One or the other." He looked around at his cronies to trigger one last outburst. "There ain't no payin' down on the principal!"

Everett formed a *T* for timeout with his hands. "So, it'll cost an additional twenty thousand to get him completely out of debt with you—is that what you're saying?"

"You move to the front of the class." Sal chuckled.

Everett looked at his watch. "I can have the money back here today." Out of the corner of his eye, Everett saw Eddie turn to face him.

"That's good, Mr. Lester. Very good." Mr. B stood, threw back the rest of his drink, and crunched the ice loudly as he took his overcoat, scarf, and gloves from Paulie. Then he raised an eyebrow to Everett. "Lemme have a word with you, alone."

Hesitantly, Everett followed the captain to the far corner.

The captain spoke in a low voice, his back to the others. "I'm a fair man, Mr. Lester. Your brother has come to me to do business." He wrapped the scarf around his neck. "As long as he does it in an honest manner—a fair and timely manner—we'll get along." He hoisted on the heavy coat. "If he continues to betray me, he *will* get burned."

He flashed his capped white teeth and lifted his black gloves up to eye level, squeezing them on, one finger at a time. "And then, I hate to think of the prospect of what may happen next. We'll need to get our money from someplace else, if you know what I mean." He began to walk away. "Let's just not go there, shall we?"

"Listen to me." Everett boiled. "I don't like being threatened, and I don't like you takin' advantage of my brother. You'll get your money. Then, I expect you to leave us alone."

The captain had stopped walking and stood for what seemed like a full minute with his back to Everett.

Everett had crossed a line, and although he instantly regretted it, he was full of electricity and ready to face the consequences.

Ever so slowly, the captain turned toward him with a face of stone. "Do the names Madison and Wesley mean anything to you? Or Sheila?"

This was bad. People like this had you executed, two behind the ear and fuhgeddaboutit. They gave you cement boots before a swim. They cut you into pieces and sent you around town in gift-wrapped boxes.

But Everett had never been one to back down. "Yeah, they do."

"What about Karen?" Mr. B said. "Does that name mean—"

In a blur, Everett was choking him by his silk scarf. "You come near my wife or any of my family and you'll regret you ever heard the name Lester."

Mr. B's men converged like a SWAT team, ripping Everett backward in a stranglehold, several delivering punches and jabbing him with elbows. Guns drawn, they hovered around the captain, making sure he was okay.

No one said a word but instead waited breathlessly for an edict from the captain, whose men surrounded a gasping Everett, panting like lions that had just been thrown a bucket of raw meat.

In short, brisk swipes, the captain brushed at his coat, tugged at his scarf to even it, and ran a hand through his hair.

"Excuse me." The graying waitress stuck her head through the curtains, drawing everyone's attention. "Heads-up—we got two cops on site for coffee, and it's gettin' loud back here."

Thank You, God!

She disappeared, and all eyes shifted back to the captain.

He shook his head and spoke through clenched teeth. "You shouldn't have done that." He motioned his henchmen toward the rear exit. "However, unlike you, I don't make fatal mistakes in the company of the wrong people."

He headed for the back door, turning around one last time. "Watch your back, Mr. Lester. And Eddie, watch yours, too. Not only do you got a debt to pay—now you got hell to pay, too."

12

Wesley and the muddy Yukon were gone from the drive-way by the time Karen, Sheila, and Madison got downstairs.

"That's funny." Sheila giggled. "Where could Wesley have gone?"

"It's like this all the time," Madison blurted. "Everything's a big mystery around here."

Sheila had gathered five or six plants on the kitchen table and was watering them and collecting dead leaves while Madison searched for something in the refrigerator.

"What else is up with Wesley these days?" Karen took a seat at the kitchen table, unable to forget the white Yukon and wanting to hear more of Sheila's perspective.

"Oh, he's your typical twenty-year-old—"

"Oh, come on, Mom."

"Well, he is, Madi! He's had some different jobs—at the BP, at Circuit City. He took a Web-design course at the technical college. And for a little while he had a job at a sub shop. He's just trying to find himself. You know…"

"He hangs out at a place called Fender's Body Shop with a bunch of dead-end losers. They're all drug addicts."

"Don't go there, Madison Kay. Wesley is a good young man. I know he smokes cigarettes and has a beer or two with his buddies, but who doesn't at his age?"

"Mother, when are you going to come to grips with reality? I can't figure out if you're really as naive as you claim, or if you're just living in denial."

Sheila rotated a planter, stepped back to examine it, and plucked more yellow leaves.

"What about David's death?" Madison came over with a plastic bottle of water in her fist. "Are you going to block that out, too? Alcohol and meth were found at the scene. I suppose David wasn't responsible."

Sheila reeled around to face her daughter. "Tom Schlater was in that car! He was older and dealt drugs. Now you leave David alone!"

"And where do you think Tom got his drugs?"

Sheila grabbed one of the plants and marched it into the family room while Madison and Karen exchanged a tense glance. Sheila returned, venting her frustration by dousing her plants, and much of the kitchen table, with water. "Karen, I want to show you the rec room downstairs when I'm done with these."

Madison sat at the kitchen table. "Mom, you know they think David was high on meth when he wrecked his Camaro. That stuff makes you feel invincible—"

"Stop it! I suppose next you're going to tell me he committed suicide in that car—while those other people were with him. That's sick. It's just sick. And the people who think it are mean. You leave David's memory alone!" She started to break up and flew out of the room with another plant.

"Oh!" Madison steamed through gritted teeth. "There's just no—"

"Calm down, Madison. She's your mother. You need to respect her, no matter what."

"No matter how deceived she is, how ignorant…how drunk."

"Yes." Karen tried to be gentle. "Honor her, just because she's your mother. At least you're generating some dialogue."

"Yeah, it takes an all-out brawl to talk about real life around here."

"Do you think you could find me a bottle of that water?" Karen was unsettled by the hostility between Madison and Sheila. Of course, she'd argued with her own mother once in a while, but nothing even close to this.

Madison got up and went to the fridge.

"Do you know where Wesley was last night?" Karen inspected the plants in front of her.

Madison came back with the water. "Why?"

"Something happened at my house. We saw a white Yukon. It's a coincidence, I'm sure."

"What happened?"

"I don't want to get into it now. Let's just say, I think whoever did what they did had to be on some kind of drugs. Was he home last night?"

"About nine-thirty or so he showed up here with a friend. I'd just gotten back from the library and was freaked out because Dad wasn't home. I was trying to call him when Wesley pulled in."

"In the Yukon?"

"Yeah."

Karen stood and took a look around the corner. "Who was he with?"

"Guy named Tony Badino. He works at that body shop I told you about. Bad news."

"Were they here the rest of the night?"

"I heard 'em leave at 11:15 or 11:30," Madison said.

"Are you sure?"

"Yeah. I didn't get out of bed, but I heard them outside. They were laughing. Then the car pulled away."

Karen unscrewed the cap and took a drink. "Has Wesley been home since you heard him leave last night and this afternoon, when we saw him in the driveway?"

"He could've been. I don't hear everything." Madison took a cookie from a jar on the counter. "Was it vandalism?"

"Yes, but worse." Karen's strength seemed to drain away as she pictured Millie's blood splattered on the snow…her lifeless body in the hole out on the ridge… Somehow, with that loss of life, she buried her dreams to have children along with her beloved dog. "I'll tell you sometime. This is all just between us, by the way."

"What really happened to my dad last night?"

Karen was spared from answering when Sheila came around the corner, the skin around her eyes and nose bright red.

"I can finish these later." She sniffed and waved at the plants. "Let me show you downstairs, Karen, while we have time."

Karen turned to Madison. "You want to come?"

"No. I'll see you in a bit."

Sheila led the way down plush carpeted steps and past framed family photographs and old-fashioned lanterns.

"Wesley's got his own apartment in there." She gestured to the left and walked to the right. "The rec room is in here."

It was a sprawling room with dark carpet, nine-foot ceilings, a big-screen TV, stereo, and speakers built into the walls.

"We have several of Madison's paintings around the house." Sheila pointed to one. "This is one of my favorites. She calls it *The Grape Picker*." The splashy watercolor showed a close-up of an old man, hunched over, holding a huge bunch of purple grapes in his weathered hand.

Beyond the entertainment area was a fully stocked bar, and hanging wine glasses. A billiard table was stationed near the bar, as was just about any game imaginable, including ping-pong, pinball, air hockey, and foosball.

"We decided to turn this far end of the room into a gym." Sheila rested her hand on the front of a large treadmill, and Karen watched her through the reflection in the mirrored walls that surrounded them. "Problem is, no one ever uses it."

They walked back through the room and got to the base of the steps.

"I guess Wesley didn't stick around." She knocked twice on his apartment door and pushed it open. "We'll just spin through here real quick."

The long rectangular room was lit only by the white light of late afternoon, which seeped through the partially opened blinds on three windows along the back wall. Sheila, who seemed as curious as Karen, turned on an overhead light and meandered through the messy kitchen, then sifted through magazines and books on the coffee table in the gathering area.

"My goodness, here it is," Sheila said to herself, then looked at Karen. "This was David's journal. I read it sometimes." She chuckled and admired it. "I guess Wesley does, too."

A phone rang upstairs; Sheila ignored it.

Karen pointed to a painting of two bare-chested boys. "Is this Wesley and David?"

Sheila nodded and walked toward it, as if she were meeting a long-lost friend. "Madison painted that from a photograph. We were in Maine one summer—Boothbay Harbor. We rented a house on a lake. It was wonderful."

"Mom," came Madison's yell from the top of the steps, "phone's for you. It's Heidi."

"Oh, I've got to take that. It's someone from work." Sheila headed for the stairs. "Excuse me, will you, just for a few minutes?"

"Sure."

"Just come up when you're done." She was gone.

Karen stood frozen, eyeing the dingy apartment. This was her chance to find out, firsthand, what David had thought of Everett and, possibly, what part Wesley may have played in his little brother's death.

Take a deep breath and exhale. She picked up the journal and scanned its pages for Everett's name.

Many of the entries praised DeathStroke and idolized Everett. The slanted, somewhat sloppy printing mentioned the band's new albums and repeated lyrics to David's favorite songs. Karen found mention of a Christmas celebration Everett had missed, as well as a cancelled ski trip, and a forgotten backstage pass. She glanced at her watch. Eight minutes had blown by. Her hands shook as she read.

I am so very confused. I barely sleep anymore. I've taken money from my mom and my dad, and even stolen from friends. I'm making enemies. My life consists of scrounging for money and getting amped on meth. I want to stop; I want to feel normal again. Let me out of this nightmare! Let me love again. Let me be a boy again. I used to be a person. I'm trapped. Can anybody help me?

Mercy, such a tragic existence. Owned by his addiction—not unlike other Lesters before him. Karen flipped to the rear of the journal and scanned backward until she saw the last bit of writing, dated just before David's death.

I am a meth junkie…body DEMANDS crank…depressing existence…jump for the Other Side.

She set the journal on the table. How would she share its contents with Everett without sending him into a deep state of dejection? After a quick visual inspection of the apartment, she went to the kitchen, where dirty dishes cluttered the countertop by the sink.

Could there be evidence Wesley was at Twin Streams when Millie died the night before? The bloody knife that was used to slit the dog's throat, perhaps? Opening and closing several drawers and cabinets, she saw only the commonplace: silverware, plastic wrap, pots and pans, coffee filters, foil, and dishes.

She longed to know more about Wesley. Was he living a life of addiction and loneliness as David had, so trapped and unloved? Other cabinets revealed nothing out of the ordinary, just pens, scissors, batteries, matches, duct tape, straws, lightbulbs, and paper towels.

Karen stood puzzled for a moment next to a cupboard that was filled with many packages of the same medicines and first-aid items, things like decongestants, sleeping pills, laxatives, hydrogen peroxide, rubbing alcohol, and numerous boxes of cold and allergy medicine. Although she found the duplicate items odd, she didn't have time to dwell on it.

Scampering back through the large apartment, the deck out back caught her eye. Unlocking the door, she stepped out. Chairs were scattered everywhere, as were ashtrays filled with damp cigarette butts. Next to one of the ashtrays she saw what she assumed was a homemade pipe. It had a thin, six-inch glass tube leading to a singed glass bowl filled with black ash and remnants of dried yellowish crystal.

Glancing around, Karen picked up the pipe, smelled its pungent contents, set it down, and returned inside.

Knowing she'd better get back upstairs, Karen headed for the steps. But a door on the way—probably a closet—forced her to a standstill. The baby Jesus figure could be behind that door, or Millie's dog tags… One quick look would pacify her.

She rested a hand on the knob. Listening intently for noise at the top of the steps and hearing nothing, she opened the door.

The room was dark and smelled strongly of dirty socks. She felt for a switch and flipped it. Fluorescent lights flickered overhead, revealing much more than a closet. It was an unfinished portion of the basement. Concrete floor. Cluttered workbench. Probably Eddie's stuff. Shelving with odds and ends, boxes of funnels, brake cleaner, and starter fluid. Jugs of antifreeze, drain cleaner, and paint thinner. But no baby Jesus.

There was one more door across the room. Padlocked. If Wesley had invaded her property, she had a right to check behind that door.

Hurriedly, she studied the unfinished walls and beams. There. A small gold key, hanging on a nail by some old wreaths. She grabbed it, rushed to the bottom of the steps once more, looked to the top, heard nothing, and headed straight for the heavy metal lock in the unfinished basement.

When she opened the door, the key still in the lock, the stench overpowered her. Don't breathe! She slammed the door shut, keeping a hand on the doorknob.

What can it be? Nothing inside a home was supposed to smell like this.

Something was dead wrong. Maybe even something dead.

She had to keep going. This was Everett's family. One last look and she'd be out of here.

Lifting her arm, she buried her nose in the crease of her elbow, hoping her sweater would filter out the fumes, Karen pushed open the door again. Still repulsed by the odor—a cross between cat urine and fingernail polish—she coughed violently.

With her free hand Karen fumbled for a light switch. Finding none, she stepped aside and let the overhead lights from behind shine into the darkness. Her eyes fell to a jumble of containers, tubes, hoses, and clamps—including a silver kettle with what looked like a candy thermometer hanging over the edge. On the ground were propane tanks, two-liter bottles, rubber gloves, and containers of lantern fuel, muriatic acid, and gasoline.

He's making bombs or drugs…

When she leaned left to allow more light into the lab, she caught a glimpse of a piece of twine hanging five feet in front of her. A light. Karen's heart slammed high in her chest as she stepped into the darkness—careful not to disturb anything—and reached out for the string.

Clunk.

Something had dropped on the concrete floor behind her. She spun, releasing her arm from her face.

It was a man, backlit and standing next to a gray duffel bag.

"Surprise."

She knew who it was when he spoke—Wesley.

13

Everett and Eddie bundled up and left Pappano's in silence.
Everett closed his eyes, relishing each step of freedom and
even the stiff, winter wind that assaulted him as they trudged the three
blocks to Karen's Honda.

On the way to the bank, Everett came close to laying into Eddie
for lying to him. The verbal lashing was right there on his tongue, but
he relinquished it to God instead. Just left his aggravation at the foot of
the cross, turned his back on it, and kept his mouth shut—at least
until he could speak rationally.

Eddie ran the extra money into Pappano's while Everett crept
along for a few blocks in the Honda. Turning the car around, he gradually worked his way back to the restaurant.

"Done?" Everett asked as the frigid air blew into the car with
Eddie's return.

"Done."

Everett looked behind him and merged into traffic. "I'll bet that feels good," he said, then winced. "Sorry. Bad choice of words. Who'd you pay?"

"Mike."

"So, you wanna talk about all this?"

"What's there to say?"

"Start with Mr. B." Everett tried to keep his voice calm. "Who is he?"

"Look, Ev, the less you know, the better. Can we just drop it?"

"No we can't! I'm involved now, man."

"That was *your* choice! You didn't have to go in, get the captain all ticked off."

"And you didn't have to lie to me!" *The nerve!*

Eddie shook his head and fixed his gaze out the window.

Everett drove and waited, quickly realizing he wasn't going to get any more information unless he kept prying.

"Look, I was there for you last night, I paid your debt, and I'm a big boy. The least you can do is tell me who these people are... He threatened Karen!"

The car rolled on in silence, and Eddie didn't flinch in their emotional game of chicken for another minute or so. Just when Everett was about to blow a gasket, Eddie put his window down several inches and started talking. "Captain's real name is Dominic Badino. They call him Brain Picker. You don't want to know why."

"What's with the *captain*?"

"He runs the show. Second in command only to the boss man. Mike, Sal, Paulie—they're all just wiseguys, foot soldiers, for the top brass."

"Why didn't you tell me this before? I could've handled it."

Eddie looked out his window at the passing buildings, and Everett wanted to pound him in the arm.

"Who's the boss?" Everett pressed.

"Guy named Frank Mendazzo."

"I suppose he has a nickname..."

"You really want to know?"

"Yeah."

Eddie looked over with a smirk. "Machine Gun."

"Machine Gun Mendazzo... *great*."

"This is what happens when you get involved in my life, brother. It's like you said this morning, we Lesters got the baggage. That'll never change."

"I shouldn't have complained this morning. I felt bad for Karen and got down on myself. I'm sorry."

"But it was real. That's how you felt. Are you supposed to suppress those feelings just because you're religious?"

"That was nothing but the enemy—"

"Who's the enemy?"

"Satan."

Eddie stared straight ahead at the red brake lights of the cab in front of them. "Well, there's one thing about you that hasn't changed." He chuckled. "It's still all or nothing with you, isn't it? You've really bought into this religious stuff, Satan and all."

What was I thinkin', mentioning a foreign concept like Satan to Eddie? "Why'd you lie to me?"

"I'm sorry about that."

"Why didn't you just tell me the truth about the vig payments and the loan—and that you were dealin' with the mob?"

"I was ashamed, okay? What do I need to do, spell it out for you? Bow down and tell you how humiliated I am?"

"Look, if it's the money, I don't care about that. It's you I'm concerned about—"

"My world's caving in, Ev."

"Man, if you want to change, there is a way. God's set me free from the addictions, all the drugs, and the bondage of all the rotten childhood memories. I've even forgiven Dad, in my heart. I wish he were still here, so I could tell him..."

Eddie pursed his lips, shook his head, and stared out the passenger window toward Central Park. "I could *never* forgive him."

"You think the old Ev could have? After all the beatings and mental abuse? But listen, bro, with God living in here," Everett rested his hand flat on his chest, "anything's possible."

Eddie flipped down his visor, looked in the mirror, and peeled back a Band-Aid. Examining a cut that had scabbed over on his forehead, he ripped off the bandage completely, wadded it up, and flicked it out the window.

"Bro, you've tried everything else. Nothing's made you whole. Why don't you just acknowledge your need for Him?" *There. It was out there for Eddie.*

Large snowflakes began falling, and Everett turned the wipers on. The Honda hummed southbound on Fifth Avenue toward the financial district and the lot where Eddie had left his car. For a few minutes, there was silence except for the muffled noise of horns and city life outside.

"Look, Ev, all that's happened to you, with your faith, is great. I'm glad that's worked for you."

"Worked for me? You say it so casually, like it's one of a bunch of options, like diet or exercise or yoga. Dude, this is the *only* thing that can transform you!"

"You sound just like Mary did when she went off the deep end, you know that?" Eddie huffed. "Exactly! Gimme a break."

Although he'd usually been inebriated when they talked, Everett clearly remembered the days when his sister would preach at him over the phone while he was on tour with DeathStroke. And here he was, guilty of it himself. Although Mary later apologized for those years of what she called judgment and legalism, Everett suddenly understood her boldness—and urgency.

It had all been about love and a faith that was real.

Like Everett's life back then, Eddie's was disintegrating. He was so fragmented and miserable, so out of control that, like Mary had, Everett feared for his brother's life. He truly believed he might be the only person who would ever have the opportunity to confront Eddie with the truth about the decision of an eternity.

"I'm sorry," Everett said. "I don't mean to sound like I've done something great by giving my life to God and that you're beneath me if you don't. That's not true. He saved me—through the love of other people. All I did was believe. I just want the same for you. I want to spend eternity with you." Tears filled Everett's eyes.

"There's been too much damage, my friend. And I got too much to do to sit back and try to talk myself into believing in something or Someone who's supposed to love me but has done nothing but fill my life with pain. No offense."

"But, man—"

"You're gonna need to hang a right on Ninth, comin' right up."

Everett lost his train of thought as he quickly maneuvered the Honda over one lane and made the right.

"Now you're gonna hang a left up here, into New York U."

"You parked at the college?"

"I can usually get away with it during the day. We'll see. Campus police may have gotten me after all this time."

Everett backed the Honda into a spot near the Amanti, which was covered in salt with chunks of snow clinging to its rear fenders and fresh snow beginning to blanket the windows.

"I gotta get that thing washed." Eddie reached for the door handle. "Listen, I can't thank you enough, bro—"

"Hold on, Eddie." Everett put the Honda in park, turned the heat down, and faced his brother apprehensively. "Tell me what's going on, financially."

"Whaddya mean?"

"I don't mind loaning you money. But it's not like you've ever needed to borrow before. Are things that tight?"

Eddie sighed, closed his eyes, and dropped his hand onto the dashboard. "We've got a lot of debt right now. Let's just put it that way."

"How's the job?"

"Job's fine. I'm just not makin' enough to support our lifestyle. Mortgage company's all over me. I got late car payments. And Sheila spends like there's no tomorrow. Clothes. Things for the house. Stuff for the kids."

"But she's working."

"At the Fashion Mart, but all that money goes right into her pocket. That's her funny money, ya know."

"Does she know how tight things are?"

Eddie groaned and turned toward the stately buildings on the snowy campus. "She says we wouldn't have these problems if it weren't for my gambling."

"Is that true?"

"It's been out of hand. I've been using a lot of my paycheck to pay debts."

"Gambling debts?"

"Yeah." Eddie faced his brother with a troubled look. "And I've borrowed against the house to pay credit cards and car payments. That's why I had to call you."

"I'm glad you did." Everett paused to gather his thoughts and sighed. "I'm gonna be honest with you. The gambling thing is first on the list. You've got to get free from that. If I find out more about it, will you check yourself in somewhere so you can kick it?"

Pulling a bulky load of keys from his winter coat, Eddie lifted up the small black remote and held down a red button. "Check that out." Steam churned from the Amanti's exhaust system as the car rumbled to life. "It starts from here. I think I left the heat on, so she'll be warm when I get in."

"Will you do it?" Everett persisted, as if he was dealing with a stubborn child.

"I told you, I've been to Gambler's Anonymous—"

"I'm talking about a *residential* program. Somewhere you stay until you're better."

Eddie dropped his head into his hand.

"I'll pay for everything," Everett said, "and I'll pay your salary and normal commission for the time you miss off work. Please, bro. You've got to do this."

"I'll lose my job if I do that."

"Tough! You'll get another one. Would you rather lose your life?"

Eddie shook his head. "My life's already ruined."

"Dude, besides God, this is the next best thing I can offer. Will you do it?"

"Look. I got a clean slate now, thanks to you. Let me just see how it goes."

"But—"

"I'll think about the treatment, Ev. Go ahead and do the research, get the details. I'll consider it."

"Until then, no more betting."

Eddie nodded. "No more."

"I'm gonna be praying for you."

"Have at it." Eddie chuckled and hoisted his hand toward his brother.

Everett clasped the hand with both of his. He wanted to pray with Eddie, but his brother was ready to go. "You take care."

"You, too." Eddie opened his door, got out, and looked back in at him. "Brrrr. I gotta make a couple stops on the way home. Who knows, maybe I'll see you back at my house."

"We'll see."

Eddie slammed the door and sauntered through the snow to the Amanti. Lifting the driver's side windshield wiper, he held up a bright pink ticket in two fingers. With a grimace, he jerked out a curse, sending hot venom into the darkening afternoon. He ripped the ticket in half, tore it several more times, and tossed the remnants into the snow. Not looking back, he rounded the door, slumped into the Amanti, gunned it backward, and roared away.

Seated in the warm Honda, Everett looked at the scraps lying in the snow. He had been the same way, not long ago. Stubborn. Rebellious. On his own.

Lord, have mercy.

14

"You better come out of there, Aunt Karen." Wesley stepped back from the doorway of the reeking lab into the fluorescent light, revealing his deathly white face.

"Wesley!" Karen tried to speak, but a whisper barely eked out, her hand glued to her chest. "You frightened me."

Between the putrid odor from the small room and Wesley's surprise arrival, a wave of nausea almost overcame her. She stepped into the light, furiously trying to come up with an excuse about why she was there. "Your mom just gave me a tour of the house."

"Where is my mother?" he sneered.

Karen didn't want him to notice her rapid breathing. "She had to take a call upstairs. I'm sorry."

Her mind blanked. *Keep talking. Say anything! Lie if you must. But just win him over.* The words were suddenly in her mouth. "I got carried away down here. Everett and I are rearranging our basement and…I just wanted to see what yours was like."

Forgive me, Lord.

She feigned a smile and waited, breathless.

Zombielike, Wesley stepped over to the dark room, banged the door closed, locked it, and put his hand in his big front pocket along with the key. Like a prisoner in a concentration camp, his face was pasty and emaciated, and there was a raw red patch beneath his left eye. He picked up the duffel bag and walked slowly back toward his apartment.

"You seen enough?" He didn't look back.

"Oh, yeah, I just loved the rec room." Karen didn't know what to do with her hands. All she could think about was changing the subject, getting back upstairs. "And your apartment is great. How have you been, anyway?"

"What?"

"How've you been?"

He stopped at the door of his apartment and waited for her to go in. "I got a splitting headache." A trace of blood glistened at the corner of his bottom lip.

"Your mom tells me you took a Web-design course." Karen couldn't help but notice that his body smelled unclean as she walked past. She meandered uncomfortably near the coffee table, hoping he wouldn't notice that she had looked at the journal.

"Yeah." He closed the door to the unfinished basement, came into the apartment, set the cumbersome bag down and approached her. "That was the extent of my college career."

The hair stood up on the back of Karen's neck. She crossed her arms and walked to the window overlooking the deck. "What types of things are you interested in these days, for work?"

He walked to the couch and plopped down, still wearing his wet, dark green army jacket, which seemed two sizes too big. "I ain't workin' now. I'd like to fly someday." He slouched low and, with an index finger, stroked hard at the raw stretch of skin that ran from the top of his nose to his hollow eye socket. "Maybe work with computers. I'm good with computers."

Her mind blanked out again as she struggled to think of something to say. "This is a nice view back here." She coughed hard, but it didn't relieve the congestion that caught in her throat.

He slouched even further on the couch and continued to rub at his chafed face.

"Well," Karen shivered, "I should probably be getting back upstairs."

He pressed his palms to his temples, closed his eyes, and shook his head.

"Your mom's going to be looking for me." She was two seconds away from dashing for the steps without another word, but he looked as if he was in pain. "Are you okay, Wesley?"

He squinted at her. "Need sleep."

"Well, don't let me keep you." Her heart surged with anticipation as she inched toward the steps. "I'm gonna talk to Madison some more."

All in one motion, he stood abruptly and glided toward her, cutting her off in the middle of the room. "What are you doin' here?" His hands were opened fully, up by her face. "Huh?"

She thought fast. "Your dad—he needed some help. Everett and Eddie are out running an errand." She nodded repeatedly in a subtle attempt to calm him and pacify herself. "I stayed to chat."

He leered at her, one eyebrow suspiciously high. "Who're you with, huh? What's goin' on?"

She put a fist to her mouth and coughed, shaking her head and concentrating hard on looking completely innocent. "I came with Everett. Just here visiting. Really."

Her gaze was met by racing eyes and almost frantic fidgeting.

"Who sent you? You wearin' a wire?" His eyes darted up and down her. "Cops put you up to this? Huh?"

"Wesley." She stiffened to stop from shaking. "This is a social visit. Okay? That's all."

With his head down, he paced fast between Karen and the stairs.

"When did we?" He spoke to himself. "That was..."

Karen just wanted out.

Wesley crossed his arms and massaged his biceps as he marched back and forth. Then he scratched hard at his scalp with fisted hands and groaned. "What the heck day is it?" He stroked the eye again and itched his stomach.

Karen wasn't sure if he was even talking to her. "It's Saturday...afternoon. Almost evening."

He slammed to a stop. "What were you doin' in there?" His small blue eyes pulsated as he pointed to the unfinished basement.

"I just ducked in. It was unlocked."

God, please, get me out of here!

He shot a confused look in the direction of the lab. "Whaddya mean, unlocked?"

"The key was in the padlock." Karen tried to remain calm. She should have known better than to lie.

"What'd you see?"

"Wesley, nothing. It looked like a junk room to me. I couldn't find the light. Why are we talking about this?"

The bewilderment on his face lit a spark of hope in her. Perhaps she could talk her way out. He was confused and paranoid, his memory jumbled.

She perked up. "Come on, let's go upstairs and see what your mom and sister are doing."

His shaved head pivoted back at her. "No! You wait." He marched toward her. "How long have you been here? What else have you seen? I wanna know! Have you heard the voices?"

Clasping her hands tightly, Karen backed away. *Where are you, Everett?*

"Wesley, I've only been here a few minutes, with your mom. She's probably looking for me. You have a great place here. It...it was nice seeing you."

With all the mettle she could muster, Karen raised her head and walked toward the steps. She heard sudden movement from Wesley's direction but did not look back.

Cl…clink.

Although she'd never heard the chambering of a round in a handgun, Karen was quite certain that's what she'd just heard.

She froze three feet from the stairs. "Wesley," she said without turning around, "I'm going upstairs now." The fear made it difficult to speak. "And my Lord and Savior, Jesus Christ, is going to protect me every step of the way."

Before she moved another muscle, a voice rang out from above. "Karen?"

"Sheila! I'm down here."

Sheila bounded down the steps. "I'm so sorry."

"I was just talking with Wesley." Karen practically hugged her drunk sister-in-law at the bottom of the steps.

"Wesley?" Sheila poked her head into the apartment. "I didn't know you were home."

Karen finally turned back around to face Wesley again.

He was on his knees, glaring clench-jawed at her as he zipped closed the gray duffel bag on the floor in front of him.

Sheila stayed to speak with Wesley while Karen made her way upstairs. Squeezing her hands together to stop them from shaking, she found her cell phone, took a tentative seat on the couch in the family room, and pushed the memory call button for Everett. It rang twice.

"Hello?"

"Ev, it's me." She practically crawled into the phone. "Where are you?"

"I'm on 87 headed back toward you. What's wrong?"

"You need to hurry!" she whispered. "I can only talk for a sec—"

"What is it? Talk to me."

"There's some kind of lab in the basement. Wesley found me looking at it."

"What?"

"He's wasted. He has a gun. I think he pointed it at me."

"Where is he right now?"

"Downstairs. I'm up."

"Karen, get out of the house!"

"I think I'm okay—"

"Get out *now*! I'll be there soon."

"Ev, listen," she whispered, eying the basement door. "Just listen. I don't want to freak him out. Sheila's downstairs with him. I think it's gonna be okay. If I leave without saying anything and he finds out, he'll lose his marbles."

"Where's Madison?"

"Upstairs. She's seen cars in and out, and guns. Says Wesley's dealing meth; he's out of his mind on it."

"I'm almost to 287. Be there in ten minutes."

"I'll be okay. I may get out. Not sure. Watch for me along the way, just in case."

"Dear Jesus," Everett broke in, "show Karen what to do. Protect her. Get me there fast… I'm coming, honey."

"Ev, one more thing." She stood and cupped a hand over her mouth and the receiver. "Guess what kind of car Wesley's driving?"

"Don't tell me it's a white Yukon."

"Try a *muddy* white Yukon."

Silence.

"I'm afraid of what I'm gonna do to him," Everett said.

Karen heard footsteps coming from the stairway. "Gotta go," she whispered.

Sheila made a stop in the kitchen and flowed into the family room, holding a long smoking cigarette at the end of two fingers.

"That Wesley." She shook her head while arranging the gladiolus on the coffee table. "He needs to get more sleep. He goes, goes, goes— up late at night. Then he crashes for a whole day. I mean, an entire day or more."

Karen looked around for Wesley or Madison but saw neither. "Sheila, what Madison said about how Wesley hangs out with a bad crowd, is it true?"

"Oh." She took a drag from her cigarette and exhaled while she spoke. "That's nonsense. What does Madison know about Wesley's world? They're complete opposites; they live totally separate lives."

"Madison's read David's journal. She says—"

Sheila swung around, the ashes from her cigarette floating to the floor. "That journal is none of your business. And neither is Wesley's personal life. Can't we just be friends, Karen? Why do you have to dig into our affairs?"

"Friends help each other." Karen stepped toward her. "Friends tell the truth."

"Tell the truth about what?" Wesley's voice echoed across the open room. Karen was certain her knees wobbled momentarily when she saw him standing barefoot in the doorway wearing a baggy fleece pullover and the same ratty pants—one arm behind his back. "What are you trying to say, Aunt Karen?"

"I was just saying…" The floor spun for a second. "After all our families have been through, we need to stick together. Help each other."

"Oh? What's your family been through?" He stepped closer.

"Everett's trial. My kidnapping." Millie's death and her infertility came to mind as well, but she was certainly not going to mention them.

"And those things are supposed to compare with our loss? With David?"

"I'm just saying, we've all been through a lot. Very emotional things. Families need each other at times like this."

"We *needed* Uncle Everett when David was still here, idolizing him. Instead, all we got were regrets. Of course, you've probably read all that in David's journal." He produced the black digest from behind his back.

Karen focused on keeping her composure. "Sheila, I haven't seen the outside yet. Would you show me around?"

Sheila was still staring confusedly at the journal in Wesley's bony hand.

"I'll take you, Aunt Karen." Madison's voice came from the banister above.

"Oh, great," Wesley huffed, as his sister made her way down the steps. "Now you two are buddyin' up. Hasn't Uncle Everett done enough damage to this family?"

"Why don't you go back to your cave." Madison headed toward the closet.

"You better shut your mouth, you little—"

"Can we not do this!" Karen tried to hold back the floodgate of emotions. "Everett and I came here today because we love you. Each of you. And we only want to help."

The tears spilled over, so Karen hightailed it for the living room, found her coat, and started to put it on.

Madison joined her in the living room. "A little fresh air will do you good. Lemme grab my coat."

Karen wiped her face with the backs of her hands, sniffed, tried to smile, and stepped just inside the family room. "Everett will be here soon. I'm glad we got to see each other. Please let me know if there's anything we can do for you."

Sheila was on the couch in tears, wiping beneath her eyes with a wadded tissue. "G'bye, Karen," she moaned. "I am glad you came, really…"

Wesley stood in a daze near the doorway to the basement.

Karen said good-bye to him and turned to leave.

"Good-bye, Aunt Karen." His voice was monotone, and when she glanced back at him, his eyes were blank. "We'll see each other again soon, I'm sure."

★ ★ ★

Madison and Karen wound around back of the house, making fresh tracks through the new snow and admiring the view of Westchester Hills and the valley below.

"What Wesley said to me in there just now, that was odd." Karen looked toward the windows of his apartment.

"He's in his own little world." Madison stared out over the white treetops. "I fear for him. And I worry for my mom and my dad and me—and other people he knows."

"Are you saying you're afraid he may hurt you or others?"

"I think of the Columbine shooters…"

"Madison, you would tell me if you knew of any evidence—"

"I'm not saying he's going to do anything like that. It's the drugs. He's messed up. Okay? He has a heart in there somewhere. When we were growing up, he watched over David and me like a hawk. He was the best big brother."

"It must be so hard for you."

"They say when a child dies, like David did, families have a hard time staying together. Marriages break up…"

"What about you?" Karen asked. "How are you keeping it all together?"

"Some days I don't."

They walked slowly along the back of the house. Karen waited, praying Madison would open up.

"Some days I wanna be the rebel; I wanna be the selfish one!" She kicked the snow. "Some days I don't want all the pressure on *me* to be the only sane one around here."

"You've had to grow up fast." Karen regretted that Madison's family had forced her into this unspoken role as overseer. She seemed so much older than seventeen.

"Yeah. My friends can't relate." Madison shook her head. "They don't know what goes on at my house."

Karen stopped walking. "I had a similar type of loneliness growing up. My dad was a pastor, and all he cared about was having a big church and a bunch of programs. He didn't even have a relationship with God."

Madison tilted her head and seemed to wait for more.

"But the difference between you and me is, I committed some awful sins to escape from my troubles—or to get back at my dad."

"What did you do?"

"Got pregnant." Karen looked at her. "Then my dad drove me to get an abortion to protect his name."

Madison actually gasped. "Oh my gosh, Aunt Karen. I'm sorry."

Karen smiled slightly and put an arm around her niece as they looked out over the valley. "It's okay. God worked it all out for good. My dad is the godliest man I know—now. And when he changed, I did too."

"I wish my dad would change. I know that sounds awful—"

"No it doesn't, Madi. It sounds honest."

Karen bent down, picked up some snow, and patted it into a snowball, praying for words that would comfort. "You've had it hard. But you know, there's a Father in heaven who wants to be your Daddy. He wants to watch over you and have a friendship with you."

She launched the snowball into the woods below, grunting then laughing. Madison chuckled, too.

"That's the only way I get by in this world." Karen clapped her hands together. "Knowing I'm loved. Knowing the God who created everything is my Father—and He'll always be there for me. You know what I mean?"

Madison swiped some snow off Karen's coat. "Thanks. Somehow it helps, shows me there's hope."

"There is, Madi. Even when things look darkest, there's hope in God."

Listen to you. You need to take your own advice! Oddly, through this new friendship, Karen was finding solace, because she was being forced to revisit her Christian roots, to remind herself of God's good-ness—in all things.

"You've fought such a good fight so far," Karen said. "I'm proud of you, how you've stayed so strong. And I want you to know I'm here for you any time you need me."

Madison gave Karen a hug. "Thank you. I may just call and cry on your shoulder sometime."

"I'll be here."

Madison pointed out to the hills. "I've tried to paint that scene a thousand times, but I can't quite get it the way I want it."

"Oh, I bet you did beautifully. I'd love to see it." Karen inspected the deck and windows of Wesley's apartment once more. "What do you say we head back up to the front of the house so I can keep an eye out for Everett?"

When they got to the top of the property, Karen scanned the large, empty driveway. "Where'd Wesley park?"

"Good question," Madison said. "He comes and goes in a zillion different cars."

"But the white Yukon is his?"

"It's a family car, but he uses it all the time. He had a car of his own once, but he wrecked it."

Karen eyed the long, four-car garage, whose doors were closed. "Would it be in there?"

"I don't know where else it would be. You want me to look?"

Karen glanced back at the still house. "No. That's okay. Let's talk some more." They sat on a cold bench by a concrete birdbath whose water was frozen. "What are you going to do this evening? It's Saturday night."

"That doesn't mean much for me." Madison chuckled. "I may meet up with some friends, but they usually end up at parties, and I'm not much of a party person."

"No?"

"Huh-uh. I don't like crowds."

"What do you do on Sundays?"

"Nothin' special. I paint a lot, or sketch. Sometimes I drive way out into the country and take pictures. Then I paint from those."

"That's cool. I'd love to go with you sometime. I'm not a city girl. I'm used to farm country. 'Keep Manhattan, just gimme that country-side.'" Karen laughed. "You're way too young to be familiar with *Green Acres.*"

"I've seen the reruns on TVLand." Madison smiled. "Do you miss Kansas?"

"I do." Karen's mind made the fourteen-hundred-mile trip in a split second. "My mom and dad still live there. I miss them *a lot.* And I had a great church there."

"Why did you move here then?"

"We still have my house in Kansas, but Ev wanted to live here, too." She peered into Madison's eyes. "He wanted to be closer to your family. He really wants your dad—all of you—to know God. And when Everett gets his mind set on something—"

"He doesn't give up."

Karen gave a big nod.

"Well, he's fighting a losing battle with this family. We've never gone to church or anything like that."

Karen heard the squeal of tires, and within seconds, Everett wheeled into the driveway. "Hi sweetie," she yelled. Then she hurried over to him and spoke before Madison got there. "Everything's okay. Don't say anything in front of Madi. Let's just go."

Everett searched the grounds, his distinct jaw jutting out beneath clenched teeth. "Where is the little—?"

"Stop," Karen insisted. "We're leaving."

Madison strolled up. "Hey, Uncle Everett."

"Hey, Madison." Broad shoulders back and slightly out of breath, Everett continued to peruse the property.

Karen turned to say good-bye to Madison, ready to invite her to church tomorrow, when she put her hands in her coat pockets and grinned.

"What's so funny, Aunt Karen?"

"Nothing." She pulled out the small black Bible. "I just want you to have this."

Madison took the book with both hands. "You always carry Bibles in your coat?"

Karen laughed, then took a deep breath and sighed. "I was very sad this morning. Scared and angry. I'll tell you about it sometime. Anyway, I was far from the house, and I took this little Bible with me. I read from it, and God came just like He always does. He reached down and comforted me... I want you to have it."

Madison stroked the leather cover. She looked up and blinked slowly. "That is so kind. Thank you. I can't promise I'll read it, though."

"No promises required."

15

When the Honda was several blocks away from Eddie's neighborhood, Everett parked it on the side of the road and squeezed Karen in his arms. They kissed and held each other in silence as the winter night settled in around them.

"I need to know," Everett finally spoke, "did he pull a gun on you?" He was determined to be calm for her, but his insides were revving in overdrive.

"I never actually saw a gun," came her muffled voice from his chest. "I heard something behind me. Metal clicking…"

"You didn't turn around?"

"I was headed up the stairs from the basement. Wesley was starting to freak out. Then Sheila showed up."

"Did you look back then?"

"Yeah. He was on his knees, closing up a duffel bag."

"I'm goin' back, babe. Not with you, but I've got to deal with this."

"Ev, I'm not positive it was a gun. Besides, you don't mess with people who are drugged out of their minds! If Wesley has a gun, he could kill you."

With Karen's head buried against his shoulder and her long velvety hair cool on his cheek, Everett stared out at some horses in the fenced field beyond the fogging window. She was right. He dumped his wrath in God's lap, and the wise thing now would be to chill.

He admired the serenity of the horses that, wearing heavy turnout blankets, wandered in a snowy pasture beneath a light shining from the peak of a barn. So carefree.

Karen explained what she'd seen in the basement and described the confrontation with Wesley in more detail. Even though he was infuriated, Everett listened intently, stroking her hair and rubbing her neck as she spoke.

"What about the white Yukon?" he finally said.

"I saw him pull up in it. There was mud all over the tires and fenders."

"Was anybody with him?"

"No, but Madison said he was with another kid last night, a bad dude. She heard them leave the house at 11:15 or 11:30."

"So they could have done it."

"Timewise, yeah."

"What do you think?"

She pulled back and looked him in the eyes. "I don't know. It's possible. Ev, he's so messed up."

"If he's doin' meth, that stuff's poison."

"Did you ever do it?"

"No. I was hyper enough. Some of our roadies did, to stay awake in the middle of the night when they had to set up the stage. They were wild things."

"Wesley looks terrible." She shook her head, remembering. "He's dirty. I mean, B.O. And he was scratching at himself like crazy."

"Crank bugs. That stuff dries out your skin. Makes you itch all over. You rub till you're raw."

"Wesley's skin was raw under his eye! And in David's journal, he wrote that he had scabs everywhere."

"I remember that from the hospital when he died," Everett said. "What else did he say in the journal?"

"I'm sorry, Ev." She hugged him and tried not to cry as she spoke. "David loved you so much. But he was a disturbed young man. You've got to know that—"

"He said I let him down, didn't he?"

Her grip got tighter. "He did, but he still loved you—so much. Right till the end."

He went limp in her arms. "Was the accident some kind of sick suicide?"

"I don't know. He believed Endora's lie about the Other Side."

"I spread that lie!" His eyes filled with tears, making the light on the barn in the distance look like a giant snowflake.

"God knows, honey." She rubbed his back, up and down. "God's working in all this."

"David wasn't a believer. He's in hell! That's *reality*. Oh, Lord Jesus, why?" He shook his head, grinding his face into her shoulder. "How many more like him are out there, who I've led to hell?"

"Darlin', don't—"

"There's no crossing back over into heaven for David." He gasped. "I read about it. The rich man's in hell; he's pleading for relief of his agony. Abraham tells him there's a divide, a great chasm." He spoke between choppy breaths. "Once you're in hell, it's forever."

They rocked in each other's arms, surrounded by steamed windows, the Honda swaying ever so slightly by an occasional car shooting past in the night.

In that solitude, Everett's mind lit up like the concert stage in Queens, and a sharp, unmistakable message pierced his soul. *There were dozens like David at your concert; there will be thousands more… Sanctify them in truth—My Word is truth.*

Eyes closed, Everett found himself nodding, vowing to rise to the occasion, promising to accept the call of a lifetime.

★ ★ ★

As Everett and Karen drove toward Twin Streams—utterly exhausted and famished—they decided they were too tired to make dinner, so they stopped in Chappaqua for a burger and fries. By the time they finished, Everett had filled her in on most everything that had transpired with Eddie that afternoon.

"He flat-out lied to you!" Karen stirred her chocolate shake with a plastic spoon.

"He was embarrassed." Everett wiped his mouth with a paper napkin. "That's why."

"Ev, this is so serious."

"Tell me about it."

"He's addicted. You've been there. Eddie's gonna gamble again, and you know it."

"I begged him to let me pay for a residential treatment program."

"I'm not sure you should have paid off that loan for him. I wish we could have talked about it first."

"There was no time to talk, honey. I didn't want to see him get hurt anymore. I figured, at least this stops it for a while."

"Yeah, but—"

"They would've killed him if he'd missed another vig payment, okay?"

Her gray-green eyes swelled. "They said that?"

"Basically, yeah."

"Who—"

"They threatened me, too." Now was as good a time as any to drop the bomb. "They said if Eddie owed money and something happened to him, they'd come after me."

She was leaning across the table now. "Who said that?"

"The captain dude, Mr. B."

"That's it. We need to get the police involved. Don't you think?"

"Honey…" He groaned and began collecting the trash on the table.

Her eyes closed, she exhaled, and her shoulders slumped. "I wish you hadn't gotten involved in this."

"How can you say that? What if you'd never gotten involved with me? Where would I be today?"

"Ev—"

"Besides, this Mendazzo family already had tabs on me. It wasn't like I showed up and they said, 'Wow, this is Everett Lester, the wealthy musician.' They did their research long before today. They knew Eddie had a brother with money."

"I'm just saying, when you were with DeathStroke, God put it on my heart to write those letters to you."

"What are you saying? I shouldn't be reaching out to my brother?"

"I'm saying, we've got to be sure the Spirit is leading us in this—that it's what God wants. Some people just reject God, and you're wiser to spend your time elsewhere."

He pushed his chair back and clasped his hands behind his head. "I really thought this was gonna be different. I'm having *no* impact."

"Ev, you're not responsible for Eddie saying yes to Christ. God is. And Eddie is."

"He told me today I was preaching at him."

"You're telling him about God the best way you know how. There's nothing wrong with that." She shrugged. "You're planting seeds, and others will water them, but God's got to cause the growth."

Everett bent forward and rested his elbows on his knees.

Karen squeezed his arm. "Back when I was witnessing to you, doors kept opening. Things were happening! You were subtly responding. Remember when I won tickets to the show in Kansas City? That was no coincidence."

"I'm confused." He set his gaze on her. "This isn't right, your having to deal with all this darkness. My dysfunctional family. Millie. The infertility—"

"Honey—"

"Just let me finish. I know it's probably not true, and you'll say it's not, but I feel like we're being paid back for my past sins."

Karen reached over and covered his hand with hers. "None of this is a surprise to God." She spoke with a courageous smile. "Why do you think all this is happening to us all of a sudden?"

"I know what you're going to say—"

"Because of the tour," she whispered. "God cares about souls. Remember that Scripture I sent you in prison? 'And they overcame him because of the blood of the Lamb and because of the word of their testimony.'"

He stared at her, absorbing the encouragement like a thirsty plant.

"Satan can't stand the thought of you sharing your testimony with thousands of people. What God's done in your life is so *radical*. And He's gonna use it for His glory."

"I want that more than anything." He touched her hand. "You know that?"

"Satan's gonna make it a war." Her eyes wandered, and she seemed to be talking to herself as much as to him. "Look how low he stoops. Trying to divide us. Scare us. Depress us." Her eyes were glassy with tears.

Everett drew closer to her. "I hate it. I've been so down. And I know you have."

"Satan wants us doubting God, doubting ourselves…" Her tears fell now.

He began to say something, but she cut in. "I know you, Ev! You're lettin' Satan play *mind games* on you. He wants you struggling over the past, weighed down by guilt…"

"What about your not being able to get pregnant?"

"What about it?" She leaned forward and squeezed his hands. "Ev, God loves us. He's taken away the stain of our sins. Do you believe it or not?"

"Out on the ridge this morning, when we buried Millie," he pulled his hands away, "I wanted a drink."

She started to speak, but this time he interrupted her.

"It was overpowering. Okay? I could *taste* it. And I was craving how it would make me *feel*. And then, when you told me about the baby, the urge got twice as strong. I knew it would help me forget and cope. How is a guy like that supposed to have an impact for God?"

"Did you have a drink? Did you go get wasted?"

"No!"

"Then rejoice, Ev! God's *shaping* you. He's getting' you ready for something big. The testing of your faith, the temptations—they produce *endurance*."

As she spoke, he could feel the wind coming back into his sails. "You are so perfect for me. Come here."

She took his hand, hopped on his lap, wrapped her arms around his neck, and gave him a kiss that was cold from the ice cream. "And you're perfect for me," she laughed, "because where else would my faith get tested so radically other than with you?"

He playfully swatted her hip. "Very funny."

She blinked those long brown lashes and flashed him that radiant smile. "You're never going to get rid of me, Everett Lester. I'm here for you till death do us part."

They drove home, hand in hand, passing only a few cars along the way. It was cold and black out as they pulled onto Old Peninsula Road.

"My folks cried when I talked to them this morning about my infertility." Karen eyed the winding road.

"I forgot to ask how that went. I'm sorry."

"There hasn't been time."

"What'd your dad say?"

"He hit a wall."

Everett searched her face by the light of the dashboard. "Really?"

"Once I told them the details, he had to get off the phone. He was crying. I mean, he was in agony. I've never heard my dad like that."

"Come here." Everett put an arm around her shoulder and pulled her close.

"Mom was trying to be strong, but she was a mess, too."

"They know how much kids mean to you."

"Mom started talking about adoption right away."

"I've been thinking about that, too," Everett said. "I guess I'm still trying to resign myself to the fact that I'll never have a precious little girl with your smiling eyes."

Karen turned away. "I'm still in a fog. Adoption's just not what I envisioned…"

"I know." He rested a hand on her knee. "Let's just let this soak in. We need to pray about it."

"The folks wanted to know if they could come a couple days early." Karen looked at him. "I told 'em yes."

"Absolutely."

"I think they'll fly in Tuesday or Wednesday."

"That'll be great. Give Jacob and me a little more time to get organized for the prison gig."

As Everett turned the Honda into the driveway, they both regretted that they hadn't left any lights on, inside or out. Twin Streams was black.

"I had no idea we'd be gone this long." He pushed the button on the garage door opener; they parked and went inside.

"I'll let Rosey out," Karen said. "She's got to be ready to burst."

"Okay." Everett turned on several lamps and plugged in the Christmas tree lights. "I'm gonna get the mail."

Heading out the side door, he strolled down the pebble driveway, which was one of Karen's favorite features of the place because it was lined on both sides by locust trees that blossomed with big clusters of white flowers in the spring.

The main house looked beautiful beneath the starry sky. It was built on a foundation of old barn stones and had six bedrooms, many with their own balconies, and a magnificent wraparound porch.

Passing the small, vacant house across the driveway, which had originally been built to house tenant farmers, Everett filled his lungs with the cold night air and cleared his head. There were no city lights to impair the view of thousands of stars, each hung by God and given its own name.

The back floodlights came on, and Everett watched Rosey prance into the snow.

Then he saw it—something standing in the yard where the manger scene once stood.

"Everett!" Karen's scream echoed from around back. "Come here, quick!"

He had already broken through the locust trees and taken off running through the snow. When he got to the backyard, Rosey was sniffing and licking the base of the baby Jesus figure, which had been returned but was barely recognizable.

Karen stood ten feet away with her hands locked over her mouth.

"This can't be happening." She stared wide-eyed, her body frozen.

Everett fell to his knees, glaring at the large words that had been scrawled over the baby Jesus in red: *You Die.*

"Freaks!" He pounded the snow with his fists, his voice booming into the night. Fear mixed with fury and boiled within him as he scanned the grounds for intruders, ready to rip the head off of anything that moved.

Rosey whined and zigzagged the area, her nose to the ground.

Convinced the culprits had fled, Everett studied the wood figure in the glow of the floodlights. Karen still didn't move. And for the next few chilling moments, Everett contemplated how on earth he would tell his wife that he suspected the horrendous inscription had been painted in blood.

16

It was after 10 p.m., but it felt like first thing in the morning to Wesley. He'd tried to sleep when Aunt Karen left that afternoon but—blast it—there was no way. The itching wouldn't stop. It felt like cockroaches were crawling all over him. And the sweats, they came in waves, like the flu.

He scrounged around in the gray duffel bag, sorting through various ammo and guns. Finding the bag of white-yellowish crystal-like powder, he squeezed it gently, put it up to his face, and inhaled.

Wesley heard a noise in the unfinished part of the basement. He busted in and flicked on the overhead—nothing but stillness. Crossing to the lab, he found it was locked up tight.

Then a smooth, mesmerizing voice spoke to him from the crossbeams. "Vengeance."

Wesley looked up at the ductwork, the wires, and copper pipes—but saw nothing.

A low, insidious chuckle came from the ceiling.

Wesley did a 360. Seeing no one, he slammed the light switch off, yanked the door closed, and leaned with his ear to it—listening.

"They're watching you," the voice whispered.

He dashed to the telephone and picked it up—dial tone.

He fumbled for his cell phone, opened it, and examined the glowing screen. Normal.

"I know you're here." Wesley twirled through the apartment from stereo speaker to stereo speaker. Nothing. He even checked the radio dial and receiver for hidden cameras or secret messages. None.

He clicked on the TV and dropped into the recliner, mashing his nagging eyes with the palms of his hands. His skin prickled, and he grated the inside of his elbows and thighs with his long fingernails. When dots of blood appeared on the raw, pink patches he'd scratched, he repeatedly slammed his forearms and clenched fists on the arms of the chair as hard as he could.

Death would be better than this.

"I. Am. Ven–geance." The loudening voice seemed to be coming from the wall.

"You're the devil! I know you are." Wesley turned off the TV and ran into the bedroom, dove onto the waterbed, and ripped at the patch under his eye with four clenched fingers.

"I'm gonna die, I'm gonna die, I'm gonna die—like David," he repeated, partly because he hoped it was true and partly to drown out the voices.

"Who says turn the other cheek?" The voice became arrogant. It was wicked and distressing—and so real it sent icy chills up Wesley's arms and coaxed him to stand and stagger toward it.

"I am Vengeance, and I own your mind, Wesley."

He dashed to the gathering room, threw the recliner out of the way, and smacked both arms against the bare wall. Canvassing it as if he were washing a billboard, he stopped suddenly—and listened.

"You are not alive, and you are not dead." The voice laughed. "You are *mine*."

Wesley jumped back. "Go away! Leave me alone, you…" He slid to his knees, ripped open the duffel bag, whipped out the Witness 9mm he'd pulled on Karen, and braced it with both hands in front of him, pointing at the wall. "I'll blow your head off, you filthy demon."

The low chuckle again. "Get your phone."

The cell phone rang.

Wesley's heart jackhammered. Out of breath, he grabbed it. "Yeah."

"Yo," Tony Badino blared. "It's time. Black Chevy Xtreme. It'll be there in ten minutes. One gram. Two hundred bucks. Plus the .38 caliber Armscor. That'll be another two fifty. That's four hundred fifty bucks you need to collect. Got it?"

"Yeah. Where you been?" The heat came again, sweat drenching his face.

"I'm workin', dude. Plus I had to run errands for my old man. We all set?"

"Yeah. Yeah." Wesley turned on the light to the deck outside his apartment and peered out, wiping the perspiration from his forehead with the sleeve of his shirt. "You remember those fire trucks I told you about? The ones I saw the other day at the house across the street—"

"Oh no. You ain't gonna start this again…"

"Dude, I think they were planting cameras in my neighbor's attic. No lie. I feel like we're bein' watched, maybe bugged. I'm talkin' federal agents. Some kind of task force—"

"Lester, listen to me. We are not bein' watched! You're freakin' out again. I'd know if there was heat at your place. I guarantee it's clean."

There was no way to stop rubbing his eye. It pricked and tingled and cried out to be scratched!

"Lester, are you there?"

"Yeah, I just feel so dang bad." He wanted to cry and explode and die—all at once. He looked at the gun in his fist, and the chill of what it could do unnerved him. "I'm goin' stir-crazy here. I need to take an ice-cold shower to stop this itching. I thought you were comin' by with some more stuff. Man…the…the…the…I told you about Everett's wife scopin' this place out. Maybe she planted something for the Feds. Cameras maybe…"

"Listen to me, you stinkin' fool. Get ahold of yourself. You got another eight minutes. Here's what you do. Right now. Take a tiny bit of that go-dust—I mean a *fraction*—from that bag you're about to sell. Give yourself a bump."

"For real?" Wesley wanted to laugh hysterically.

"Do it. You need it. These slam-heads comin' over now are clue-less. They ain't gonna weigh it or nothin'. Go get yourself some of that chalk, but only just enough to get you heated. You hear me?"

"Oh, yeah, Tony, yeah. Thanks, dude, thanks. I owe you."

Hands trembling at seizure magnitude, he slid the phone into the pocket of his baggy pants and went for the bag. Within seconds he was set up at the small kitchen table with a mirror, razor blade, straw, and the gram bag he was about to sell. If he had any saliva, his mouth would have been gushing, as the thrill of what he was about to do pro-duced in him a complete and utter sense of ecstasy.

He could do little to stop his hands from shuddering, and every once in a while his whole body jerked. But he was used to the symp-toms and, in no time, had anxiously scraped together two imperfect lines of meth on the surface of the mirror with the razor blade, each about two inches long.

"I'll make you go away," he yelled at the wall in the other room, then erupted in his own sadistic laugh.

Bent over the mirror with the straw snug in his right nostril, Wesley ran the tooter the length of the first line, making every particle disappear.

The rush came like a roaring waterfall. *Oh yeah, baby.*

After exhaling, he breathed in again through his tingling nose, feeling his head drop backward and hoping the meth would crystallize in his brain so he could feel that way forever.

Sheer flipping euphoria.

"I'll teach you to mess with me!" He vacuumed the next line with the opposite nostril and hunched over the table, giggling, a sense of well-being engulfing him.

Boomity-boomity-boom. In a flash Wesley's coat was on, the gun and gram were in a plastic bag, and he was out at the street. The black Xtreme came like clockwork. Two girls, a guy, and a dog—all white. Looking to get cranked up.

The dude in the Xtreme was a smart mouth, tryin' to show off for the ladies. It didn't matter. Nothin' did. Wesley was flying high, and there were no more voices. He kept his own mouth shut, produced the white bag from the waist of his pants, got the four fifty, and made for the house. Easy money for him and Badino.

Back inside his parents' part of the house, it was warm, dark, and smelled like, what? Chinese? Wesley nudged his boots off by the rug in the kitchen and crept out to the family room. A lone spotlight lit up the large painting of Madison's over the fireplace—of a barn, a field, and a stormy sky.

He stopped on the big, soft Oriental rug in the middle of the room, admiring the watercolor, feeling his face grow warmer, hearing the tap-tapping of his racing heart and enjoying the keen sense of alertness and sensitivity to the once-again-conquerable world around him.

The sound of a TV came from back in the den. He walked that way. Dim light sliced through the small opening leading into the room.

Wesley went closer, right up to the door. His dad was alone, seated on the leather ottoman two feet from the TV, his elbows resting on his knees, and his hands in the prayer position in front of his face. Only he wasn't praying. He was concentrating on a basketball game.

"No, no, no." Eddie raised a fist toward the TV. "Don't give him that! How can you leave the best guy in the NCAA wide open from twelve feet? Gimme a break!"

Several bandages dotted his face. He wore shiny blue sweats. And he was glued to the game with such intensity, there simply had to be more at stake than just good old Ohio spirit. Besides, Eddie had attended Ohio Wesleyan, not Ohio State. Something funky was going on in the old man's world.

"Come on, Buckeyes. Make it happen. Work it in. There he is, wide open! That's right…yes!" With the basket, Eddie stood abruptly, pumped his fist, and then swigged from a glass that was forming a ring on the TV. Setting it back down, he paced in front of the tube like a coach in front of his bench.

Wesley headed for the stairs to his apartment, trying without success to recall the last time his dad had paid as much attention to him as he was that game. But this was old news. Been that way all his life. Nothing was going to change. Forget it.

Crossing back through the family room, he became curious about his mom's whereabouts. Grabbing the banister, he leaped up the stairs two at a time. Passing David's old room, a bathroom, and Madison's room—where light shone from beneath the door—he went to the end of the hall and tapped on the door of the master bedroom. No answer.

After knocking again, he turned the knob and pushed the door open. The smell of his mother's perfume was strong. Although there was no sound, the bluish glow from the home shopping channel on the wall-mounted TV lit up the elegant room. Near the TV, half covered in gold satin sheets and a down comforter, Mom lay on her side, black sleeping mask covering her eyes. She looked tiny in that enormous bed.

Wesley crept to her side. A flask of something—it smelled like whiskey—lay on the nightstand, along with three bottles of prescription medicine. Two of them were open. There were still plenty of pills in all three.

He tucked her arm that was hanging off back onto the bed and pulled the soft covers up to her chin. She didn't move. He stood over her and stared at his mother. After a few seconds, he lifted the mask to the top of her head so he could see her whole face. He kissed her softly on the cheek, smelling the whiskey that seemed to ooze from her pores.

"What are you doing?" came Madison's loud whisper in the doorway.

He pulled the mask back down over his mother's eyes, went to the door, and exited in front of his sister.

"Checkin' on Mom." He walked back toward the steps.

Madison shut the door quietly and followed him as far as her room. "She passed out again."

He kept walking.

"Who was that you met out front?"

He turned around and faced Madison. "None of your business."

"Yeah, it is my business. You know why? Because as long as you keep doing whatever you're doing, I've got to stay here."

"Oh, really?" He walked toward her. "Why's that?"

"'Cause I'm afraid someone's gonna get hurt. What was in the bag?"

He entered her room and nodded toward the window. "I saw you and Aunt Karen looking down at me today."

"So?"

"So, did she tell you?"

"Tell me what?"

"Never mind." He started to leave, thinking Aunt Karen might not know he was at Twin Streams after all. But he stopped when he saw the small black Bible on her dresser. Picking it up, he leafed through the first few pages, saw Karen's name, and smirked.

Madison pointed to the rash around his eye. "What did you do?"

"She gave this to you?" He wagged the Bible at her.

"Aunt Karen's sweet," Madison said. "So's Uncle Everett. No matter what you say. Your eye is a mess, and your wrist is bleeding."

He looked down and wiped the blood on the front of his shirt. "No worries."

"She said something happened at their house last night." Madison took the Bible out of his hands and set it back on the dresser. "And that they saw a white Yukon."

"What happened?" His mind flashed back to Twin Streams, the manger scene, the dogs—how berserk Badino had gone.

"She wouldn't say. Was it you?"

He walked out into the hallway.

"You were with Tony Badino last night," Madison prodded. "He's supposed to be nuts. I heard he's into Satan worship."

"What? Where'd you hear that?"

"A friend who would know."

He blew it off. "What's goin' on with the old man? You see he got banged up?"

"Yeah." She plunked down on the bed. "Said somebody tried to take his wallet on the subway."

"Right." Wesley leaned against the doorframe. "And he fought back?"

"I don't know what's goin' on, but whatever it is, Uncle Everett bailed him out. You need to be nice to him and Aunt Karen. They're good people."

"What makes them good? Tell me!" He thrust a finger at the Bible. "Is it 'cause she gave you a book?"

"They care about people like us. People who don't care about them or deserve to be loved."

"It wasn't always that way and you know it."

"Well, it is now."

"Oh, and that means we automatically forget how he left David high and dry? Misled him? The poor kid was crazy! He thought he was going to another world! And you just want to let it go?"

Wesley's insides were churning like the pistons in a roaring engine.

"Uncle Everett's sorry. They both are."

"Sorry ain't good enough."

"Oh, what a jerk. You've never made mistakes? What more do you want them to do?"

"I'm not sure yet."

He could almost hear the voice, the one in the wall, calling itself Vengeance.

Maybe that's what he wanted. Maybe he wanted Everett Lester to pay.

Back downstairs Wesley stalled, fearing the dreaded voice would come calling again when he returned to his apartment. He pulled the fridge door open, lighting up his parents' kitchen. Nothing appealed. He meandered to the front door, staring out at what many would call "the perfect home." *Little did they know.*

He headed for the den to take one more peek in on his dad. Putting his face up to the light, he peered through the crack. But he got too close and the door opened about four inches, squeaking slightly. He turned and crept away.

"Wes?" his dad called.

Wesley froze, then turned around slowly.

His dad stood in the doorway, silhouetted by the light from the den.

"What is it, son?" He turned sideways and raised his arm toward the inside of the room. "You want to come in?"

Wesley walked toward him and hesitantly stepped into the room.

"Buddy, what'd you do to your eye?"

"Some kind of rash." Wesley pulled his sleeve over his wrist. "It's been itching. No biggie."

His dad examined him, up and down, slowly—but not too closely. "It looks really bad. Maybe you need to go see Dr. Wegryn. He may want to give you some steroids or something to knock that out, whatever it is."

Wesley shrugged, just to give him some kind of feedback. He eyed his dad's face. "What happened? The cuts?"

Dad sloughed it off. "Some pickpocket tried to lift my wallet on the subway."

"And."

"I tried to fight him off. Other people helped. He took off."

"Did you get the wallet?"

"Yeah, luckily."

Wesley looked at the TV, which made his dad fix his gaze back to ESPN also.

"Ohio State–Michigan." Dad sat back down on the ottoman. "Sold out in Columbus. Nineteen thousand, two hundred people. It's half-time."

"Who's winning?"

"Buckeyes, but not by enough." He laughed.

Wesley took a seat on the couch as the third quarter got under way.

"Yeah, sit." His dad shot him a glance, then was drawn back to the tube. "Come on now, Buckeyes, break this thing open." He reached for his drink, but it was empty, so he set it back on the wet ring. "This kid Poorman is playing a heck of a game. He's hit, like, four three-pointers."

Wesley couldn't care less. His knees bounced. He examined the dried blood on the inside of his elbow.

What are you doing here, anyway? "That's enough for me." He rose from the couch.

Dad's eyes didn't leave the screen. "You just sat down."

"I know. I'm beat."

"Okay, my man." His dad gave him a momentary look. "Sleep well."

Wesley stood there for a moment, saddened by the cold but familiar reality that he'd received the extent of his father's attention. "'Night," he said, as his dad cursed at an Ohio State turnover.

Wesley headed toward his apartment.

For once, I wish we could just sit and talk. No TV, no newspaper, no rushing out the door. Just talk. Is that so much to ask? Maybe I could even tell him how scared I am. Of the grip this drug has on me. Of the voices. Maybe he could even convince me I'm not losing my mind.

17

Even though the shades were drawn, light had filtered its way into the master bedroom at Twin Streams by the time Karen finally awoke Sunday morning. Before she even opened her eyes, she was back out in the yard the night before, gawking at the baby Jesus figure and the haunting words in red, pouring out her soul to the police, and watching them take pictures and drive away with the evidence in tow.

A blanket of desperation covered her body. Oh, how she wished her infertility were only a bad dream. But she was awake enough to realize that was not the case. Perhaps God would change His mind and knit Everett's baby together in her womb.

Oh, Lord, please, let me get pregnant, someday, some way…

She lay still, listening to the furnace chugging along—as it had all night—trying its best to keep the somewhat drafty old house warm during the New York cold snap. With a harsh cough, Karen swallowed back the pain in her throat and noticed how dry the insides of her nose and mouth had become overnight. She opened her eyes, and Everett wasn't on his side of the bed.

I hope he's making coffee.

But he was supposed to be at church. She shot up and looked at the time. "Ev?"

A white piece of paper was folded up next to her clock. "Karen" was written on the outside. She unfolded it.

Good morning, babe!

I couldn't wake you. You needed the rest. Be strong in the Lord. Everything's going to be okay. We'll find out more soon.

The coffee's on, and I'm headed for the first service. I'm nervous but excited. Say a prayer for me, if you're up in time. I'll see you at the second service. We can sit together after my song. Stay warm. Be careful; the roads might be icy.

Love ya,

Ev

Karen was glad she'd slept in. She stretched and yawned, relishing the light and the hope of a new day. "Father in heaven," she prayed, eyes closed and hands lifted, "let Your Spirit flow through Ev this morning. Give him peace. Let him feel Your love. And, dear God, let the words and music penetrate people's souls. Also, protect us from evil..."

Putting on her robe and slippers, Karen greeted Rosey in the kitchen and poured herself a cup of coffee. Everett made it strong, and she had come to like it that way. Rosey remained sitting at attention by the refrigerator, looking deprived. Karen went over to her bowl, bent down, and felt it—still slimy.

"You rascal." Karen snickered at the dog. "You really are the Pretender. Daddy already fed you, and you know it." The Pretender was a nickname Rosey's breeders had given the collie, because she pulled the same "deprived" trick on them when she was a pup. Karen sidestepped the memories of Millie that sought to fill her mind.

The red needle on the thermometer outside the bay window pointed to seven degrees. "Brrrr." She let Rosey out, feeling her stomach turn slightly when she saw the spot where the baby Jesus figure had been returned, and beyond that, out to the ridge and Millie's fresh grave.

Even Rosey appeared somewhat shocked by the quiet cold as she walked gingerly on the icy grass, did her business quickly, and made a beeline for the back door.

The *Bedford Post* was on the island in the kitchen, still in its clear, wet plastic bag. Karen got it out and took it to the kitchen table. Although she didn't need to clip coupons anymore, it was a habit and something she enjoyed doing as she went through the Sunday paper. Fifteen minutes and a second mug of coffee into her review of the paper, she zeroed in on a story in the local section under the heading "Police Reports."

IN-STORE DETECTIVE ATTACKED AT WAL-MART

WHITE PLAINS—An in-store detective for the local Wal-Mart is in stable condition after being assaulted in the parking lot of the store Friday evening when he confronted two would-be shoplifters as they left the store.

One of the two suspects kicked the detective in the throat while the other ran for a white GMC Yukon, in which the two escaped. During the fray, the attacker dropped several boxes of cold medicine, the ingredients of which are commonly used to "cook" the fastest-growing social drug in America: methamphetamine.

The men were described as Caucasian, in their early twenties, and both about five feet ten inches tall and of average weight. The attacker wore a black trench coat and gray stocking cap while the driver was wearing a baggy green army jacket.

She pulled back and stared in disbelief at the headline again.

Wesley.

All she could think about was the day before. Him scaring her from behind in the basement, then plopping down on the couch in his apartment—wearing a wet green army jacket.

Karen checked the wall clock. She couldn't disturb Everett now. Adding some coffee to her mug, she went to the desk in the den, got on the Internet, and searched for *methamphetamines*. Within seconds, she was scanning feature stories, drug prevention sites, and law enforcement pages—and with each item she read, an alarm rang louder in her ears.

Meth could be smoked, swallowed, injected, or snorted. The powerful stimulant actually overwhelmed the brain, spinal cord, and central nervous system. The intense high users got could last days and usher with it chilling side effects, such as extreme paranoia, frantic physical activity, a false sense of power, unpredictable rage, heart failure, and even suicide.

Karen was glued to the computer as time flew. With each website she visited, she uncovered more explanation about Wesley's eerie behavior and more confirmation about what she'd seen in his basement.

Meth labs didn't take up much room and could easily be set up in apartments, sheds, motel rooms, barns, garages, vacant buildings, vehicles, and yes, in basements. The drug could be cooked in as little as three hours using everyday household products.

Karen wanted more coffee but couldn't pull herself away from the wellspring of information being illuminated before her eyes. After some almost frantic searching, she finally drilled down to a page that offered police photographs and—*BAM*—the images hit her like a locomotive. Meth supplies, meth pipes, and meth labs. The pictures may as well have been taken in Wesley's apartment.

Karen glanced at the grandfather clock. Time to get ready for church soon. She began down another rabbit trail. Searching specifically under "meth explosion," she was blown away by the results.

The websites of TV stations and newspapers all over the country popped up—reporting up-to-the-minute instances of meth lab explosions. In many stories, the people involved were badly burned, maimed, and even killed, while the lucky ones were in shock or slightly injured.

The deadline Karen had set for herself to get offline was just three minutes away. The last story she found explored some of the utterly sick things people had been known to do while flying high on meth. One user outside Chicago parked his car on train tracks to commit suicide but fled the scene on foot at the last minute, causing the commuter train to ram his car, killing eight people on board. Another small party of users in Oregon got lost in the woods during a snowstorm; they were so discombobulated that they couldn't describe to 911 operators where they were, and all perished.

Other "tweekers" committed dastardly acts that hurt others, like throwing babies from moving vehicles and locking children in attics. One of the strangest accounts was of a group of young users in California who actually pierced their shoulders with meat hooks and dangled their tattooed bodies from bamboo tripods off a local sandbar, all in the name of "fun."

When Karen arose from the computer, she was light-headed. Her coffee was cold and so was her heart. She set her cup in the sink, stopped, and stared out at the cold white landscape. The pages of David's journal came back to her, as did his desperate cries for help. She wanted desperately to speak with Everett, but she couldn't. So Karen headed for the bedroom to get ready for church.

Although Everett had grown accustomed to having all eyes on him as the lead singer of DeathStroke, it didn't help when he was about to jam before six hundred onlookers at his church. In fact, he wanted to crawl within himself and hide.

The place was decked out for Christmas with poinsettias and greenery, candles, and a large manger scene. Karen had come in several minutes ago and sat about fifteen rows back.

Everett's stomach gurgled as he made himself smile at the blur of faces, took a seat on the wooden stool, and adjusted the microphone in front of him. Yes, people were watching, but they weren't just any people—they were Christians.

He'd checked himself in the mirror just before going on, making sure the baggy long-sleeve top he wore covered his remaining tattoos, and that his hair was just right.

But they still knew his story.

As their eyes bored into him, were they judging him for his seedy past? Did they really believe a sinner like him could be one of them? Were they waiting for him to slip up, to say or play something "ungodly"?

Everett forced a smile, nodded a hello, and adjusted his acoustic guitar. As a hushed sense of anticipation blanketed the sanctuary, another jolt of anxiety rocked him. He folded inward, frightened, as if he were perched on a ledge atop an eighty-story building. He couldn't seem to look beyond three feet from his face. He wanted to be anyplace but here.

He searched for his sister's words like a heart patient grasping for nitroglycerin.

"God made you precisely the person you are."

His eyes found a boy sitting with the youth group, near the front.

"For His purpose."

Arms crossed. Head down. Black T-shirt.

"Don't worry about what anyone else thinks."

Curly, bleached-blond hair on top, shaved sides.

"Be yourself, Everett Lester."

Earrings.

"Meet them right where they are."

Chains.

"Share with them."

Tattoos.

"They'll listen to you."

"Whoever you are," Everett moved the mike slightly, and his deep voice echoed, "we're glad you're here."

"Be transparent."

"Before I became a Christian, I was the leader of a band called DeathStroke." Mention of the band brought a smattering of laughter. "Ah, some of you have heard of it." A sense of relief came with the laughter.

"During my years with the band, I thought I was something special, someone very powerful. The world made me feel extremely important." He took an anxious breath. "Since then, though, I've learned something I believe God wants each one of us to understand. And that is, we're nothing without Him."

The truth of Mary's words was seeping in, taking hold.

"Life is fragile, guys. Think about it. Our bodies are nothing but flesh and blood, bones and water. We breathe and walk and run and laugh—we are sustained minute by minute because He says so."

A hum of verbal agreement arose throughout the auditorium. He looked around, low and high, in silence; even shading his eyes to see the faces surrounding him, looking back at him with love and care and a sense of anticipation.

"I wrote this song in prison when I was on trial for murder. It's all about this realization that He is everything and I am in awe of Him."

He closed his eyes and began strumming. "Many of the words and ideas for this song come from the book of Job. Job says, if God determined to do so, if He should gather up His spirit and His breath, all flesh would perish and man would return to dust. Imagine that. God's indescribable. Close your eyes and listen. This song is called 'Now I See You.'"

Working the strings hard and fast, the song came alive—sharper, richer, louder. Everett's head and shoulders bobbed with the music.

The vibration of the acoustic strings filled the room like a melodious fountain, bringing a smile to his face. At that moment, Everett knew it wasn't him playing, and it wasn't his voice that thundered so deep and strong.

Where were you when I laid the earth's foundations?
When I said to the sea,
"Come this far and stop right there"?
Have you ever in your life
said, "Let it be morning"?
Or caused the sun to set in its place?

What about the rain—who's its father?
Hey, who put wisdom deep inside?

Can you bind the chains of the constellations?
Can you loose the cords on all the stars?

I lay my hand on my mouth.
I am insignificant.
Insignificant.

I had heard of you with my ears,
But now I see You,
Now I see You,
For who You are,
For who You are...

You are marvelous and mighty,
You are the King of kings,
You are far beyond description,
You alone can do all things.

You are the Maker and the Ruler,
The God of heaven and earth.
You are Father of all creation,
You gave me second birth.

Now I see You,
Now I see You,
Coming in the clouds,
A whirlwind in the night.

Now I see You,
Now I see You,
Father of all nations,
The One who gives me life.

It wasn't until the song was finished that Everett opened his eyes and looked around. Every person was standing. Many of the faces glistened with tears. He found Karen in the audience on her tiptoes, waving like a schoolgirl, dabbing her eyes with a tissue. Then he turned to the boy in the black T-shirt. He wasn't clapping, but he was standing, and his eyes were fixed on Everett.

Touch that boy, Lord. Draw him close.

Setting his guitar on a stand, he joined Karen amid the congregation. They hugged. "It was awesome." She squeezed his hand as the worship team took the stage.

"Thanks," he whispered. "You okay?"

"Fine." Her eyebrows arched.

"What is it?"

"Found some stuff in the paper and on the Internet," she murmured. "I'll tell you more later."

"Give me the upshot."

"It all points to Wesley…"

18

Tony Badino's old blue Monte Carlo smelled like gasoline and roared like a stock car. Wesley was in the cold vinyl passenger seat up front, where he'd just burned his finger on a blistering pipe they'd used to smoke several chunks of meth in the parking lot of a White Plains bowling alley.

"Why don't you get the heat fixed in this thing?" Brubaker rubbed his hands together in the backseat. Tony shot him a nasty look in the rearview mirror, gunned the Monte Carlo onto the street, grabbed a Marlboro, and lit it while steering with the insides of his elbows.

Wesley cranked up the stereo to the screams of AC/DC, which blared from two homemade speakers mounted in the rear window: "I'm rolling thunder, pouring rain. I'm coming on like a hurricane. My lightning's flashing across the sky. You're only young but you're gonna die. I won't take no prisoners won't spare no lives. Hell's bells...hell's bells."

In the blur of the rush, Wesley stared out the passenger window. Something about the winter made his brother's death even more unbearable. Guilt cried out from the frozen ground. Wesley's soul was barren. There was nothing to live for anymore, except getting stoned. And even that was killing him slowly.

What if he were to murder Everett Lester?

Maybe that was his calling.

Vengeance.

Nothing would matter once he did the deed. The cops could do whatever they wanted to him.

I'm gonna die, anyway.

Would the heaviness clear once he pulled the trigger?

If not, maybe he'd just turn out his own lights, as well.

Tony bounced the Monte Carlo into a plaza in the suburbs and jerked to a stop in front of a long, gray, one-story building called Shooters.

"Grab your toys, fellas." Tony got out of the car and headed for the trunk. "This is my treat. All you can shoot, on me."

Each of them hoisted a heavy duffel bag from the trunk and strutted into the shooting range as if they owned the place. A muscle-bound guy with a baby face and a gray T-shirt walked toward them behind the long glass case.

"Hey, Badino." He held up a thick hand. "What can I do for you?"

"Hey, Dennis." Tony's eye twitched as he spoke. "We need ammo and range time. You got lanes open?"

"Yep." He turned to examine the small, closed-circuit black-and-white TV screen. "I only got one guy in there. You'll pretty much have the place to yourselves."

"Excellent," Tony said. "Give us, let's see, three boxes each of twenty-twos, thirty-eight specials, nines, and forty-fives. And I suppose Bru is gonna need some twelve gauge."

The guy raised an eyebrow, wheeled around, and got busy gathering the ammo, whistling.

Wesley and the others dispersed like kids on a treasure hunt. Tony admired the wide assortment of knives locked in a showcase across the room. Brubaker wandered along the front of another long showcase, admiring the dozens of shotguns, rifles, and carbines that hung on the Peg-Board behind it.

Wesley went straight for the main display case, which was packed with several hundred new and used Taurus revolvers, Walther semi-autos, Cobras, Sigs, Colts, whatever you wanted.

"Okay." The big guy clunked the last boxes on the showcase and pushed a clipboard toward Wesley. "If you guys will each sign in, you'll be ready to go. You need eye or ear protection?"

Tony marched over and took the pen and clipboard. "Nah. We got all that."

"If you're going to be shooting a twelve gauge, be sure to use the rifle range," Dennis said. "There's a door beyond the regular stalls."

Brubaker signed next and held out the clipboard. "Wes." He set it on the counter.

Wesley, who had wandered over to the knives, approached hesitantly as Tony and Brubaker opened the white door that led to the range. *I'm not signing that thing! It's probably a background check or some kind of straight line to the cops.*

"What's this for again?" Wesley motioned to the white paper that awaited him on the clipboard.

"Liability release." Dennis handed him the pen and smirked. "Basically says if you shoot yourself, it's not my fault."

"So, it's not like a background check or anything." Wesley stroked under his eye with his index finger. "You're not gonna register my name or something…"

"That's only when you buy a gun." Dennis scowled. "You've shot here before, haven't you?"

"Yeah, yeah." Wesley perused the form, looking for a place to sign. "I just…it's fine…fine."

"Bottom right." Dennis pointed.

The instant Wesley entered the concrete vestibule, a loud, slightly muffled crack exploded, and he cursed himself for forgetting to put his earplugs in. Dropping his duffel bag, he unzipped a side pocket, found the plugs, put them into his ears, then picked up his gear and entered through the next door.

The place looked like a basement—dark with low ceilings, several chairs and tables scattered about, and eight stalls. It smelled like sulfur. Wesley set his bag on the stomach-high shelf at a stall in between Tony and Brubaker. He looked around behind him, up high. There it was: the small, bubblelike, closed-circuit camera that fed their pictures to Dennis. The only other guy in the range was in the stall at the far end.

The rattling blast of Tony's Tech .22 startled Wesley. He leaned around the corner. The black gun spit fire out front and hot .22 cartridges out the side, several hitting Wesley as they ricocheted off the dividing wall and bounced to the concrete floor.

The surprise blast from Brubaker's Mossberg—a long, black, gangster-looking pump action—shook Wesley's lungs.

"Yeaaaaaaah," Brubaker screamed.

The sound and vibration of the thing literally commanded that you pay attention to it.

"You're not supposed to shoot that in here!" Wesley pointed to the shotgun and waved toward another door in the room. "There's a range for long guns."

The shooter at the other end leaned back out of his stall and eyed Brubaker.

Wesley stepped back into his stall, glad to separate himself from the nutcases on each side of him. He glanced back at the camera, then picked up the magazine for his Witness 9mm and began thumbing bullets into its spring-loading chamber.

"What happened to the Glock?" Brubaker ducked his head around the corner, laughing. "Isn't that what your uncle used to kill that psychic, a Glock?"

Wesley nodded but didn't look at him. "That's why I got rid of it." Then he slammed the magazine into the handle of the Witness with the palm of his hand. Fixing the big gun in front of him and aligning its front and rear sights with the target, hanging close to the thirty-foot marker, he squeezed the trigger. *Crack!* The gun jumped in his hands.

That's Uncle Everett.

Crack—it jumped again.

I got him cornered.

Crack—jump.

You're gonna pay for killin' my brother.

Crack—jump. *Crack*—jump. *Crack*—jump.

Blasting away gave Wesley a rush. Each shot was loud, even through the earplugs, and seemed to rattle every bone in his chest.

Just think what it would do to human flesh.

BOOM.

The feel of the explosion. The shock of the recoil. The smell of burning powder. The downright authority he had when those burning cartridges ripped out the side of the gun.

Ecstasy.

Wesley unloaded the magazine from the Witness, hit the return switch, and looked down the dark lane as the white paper target floated back to him like a ghost on a wire. Not bad. Granted, he hadn't formed any tight clusters around the guy's heart or face, but he'd pretty much filled the paper with holes. Certainly enough to send an uncle to his grave.

The guy at the far stall had packed up a blue shoulder bag and was leaving. "You shouldn't be shooting that twelve gauge in here," he said to Brubaker, voice raised, but he kept moving.

Brubaker cackled, pumped the Mossberg just as the guy reached the door, and fired from his waist, the gun exploding with light and smoke and recoiling more than a foot. The man flinched and flung the door open at the same time, glared at a hooting Brubaker, and took off.

Tony tapped Wesley hard on the shoulder. "Put another target up and try this." He placed a big, shiny, black-carbon steel gun in Wesley's hand. "It's loaded."

"What is it?"

"Para-Ordinance forty-five caliber! It's got a laser. Here." Tony took the gun back and hoisted it out in front of him. "Look down there."

Wesley saw a shaky red dot light up amid the black rubber plugs at the far end of the range. "You put your finger here, along the slide." He pointed the gun straight up to show Wesley. "Hit this switch with your index finger, and the laser comes on. Wherever the light is, that's where your round's goin'."

"Bad." Wesley took it out of his hands. "How much did it run ya?"

Tony nodded with a grin. "Enough." Then he disappeared around the corner.

Wesley clipped another target onto the metal plate hanging in front of him and sent it back to the thirty-foot range.

"What's that?" Brubaker came from the other side.

"It's got an internal laser." Wesley aimed, turned on the laser, found the target's head, and—*boom!*

Wow. Smooth.

He aimed at the target again—*boom.*

Again—*boom.*

Then, nothing.

He tried to pull the trigger repeatedly, but it wasn't budging. Not wanting to break Tony's expensive toy, Wesley took it around the corner to him. Brubaker followed. Even though they were the only three left in the range, they kept their ear protection on, which made everything seem fuzzy and muffled.

Wesley spoke loudly to Tony. "I thought you had this thing loaded. I only took three or four shots…"

Tony glared at him, snatched the gun, aimed across the lane at Wesley's target, turned on the laser, and attempted to pull the trigger—nothing.

"What the heck did you do, Lester?" He tried to move the slide back but couldn't. Pointing and attempting to fire again, the gun appeared broken. Pushing a metal switch, the magazine popped out the bottom of the handle. They checked it. Still loaded with at least six bullets.

Tony knocked the magazine back into the handle and bore down on the gun. With the strength of both hands, he tried to cock it by racking the slide. Wesley reached over to make sure the gun wasn't locked, then pushed the laser button.

"What're you doin'?" Tony winced.

"I dunno." Wesley started to take his finger off the switch, noticing that the red light lit up the inside of his skinny wrist.

BOOM.

At first, Wesley thought his wrist snagged on something or was hit by a stray bullet casing. It was hot and hurt like a bee sting. But the unreal image in front of him screamed otherwise. Blood spouted everywhere. He moved his arm. The fountain was coming from him.

Tony stood frozen, his eyes bulging like marbles. Brubaker fled the room.

"Towels," Wesley barked, trying to cover the fountain with his other hand and sending Tony into action.

Trying to swallow, stay calm, and get a grip on what was happening, Wesley knew his energy waned. The wrist was numb. Everything ramped down to slow motion. He was looking through a haze. His knees buckled. Confusion set in.

The door flew open, and the big guy, Dennis, ran in with a frantic Brubaker behind him.

"Let's see it; let's see it." Dennis took charge, holding Wesley tightly at the shoulder and elbow. "Okay, okay, okay. We need to get you to a hospital. Paramedics are on the way. Let's hold it high till they get here."

Tony rushed in with two towels. Dennis pressed one firmly against the gushing wound.

"Let's sit you down." Dennis guided him to a chair and kept the arm up. "How you feelin'?"

He was hot, hot, hot. And spinning—the room was spinning. He was dizzy and nauseous and having trouble swallowing, breathing. Idiot! He couldn't believe he messed up in front of Tony. Now his parents would have to get involved. And blood was everywhere. And his chest hurt bad. And there was meth in the car. And all these guns.

Blackout.

19

"Why haven't the police gotten back to us?" Everett paced in the kitchen at Twin Streams Monday afternoon. "I should be practicing...I just can't concentrate."

"Maybe you've done enough for today." Karen didn't look up from the scarf she was knitting at the kitchen table. "Why don't you go for a walk, get some fresh air?"

"I've barely done any work, and I've gotta have those new songs concert-ready for the prison show," he insisted, not expecting any response.

With Rosey curled up at her feet and her long, pink needles weaving in and out like a machine, Karen seemed determined to lose herself in her knitting.

While they waited Sunday afternoon for the police to call with forensic results from the baby Jesus figure, Karen and Everett had worn themselves out talking about what she'd found on the Internet, the Wal-Mart article, Madison's description of Wesley's activities—

and how it all lined up perfectly with the meth horror stories Karen had found online.

The whole mess shook Everett's very soul. He wanted so desperately to help Eddie and his family, but the mission was proving hopeless. Karen's patience was waning, and so was his.

"I can't wait around anymore and do nothing." Everett snatched his car keys from a hook on the wall. "I'm gonna go pay that little weasel a visit."

"No you're not!" The scarf and needles collapsed in her lap as Karen jumped to her feet. "Not before we think this thing through...and find out more—"

"What more do you want?" He pointed toward the backyard. "Millie's dead. The Yukon was here. We know Wesley hates my guts. He pointed a gun at you, and you know it! Now he puts the baby Jesus figure back with blood all over it... You just don't want me to go over there."

"Is that so stupid?" She approached him, reaching for the keys, but he yanked them away. "You need to cool down, Everett. Wait till we hear from the police. They'll be able to help us."

She turned her back on him, apparently having faith that he would stay, and she flipped on the gas burner holding the silver teakettle.

"What if the cops don't come up with anything?" Everett dropped onto a chair at the kitchen table. "Then what do you propose?"

"Look, honey, this meth is a new animal." She crossed her arms and leaned against the counter. "These people are so revved up on dopamine and adrenaline, you don't know what they're going to do. Rob you. Kill you. They don't know themselves. They'll do anything to get more of the stuff."

She took a seat next to him. Rubbing her eyes, she leaned forward on the table with her hands together, covering her nose in the prayer position. "Part of me says you should sit down and talk with Wesley."

She gazed straight ahead, out the bay window to the white acreage beyond. "Just be honest. Have a heart-to-heart. Tell him what I saw in the basement, what Madison told me. Talk about the journal and his feelings toward you. And confront him about Millie and the manger scene."

"What about Eddie and Sheila?"

"They can be there, if you want. I will, too—"

"Great. I can only imagine *that* conversation."

She slouched back in her chair. "Another part of me says to drop the whole thing." Her eyes met his. "Act like nothing happened. Stay away from them. Ride the storm out."

"How can you say that after—?"

"We're discussing options, that's all." She leaned toward him. "We've got a tour coming up. It's something that's going to lead who knows how many people to Christ—"

"You know that's everything to me."

"And I don't want to jeopardize it!" Karen said. "I just feel like we're dealing with Satan and his demons here, Ev. I *know* how much Satan hates the thought of it."

The teakettle whistled. Karen poured two cups of instant coffee, grabbed her journal from the kitchen desk, and sat down. "It's like Pastor Steve said yesterday." She scanned the journal as she leafed through. "'Our struggle is not against flesh and blood, but against the rulers, against the powers, against the world forces of this darkness, against the spiritual forces of wickedness in the heavenly places.'"

"But God's bigger than Satan."

"Of course He is, honey. But sometimes… Do you remember that verse we chose for the front of your memoirs?"

"'In a great house there are not only vessels of gold and silver—'" Everett said.

"'But also of wood and clay…some for honor and some for dishonor.'"

"Yeah, but we used that to describe Endora and Zane Bender. I mean, they were into mysticism and witchcraft."

"Just a sec," she mumbled, turning the pages of her journal. "Here it is. Listen to this, babe. 'The Lord has made everything for its own purpose, even the wicked for the day of evil.'"

"Wait a minute." He shoved his chair back. "This is my brother we're talking about, and his son. My own flesh and blood—"

"I know." She inched closer and took his hand. "And I know how much you love them. That's why we're here." She shook her head sympathetically. "And listen, I'm not saying we don't keep reaching out. I just want us to weigh all the options."

"I mean, let's face it." He moved his hand away. "When you quote verses like that, you're making it sound like Eddie and Wesley were designed by God for evil. Is that what you're saying?"

"Honey," she shook her head, "I'm not God. I don't know what He's doing. I just remembered those Scriptures. They came to my mind and I wanted to share—"

"Yeah, well, you wanna know what Scripture comes to my mind?" He leaned his elbows on his knees. "The one you just read on the ridge. Love your enemies. Do good to those who hate you, pray for them." He stared at her.

"I know." She shifted in her chair. "I know what it says—"

"What good are we doing if we only love the lovable?"

"I get your point, okay? I'm just frustrated. I didn't mean to hurt your feelings. I don't want to argue."

"I'm frustrated, too!" He clenched his fists. "I'm torn between loving these people and wanting to *rip* their heads off."

Karen sighed and dropped her forehead into her hands as she leaned on the table. "I'm bitter about Millie…I'm shocked Wes would pull a gun…I'm thinking about the baby Jesus…" She began to sob. "I'm just so mixed up."

Everett knelt beside her and put his arm around her shoulders, knowing, too, that she was saddled with the sorrow of infertility. "I'm sorry, hon. Sorry about everything." He wrapped his arms around her waist. "I love you so much."

"We've got to pray, Ev." She cried. "I just don't have the answers.

Back when I wrote those letters to you, it was different somehow. I had faith you were gonna be saved."

"I know, but the results are in *His* hands. We just have to be obedient and share His love—almost blindly."

"You're right." Karen nodded with her eyes closed. "You're teaching me now." She took in his face. "You've grown so much—"

The phone rang. Everett remained there for two rings, then eased up, kissed her forehead, and went to the granite-top desk that was built into the wall of the kitchen.

"Hello."

"Hi…Uncle Everett?"

"Madison?"

Karen looked over, wiping her tears with the sleeves of her sweater.

"Yeah, it's me. Um, is Aunt Karen there by any chance?"

"She is. Hold on." He covered the phone while Karen got a Kleenex and blew her nose. Then he handed her the phone, squeezed the back of her neck, and picked up his mug.

"Madison…hi." Karen headed for the family room with the phone, sounding congested. "Of course I've got a second…"

Everett was petting Rosey when Karen rushed back into the room, snapping her fingers.

"Uh-oh." She eyed Everett. "Which hospital?"

Everett mouthed the word *Eddie?* but Karen shook her head.

"Okay, I know where it is," she said. "Of course I can come. Are your mom and dad there?" Karen paused, then frowned. "Well, you keep trying him and we will, too. We can be there right away. And honey, we'll be praying." She turned the phone off.

"Wesley?" Everett asked.

"Yep." She clasped Everett's hands. "He's okay, but he's been shot in the wrist. He and some friends were at a shooting range. It was an accident. The bullet went right through, missed the bone completely. He's gonna make it."

"Oh, man... what about Eddie?"

"They can't find him. Can't reach him by phone. Don't know where he is. Sheila's at the hospital."

"We better get down there."

"Who knows," she started for her coat, "maybe this is the beginning of the answer to our prayers."

Forty minutes later, Karen rubbed Madison's back as they sat next to Wesley's hospital bed on the second floor of White Plains Hospital Center. Everett stood nearby, his arms crossed, and his energy sapped from the recent emotional upheaval. The room was still and dark except for the fluorescent light that glowed and hummed ever-so-quietly beneath some dark cabinets over by the sink.

As he slept, dark shadows filled Wesley's deep eye sockets and accentuated the hollow cheekbones on his ashen face. Sheila had fallen asleep with her head back in the chair next to the bed. Her nose was red and her mascara was slightly smeared. She clutched a box of tissues in her lap.

"The doctors said it was painful," Madison whispered. "He's been on an IV since they brought him to the room."

Everett noticed the white gauze wrap that covered about four inches of Wesley's wrist. "His hand and arm look pretty good."

"Both sides have started to bruise where the bullet went in and out." Madison's whole body relaxed and she seemed to breathe easier.

"We couldn't reach your dad," Karen said.

"I know. I tried him again just before you got here... Whatever."

"So," Everett gestured to Wesley, "they were at a shooting range?"

"Yeah." Madison turned to Karen. "He was with that Tony guy I told you about. And another guy. A gun jammed. Wes and Tony were working on it at the same time, and it went off. The owner called 911."

"Were the police involved?" Karen asked.

"No," she checked her mom and lowered her voice, "but the doctors did tests. They told my mom meth was in his system."

Karen shot Everett a glance. "Has the doctor informed the police yet?"

"She already did. But they told her that, because the guys are adults and the shooting was an accident—and no meth was found at the scene—they couldn't do anything…"

"The cops around here are overwhelmed," Everett said.

"I don't know if that's good or bad." Somebody tapped on the door, and Madison went to answer it. "Sometimes I think it might help if Wesley got thrown in jail for a spell."

She opened the door slightly. Everett heard a low male voice on the other side. Madison conversed with whoever it was for several moments; then she shut the door gently and turned back into the room, wide-eyed.

"That was Tony Badino's father. He got a call from someone," Madison said. "There was some confusion. He thought his son had been shot. The nurses told him about Wesley, and he recognized our last name—"

Badino… "Wait a minute." Everett ran a hand through his hair, took several steps toward the door, and stopped. "Who's Tony Badino?"

"The guy Wesley's been hanging out with," Madison said. "The crazy one."

"I told you," Karen added. "He was with Wesley the night, you know…at our house."

Everett shook his head, trying to clear the haze.

It can't be. "You didn't say his name was Badino." He headed for the door.

"Why?" Karen followed. "What's going on, Ev?"

He opened the door and stuck his head into the light of the hallway, looking to his left. Empty.

"Well, well," came a deep voice from the other direction, "if it ain't the world-famous rock star. I had a feelin' you'd be here."

Everett turned the other way to face the finely dressed Dominic Badino and his two dark henchmen. He leaned back into the room and said to Karen, "I'll be right back. Sit tight."

"What's going on?" Karen insisted.

"I'll tell you in a minute. Be cool."

Everett went into the hallway. It was all clear except for the Sopranos.

"Madison's a fine-looking young woman," Badino remarked from behind charcoal-tinted glasses. "Is your nephew all right?"

Everett's jaw tightened and his fist clenched. His impulse was to hammer the captain, but he rethought it when he sized up the tall and short guys wearing black raincoats, whom he recognized from Pappano's. "He's going to make it," Everett managed.

"I got a false alarm about my boy." He turned to his bodyguards, who were both on cell phones. "At least we think it was a false alarm. We're still puttin' the pieces together. Sounds like it was an accident. I can't get ahold of my boy. The little—"

"I didn't realize Wesley was friends with your son."

"Tony's been runnin' with your nephew for a while." Badino laughed. "Gotta keep track of these things, Mr. Lester. By the way, I hear your brother's on a winning streak."

Everett heard the words, but they didn't register. "What do you mean?"

The short, wiry, older wiseguy interrupted. "Excuse me, Mr. B. I finally got Mrs. Badino. The boy's fine. He's been in touch with her. Everything's okay. He's got his phone back on when you're ready to speak ta him."

"Okay, Rocko. I'll talk to him in a minute."

"What were you saying about Eddie?" asked Everett. "The winning streak?"

"You don't know?" Badino smirked. "I'm tellin' ya, your brother's got the fever, and when that happens there's no truth. No truth. You can't believe anythin' he tells you." Badino chuckled. "Not that it bothers me. If your brother's bettin', we're ultimately makin' money."

Everett was sick of this big talker. "Would you just tell me what he's doing?"

"You gave your brother twenty grand to finish off his debt with us, right?"

Everett nodded.

"He bet it." Badino took pleasure dropping the nuke. "Mike said he placed the bet while you were waitin' in the car for him last Saturday. Talk about dirty pool."

Everett's face burned. His fingernails dug into the palms of his hands.

"He won that night." Badino brushed some lint off his coat. "Ohio State over Michigan. So he was up twenty grand. 'Course, he bet it all Sunday and won on the Giants; up forty. Then he took the Raiders in the afternoon and won that. Up eighty. That's the last I heard."

Everett was cold to the core. He cupped his hands to his mouth and blew into them. "Mr. Badino, I've tried to help Eddie. I've offered to put him in residential treatment. He won't go—"

"'Course he won't. He's full tilt. I told you that."

"But what I'm saying is, you can't hold me responsible for his behavior—or my family."

Rocko's eye's flared as he made for Everett. "How dare you…" But Badino raised a thick arm, stopping the little maniac with the back of his pudgy hand.

"Don't you dare tell me what I can and cannot do." Badino's mouth barely opened as his small black eyes met Everett's. "This is like havin' a child who vandalizes, Mr. Lester. If that pipsqueak can't pay for the damage he does—his parents will. And we're lookin' at you like his parent, you and Karen. Unless, of course, you want us to approach his real mother, Doris, who I happen to know is very sick with emphysema in northeast Ohio. Now, that wouldn't be a very pleasant visit—"

All sound faded and everything seared white in Everett's head. He tore into Badino, whipping him around by the lapels of his coat. "Leave my mother out of this. And my wife!"

Rocko's knee slammed Everett's groin, and he groaned as he collapsed with his head down to his knees.

The door to Wesley's room swung open. Karen was in the hallway. "Leave him alone. Help! Somebody!"

The tall bodyguard swung Karen around and clapped a big hand over her mouth. Her eyes were huge as he muffled her screams. Everett lunged at the goon, ripping his arm away from Karen's mouth, and jacking him with a right hook to the side of his face.

"Heeeeelp!" Karen squirmed away.

Madison was in the hallway now, running in the direction of the nurses' station.

The goon was about to bash Everett. "Why, you miserable—"

"Enough!" Badino barked. "Outta here—*now.*"

The dude rammed Everett into the wall, and he crumpled to the ground. The three men regrouped and headed toward the dark end of the hallway.

"As long as your brother keeps betting," Badino seethed as he walked backward, while the goons jogged toward the exit, "we're gonna be an intimate part of your life. Get used to it, Lester. Tell your wife and mother to get used to it, too."

20

Just when Everett was ready to collapse back in Wesley's dark hospital room, the turmoil fired back up.

"I want to know, straight out, what my dad is into," Madison demanded as she stood in the middle of the room. "What's he doing? Dealing drugs? Insider trading? What?"

Wesley slept in the same position as before the altercation. His mother was wiping her face with a steaming washcloth at the sink.

"Go ahead." Sheila spun around. "Tell her what you've found out. I don't care anymore. I can't go on like this. It's like I don't even have a husband. I wish I didn't. What good is he? Where is he now, when we need him?"

Sheila dried her hands with a paper tower and walked to Wesley's bed, where she stroked his head with trembling fingers.

Everett wanted to crawl away, despising the fact that he had to convey such disturbing news to his niece. "Your dad's been gambling." He approached Madison. "It started at the casinos, but a couple of months ago, he took it to another level; he got himself a bookie."

The girl just stared, her mouth sealed shut.

"Eddie said he didn't know the bookie was part of a, kind of a crime operation."

"Oh, he knew!" Sheila insisted.

"What are you saying?" Madison asked. "Mafia?"

"Some kind of organized crime family, yes," Everett explained. "The men here today were from that family. Tony Badino's dad, Dominic, is the captain."

"How do you know all this?" Karen asked.

"They were all at the restaurant Saturday when I went with Eddie to help him pay his debts. Badino is highest in command next to the boss."

Karen stuck her hands on her hips. "He's the one who threatened you?"

"More than once."

"Why would he threaten you if my dad's the one in trouble with them?"

"I'll tell you why, Madi." Sheila jabbed into the air. "Because if your dad doesn't pay what he owes, they'll come after your uncle for the money. Or you, or me, or Wesley—or Karen. Let's just face it, Everett, your brother's a self-centered *loser*. He doesn't give a flip about what happens to us. We've got creditors calling at all hours. He's completely gone off the deep end. And I'm not going down with the ship."

Everett understood Sheila's bitterness and wondered how much of Eddie's behavior contributed to her alcoholism.

"Mom, he needs help," Madison insisted. "We can't just—"

Wesley's harsh cough startled everyone as he lurched forward—hacking, straining, and red-faced. He scrambled to get out of the bed but was held back by the IV hooked to the silver stand next to him.

With fiercer hacking, it looked as if he was going to get sick. "Get him a wastebasket." Everett grabbed the IV stand and wheeled it around the bed, not wanting the boy to undergo the embarrassment of getting sick in front of them. "C'mon, Wes, let's get you to the bathroom."

Wesley pushed away the wastebasket Madison held up, made it to the restroom with the IV stand, and waved Everett out. Within seconds, violent heaving echoed from behind the large bathroom door. "Should I go in?"

"Leave him alone, Mom." Madison shook her head. "He doesn't want you in there."

Sheila found the call button on the side of the bed and pushed it repeatedly. When no response came within thirty seconds, she bolted for the door. "I'm going to get help."

Minutes later, Madison's cell phone rang. She examined the caller ID and glanced at Karen before answering. "Dad? Where are you?" She bit at the cuticles of her fingers while listening. "Yeah, well, your remaining son is in room 224 at White Plains Hospital. He got shot in the wrist. He's gonna make it, but it sure would be nice if you could be here."

She listened with her eyes closed. "There are always excuses…" She crossed to the window. "No, we don't need anything. Just get here, for Wesley."

By the time she hung up, the bathroom was silent.

Sheila entered the room. "The doctor will be here in a minute."

"Dad's on his way," Madison told her.

"Where's he been?"

"Said he's been working all day and didn't realize his phone was off. When he finally turned it on, he had twenty-three messages."

"Uh-huh," Sheila said. "I've never heard that one before."

The hospital phone on the table by the bed let out one low but annoying ring. Everett picked it up. "Hello."

"Wes? That you?"

"No…Wesley can't come to the phone. Can I give him a message?"

"Who's this?" the blunt voice asked.

"A relative." Everett turned his back to those in the room and lowered his voice. "Who's this?"

"Oh, ho! I know who this is," came the deranged voice. "Glo-ray, glo-ray, hallelujah! Out of the darkness and into the light. This is Everett Lester, ain't it?"

A flash of chills engulfed Everett. "It is."

"It is, or 'I Am'?" Hideous laughter blared from the other end. "Is this the great 'I Am'?"

Everett dropped his head, closed his eyes, and tried to remain calm.

"Are you there, I Am, or did you disappear on me?"

"I know who you are."

"Oh, that's right, you know all things."

"Tony Badino," Everett said quietly.

Long pause. "Wrong! This is the ghost of your nephew, David Lester, askin' why you led me astray. Why you promised me the Other Side. Now I'm dead. I don't exist no more. I'm cryin' out from nothingness, reminding you that my blood is on your hands. Does that haunt you at night, I Am?"

"Why are you doing this?"

"Because, I *can't stand* people like you, leading others astray."

Even coming from a deranged idiot like this, the words battered Everett's psyche. He waited for more.

"First it was the Other Side," Badino seethed, "some make-believe oasis for everybody who dies. Now it's even worse—a selective utopia for Jesus freaks only."

"If you don't believe the way I do, that's your business—"

"You're right! It is my business, and I'm gonna make it other people's business, too. People need to know the truth. We exist for the here and now! This life is *it.*"

"That talk's from hell."

"There is no such thing."

"I'm not going to argue with you."

"The point is, Lester, you shouldn't be able to just spout your dead-end lies and promises of paradise to the whole world and go on your merry way, leaving a trail of corpses. You gotta answer to somebody!"

"To you?"

"That's right!"

"Why you?"

"Because I'm an authority on the subject."

"Yeah? Why's that?"

"'Cause I lost somebody because of religious zealots like you. Three years ago. Her name was Erica Santose."

"That's what this is about? You losing your girlfriend to Christianity?"

"Shut up, jerk! She's dead!" Tony breathed heavy. "I was gonna marry her. She got baptized at a *stinkin'* revival. They promised her new life—all the things you promise. She got blindsided by a drunk driver on the way home that very night. Some new life your God gave her, huh?"

A thousand images of Liza Moon, an old girlfriend, spun in Everett's head. Before Karen, she'd been the one—until she overdosed. Her death—the loss—resurrected itself in the pit of his stomach, and he felt for the kid.

"Okay, look, I'm sorry about your friend—"

"Sorry ain't good enough, Lester. You need to *pay*, for Erica, for David…"

Badino's voice was intense, and his gall troubled Everett's spirit. "God will judge me, Tony, just as He'll judge you."

"No! Don't do that. You hear me? Don't you dare try to feed me your hypocritical self-deception."

"Jesus loves you—"

"Don't give me that! You've been brainwashed. You're pitiful."

"But there's peace in my heart," Everett said. "Even now, while I face your wrath, I have a high tower. I take all my troubles to Him."

"No! I told you not to do that. You're lying. I won't listen. Nothin' you're talkin' about satisfies."

"Yes it does, Tony. Jesus satisfies. His Spirit lives in me. I'm His child—"

"That's a crutch for losers like you who don't know how to cope with reality."

"But He forgives my sins," Everett pleaded. "He makes me whole."

"You rely on invisible myths and spiritual pipe dreams, but *I'm* the captain of *my* soul."

Everett dropped his head and shook it. "No—you're not. You're mistaken. Tonight, you could lose your life. And then you'll face the real Captain of your soul…"

He took a deep breath and pressed the phone hard against his ear. He still heard movement, breathing. Waiting through the silence, he sensed the attention of those in the room but did not turn around. His ears were ringing, and the ground spun slightly from the intensity of the conversation.

"Lemme tell you somethin'," the nasty voice rumbled like a beast. "You know what satisfies? Indulgence. Vengeance. *Sin.* Sin rules, Lester. Sin reigns. And sin is gonna ruin you. You know why?"

Don't listen. You don't have to play his game. "I'm going to hang up now—"

"'Cause you're a creature of habit, just like me! You think your house is swept clean, but the unclean spirit that left you ain't gonna find no rest. He's comin' back. Haven't you read your Bible? Matthew twelve. He's comin' back with seven spirits more wicked than himself. And they're gonna rock your world, man. You'll see."

Everett had read the words Tony quoted but had no idea what they meant. There was a slight commotion behind him. He turned to see the doctor helping Wesley back into his bed. Sheila and Madison were by his side. So was Karen, but she was searching Everett curiously as she did.

"Bad dogs like you always return to their vomit, Lester. You just wait. All it takes is one time. One slip…"

"Look, Badino, you're confused and you're angry. I don't want any trouble with you—"

"But what if we want trouble with you, huh? What if we decide to make hell for you and your sweet little wife?"

"Who's we?"

The phone went silent.

Everett waited.

"Me and my legions, of course." Tony's voice suddenly sounded like a jovial romper-room teacher leading kindergartners.

"Legions?"

"That's right. What if we decide David's and Erica's deaths will not be swept under the rug? What if we *hate* what you're doing so much that we—"

"I'll get the police involved."

"You're going to fight a spiritual battle with flesh and blood? Good luck. Besides, they won't have anything on us."

"What about your father? What will they have on him?"

There was a loud rattle, a click, then silence. With the phone still glued to his ear and his hands trembling, Everett looked around. The others were tending to Wesley, but Karen approached as he placed the phone back in its cradle.

"Who was it?" she whispered, running her hand down his back.

"Tony Badino." He squeezed her hand but didn't want her to feel his shaking, so he let go.

"What was it about?"

The doctor—a pretty woman of fifty or so with fair skin, stylish white hair, and blue eyes—was examining the wound on Wesley's wrist.

"Satanic." Everett leaned down to Karen's ear. "I'll tell you, I'm ready for us to get out of New York, get on the road."

"You look terrible." Karen touched his face. "You're pale."

"I feel clammy, like I just gave a gallon of blood."

Sitting on the bed and rebandaging the wound, the doctor faced Sheila and Madison. "This is going to be fine in no time." She patted Wesley's upper arm and pivoted to face Everett and Karen, who stood near the foot of the bed. Reaching out her hand, she shook with Everett. "I'm Rebecca Denton, Wesley's doctor."

"Hi, I'm Everett." He tried to smile. "This is Karen, my wife."

"I've met Karen." She grinned and stood. "And I recognize you." The doctor put the lid on her pen and dropped it in the pocket of her white physician's coat. "It's amazing how little damage the bullet did. He's lucky. In fact, it may be the thing Wesley needed to get him in for a much-needed doctor's visit."

"I told Dr. Denton she could speak freely," Sheila said, almost frantically. "We're all family. Wesley's okay with it."

Wesley rolled his eyes and looked out the window.

"We've talked a little about this, but I'm going to be frank with you." Dr. Denton examined each person. "Wesley's methamphetamine habit is doing some serious damage to his body. It's been going on for quite a while."

Wesley mumbled something about Sherlock Holmes, but it didn't faze the doctor. "I'm concerned by what I see and hear going on in his body and by what he's told me. He realizes the meth is tormenting him, that it's taking its toll."

"I've ignored it." Sheila snatched another tissue. "We lost a son a year ago. It's set me back."

"Wesley told me about that."

A rap sounded at the door, and Eddie hustled in wearing a navy suit out of the pages of *GQ*, with a dark overcoat slung over one arm. No bandages were on his face anymore, just small scabs. "Where's my man?" He glanced at the others and headed for the bed. "Look at this guy." He rubbed hard at the brown stubble on Wesley's head. "Unstoppable. Even bullets don't slow him down."

Wesley's lip turned up, and he yanked his arm away when Eddie fumbled for the bandage on his wrist. Ignoring his son's coldness, Eddie said his hellos and introduced himself to Dr. Denton, who didn't appear impressed.

"Shall I continue?" The doctor looked at Sheila then Everett.

"Yes." Sheila sat on the bed and addressed Eddie. "We're talking about methamphetamines. I've been pretending this wasn't happening. I think you have, too. Dr. Denton says it needs to be dealt with."

Eddie grimaced and opened his mouth, but Dr. Denton jumped in.

"This drug is on the rampage in New York, and it's a killer, both of lives and souls. First, it's addictive as all get-out. Second, heavy users are losing their minds. They're racked with chronic depression and hallucinations. The drug ramps up the neurological system so high it can literally make your heart explode. We've seen brain damage, lung disorders, fatal kidney disease. I don't think there's a more dangerous drug out there right now."

Eddie scratched his head and stuck his hand on his hip. "Wait a minute. When did—?"

But his son's voice claimed the floor. "Not to mention the fact that it makes you do things…"

"You don't have to do this, Wes! Your mother's cooked this up—"

"Dad, would you be quiet! We're finally getting somewhere here. Or is dealing with this gonna be too much of an inconvenience for you?"

"Don't talk to me like that, Madi."

"People. There are no comparable options here, not even close." Dr. Denton picked up her clipboard from the counter. "Wesley needs help—now. In two days or less, he's going to hit a cycle of withdrawal symptoms of nightmare proportion. He needs proper care."

"Now, come on." Eddie raised a hand toward his son. "Is it that bad, Wes?"

Sheila shot to her feet, and Madison got in Eddie's face. "I can't believe you! Are you on drugs, Dad?"

With an open-mouthed smile, Eddie feigned innocence. "All I'm saying is, let's ask Wes how bad this really is."

Wesley's nostrils flared as he jerked his head away from his father. His eyes pierced like lasers, and his jaws ground together, muscles flexing. When he closed his eyes, a lone tear trailed down his cheek.

Sheila fell back to the bed, sobbing, and wrapped her arms around him. Madison squealed something and buried her head in Karen's arms. Everett could only meet Eddie's confused eyes with an unflinching glare.

"Look." Dr. Denton exhaled heavily. "I know a program in Stamford. It's been extremely successful at getting meth users clean and back on their feet. It's called Horizons at Harbor View. Wesley could be admitted today. It's a two- to four-week program. He could be out in January, start the New Year off right."

If it weren't for Dr. Denton, war would have broken out in that room. She kept things moving nicely. "How 'bout it? I can call and make sure there's an opening." She reached for the cell phone in her coat pocket.

Eddie held up his hands. "I'm just asking, are there any other options?"

"None even close to this one." Dr. Denton didn't make eye contact with him. "This deals with the disease of addiction. It helps patients identify usage triggers and develop new social skills. It gives them a thorough relapse prevention plan, teaching coping skills. Wesley could try Crystal Meth Anonymous meetings, but I really don't think he's a good candidate for that."

"How do you know?" Eddie squirmed.

"She talked to me!" Wesley exploded. "She sat on this bed and asked me questions. Okay? She listened for an hour. She *listened* to me!"

"He's going to Stamford," Sheila blasted to her feet, "and that's final."

Eddie marched to the window, pulled out his cell phone, and started jamming buttons. "Fine, make the call."

21

The midafternoon sky had darkened, and the snow fell heavy and thick in the fifty minutes since Karen left Twin Streams to pick up her parents, flying in from Kansas City International. With only a few days left before Christmas, parking at LaGuardia was dreadful.

Wiping her feet on the soaked mat and checking the arrival monitors once inside, Karen found that American flight 2822 would be pulling up to gate D in the Central Terminal Building about forty minutes late.

Not too bad.

Having met Everett at LaGuardia on a handful of occasions, Karen was somewhat familiar with the layout. She strolled past the busy postal kiosk and the gents at the shoe-shine stand by the souvenir store and ducked into a restroom.

When she came out, Karen stopped for a moment to get her bearings. Since she couldn't go to the terminals, she set out to find something to drink in the central hub of the airport. She got in line at

Starbucks behind about eight people. While reviewing her grocery and
to-do lists, the phone in her purse played "Silver Bells." "Hello?"

"Hey, honey. Where are you?"

"Hi, Ev. I'm at Starbucks in the airport."

"Good. Can you believe all this snow?"

"It's getting slick out there," she said. "This place is a zoo."

"Listen, babe…one of the detectives called a minute ago."

Her whole body came to attention. She covered her free ear.
"And?"

"Well, they couldn't get any clues from the footprints, because so
many tracks were already out there."

"What else?"

There was a pause, too long of a pause for it to be anything good.

"The letters were painted in blood, babe…from some kind of animal."

Another blow. Deflated, she staggered out of line to the closest
table and dropped into a chair.

"Believe it or not," Everett said, "the detective told me they see
this fairly often—"

"Oh, right." *A real comfort.*

"Usually kids playing pranks."

"Did you tell them about Wesley?" she asked.

"No, I wanted to talk to you first. Look, I'm ready to go straight to
Wesley and Eddie. That's what I think we should do."

There were so many variables, so many people and feelings
involved. She couldn't seem to muster any words.

"I've got to talk to Eddie anyway, babe. Something else happened…"

Her head dropped. There couldn't be more. "What?"

"I just went to get the paper and take Rosey out, and I found an
envelope from him in my coat pocket. It had twenty grand in it."

She stared at the masses of people moving past and tried to mentally juggle all the tribulations pressing in on them.

"He must have put it in there at the hospital," Everett said. "And a note on the envelope said the other twenty-four thousand is on its way."

"Eddie's gonna die," she finally managed. "And that mob he's involved with is going to come looking for us."

"I tried to call him. Got his voice mail. I was straight with him. Told him we saw Dominic Badino at the hospital and that we know he's betting again. I let him know he's putting us in danger."

Knowing how unreliable and selfish Eddie was, that didn't help one iota. "It's time to get the police involved, Ev."

"Karen—"

"What?" She couldn't believe she'd just yelled in Starbucks; her face heated and her voice dropped. "We need to get on record with the threats Badino's made."

"Honey, there were no specifics, and it's his word against mine. Besides, you can't call the cops on the son of a *mob captain*."

"Maybe you can't, but I can!"

An awkward hush followed. Enough had been said for now. Maybe too much.

"Look, I need to process all this," she said.

"I'm sorry to drop this on you right when your folks are due in."

"I'm getting used to it." It was a mean thought, never meant to become words. The silence that followed was like watching a bomb drop in a documentary. She knew the fallout was imminent, and it came in the form of a quick and quiet good-bye from Everett.

She'd wounded him. *Is that what you wanted?* She felt crippled herself, almost sick inside. She closed her eyes and asked God to forgive her. And then she lifted her head and tried to keep going.

With a tall mocha in hand, Karen made her way to the center of the airport hub. She chose a chair that faced the huge flight schedule board that would keep her abreast of any further changes in her parents' flight, now due to arrive at 2:36 p.m.

The rich coffee warmed Karen. She shed her denim coat and watched the people go by. Many, it appeared, carried burdens as heavy as their winter jackets and suitcases—solemn-faced, not saying hello or even making eye contact. They were fixed on their destinations, on their own little worlds. Others seemed completely tuned out to humanity, thanks to their laptops, cell phones, and iPods. What a wonderful thing technology had done for mankind.

Seeing a pretty brunette with a bandage on her forehead in the bookstore across the way sent Karen back to the night Eddie had shown up at Twin Streams with his wounds.

Oh, Lord, help my love for people not to grow cold. I can feel it happening. I'm frustrated with Eddie and Sheila, their immaturity. I'm tempted to hate Tony Badino, Wesley—whoever killed Millie. So many are owned by Satan, blinded by him. Let me have Your compassion. Live in me. Let me love them like You do.

Her eyes caught the gaze of a young man in a long black trench coat. He, too, was in the bookstore about twenty-five feet from her, holding open an issue of *Hot Rod* but staring directly at her. His brazen gaze scorched her face. She buried her attention in her purse and began digging around in it, as if she were searching for something.

You're just paranoid.

She made up her mind to take another glimpse. His eyes still locked on hers like a warhead on its target. He had small, taut features and a tough yet boyish face. She took inventory of his attire—faded jeans torn at the knee, brown work boots, gray ski cap, and several layers of shirts beneath the long coat.

Digging once again in her bag, she pulled out her cell phone, opened it, and pretended to push buttons. Putting the phone to her ear, she glanced up again.

He was gone. *Nowhere in sight.*

With slightly trembling hands, she sipped the cooling mocha and searched the flight board again. Still 2:36.

"Dat?" A tiny girl with shiny brown hair appeared, holding up an index finger and pointing to Karen's cup. "Dat?"

"That's coffee." Karen turned the cup toward the girl, who wore a light pink winter coat with white fur around the hood.

"Coffee?"

Karen met the proud green eyes of the girl's smiling young mother perched on the edge of her seat, her arms half-outstretched. "She's just starting to walk," said the redheaded father, standing behind the mother's chair, wearing an equally proud grin.

"How are you today?" Karen spoke to the girl in a singsong tone while simultaneously inspecting the area for black trench coats.

"Ta-ti." The little girl nodded repeatedly. "Ta-ti."

How adorable.

"*Ta-ti* is grandma," the woman interpreted. "Grandma and Grandpa are coming for Christmas, and her birthday."

"Ah," Karen said in a tone that got the girl's attention. "And what is your name? Can you tell me your name?"

"Say-wa."

"Sarah? That's my mother's name. That's a pretty name."

The girl blinked and nodded her approval.

Karen turned back to the parents. "Is she your only child?"

"So far." The woman laughed. "We hope to have more. What about you?"

Karen's smile melted. "I don't...we don't have any—yet."

"Well, enjoy it while you can," the father advised. "They sure keep you busy."

For that kind of busy, I'll trade you any day.

Karen grinned at the father. "How old is she?"

"She'll be twelve months Christmas Day."

"Oh, Sarah. You and Jesus have the same birthday. How special."

"Silver Bells" played again. Karen excused herself and opened her phone. It was Madison.

"I'm so excited. We got Wesley registered at Horizons at Harbor View. The people are really friendly. And it's like a resort, all decorated for Christmas, with a fire in the fireplace. Even has a view of Long Island Sound."

"That's great news." Karen scanned the area again. "Is it far from you?"

Karen barely heard Madison describe the location of Horizons; she was more focused on searching out each piece of black clothing and its respective owner.

"Can you believe it?" Madison's voice brought her back. "Aunt Karen?"

"I'm sorry." Karen pressed her fingers to her forehead. "I missed that."

"A girl! Wesley met a really sweet girl while we were getting him situated. Her name's Cassidy, and she's from Schenectady. She's been there about ten days. I've never seen him take to anyone like that. We can't see him or talk to him for at least a week. That means he'll be alone for Christmas, maybe New Year's, too."

"Oh, that's *good*." Karen's fears subsided momentarily as her gaze settled on little Sarah, who was half-eating, half-sucking Cheerios from a plastic yellow container clutched like a football in her tiny arm. "How did it go with your mom and dad?"

"Mom and I drove Wesley to Horizons. Dad drove separately. I hate it that they can't even stand to be in the car together."

"That is so hard," Karen said. "I don't know exactly how you're feeling, sweetie, but God does. And I've been praying you'll get to know Him."

"Thanks. I've been reading the Bible you gave me."

"Oh, Madi…" Karen lost her breath for a second. It was all the emotion—of everything—seeping over the top. "That makes my day."

When Karen hung up, Sarah held out her tiny wet hand, offering a Cheerio. Karen put it up to her mouth and pretended to eat it. Then she glanced at her watch and decided to head over to the passenger arrival area.

After sharing a pleasant good-bye with the little girl and her parents, Karen tossed her empty cup in a trash can, then made the short walk toward a bright, open area where hundreds of people congregated beneath a line of glowing arrival screens, about forty feet from the escalators.

Karen watched the weary travelers emerging from the escalators: men and women in business suits, casually dressed people yakking on cell phones, young people wandering inquisitively wearing headphones, and old people clinging to each other for dear life.

Then she saw the gray ski cap. The long black trench coat. And the eyes. The penetrating eyes—sizing her up like a predator does its prey.

Her head dropped, staring at the scuffed floor. He was just another New Yorker there to pick up a friend. He had to be. She twisted her watch, adjusted the shoulder strap on her purse, and prayed she was just being obsessive.

Okay, just look around, calmly. She peered up at the array of arrival details on the board, then glanced back to the open space to the right of the escalators.

He leered at her with those little eyes and that cocky demeanor— a leg slung over the arm of a red vinyl chair.

Karen held his gaze as long as she could, but it was like holding her hand over a flame. When he eased his head back and grinned seductively, she spun completely around toward the restrooms. She squeezed her fingers and sought solace amid the sea of faces surrounding her but found none.

She checked her watch—2:40—then the arrival board; her parents' flight was in. *They'll deplane, get the train…another ten minutes.* She let her eyes drift back to the red chair.

Empty.

She froze, unable to turn her head. She was certain he'd be right there. She stared at the escalators, but the people pouring off were only a blur. Her mind whisked her back to Twin Streams—the splattered red snow…Millie's blood-caked body…and the words *You Die* scrawled in burgundy.

"Excuse me," came a male voice from behind, along with a tap on her arm. Her shoulders lurched. She clutched her purse and forced herself around. "I'm sorry." A slight man of Middle Eastern descent smiled at her with brilliant white teeth. "Do you have the time, please?"

Karen heaved a sigh, gave him the time, and chuckled at herself.

It was times like these when she was glad no one but God knew her every thought. She relaxed in the security of the masses and swiveled to face the escalators.

There he was. Again.

Within six feet. *Glaring.*

She bumped into the woman next to her. Her mother's red coat caught her eye first. Then her broad-shouldered father in his black leather jacket and assuring smile. Karen's hand rose, and she heard herself squeal.

She was weak and dazed, but she kept going, excusing herself, weaving around bodies, bumping hard into several, frantically making her way into the opening. Into the warm embrace of those who'd always kept her safe.

22

Wind swirled the snow around outside the bay window at Twin Streams. After seeing the ghostlike reflection of headlights on the wall, Everett had passed through the busy kitchen and peered out at the night. By the time he got there, the headlights became taillights, gliding down Old Peninsula, over the hill and out of sight.

Ever since his disturbing phone conversation with Tony Badino, Everett couldn't get the kid out of his head and was glad to finally be talking about it with Karen's father, Jacob, who had become his spiritual mentor of sorts.

Karen's dinner of baked chicken and mashed potatoes had garnered positive reviews from her parents. But something in their countenance—perhaps their quieter-than-normal manner—made Everett suspect they'd already spoken at length with Karen about her infertility on the way home from the airport. It hadn't been mentioned during dinner.

Everett made coffee while Karen and Sarah tidied up the kitchen, gabbing like long-lost roommates while upbeat Christmas carols played over the home stereo system.

Jacob sat at the kitchen table, studying Everett's Bible. "Is this it? 'When the unclean spirit goes out of a man, it passes through waterless places, seeking rest, and does not find it. Then it says, "I will return to my house from which I came"; and when it comes, it finds it unoccupied, swept, and put in order.'"

"That's exactly what Badino quoted to me," Everett said. "Keep going."

Jacob looked back down and followed his finger. "'Then it goes and takes along with it seven other spirits more wicked than itself, and they go in and live there; and the last state of that man becomes worse than the first.'"

"Okay, translate it for me."

"Well, first of all, if he was implying this is going to happen to you, Ev, he's wrong. Jesus was talking about people who try to become *morally reformed* but not born again."

"What's it mean, about the unclean spirits?" Everett asked.

"Say a person cleans up his act. He gets rid of some of the bad things in his life, and what happens? The unclean spirit goes out of him. For a while, he does better. But Christ hasn't been invited to live in that person, so he's plagued much worse than before."

Everett shuddered. Had unclean spirits haunted him at times and made him question his own salvation? His past—the women and drugs, the violence and vulgarity—seemed too despicable to be swept under God's rug of forgiveness.

But Christ lives in me. I am forgiven. Why do I doubt?

In many ways, Everett was still at war—with temptations and feelings of inadequacy, like he wasn't pure enough to wear the name Christian. But he was too embarrassed to share such things with Jacob.

Karen topped off their coffees. "I want to know how Tony Badino knows Scripture like that. He mentioned Job and dogs returning to their vomit. He knew God was called I Am; it's just plain creepy."

Sarah came over with a dish towel draped over her shoulder. She looked radiant, her blond hair short and shiny. She stood behind Jacob and rested a delicate hand on his big shoulder as they deferred to Everett.

"Don't look at me." He straightened his posture and held up both hands. "I have no clue. The guy sounds like some kind of antichrist to me."

"He said his girlfriend was baptized before she died." Jacob sipped his coffee. "Maybe that's what got Tony interested in the Bible. Maybe he sought God afterward, or before, leading up to her conversion."

Karen wiped the counter. "All I know is, nobody just knows Scriptures like the ones he mentioned unless they've spent time in the Word."

"Well," Sarah said, "I can't imagine Dominic 'Brain Picker' Badino leading family devotions in front of the fireplace."

The laughter cleared Everett's head, and he was suddenly whole again. Indeed, most of the time he was sound and walked in the Spirit. It was the other times, those brief sieges, when he would momentarily be overcome by the lies of the flesh. He hated himself for those times and silently cursed Satan for ravaging him with feelings of guilt and inadequacy.

Being with Jacob and Sarah took him back to their comfortable home in Topeka and to his rental house in Bal Harbour, Florida, where he lived during the Endora Crystal murder trial. Wherever these people were was a bastion of love. They were the family he'd never known as a child, growing up in a dysfunctional home in the shadows of Cleveland's refineries.

Everett saw the reflection of headlights in the window but ignored it this time. Karen and Sarah wrapped Christmas presents on the floor by the fireplace in the family room, with Rosey nestled up next to them.

Everett showed Jacob the new recording studio in the basement.

The cushy spread contained all the latest electronic equipment, with walls and ceiling made of state-of-the-art soundproofing materials.

"Karen seemed a little out of it when she picked us up today," Jacob said as they stood over the massive soundboard.

"Out of it?"

"Kind of distraught. We thought it might be because of the doctor's appointment and all that's been going on around here lately."

"We've been under the gun, no doubt. It's been a stressful couple weeks."

"I'm sorry Karen can't conceive, Ev." Jacob's eyes met his. "You know it's my fault."

Everett looked up several inches into his father-in-law's beaten eyes and shook his head. "It's nobody's fault, Jacob. It's just God's plan, I guess."

"She's always loved children. Well, you know that…" Jacob panned the studio, perhaps to avoid eye contact or to stop a tear from falling. "She used to help in the nursery when she was young, just loved those babies." He peered through the polished glass into the recording studio at the various microphones and guitars, smoothing his thick brown mustache.

"Who knows? We may adopt," Everett said. "But I'm not going to stop praying for our own."

Jacob turned back to him. "We're not either."

"Can I ask you a question?"

"Sure." Jacob crossed his thick arms and leaned back on the desk.

"Karen's infertility." Everett sat in the swivel chair, rolling it back several feet. "Millie. The stuff going on with my brother and Wesley. I just want to know, does God pay us back for our sins? The bad things we did before we were saved? I mean, you mentioned Karen's infertility being your fault, but you're the godliest dude I know."

"What I meant was, I'm the one who drove her to get the abortion, to protect my image." Jacob folded his arms and stroked his cheeks with a large hand. "I was a legalistic hypocrite. The abortion never should have happened."

"But there's no payback?"

"Ev, when Christ came, He did something that had never been done before. He forgave sin completely. You need to remember that."

"What about when I sin now?"

A heavy crash thundered from above. Then barking.

"Evvv!" Karen's shriek sent the men in motion.

Everett dashed to the stairs, took three at a time, and bound through the kitchen with Jacob right behind him to the family room. They found wrapping paper, ribbon, tissue, and packages, but not Karen or Sarah.

"Karen!"

"Here, Ev. Living room!"

Everett led the way but stopped cold at the beige carpet leading inside. The floor was covered with shards of sparkling glass as a frigid wind blew the white curtain sheers into the room.

Karen and Sarah ran to the men from their position in the foyer. "There's a brick." Karen pointed, out of breath. "It came through the window. We were wrapping—"

"Are you okay?" Jacob squeezed Sarah's shoulder.

"We're fine." Karen was shaking, talking fast. "We let Rosey out, to keep her away from the glass. There's something written on the brick."

Everett released Karen and stepped through the broken glass, picked up the brick—which was lying on its side—and examined it.

"A cross." He faced the large, white painted cross toward the other three, then looked on the back of the brick. "*Abaddon.*" He turned it again to show them how the word had been finger-painted, savagely, in white across the length of the brick.

Sarah looked at Jacob. "What's it mean?"

"Destruction." Jacob took the brick from Everett. "That's Abaddon in Hebrew. *Ruin.*"

Everett pumped a fist. "When's this gonna end?" He stomped to the window. "Why us? What the heck's goin' on?"

"Keep your cool, son." Jacob eyed the brick. "Were you ladies able to see anything?"

"By the time we figured out where it had come from or what it was," Sarah held up her hands, "there was no one out there."

Everett stalked into the foyer, turned on an outside light, threw open the front door, and disappeared into the night. The wind was bitter cold. The ground was so frozen, he couldn't see any footprints. Rosey was sniffing up a storm, but whoever had done the deed was gone.

"This looks like an inverted cross." Jacob tossed the brick lightly in his hand as Everett came back in and bolted the door.

"What's that mean?" Karen put her arms around Everett's waist.

"It's a symbol," Jacob said, "ridiculing Christianity."

"Tony Badino did this." Everett pulled away from Karen and seethed through clenched teeth. "I'm gonna find that little whatever he is and deal with this!"

"Just calm down, Ev," Jacob said. "You can't go off half-cocked. We need to call the police, then get something to cover this window."

I should have called them a long time ago. Everett took off for the garage. Two minutes later he rejoined the group in a huff, with his arms full.

"Here." He stuffed a large piece of wadded blue plastic in a chair in the foyer. Then he set down a hammer and a cardboard box of nails. "This is to cover the window. There's a ladder in the garage." He took off toward the master bedroom.

"Babe, don't do this. Please!"

"You're not going to solve anything tonight," Jacob's voice followed him. "Let's just file a report and think this thing through, buddy. We'll come up with a plan . . ."

When Everett emerged from the walk-in closet, Jacob stood there, staring at the black gun in his hands. "What do you think you're doing?"

"I'm leaving this for you, in case Badino comes back."

"I didn't think you'd ever own another gun—"

"It's for protection. You don't know how many threats we've had." Everett held up the semiautomatic and its magazine in separate hands. "If you need it, it'll be in the cupboard, up high, in the kitchen."

Everett huffed past him, but Jacob followed. Once in the kitchen, Everett put the artillery up high in the cupboard without the girls knowing it.

"What do you think you're going to accomplish? Where are you going?"

"Badino's house."

"Are you, crazy? After all that's happened with Eddie? This is the Mafia we're talking about."

"I don't care anymore." Everett marched to the hall closet and got his coat. "I've let it go long enough. Millie's dead. My wife's scared to death. I'm goin' after this guy."

"No you're not!" Karen rushed in, with Sarah five feet behind her. "Stop this, Everett! Don't be like this. Vengeance isn't yours to repay, it's God's. We'll be okay. It's a broken window…"

"And what will it be next?" Everett roared. "You—dead? I'm sorry, but I'm not gonna wait around for that." He grabbed the keys from a wall hook near the door to the garage. "Call the police. File a report. Tell 'em who we think is responsible. But don't mention where I am."

As he hit the garage door button and strode to the car, Everett heard Karen wailing.

"This is not God's way, son," Jacob's bold voice came toward him in the cold garage. "I know what you're feeling, but striking out in anger isn't going to accomplish anything good. You could get yourself thrown in jail, or worse."

Everett's flesh took over. He knew right from wrong. Knew what Jacob said was true. But it all blew away. He was not like Jacob. Would never be the perfect Christian. He was Everett Lester. The confused kid from the wrong side of the tracks. The kid who knew how to fight.

"I'm sorry, Jacob." Everett gave him one last glance. "I'm not wired to sit around and watch people harass me and haunt my wife." He bent into the Audi, revved it to life, flew backward, and spit stones as he took one last look at Rosey in the headlights.

Now I'm the stalker—and I'm comin' for you, Badino.

23

As Karen and her mother swept up the glass, and her father balanced the ladder outside the living room window, Karen's heart leaped when she heard Rosey barking and a car rolling over the gravel driveway. She dropped everything and dashed to the front door.

But she could tell from afar that it wasn't Everett's car.

"Who is it?" Mom said, as Dad came into the house through the front door.

"Not sure." He headed for the kitchen. "Keep an eye on it."

"It looks like a Volkswagen." Karen stood on her tiptoes, peering through the glass in the top of the door. "Convertible. I don't know anyone who drives one."

"Let me go out." Her father rebuttoned his coat and went out the front door and down the sidewalk toward the garage. Meanwhile, Karen led her mom through the kitchen and into the garage, so they could peek out.

"My gosh, that's Madison." Karen unlocked the side door and headed into the brisk night.

"I'm sorry, Karen." Madison sniffled, appearing tiny next to Karen's six-foot-four father. "I didn't know you had company."

"Stay down now, Rosey." Karen shivered. "You remember my dad, Jacob, from the wedding? And my mom, Sarah?"

"Yes." Madison followed Karen and Rosey into the garage. "I'm sorry to barge in."

Once everyone was standing within the golden glow of the kitchen, Madison's eyes appeared bloodshot. Her face was pale, and her mascara was smudged beneath her right eye.

"I won't stay long." She kept her head down.

Karen was about to give her parents some kind of signal to ask them to leave Madison and her alone, but it wasn't necessary.

"Jacob and I have got some things we have to get done." Her mother forced a chuckle and led the way out of the kitchen. "If you'll excuse us…"

Madison shot them a half smile, and they were gone. As soon as Karen put an arm around her, she unraveled.

"I'm pitiful," she cried, "to come here like this."

"I'm glad you came." Karen held her tight. "I need some company now, too. Let's go in the den. You can tell me all about it in there. Do you want some hot tea or cocoa?"

Madison shook her head and took Karen's hand.

In the den Karen laid Madison's suede coat over an ottoman and noticed how beautiful her niece looked—shiny black slacks and boots, a pink and white sweater, and perfume that smelled like lilacs. Rosey sniffed the coat.

"You look like you've been out on the town." Karen patted the seat next to her on the couch.

"I was on a date." She sank next to Karen, shivering, with her arms folded. "I haven't been on one for so long. This guy seemed differ-ent…"

Red flags started flying.

"We had dinner. It was fine." Madison began to break up. "Then he wanted me to go to his house. His parents were away. I said no. But he said he just wanted to play some music and talk."

Karen's soul cried, *No!*

Madison's head dropped, and her shoulders began to shudder. "I trusted him, Aunt Karen."

"Oh, Madi." Karen held her softly. "Are you okay?"

"Who can I trust?" she wailed. "I have no one. I hate this world! There's no light, no joy—not like you have."

"Madison," Karen gripped her niece's firm arms, "did he hurt you in any way?"

"I got out." She shook, probably with the same resolve it took to get away from the monster. "I'm okay. I just…I'm so tired."

Karen held her for what seemed like minutes. "I'm so sorry, honey. It's going to be okay. I'm here for you."

"You're all I have. My parents are just—sickening. My brother… It's so depressing. I don't wanna get out of bed in the morning. But I have to. I'm responsible for everybody! I don't know how much longer I can do it."

As Madison let her sorrow spill, Karen heard her dad's hammer pounding in the distance, as if someone were banging on her chest. She closed her eyes, rested her head on top of Madison's, and cried out to God in silence. *Oh, Lord, help! Give me the words. Help me lead her to You. I'm so confused. Please, protect Everett…*

"I've been reading that Bible," Madison blurted out. "You really believe it's the truth?"

Karen sat up and ran her fingers through the back of Madison's frizzy hair. "Yes, I do. That's what gives me hope."

"It makes me feel better, when I read it."

The words floated out there for a second, and Karen examined each one. "There's a reason for that. God's showing you how He wants you to feel, all the time. Safe. Secure. Loved. That's what happens when you invite Him in, sweetie. He becomes that Father we talked about, that close friend."

"I don't know if I can trust that, or if I even have the energy to put into it." Raising her head, Madison's pretty face was pink and wet and sadly distorted from anguish. "I don't want to get hurt anymore. All I want to do is be here with you."

Karen stood and gently guided Madison's legs onto the couch. She adjusted a pillow beneath her head and draped a throw blanket over her. "You can stay here as long as you want," Karen whispered. "I'll be here for you. We all will." Then she kissed her lightly on the forehead, dimmed the lights, and went off to worry about her husband.

Everett drove at the speed of his racing heart. Just thirty minutes and he was swinging the slate-blue Audi into Tony Badino's neighborhood in Pelham Village, a middle-to-upper-class section of town northeast of the Bronx. Gliding past a mailbox decorated with a glowing white wreath, he eased to a stop just down the street from Badino's stone house at 944 King's Court.

No cars were in the driveway, and Everett couldn't tell if any were in the detached two-car garage out back. Yellowish lights glowed from within. Turning off the car, he monitored the grounds for any sign of movement—cars, people, whatever.

He could still feel the December air whipping through the living room at Twin Streams; see the brick with its shrewd white paint lying on the carpet amid the shattered glass. He relived the terror when the Yukon invaded his property and smashed the manger scene. And Millie, poor Millie—she couldn't even whine.

Everett was ready to make some noise. But with a hand on the door handle, he stopped. *This can lead to even more trouble.* Firing the Audi back up and hightailing it home would be the safe play, the wise play, probably what Jesus would do.

But he wasn't Jesus, and he'd taken enough *bullying*!

Drawing a deep breath, he popped out of the car. Looking around three hundred and sixty degrees, he locked the Audi and hoofed it down the street, crossing as he did. As he marched up Badino's driveway, the moon was bright, the asphalt was wet, and he could see his breath.

Up five stone steps quickly, he ignored the faint orange light from the doorbell button and rapped loudly, then stood back from the door. His weight shifted repeatedly from one foot to the other, adrenaline pumping.

Within seconds, a dim white light flicked on above him, and a brunette peered through the glass. "What do you want?" she yelled.

"I'm here to see Tony."

The door opened four inches but stopped abruptly at the end of a six-inch gold security chain. "He's not here." The pretty lady shook her head. "Who are you, may I ask?"

"Everett Lester. Are you Mrs. Badino?"

"I am. What is this about?"

Everett looked out at the still street then back at her. "I just really need to see Tony. Do you know where he is, ma'am?"

She squinted. "Why do you want to know? Are you with the police?"

"Do you know when he'll be home?"

"I have no idea."

God's trying to protect me. Maybe I should just leave. "He does live here, right?"

"Most of the time. But we don't see him much. He has his own quarters," she eyed out back, "above the garage. *Who are you?*"

You can still bail... "I'm the uncle of one of Tony's best friends, Wesley Lester."

"Doesn't ring a bell. But you seem familiar..."

"I was in a band. DeathStroke. My name's Everett Lester."

Her head practically hit the door. "I knew I'd seen you. *People* magazine, *The Enquirer*. You quit the band and became religious. Then you were involved in that big murder mystery, with that psychic—"

"Mrs. Badino," Everett looked around, "may I come in for a minute?"

"Oh, dear." She glanced at her watch and twisted the tip of her index finger between her front teeth. "I know it's cold out there. I guess it's all right, just for a minute."

The door closed, and Mrs. Badino fluffed her hair and welcomed him into the small foyer, but no further. The wood floor squeaked when Everett stepped in, and the place smelled like cigars. The ceiling was low, and he could hear the ticking of the ornate grandfather clock.

"I've spent my whole life in the church. Never miss." Mrs. Badino was slim and pleasant; she wore very little makeup. "Saturday night's when I like to go. It's just a few blocks from here. Christ the King. You know it?"

"No, I don't. What about Mr. Badino and Tony?"

"Oh, they don't go." She waved a hand and straightened a mirror on the wall. "Tony did. He was interested for a short time, several years back."

"He had a girlfriend…"

Her head snapped back to him. "You know about Erica?"

"A little."

"Why, you must know my son quite well. He usually doesn't open up." She clasped her hands in front of her and gazed off. "Erica was a fine young lady."

"She became a Christian," Everett said.

"Yes." She shot him a closed-mouth smile. "She actually started exploring religion six months or so before that night she was baptized—the night she died." The smile disappeared, her eyes drifted, and her upbeat voice went monotone. "Tony'd been a different person that summer. He asked to come to church with me. He wanted to know what I believed. He went to Erica's church, up until she died."

She came back to the present. "Would you like to sit down? Have you come far?"

"I'll sit for a minute." He followed her into the family room, which featured two matching couches, facing each other and centered on the fireplace. "We live up in Bedford. So it's not that far."

"Oh my, Bedford. You're neighbors with Martha Stewart then, aren't you?"

"Yes, she lives up there." He chuckled and found himself losing his edge.

"Do you know her?"

"I've met her before around town, at a social event or two." *What am I doing here? I haven't accomplished a thing, and now she knows my name.*

"Tell me, what is she like?"

"She seems very kind, genuine."

"Well how 'bout that!"

"Do you have other children, Mrs. Badino, besides Tony?"

"Please, call me Margaret. Tony's our only child. Sometimes I wonder if that's... Oh, never mind."

"You wonder what?"

"Oh," she managed a smile, "sometimes I just regret not having more. I wonder if Tony would somehow be different if he'd had brothers or sisters. He's a very independent young man. Being a friend, you must know that. He's very secretive. And his health habits."

She winced. "He's just not...he doesn't eat right. The only exercise he gets is crawling around those broken-down cars all day. And he's up until all hours. I see the light on in his apartment."

"He works at that body shop, what's it called?"

"Fender's. In Eastchester. Can I get you something to drink, Mr. Lester?"

"No, thank you."

She crossed her arms. "He's also been doing a little work with his father, so I hear. They don't tell me much, though."

"Oh, really? Doing what?"

"I think he's just running errands, trying to make some extra money on the side."

"What does Mr. Badino do?" *This'll be interesting.*

"Oh, sheesh—what doesn't he do! He's an entrepreneur, so he's into real estate, restaurants, entertainment, waste management, you name it…the vending industry."

All so proper and businesslike. "Tell me, Mrs. Badino—Margaret—has Tony ever mentioned my nephew, Wesley Lester? They're quite close."

She frowned. "Like I said, Mr. Lester—"

"Everett."

"Everett, I don't see a whole lot of Tony, so I don't know who his friends are anymore. I've been getting to the point, quite honestly, where I don't think he has any. It breaks my heart."

She seemed to fade out momentarily, as if talking to herself. "Ever since Erica died, he's gone into his own little world. It's almost bizarre. But what can I do? He's an adult, for Pete's sake. He's twenty-one. On his own now."

"He is an adult." Everett stood and so did she. "But he'll always be your son, won't he?" *In other words, don't bury your head in the sand.*

It was quiet as she followed him to the door. Should he say more? His conscience urged him to confront her about her dangerous son. Everett turned to face her before leaving, and suddenly she looked hollow somehow—wrinkled and frightened.

"Margaret, you asked earlier if I was with the police." He studied her, but she didn't make eye contact. "You mentioned Tony staying up all night, being gone for days. Ma'am, if you suspect anything—anything that could bring harm to other people—you should call the police. Call me if you want. But do something."

Her mouth hung open, but no words came. Everett asked for a pen and paper, scribbled his phone number, gave it to her, and rested a hand on her shoulder. "Thank you for inviting me in. I can't tell you why, but it may be best if you don't mention that I was here."

Margaret could only purse her lips and lift a hand as she ushered him into the night. And Everett left wondering how close she was to her husband. Did she tell him everything? Would she say that a man named Everett Lester had come calling?

Time would tell.

As Everett hurried along the driveway toward the street, he was dumbfounded by Margaret Badino's kindness. He glanced back at the garage. What was it like up in Tony's nest? Was there a meth lab? Evidence of some kind of bizarre Satan worship? Once to the car, he started it, cranked up the heat, and got on his cell phone with Karen.

"Hey, it's me," he said, still breathing steam inside the car.

"Thank God! Are you okay?"

"I'm fine." He heard her yell to the others that he was all in one piece. "Leaving Badino's place down in Pelham Village. His mom was the only one home. Believe it or not, she's a nice lady."

"You went in her house?"

"Yeah, I'll tell you all about it. I just wanted you and the folks to know I'm okay. Back to my senses. On my way home. I'll give you the details when I get there."

"Okay. Listen, Ev," she whispered, "Madison's here. She's upset. She went on a date earlier, and the guy tried to force himself on her."

"What?" he yelled. "Who was it?"

"No one we know. She's sleeping now, but we had a chance to talk. I'll tell you more later. Hurry up and get here!"

"Love ya. Bye." Everett tossed the phone on the passenger seat. *Poor Madison.*

As he reached for the headlight switch, a car careened around the corner with its tires screeching three blocks away. Thinking it might be Tony, he turned off the ignition, ducked, and lay still—peeking just over the dashboard.

The headlights of the approaching car were dim and yellowish and spread out wide, probably an older model. The car came toward him, slowed, then swung wide left before wheeling right and pulling into the Badino driveway. Two figures sat in the Monte Carlo. He assumed the driver was Tony.

Both young men got out of the car, the driver wearing a long black trench coat and a gray ski cap, the tall passenger wearing a baggy three-quarter-length hiking jacket and a dark baseball cap.

Too bad his window wasn't down. Everett couldn't hear them as they met at the rear of the car, talked for a moment, then opened the trunk and peered in—moving something around inside. The tall one pointed to the driver's stomach, then reached over and parted the black trench coat.

The shorter one, likely Badino, hit his hand away and threw both arms into the air. Then he reached into the trunk, hoisted a backpack onto his shoulder, banged the trunk closed, and huffed toward the side door of the garage, with the gangly guy in tow.

The second the men were inside, Everett unfolded out of the Audi, nudged the door shut, and took off down the street. He scampered through the Badinos' yard to the far side of the driveway, along the trees and bushes that separated their lot from the neighbor's. With his eye on the windows of the house every step of the way, Everett made it to the Monte Carlo and the garage. Lights were on upstairs now.

Seeing no way to get up to the second-story windows in the garage, he dashed around back. He found a five-foot chain-link fence, boxing in three large garbage cans, a wheelbarrow with a flat tire, and a dilapidated push mover. Looking up, he saw a window and a two-foot ledge running the length of the garage.

Everett mounted the chain-link fence, then managed to stand while balancing against the side of the garage. *Just don't fall.* Reaching the ledge, he hoisted himself up and planted his bottom on the wet, narrow shelf.

It was cold. He sat still, contemplating whether to keep going. The window was ten feet away. *It can't hurt to look.*

In the seated position, with his legs dangling over, he shimmied along the ledge toward the light. Once he got right next to the window, he rested with his back to the wall. It was an awkward position. There wasn't enough room to get up on the ledge and look straight into Badino's apartment. He would have to crane his head around backward to see inside.

Here goes.

The room was washed out in a pale yellow glow from a dull overhead light. His eyes adjusted. The young men came into focus, oblivious to his presence.

The dreamlike scene before him registered in his brain, forcing him to jerk his head away, retch, and then catch his breath before peering in again.

24

Officers with the Bedford police took a full report at Twin Streams, noting Karen's suspicions that Tony Badino might be behind both vandalism incidents. She did not mention Wesley.

The two middle-aged officers took photographs of the painted brick, then helped her father tightly cover the hole in the living room window. As they did, Karen explained to Madison what had happened the night Millie was killed. Once the officers helped Dad put the ladder away, they vowed that Bedford's finest would patrol the area more frequently. Then they were gone.

Karen walked into the family room from the kitchen. Madison was cuddled up in her stocking feet on the couch, with Rosey at her side. Karen's parents were nestled on the loveseat.

"That was Gray Harris." Karen set the phone on the coffee table, eased down next to Madison, and petted Rosey. "Final band practices are confirmed, starting the day after Christmas, right through the New Year's Eve event in Miami at the prison. Then we practice daily, right up till the tour launches. It's getting exciting."

"Did you say prison?" Madison asked.

Karen nodded. "Down in Miami-Dade, where Ev did time during the Endora trial. It's the final test run before the tour kicks off."

"I can't wait," Mom said. "Jacob and I are going, and Karen—"

"You hope," Dad said.

"They haven't actually cleared Mom and me yet," Karen said. "We want to help with counseling, but they may not allow women to do that. We're still waiting to hear."

Madison squinted. "Sounds dangerous."

Karen checked the clock on the mantel. Everett should've been home, but she dismissed the idea of calling him. He'd probably stopped for gas or gone to the store.

"Madison, what are your plans for Christmas?" Mom asked.

Madison's gaze skipped from person to person. "Plans? You mean like a family gathering or something?"

Mom nodded. "Will you be with family? I just wondered what you'll be up to."

"We don't really do Christmas." Madi sighed. "My parents give us money or a few big gifts, and sometimes we go to the movies Christmas day. That's about it."

"Maybe you'd like to come with us tomorrow night," her mother said. "We're taking Everett and Karen to dinner at their favorite restaurant, then we're going to the candlelight service at their church. What time does it start, honey?"

"Second service starts at nine. That's the one we'll go to."

"That's nice of you." Madison's cell phone rang. "Excuse me. I better grab this. I'm sorry." She headed for her phone, and Rosey followed.

Karen couldn't help but listen.

"No, Dad, I haven't seen her," Madison spoke into the phone while looking at the Christmas tree. "Maybe Mom's out with her girlfriends."

Karen had found herself connecting with Madison and taking great satisfaction in their relationship. She could relate to the girl. After all, Karen's teenage years had been similarly filled with hypocrisy and turmoil—until her father's Damascus road experience.

Although Karen found it difficult to fathom the pressure her niece was facing, she could certainly relate to what had happened to her earlier that evening, with the boy. However, unlike Karen, Madison hadn't allowed herself to be used for some twisted attempt at rebellion. She was not only mature, but virtuous; a flower among thorns.

"I'm at Uncle Everett's." Madison wandered with the tiny phone. "No. He's not here."

Karen's father said something, but she was too busy eavesdropping to catch it.

"Karen." He chided her with a glance. "How far is it to Pelham Village?"

"I told you, Dad, thirty minutes or so." She looked at her watch. "Everett must've stopped somewhere. I'm not gonna call him again. He's a big boy."

After speaking to Eddie for several more minutes, Madison dropped the phone in her purse. "Well, my dad talked to a nurse at Horizons. Wesley's had a rough day. He's going through the worst of the withdrawal now."

"I can't imagine." Mom shook her head.

"He was also looking for Uncle Everett," said Madison. "Said he had some earth-shattering news to tell him. That's my dad for you, either high as a kite or in the depths of despair. It runs in the family."

Karen caught her dad's gaze. She had seen the thoughtful smile on his face a million times. That's how she knew he was about to do something unusual.

"Madison," Dad moved to the edge of the loveseat, "with all that you're going through…" He glanced at Mom and Karen. "Can we pray for you? I mean, can we gather around you right now just real casually and lift you up before God?"

Madison's eyes darted about. Karen reached over and placed a hand on her knee.

"Sure," Madison whispered. "I guess so."

Mom moved next to Madison, and Dad sat on the very edge of the couch beside her as well. It was quiet for a moment. "Lord, Madison has her whole life ahead of her, but she feels trapped by the poor choices of her family."

Karen squeezed her niece's knee, and Madison's trembling hand covered hers.

"Any fears she has, any doubts, any hatred, any uncertainties—we pray they'll all be washed away in the flood of Your presence. We pray for her family, that they'll grow weary and fed up with themselves and their ways, that they'll turn to You for a better way.

"You know about the evil that's risen up against us." Dad took a deep breath and exhaled. "Bloodthirsty men hate people of integrity and seek to kill the upright. Lord, we need Your protection. Destroy Your enemies…"

In the stillness that lingered following the prayer, Mom spoke to Madison about the Christmas Eve service while Karen made one more silent appeal. *Please keep Ev safe, Lord. Bring him home to us soon…*

The blood grabbed Everett's attention first. A crimson stain the size of a Frisbee and shaped like a cauliflower—soaking the stomach area of Tony Badino's white thermal top. Then Everett gagged when he noticed the bits and pieces of intestine or brain or whatever gruesome thing it was that had sprayed Tony's shirt and pants. His hands, too, were tainted red, as if he'd just painted a wagon.

The tall guy looked on as Tony ripped the shirt off and stuffed it into the black duffel bag at his booted feet. Everett blinked twice to make sure he was seeing straight when he spotted the long black-and-red inverted cross on Tony's right bicep. Only this one wasn't just a cross; instead, the long part was hooked, like an upside-down candy cane.

Tony dropped to the floor, stripped off his boots, and tore the pants from his legs—into the bag. His body was white, lean, and muscular. A long silver chain hung from his neck, with dog tags bouncing against his young chest. Badino had another tattoo—this one of a small inverted cross—on the inside of his left wrist.

Tony's facial features were small and taut. He wore a constant scowl, and one of his eyes twitched. On his way into another room, he picked up his black trench coat, said something, and threw it at the tall guy, who examined it closely.

The room was a pigsty. An unmade mattress on the floor, boots, shoes, and dirty laundry everywhere. Gun and pornography magazines strewn about. Bags of junk food, dirty dishes, and beer bottles lying throughout.

The tall kid was moving a mile a minute. Done checking Tony's coat, he threw it onto the bed, undressed, and stuffed his clothes into the duffel.

Tony came out, patting his face and neck with a green towel. Rummaging through a nightstand full of junk, he found a smashed pack of Marlboros, tapped one out, and stuffed it into the corner of his tiny mouth. Finally finding the Zippo in his black coat pocket, he lit the bent cig, took a massive drag, dropped it in a glass ashtray on a cluttered dresser, and exhaled like a dragon.

Opening several drawers, Tony fired clothes at his tall buddy. They got dressed. Everett heard the hint of a ringing phone through the window. Tony snatched it from the black coat. As he talked and paced, the tall guy meandered about, glancing at one of the girlie magazines then flicking through a muddled pile of CDs on top of an old console TV. Tony covered the phone and barked some instructions, and the dude dropped onto the mattress and went through the inside pockets of the black coat.

Pulling out a small silver pipe and a plastic bag of white crystal, the tall dude loaded the bowl. Still on the phone, Tony gave him a thumbs-up and threw him the Zippo. Soon, the crystal was cooking, and both young men were seated on the low bed with their knees high, toking away.

Everett longed to know what was in the trunk of the Monte Carlo. Should he make a run for the trees next to the car? Or maybe just get to the Audi while the getting was good? But he couldn't do either; he was mesmerized by the scene: two friends getting stoned after just changing out of blood-and-flesh-soaked clothes. The sheer hideousness of it forced him to keep watching.

When the tall guy dropped to one knee and reached for his jacket, that should have been Everett's first clue to hightail it. But it didn't register. Within seconds, the two goons had their coats and hats on. Tony hoisted the duffel bag onto his shoulder, and they were through a doorway.

All in one motion, Everett bounced off the top of the fence, leaped to the ground, and took off for some bushes at the side of the garage. He'd barely made cover when the two came chuckling their way out the side door and to the rear of the Monte Carlo. Tony put the key in and popped the trunk.

"Help me here, Bru." He leaned in.

The tall dude bent in as well. Together, they lunged at whatever was inside and practically fell over laughing.

"Gettin' heavier by the minute," Tony cracked.

"I'm serious!" Bru hooted.

"Come on, roll 'em," Tony commanded. "Let's go."

The Monte Carlo rocked as they shifted the cargo in the trunk.

"Lemme lift this." Tony wrestled with something.

It was a shoe. A shiny brown dress shoe. And it was attached to a leg. The leg of a man! At least that's what Everett thought he saw. It happened so fast; it was but a flash. Had he really seen it?

"Now, go 'head." Tony forced something in the trunk. "Drop 'er in."

The tall guy lifted the duffel bag over the edge of the trunk and dropped it inside.

"We're outta here." Tony slammed the trunk and went for the driver's seat while his buddy scrambled for the other door.

Everett crouched and tried to become one with the wet ground as the Monte Carlo came to life and backed out of the driveway, lighting up the entire landscape where he hid.

You don't see me; you don't see me!

As soon as the car was on its way down King's Court, Everett sprinted up the driveway, cut through Badino's yard, hit the unlock button, and climbed into the Audi. *Hurry!* Within seconds he was roaring down the empty road, searching for the red taillights of the blue Monte Carlo.

He caught up with them at a four-way stop near an affluent suburb called Pelham Manor. Keeping his distance and praying they'd get to a more congested area so he wouldn't be so noticeable, Everett felt for his cell phone.

"Where are you?" Karen answered. "I've been worried!"

"Can only talk a sec." Everett caught his breath. "I'm following Tony Badino and another kid—"

"I thought you were coming home!"

"I was, but Tony showed up with another doper. They're high on meth, and I think they may be about to do something… I just need to follow."

"Why are you doing this, Ev?"

"I watched through a window. There was…it looked like blood on their clothes, and I think a body's in the trunk."

"Everett, call the police!"

"Don't worry. I'm not gonna do anything stupid."

"You already are if you don't call the police!"

"I'm not gonna call till I know we can nail this dude."

"Ev!"

"I'm going to call them! I just need to follow and be sure. I'm not going to approach them."

Karen sighed. "Where are you?"

"We just turned north on River Parkway."

"Don't let them see you, do you hear me?"

"I won't. I'll talk to you soon."

"Honey, wait." She paused. "I love you."

"I love you, too, babe."

"We're praying…"

It began to drizzle as Badino's car hit a main highway, and Everett tucked the Audi in among several other cars. Tony must have been doing about sixty-five miles an hour. Everett did the same, only one lane over and sixty feet back. As he adjusted the wipers, he debated calling the police.

I'm not positive it was a body.

Without using a blinker, Tony rocketed off River Parkway and veered onto Cross County Parkway, heading west in a hurry. Following, Everett began to do the map in his head.

Okay, into Mount Vernon to Yonkers, then… Oh, dear God, help me. We're headed straight for the Hudson River!

25

Wesley had no clue what time or day it was. His clouded head, parched lips, and sore throat told him he may have slept through winter. His heavyset, energetic nurse, Veronica, wheeled him down the long hallway to the quiet, low-lit lounge. On the way, he passed solemn faces, some people talking, some crying.

There was no laughter.

Veronica told him it was late Tuesday night. Whatever. He really didn't care about time frames. All he knew was that Veronica, with her red cheeks and bright smile, had come to the rescue. She'd gotten him out of his suite, as he requested. The room had begun shrinking, and he'd started to hear the voice again, the one calling itself Vengeance. It flustered him so bad, he was afraid what he might do to himself.

No matter how long he'd lain on his bed, sleep wouldn't come. He'd constantly been getting up, rifling through magazines and newspapers, itching, washing his hands, pacing, and picking at his skin. He shuffled through one song after another on his iPod when Veronica finally came in with some meds, offered to wheel him to the lounge, and left him there.

The drugs were kicking in, taking the edge off.

Mellow was how he was beginning to feel as he reached up from his wheelchair and pressed his fingers against the huge picture window. Cold. The winter rain pounded the concrete patio outside. Showering the earth. Replenishing the Sound beyond the glass.

Through the splattered window, he made out a long, horizontal strip of lights—many of them Christmas red and green—from across the water on Long Island. Through the droplets, the lights shone like tiny spiderwebs, reflecting off the dark waters that headed out to the Atlantic.

It was a peaceful place, and Wesley decided if he had to live, it would be here. He could stay here on meds for a long time. In fact, he didn't know where else he could survive. His life had become one of constant upheaval as he either warded off the evil spirits and the insatiable desire to get high, or gave in to the monster and suffered the unbearable physical and mental consequences.

He'd made a fool of himself earlier, flipping his food tray, threatening the unit supervisor, and begging for a bump of the drug that had become his master. It'd been pitiful but was probably not altogether uncommon at Harbor View.

"I hear you had a rough day," came a pleasant female voice from behind. "You doing okay now?"

Without turning around, he listened to Cassidy's footsteps. "Can I sit?" She stood over him. He liked it when she was near. He nodded and continued staring out at the blurry night.

"My first few days were bad." She pulled a chair next to his wheelchair. "I told you what I did... It's gonna get better."

I doubt it. He glanced over. Her face was fair, and she had marble brown eyes, and pretty black eyebrows, which matched the color of her short, messy hair. He wondered if he'd see her when they got out, or if this was one of those foxhole friendships.

"It's nasty out there, isn't it?"

"I like it." A wave of heat rolled over Wesley's tired body.

"The rain, you mean?"

"Yeah. And the Sound…"

"What do you like about it?" she asked.

"The lights. They're distant. You can admire 'em from over here without having to get involved."

"No commitment, huh?"

He nodded. "That's right." Her cheeks were wide and tapered down to a cute pointy chin, and she had big dimples that came easy. There was a small gap between her front teeth, and she had a tattoo that looked like a leafy bracelet around her left wrist.

"We've gotta make up our minds that things are gonna be different when we get out," she said. "That's gonna take commitment, and a Power beyond ourselves."

"I can't do it."

"Yes you can, Wes. I can, too. The key is cutting the cord to the bad relationships."

"Good girl for listening to your counselors." Wesley gave her a crooked grin. "I can tell right now the desire's still gonna be there. It's there *now*. I'll never forget what the high is like, never be able to erase it from my mind. It's too outta-this-world."

"Give it time. I thought the same, but the cravings are going away a little more each day."

"I can't function outside this sanctuary without meth, okay? No matter what the lecturers say."

"Well, with that attitude—"

"Hey, I'm just bein' honest. My issues…they're gonna drive me to it."

"You gotta let all that go." She chuckled. "I've been reading my Bible a little bit."

"Don't even go there, Cass. I've got a mess on my hands. My family's had it with me."

"They're still going to love you."

"I've made enemies of some relatives…"

"What'd you do?"

"Pulled a gun on my aunt, among other things."

She rested a hand atop his shoulder. "You know, Wesley, people can be pretty understanding. Especially if you go to them and say you're sorry."

"I got friends outside here." He exhaled loudly. "One in particular. He's gonna drag me down."

"Not if you say no. Not if you stop the relationship. That's what I'm gonna do."

He smirked. "You don't know this guy. He's a psycho."

"You know what? I don't buy it. I don't think any of those things are what's really worrying you." She stood, crossed her arms, and looked out at the rain. "Do you want a Coke or something? Coffee? Candy?"

"Whaddya mean by that?"

"I mean, I think there's something else bugging you." She peered down at him. "Something you're afraid of. And it haunts you so bad, you feel like you're always gonna need meth to hide from it."

He gripped the wheels of his chair and rolled it back and forth slightly. "What gives you the right… How is it you think you know so much about me?"

She turned back to the window and laughed. "Well, just think about what I said. Maybe you'll face reality someday, after I'm gone."

"I didn't know they hired you as one of the counselors." He dropped his head to his chest and shook it, then looked back up at her. "Whaddya say we drop this and go find me a smoke?"

She continued to scan Long Island Sound for what must have been a minute, then turned to him with a close-mouthed smile and stepped behind him to take the handles of his wheelchair. She exaggerated a grunt and backed him away from the window. As the chair swiveled and his view of the rainy night disappeared, he pondered what Cassidy had said, about the fear—about the haunting.

The meth he'd sold to his brother, the fact that he'd played a part in David's death, it ate at him. Was it real—the guilt? Was he at fault for ending his brother's life? Wesley had lived in such a wasteland since the grim day the Camaro crashed, he really couldn't decipher truth from falsehood. All he knew was, Vengeance continued to speak to him, assuring him that if he would end his Uncle Everett's life, all his sins would be erased. And, perhaps, Wesley could be a human being again.

But he didn't want to kill, didn't want to hurt anyone. Not really. The meth was in his system, part of him. Distorting things. Causing the voices. Messing up his family. And even as he glided down the peaceful hallway lined with Christmas cards, tiny lights, and tinsel in one of the finest treatment facilities in the country, Wesley knew deep down he would never kick the meth.

Never.

Once the Monte Carlo turned off Cross County Parkway, nothing was familiar to Everett. The blue car made a series of turns on main highways and back roads, and all Everett could do was follow and try to catch the name of a street here and there.

On and off, the skies opened up, and he was forced to flick his wiper blades to high as he struggled to follow Badino's car without being spotted. He sensed they were heading north, running parallel to the Hudson, and kept peering out the driver's side window, certain he would see the river. They just passed a city college and a small park, and he saw the shimmering water beyond.

The Monte Carlo reduced its speed and hit a series of dark back-streets. Everett's chest tightened. He was the only car left behind them, which forced him to drop way back. As he did, he reached for the cell phone, opened it, and dialed 911.

"911. What is your emergency?"

"I need to report some suspicious activity."

"Go ahead, sir."

"An older-model Monte Carlo, blue, just got off Cross County Parkway, and it's near the river, headed north on Warton Avenue, I believe."

"What's going on, sir? What's the car doing?"

"The drivers are using methamphetamines. In the trunk is a duffel bag. It's got bloody clothes in it. And I believe there's a dead body in the trunk. I'm following. I've got to go now. I'll call back."

"Sir, what is your—?"

Everett turned off the phone, tossed it on the seat beside him, and slowed to a crawl. The Monte Carlo must have been moving at less than ten miles per hour. The rain plastered the leather top of the Audi, reminding Everett of the time he and Eddie had camped out as boys.

A fierce thunderstorm had arisen, pelting the canvas tent with rain. Neither his mother nor his father even checked on them. Everett could almost taste that same fear and vulnerability as he squinted through the blurry windshield and kept driving.

He couldn't continue much longer like this, on these desolate roads, or Badino and company would realize they were being followed. Everett cut his headlights, and the second he did, the Monte Carlo stopped, dead in the middle of the street. And so did his heart.

Opening his window slightly, Everett pushed his head against the splattering rain and listened. He could only keep his wipers on intermittent, because he didn't want the creeps to hear him back here.

Both doors of the Monte Carlo banged open at the same time. Everett was ready to bolt, but no, they hadn't seen him. Tony raced around the driver's door to the front of the car in the path of its headlights and fell to his knees, his long, hunched shadow extending eerily into the night.

Meanwhile, the tall guy opened the trunk, ripped out the duffel bag, and ran it around to the front of the car where Tony was crouched over. The tall guy dropped the duffel and bent to help. Together, they pulled and jerked at the pavement.

What the...

A manhole cover. They lifted it and set it aside. In a split second, the duffel bag was gone—into the hole. Then both men dashed to the back of the car, one on each side. Leaning into the trunk, the tall guy muscled the limp body under the armpits out of the trunk. Tony locked his arms around the knees and lifted.

Everett found it difficult to take a breath. He snatched the phone and hit redial.

"911. What's your emergency?"

"I just called a minute ago," he whispered frantically. "Blue Monte Carlo. Warton Avenue. They're dumping a body in the sewer system. Hurry!"

With the sagging corpse between them, Tony and the tall guy took small, fast steps around the passenger door into the dreamlike path of the headlights. It took but a few seconds, and the man was gone. *Ploop.* Headfirst into the hole.

Within seconds, the lid was back on, the red brake lights flashed, and the car was moving.

God help me.

Everett zipped the Audi to within a few feet of the manhole cover and waited till the Monte Carlo was out of sight. Jerking the parking brake and finding the door handle, he raced into the rain.

On soaking knees he fought the heavy lid from its hole. *So heavy.* Sliding it aside, he peered into the dark abyss. Nothing. But when he heard the raging current, he knew the body and the bag must be gone.

The scene lit up. Everett whipped around. Bouncing headlights—wide and yellow—catapulted toward him from the direction of the Monte Carlo's exit.

He froze like a deer.

The roaring car hit the last curve before the manhole cover.

Sweeping light flooded the scene. The nightmare became reality.

It's them!

No time to get in the Audi.

Pop!

The sound of the gun blast was muffled by the relentless rain. But Everett saw the flash from the passenger window of the approaching car.

He dove and hit hard, rolling across the flooded pavement.

Pop. Pop.

To his feet he scrambled, running low, into the grass. Down a slope. *Whoa!* His feet slid out from under him. He landed hard but bounced up, taking an incline and heading into the open.

Behind him, the Monte Carlo screeched. Then a loud crunch.

Everett ran with all he had, dodging trees at the last second because of the darkness.

Small, white lights were visible in the distance. *A house?*

BAM. BAM.

A different gun. Louder. Bigger.

Badino.

BAM. Pop, pop. BAM.

Watch out for the trees!

He darted through the black night. He could barely see. The open landscape jumped up and down with each soggy footprint. Trees and grass, trees and grass. His body was heavy and sopping. The house or barn or whatever it was remained frustratingly far off. He squinted for someplace to hide. Anyplace.

Turning back, he saw a flash in the distance. Seconds later, a blast from the gun. *Good.*

He was getting away. Farther and farther from the killers.

Keep running!

The tree clobbered him in midstride, and his whole world went from fifteen miles an hour to zero in less than a second.

He was on his back. Could not breathe. The cold ground soaked into him. He fought to suck air into his lungs.

Small, white stars whirled in the blackness. The opening in his throat had shrunk to the size of a straw.

Pain. In the chest. Bad pain, deep inside.

Breathe!

Voices. Beyond the trees and grass and rain. Getting closer. He couldn't suppress the strangled gasps that bellowed up from deep within his chest.

He had to get air!

But they were coming. And so were the sirens. He heard them now. Just before everything somersaulted to black.

26

Wrapped in a heavy, black wool blanket with the letters *NYPD* embroidered in yellow, Everett absorbed the warmth and sweet aroma of pipe tobacco in the backseat of the patrol car. Groaning from the splitting pain in his chest, he examined the laptop computer mounted to the dash, and then the fifty-something officer, Harry Barnett, who stood in the rain out in front of the squad car's headlights.

Barnett had found him sprawled out at the base of a sugar maple tree several hundred yards off of Warton Avenue. For the past ten minutes, the veteran officer had been shining his powerful flashlight into the sewer hole that Everett had left uncovered and was just returning to the car.

"We're gonna have to wait till this rain stops and get a crew on this." He dropped into his seat and pulled the black NYPD poncho over his head. "Probably first thing in the morning." He threw the raincoat to the floor beside him. "That water's raging in there now. How you feeling, Mr. Lester?"

"Considering the alternatives, like a million bucks."

"Paramedics should be here soon."

"I don't know if there's anything they can do. It feels like cracked ribs or something."

"Well, you need to get checked out either way. How's the head?"

Everett ran his fingers over the hard lump. "Feels fine."

"You're gonna have a pretty good egg up there. Lucky the skin didn't split open."

"How's my car?" he asked.

"Pretty bad. Maybe totaled. Good thing is, we'll be able to get some decent paint samples of the Monte Carlo."

While Barnett warmed his tough hands, lit his cherry-colored wood pipe, and scribbled on a form attached to a clipboard, Everett explained everything that had happened that evening, starting with the brick through the living room window at Twin Streams. He repeated the facts about Millie's death and the manger scene and his suspicion of Tony Badino. Through it all, Everett made no mention of Wesley or Dominic Badino.

"What'll happen next?" Everett asked, feeling a tinge of fret as he contemplated possible repercussions from the Badinos.

"Like I said, we'll start a full-fledged search for the body and the bag when it's light." Barnett stroked his thick salt-and-pepper mustache, which was the same color as his curly hair. "This rain's supposed to stop sometime tonight. We're gonna want to bring this Tony Badino in for questioning, search his place."

Everett stared at Barnett's face in the rearview. He knew this was coming, and the reality of it made his stomach ache.

Barnett said, "You don't know the name of the other individual, the tall one?"

"No."

"We'll get it. Meantime, you just need to sit tight. We'll let you know if we need anything else."

Everett heard sirens.

"That's our ambulance."

Everett sighed as he shifted position to see the approaching vehicle and finally caught a glimpse of the crumpled Audi. "Will Tony Badino know I'm the one who filed the report? I mean, can we keep it anonymous?"

"Okay, your name's on this report, has to be." Barnett's eyes met Everett's. "You're the only witness we have. You're what's makin' us ramp up to do a manhunt. So, this is your baby."

Great.

"Now, because it's gonna be an open investigation, at least for a while, the public won't be able to get their hands on this report."

Everett closed his eyes and slumped back in the seat.

Thank You, Lord.

"But I'll tell ya, Mr. Lester." Barnett tapped the spent tobacco into an ashtray. "If you're right about the body and the bag of clothes, then you're gonna be needed as a witness—*the key witness*—to bust these slimeballs. So, I guess my advice to you is, get ready for the ride."

A hot mass of bile swirled at the base of Everett's throat as two paramedics in rain gear headed toward the patrol car.

I guess I better get ready for the ride.

Everett awoke early on Christmas Eve, even after the late-night X-rays in the emergency room at Yonkers General Hospital. Karen and Jacob had met him there and waited out the results and prognosis: a hairline fracture to the sternum that only time would heal.

Certain movement sent riveting pain down the center of Everett's chest. Wearing black flannel pajama pants and a torn gray sweatshirt, he stood at the bay window in the kitchen and scanned the dark backyard. At least there had been no more vandalism. He turned off the floodlights.

Rosey was ready to go out, but first he rose to his tiptoes, letting out a painful groan as he reached for the kitchen cabinet and brought down his heavy Glock in one hand and its magazine in the other. Everett and Karen had filled out two police reports within twenty-four hours, naming the Badinos in each, and Everett was concerned for his family's safety.

He slid the magazine into the gun grip and locked it into place. Bracing the weapon in front of him at arm's length, he pointed it at the microwave, the dishwasher, then outside. *If I have to, I'll use this thing.* Thumbing the release button, he sent the magazine springing into his hand.

After placing the gun back in the cupboard, he loaded the coffeemaker. Letting Rosey out, he gingerly made his way to the end of the slushy driveway, where he bent down to retrieve the newspaper.

He read the headlines at the kitchen island while waiting for the Bunn to finish brewing, making sure there was no news of his adventure the night before. There wasn't. The paper predicted clear skies and a high of forty-four degrees. Perfect weather for finding dead bodies.

He filled a white thermal mug with coffee, grabbed his Bible from the kitchen desk, then went into the den with Rosey and closed the door. Turning on the standing lamp and easing into the recliner, he sat for a few moments, sipping the coffee.

You've interrogated the wife of a mob captain—in his own home.

He ran a hand through his hair and pictured Eddie's trampled body lying in the puddles at Mars Hill Racetrack, trying to deny the hollowness that ate at his insides.

You've narked on the meth-smoking, cold-blooded-killing son of a mob captain.

The heated meetings and sober threats of Dominic Badino and his henchmen overcame him.

This is bad.

For a moment, he was back on the cold, wet ledge outside Tony's apartment, staring in at the blood and gore, at the red and black inverted cross emblazoned on the rebel's bicep. Jacob had told him later at the hospital that the tattoo—with the hook at the end—was a "cross of confusion," an insignia once used by the Romans to symbolize the questioning of Christianity and the deity of Christ.

He cupped the top of his forehead with a weary hand, pulling it away to see the perspiration. And he'd forgotten about the grotesque-feeling lump.

He was numb and distracted. He could taste the danger. The foreboding. Not only for him, but for Karen and her parents.

Just one drink would make all this so much more bearable.

With hands trembling slightly, he opened the leather Bible to the bookmark in Revelation, where he'd left off the morning before. But how did this pertain to him today?

A fat, gold envelope on the desk caught his wandering eye. He set the Bible on the ottoman and went to the package. It was addressed to him with a return label from Jeff Hall, former president of the DeathStroke fan club.

Taking it back to his chair, he tore the envelope open and pulled out a stack of letters and cards held together by a rubber band. On top was a yellow sticky note:

> *Everett, as per your request, here's a quarterly sampling of the letters, e-mails, and blogs we've been seeing of late. Hope all is well. Jeff.*
>
>   *P.S. Best of luck on the LW tour!*

Unfolding the first note that fell into his hands, he read: *"Ha ha! What a dumb, messed-up idiot you are, Lester. No matter what level of forgiveness you seek, you'll be going to hell for murdering Endora Crystal, and for obliterating so many minds along the way. Nice job, jerk. I'll save a seat for you in hell."*

Everett's hand went limp with the note in it. He shook his head. The voice in the note was bitter and frustrated, much like his own used to be. This was the kind of person Everett wanted to reach.

Hoping for something more positive, he pulled out several sheets of paper stapled together. It contained blog messages found on a popular rock music website. He perused the string:

"What an idiotic reason to leave the band. He was impacting millions of lives before; now what's he going to do…teach Sunday school? I'm thoroughly disappointed. I can't believe he would leave for such a stupid reason."

Everett sighed deeply and continued down the page:

"I wish him all the best and look forward to his music, as long as it's not that Christian bubblegum stuff." That one got a chuckle.

"Hey, all I know is, I still got Marilyn Manson!"

"He's doing what's right for him. Can't you see that's all that matters? Anyone who can't respect or understand that has got major problems." You tell 'em.

"Why does god have to mess up all the good things in life? R.I.P."

"Calm down. Bands and singers come and go. What did you think, they were going to last forever?"

"He found the number one God." ☺

"What's wrong with him? He didn't have to leave the band. It's not like DeathStroke was satanic or anything. Hopefully the band will continue cranking out great music without him."

"Don't hold your breath, he was DeathStroke."

"In case you didn't know, the band has a new lead singer, Maxx Syphon. He jams."

"FYI…Maxx Syphon can't carry Everett Lester's guitar pick." He smiled at that note.

"Everett Lester is the most insecure wimp on the face of the planet. How can he trade what he had with DeathStroke for…what? Some myth you can't even get your hands around? He'll be sorry. Another year and you'll see him begging to do jingles for cereal commercials."

Closing his eyes, Everett sank back into the chair. So many people, believing so many lies. They need Truth. They need one of their own to show them how God's love can change their miserable lives.

He knew he needed the strength and promise only the Bible could give, but his head felt like a minefield of worries and doubts. He still had songs to iron out for the tour… He had a family to protect from who knew what kind of evil… Karen was walking through a nightmare… And he felt about as mentally stable as a schizophrenic.

I'm afraid.

Not only about all the hell that was breaking loose.

I'm afraid of myself—of what I might do…

He could find an open bar somewhere or buy a bottle.

Everyone's still asleep.

Drive around with it. No one would know.

Clenching his jaw, he sat on the edge of the chair and ran his hands through his hair. As he did, a razor-sharp pain split his chest. He groaned, "This is nothin' but the enemy."

The Bible sat open.

Leaning over it, he found the word fear in the topical index and its definition: "Anxiety caused by approaching danger." He looked up one of the suggested verses. "When evildoers came upon me to devour my flesh…they stumbled and fell. Though a host encamp against me, my heart will not fear; though war arise against me…I shall be confident… For in the day of trouble He will conceal me in His tabernacle; in the secret place of His tent He will hide me; He will lift me up on a rock."

Everett eased to his knees and leaned on the ottoman and Bible. "Forgive me for being scared, for wanting to escape through drink…for worrying about these wicked people and what they may do… Fill me with Your Spirit again, Lord."

A passage surfaced in his head, like a submerged buoy popping up in the ocean. He found it and whispered: "'The Jews were just now seeking to stone You, and are You going there again?' Jesus answered, 'Are there not twelve hours in the day? If anyone walks in the day, he does not stumble, because he sees the light of this world. But if anyone walks in the night, he stumbles, because the light is not in him.'"

Everett buried his head in the Bible. "Why should I be scared? I'm representing You! You've put this desire in my heart, to reach the unsaved. If You're with me, I can go wherever I need to, wherever You send me, in the open, no fear! My life's in Your hands. Whether I live or die is up to You. Your will be done."

The phone startled him, yet the second he heard the ring he was determined to pick up before it woke anyone. He braced his chest with a flat palm as he stood and went for the phone.

"Is this Everett?" came the timid voice.

"It is. Who's this?"

"It's Mrs. Badino...Margaret." She was out of breath.

Uh-oh. "Margaret, what is it? Are you okay?"

"Yes." A horn sounded in the background. "I'm sorry. I'm at a pay phone. I felt I needed to warn you."

The words hit his gut, as if he'd had the wind knocked out of him. "About what?"

"I mentioned to my husband that you were at the house last night looking for Tony, and he—"

Everett's body went limp, though he kept standing.

"Mr. Lester, he was furious. I don't understand why. I've never seen him respond like that. I don't know what your history with my husband is—"

"So, he was upset with me for coming into your home?"

"Yes, he was. And he didn't know why you were looking for Tony. This bothered him immensely. I told him I thought the two of you were friends..."

His eyes closed, and he dropped his head. "Why are you using a pay phone?"

Silence.

"Hello?" Everett pressed the phone tight to his ear.

Her voice broke the silence, stronger and louder than before. "There's one more thing you should know." The line was quiet again for a moment. "My husband got a call in the middle of the night. He got dressed and left the house. You told me if I suspected anything—"

"To call me. What is it Margaret? What happened?"

"Several hours after Dominic left," she sniffed, "at four or so this morning, a group of men came to the house. They went through Tony's apartment and took a bunch of things with them."

"What did they take?"

"I'm not sure. Everything was in plastic bags and boxes."

"Who were they? Did you recognize them?"

Again, a prolonged hush. Everett forced himself to be patient.

"I've seen at least two of them before," she whispered. "They're associates of my husband."

"What kind of associates?"

"Look, Mr. Lester, I've said enough. I don't even know why I'm calling—"

"Because God wants me to know what you're telling me."

"I don't know what it means…"

"I don't either, but I know it's important. Where's Tony now, Margaret?"

"As far as I know he's still asleep."

"He didn't leave with the men?"

"No."

He sighed. "Do me a favor. Keep your eyes peeled for anything else. Keep my number."

"Okay…I'm nervous."

"Are you in danger?"

"Our phones are tapped. My husband does it. That's why I couldn't call from home."

"I see."

"Dominic loves me very much. But it's Tony… I'm afraid to ask what you know about my son."

Everett breathed deeply and treaded carefully. "I don't know anything for sure, Margaret. All I know is, you've been very kind to me. Thank you for calling."

"I've failed as a parent; I know that."

"You can't—"

"Tony's in trouble, isn't he, Mr. Lester? Has he hurt others? Something in my heart is just grabbing me and shaking my insides, saying, 'Be careful. Beware. There's poison in your midst.'"

And Everett knew she was right.

Poison.

27

By early afternoon Karen noticed a slice of sunlight brighten the kitchen at Twin Streams. The grounds outside were saturated from the previous night's rain, and the melting snow trickled and swirled along streams and paths of their own making. The day had passed torturously slowly, for it was a time of waiting.

Karen had been to church earlier, where a dozen teenagers from the youth group helped her set up for that night's Christmas Eve services. Now she and her mom attempted to relax with tea in the family room, playing double solitaire and awaiting any news from the police about what they prayed would be Tony Badino's arrest.

Although the basement music studio was about as soundproof as one could expect, Karen could feel the slight vibration beneath her feet of Everett's vocals and guitar, as he practiced for the upcoming tour. She'd come to love his new music, which she secretly believed had the potential to impact millions of people worldwide.

"I hope Madison comes tonight." Karen played an ace of clubs.

Sarah smiled and examined her cards. "She reminds me of you. Always wanting everyone to be happy. The peacemaker."

"I want her to find Christ."

"I know." Mom nodded and locked eyes with Karen. "Be patient. Pray. Love her unconditionally, just like you did Everett."

The music stopped below, and Karen heard footsteps in the stairwell.

"Hey, ladies." Everett drifted into the room, kissing Karen on top of the head. "I can't wait any longer. I'm gonna call the cops and find out what's going on. Is Madison coming tonight?"

"Haven't heard from her," Karen said. "We should call and check on Wesley, too."

"I'll do that later," Everett said on his way to the kitchen.

Karen got up, walked to the bay window, and nestled next to Everett. They faced each other, and he took her hand, brought her close, and slow-danced her around the kitchen. She laughed, knowing her mom was watching from the adjoining room, yet didn't take her eyes off his.

When they stopped, he gave her a long kiss and gazed into her eyes. "You mean the world to me, babe."

His words filled her up. "I love you," she whispered.

"We're gonna make it, aren't we?"

She nodded. "Yeah. We're gonna make it."

He hugged her, then squeezed her waist and headed toward the hallway.

"You're in a good mood," she said.

He stopped at the doorway and looked back at her. "That's 'cause they're gonna nail Tony Badino today." Then he left, and Karen rejoined her mom.

"If you play the eight of spades," Mom said, "I'll be able to turn over my last card."

"Hey," Everett called out from the other room, "Madison's here."

Karen and her mom met her at the Beetle and walked her to the front door, pointing out the new glass in the living room window.

Madison was quiet, chewing gum and listening to the mother-and-daughter tandem rave about what they were going to order for dinner that evening at Beau's Tavern.

Madison set her coat over the back of a chair. Karen had failed to notice before how lean her niece was in her formal brown slacks and a furry, off-white sweater. She used quite a bit of makeup and glossy brown lipstick, but it was tasteful; she was radiant. Karen hoped she planned on going to church with them after their big dinner out.

Mom went to the kitchen to pour Madison a cup of green tea while Karen put an arm around her niece and guided her into the family room. "So, what happened when you got home last night, anything? Were your folks there?"

"Dad was asleep; Mom wasn't home yet." She didn't make eye contact. "I couldn't sleep. I was up reading when she got home at like one-thirty."

One-thirty? Grow up, Sheila.

"She saw my light on and came in," Madison said. "She'd been drinking, of course. Made some snide remark about the Bible you gave me—that's what I was reading. I just couldn't face her. She never remembers anything the next day."

Madison shook her head, as if shedding the memory. "What's new in the Badino saga?"

"Madison," Karen frowned, "haven't you got enough on your mind without worrying about that?"

"I want to know, Aunt Karen." Madison leaned close. "I have a right to know. He's hanging with *my* brother. What goes on with him affects me, my mom, and my dad."

Madison was mature beyond her years, and Karen relished their growing friendship. A true bond was forming. She told her about the call Everett had received from Margaret Badino that morning.

The back porch door rattled, and Dad came in with a burst of fresh air. "Hello, ladies." He bent over on the rug and began taking his boots off.

"Where have you been?" Mom asked.

"Walking. Look at it out there. Gotta take advantage of the sun when it shines in these parts in late December, don't we?"

Everett entered the kitchen, holding a piece of paper in his hand, but Karen couldn't read the blank look on his face. She gave him a "what's up?" expression, and he looked questioningly toward Madison. Karen nodded, assuring him it was okay to talk.

"Folks, I've got an update on what's going on with the police," Everett said.

Karen took several steps toward Everett. *Lord Jesus, let it be good news.*

"The upshot is the police and a scuba team have been hunting for the body and the duffel bag since mid- to late-morning. So far they haven't found anything, *but* this detective assures me if anything's down there, they'll find it. So, that's good news."

"Hurray." Mom held up her cup of tea. "Let's keep praying."

"They even have people from the city water department working with them," Everett said.

"It sounds as if they're going at it with all they've got." Dad nodded. "This could be really big."

"Yeah, and that's not all." Everett breathed deeply and paused. "Detectives are interrogating Tony Badino as we speak." His head dropped to his chest.

Perhaps for the first time, Karen more fully grasped the pressure he'd been under. She leaned into him, and her parents closed in as well. Karen reached out and took Madison's hand, drawing her into the circle.

Her father extended his big hand toward Madison's and held Mom's, too. Everyone was linked as Dad closed his eyes and leaned his head back. "Oh, God." He sighed. "This is exciting. We see You working. Please, intervene in what the police are doing *right now*. Lead them to the body and the evidence. Let justice be done with Tony Badino and his father. Let the truth come out…"

Karen rested her head against Everett's arm. The house was silent, except for Rosey's toenails clicking on the tile floor, then the sound of her lapping up water from her bowl.

"Lord." Mom cleared her throat. "We lift up Madison's mom and dad to You."

Madison squeezed Karen's hand, and the grip stayed firm.

"We ask that You'll restore their marriage. But even more important are their individual hearts and souls. Same with Wesley. We want to see him free from drugs and living well, but You have even bigger hopes in mind; dreams of heaven for him…"

Madison's hand went limp in Karen's. "What about me?" Her high-pitched squeal forced Karen's eyes open. "You guys are praying like I'm one of you." Everyone was looking at her now as she sniffled, breathed in chops, and spoke in spurts. "I'm not…I don't think I'm a Christian even. I've only been to church at weddings…"

Dad lifted Madison's delicate hand in his, and a huge smile broke out beneath his thick mustache. "Do you believe in God, Madison?"

"I know there is a God," she stammered and turned to Karen. "I've been reading the Bible, devouring it." She showed a tentative smile. "I do believe in Jesus. *I do*."

Everyone melted down right there. And there was laughter.

Karen's father was a rock—a glowing, beaming rock. "Can we say a prayer with you, to invite God into your heart?"

"Yes." Her lower lip quivered, and she wiped her nose with a tissue Mom handed her. "Please."

Just before Karen closed her eyes, she took in each wet face, smiling gloriously, rejoicing with the angels.

★ ★ ★

Later that afternoon, they meandered back toward the house after plac-ing the tombstone on Millie's grave. Karen felt spent, yet oddly refreshed.

It didn't feel like Christmas Eve; there had been so much disrup-tion. But Madison certainly was enjoying the stroll, listening intently and laughing often. That filled Karen with joy and a sense of satisfac-tion, accomplishment even.

What bothered her was Everett's demeanor: carefree one minute, withdrawn the next. He had suggested they get back to the house quickly, and Karen knew it was because he was concerned about some sort of retaliation from the Badinos. His anxiety wasn't making her feel the least bit secure.

She stuck her hands in the pockets of her denim jacket as they walked, fingering a piece of paper. Something was wrapped inside it. Something hard. Coins maybe?

"Ever since Everett told me about Beau's famous blackened grouper, my mouth's been watering for it," her mother said. "I mean it; I can't wait."

Karen pulled the folded clump out of her pocket. The white note-book paper struck her as foreign. When she unfolded the paper, everything came to a halt. The ground spun far away, as if she'd put on someone's strong prescription glasses.

"What's the matter, sweetheart?" Her dad held her up with a strong arm. "What is that?"

She dropped the note into his hands and fell to the ground. The wet, cold earth seeped into her corduroys.

"Karen!" Her mother yelled. "What is it, honey? What's wrong?"

Everett was hovering over her within seconds, urging her to breathe deeply.

Her father was on the ground next with the crumpled paper in his fist. "You're gonna be okay. Everything's going to be fine. Just tell me, where did you get this?"

"What is it?" She heard Everett grab the paper. "Millie's ID tag…"

She just had to rest. Didn't have the energy to explain that this was the coat she'd worn to the airport to pick up her mom and dad, or that she hadn't worn it since.

Things were beginning to fade as Everett read the note: "'How does it feel to lose something you love? Your so-called God allowed this.'" And then he must have seen the inverted cross, as she had. "'To hell with your God, and with you, his followers.'"

It was the guy in the gray ski cap. A buzzing sound drowned out Everett's voice. The one following her at the airport.

Her head filled with pressure, and the ground spun. She couldn't hold on any longer; her eyes closed.

It was Tony Badino…

And then—nothingness.

28

By the time they got Karen back to the house, she was coming around. Everett laid her on their king-size bed and stroked her forehead while Sarah rummaged around in the large master closet for some dry clothes.

"You fainted, babe," he whispered.

She blinked and licked her lips. "The note...it freaked me out."

"We're gonna get you changed into something warm."

"Okay."

He stroked her soft hair. "Are you all right?"

She closed her eyes, nestled her head against his hand, and smiled. "I'm fine."

"You should sleep awhile." He stood, still gazing down at her. "I'll check back on you in a little bit."

"Ev." She touched his arm lightly. "There was a guy following me at the airport."

"What?" He bent back down and leaned close to her pale face. "Honey, you're still out of it. Let's just—"

"Listen to me. I want to tell you this now. It had to have been Tony Badino."

Everett cringed at the mention of Badino's name. "Why didn't you tell me earlier?"

"I thought I was being paranoid."

"What'd he look like?"

"Midtwenties. Mean little face. Gray ski cap and a long black trench coat."

"That's him." The gears in Everett's mind spun out of control. "Did you wear the denim coat you had on today to the airport?"

"Yeah. Today's the first time since then. He was watching me from a bookstore. Then when I was waiting for Mom and Dad at the top of the escalator, he was there."

Watching my wife! "Did he say anything?"

"No. I remember bumping into some people when I saw my folks. I was kind of in a hurry. He may have dropped the dog tags in my pocket then."

Jacob's deep voice came quietly from behind. "He hates God." He padded into the room in his baggy gray socks. "I saw it so many times when I was in ministry. People get mad at the church, at the pastor, or at Christianity altogether—and they end up hating God."

Sarah appeared in the bathroom doorway with a sweatsuit for Karen.

"This guy's girlfriend finds Christ. He sees a change in her. May have piqued his interest even. But then she dies and he's ticked at God. All of a sudden, everyone who believes becomes the enemy, especially prominent pastors—and born-again rock stars." He glanced at Sarah. "We had our share of nutcases in and out of the church."

"Tell me about it." Sarah rested her palm on Karen's forehead. "Whenever you're bearing good fruit, there are trials. Look at what you guys are about to embark on—a missionary tour that's gonna blow the lid off of Satan's plans for many, many lives."

Jacob shook his head. "There's gonna be heavy-duty persecution."

Sarah stood. "Okay, enough of this for now." She shooed Jacob and Everett toward the door, walking with them. "Let's let this girl get out of these wet clothes."

"I'll be out in a few minutes." Karen raised her head. "I wouldn't miss tonight for anything."

"Don't worry about tonight, babe. Just take it easy." Everett closed the door and followed Jacob and Sarah to the kitchen.

"How is she?" Madison asked from a chair at the kitchen table.

"Feisty as ever." Everett sauntered up behind Madison and leaned over her shoulder.

With a pencil held loosely in her right hand and a gray eraser in her left, she sketched a picture of the view outside the kitchen window.

"That's incredible, Madi. Karen said you were talented, but I had no idea…"

Sarah and Jacob wandered over, too. "That is beautiful," Sarah said. "Is this something you're pursuing as a career?"

"I'm not sure." She kept working with her head down. "I'd like to, but it all depends."

"That's a real gift, to be able to draw like that," Jacob said.

"I'm tellin' ya," Everett said, "this girl's got it goin' on!"

Jacob found a sliced carrot in the fridge, snapped off a bite, and spoke with a mouthful. "It's so cool to see the different gifts God gives us."

Everett's head jerked toward the pounding at the front door. His heart slammed into his throat, then dropped back down into position but continued ticking like a bomb.

Madison and Sarah sat frozen at the table while Jacob took several steps toward the kitchen cupboard where the gun was stashed, but he stopped short.

Everett peered through the sheer that covered the narrow, vertical window next to the door. "It's Eddie." He unlocked the deadbolt and opened the door. The cold air rushed in and so did his brother.

"Whaddya think you're doing?" He was five inches from Everett's face, seething through clenched teeth. His brown eyes were sunk deep in their sockets, and he was unshaven. "What'd you do? Huh?"

Everett looked toward the others.

Eddie's eyes followed. "Jacob. Sarah." He nodded. "Madison…" His voice went soft, and he put his game face back on. "Look, I gotta talk to Ev alone. I'm sorry. It's urgent." Out of breath, he turned back to his brother. "Where can we go?"

"The den, I guess." Everett led the way.

"Do you want me to come, Ev?" Jacob caught Eddie's gaze. "I know everything that's going on."

"Just give us a few." Eddie continued toward the den, wiping his mouth with the back of his wrist.

With a bob of his head and a raised hand, Everett assured Jacob it was okay.

Madison remained red-faced at the kitchen table, and Eddie made no further contact with his daughter as he marched past.

Everett closed the door behind his brother, who didn't bother to remove his winter coat and still clutched his leather gloves in one fist. Everett started to speak but was cut off.

"What in the world do you think you're doing, messing with Dominic Badino? Are you crazy? What his wiseguys did to me, that knot on your head—*it's child's play!* These guys chop off hands and feet. They'll dismember you, put the pieces in a burlap sack, and scatter your remains along the Jersey Turnpike!"

"I was following his son, not Dominic," Everett said. "I don't give a flip. It doesn't matter—"

"You're really one naive idiot, Ev, you know that? Ever since you got saved it's like you just fell off the turnip truck. You're in hot water, understand? Boiling hot water."

"Why?" A wave of panic rocked Everett. "What'd you hear?"

"You filed a police report last night—" Eddie spun away, hands on his waist—"accusing the son of carrying a stiff around in his trunk and dumpin' it in the sewer in Yonkers."

"I saw it! He and his buddy chased me; they fired at me. How'd you find out?"

"I just did."

"Well, they're going to find the body." Everett approached the window Eddie was staring out. "I called down there today. They've had teams working on it since morning. And Tony Badino's in for questioning."

Eddie smacked his gloves to the ground, swiveled, and grabbed Everett's shirt at the neck. His brown eyes danced wildly. "What do you think this is? You think this is a game?"

Everett groaned as Eddie's knuckles pushed hard against his throat, shoving him backward into furniture, disturbing his cracked sternum. "You think you're on some kind of crusade to tidy up society like some Christian superhero?"

"Tony threw a brick through our living room window last night!" Everett grabbed his brother's wrists and stopped himself from being pushed any farther. "And he's the one who cut Millie's throat. He was with *your*—"

Three knocks sounded at the door. "Ev, is everything okay?" Karen called.

Eddie shoved him and let go.

"It's okay, babe. We're fine." He breathed hard, his chest aching. "Be out in a minute."

"What you *don't* know," Eddie spit out as he jabbed a finger at Everett, "is that Dominic Badino's henchmen fished that stiff out of the sewer before sunrise."

"No way! There was a bag of bloody clothes—"

"They got that, too," Eddie said. "No body, no evidence—no crime."

"How do you know all this?"

"Never mind."

"No! Tell me how you know!" Everett grabbed Eddie's tie and pulled it tight against his throat. "I'm sick of you lyin' to me. I moved to this town to be near you. To help you!"

"Get your hands off me." Eddie squeezed Everett's wrist. "I won't ask for your help again."

"Look, they're gonna *find* evidence." Everett released him. "At least meth."

"Forget about it!" Eddie pounded the windowsill. "Badino's thugs went over the kid's place with a fine-tooth comb before sunup."

"There's gotta be blood stains in the trunk—"

"The car's gone," Eddie spoke like an all-knowing madman. "Badino's men took it. Nobody'll ever see it again."

"But—"

"What you don't realize, brother, is that what's true and right ain't always true and right." Eddie quit fighting now, and his voice weakened to a monotone. "Even if they do find something on the kid, his old man owns half the NYPD."

Everett shivered. "You've gotta be kidding me."

"He can make it so that police report never existed; same with the officer who filled it out; and same with the witness who claims he saw the crime. That's you."

Everett covered his mouth, then dropped his hand. "You're in deeper than you're telling me."

"You worry about yourself." Eddie bent over to pick up his gloves. "This is the real deal. You're way out of your league. They may not come after you now, while this thing's hot, but they'll come—when you least expect it, and from someone you least expect."

"But if Tony goes free—"

"No." Eddie shrugged and laughed nervously. "It doesn't work that way. They're not gonna let this die. I guarantee it. You went to the captain's house lookin' for trouble. You fingered his son! In the mob's eyes, this is unforgivable."

"So, what do I do?" Everett yelled. "Go to Badino? What?" He nearly smacked his brother. "You tell me, since you're so involved with this gang—"

"Are you nuts? He'd have you stuffed on the spot. You need to look into witness protection or something. But watch your back. You still got a gun?"

Everett didn't want to admit he did, and instead pivoted away.

"If you don't, you need to buy yourself one." Eddie slapped something bulky against the back of Everett's shoulder. "I know you can shoot."

Without looking back, Everett covered the package with his hand. "What's this?"

"The rest of the dough I owe you. Twenty-four grand."

The money was in a fat white envelope. "How long can you keep winning?" Everett turned to face his brother. "Huh? Forever?"

"I knew the bad beat was gonna end."

"Stop, Eddie, while you're ahead." But Everett knew his plea wouldn't penetrate; Eddie was as stubborn as their father had been.

As Eddie reached for the doorknob, Everett wanted to tell him that Wesley had probably been with Tony in the white Yukon the night Millie died. But he kept his mouth shut and watched his brother open the door, walk past his daughter, and amble out of their lives.

Madison scrambled to her feet seconds after he was out the door. "Dad, wait!" She ran into the cold without her coat. Everett watched from the window as Eddie turned and faced his daughter on the front sidewalk. He looked down at her as she spoke, steam filling the air between them.

After several moments, he grasped her hands at chest level and began to warm them in his. She continued peering up, directly into his aging face—talking, nodding, sharing. And then Eddie engulfed her in his arms, and she hugged him back tightly. For minutes, they held each other, swaying back and forth in the wind that had whipped Eddie's coat collar up against the back of his graying head.

When finally they parted, both faces glistened. Eddie took his glove off and wiped her cheeks with the back of his fingers. Then, with an arm around her shoulder, he walked her back up the sidewalk to the door.

Madison's mascara was running when she came back in, but her brown eyes were open wide and shining. She nudged the door closed, crossed her arms, and stroked her biceps as she strolled toward her extended family.

"I had to tell him how much I love him, no matter what…" She smiled and cried at the same time. "I mean, that's what Christmas is all about, right?"

29

Something wasn't right. Everett was despondent. He couldn't play the music, couldn't even make himself smile. As the band prepared to take the stage in the center of the atrium at the Miami-Dade detention center on New Year's Eve, Everett asked for a few minutes to himself.

His old friend Donald Chambers, one of the head guards at the maximum security prison, led Everett beyond several roped-off areas to his own office cubicle in the bowels of the complex.

Chills engulfed Everett along the way as the prisoners chanted at the top of their lungs, "Les-ter, Les-ter, Les-ter." He wished Karen and Sarah could be here, but the prison had refused to allow females to interact with the inmates.

"Reminds me of old times." Donald smiled.

"Yeah." Everett took a deep breath. "Sure does."

"It's good to see you again, Ev. You okay?"

"I just need a few minutes to get focused."

Sitting alone in the charcoal-colored swivel chair at Donald's cluttered desk, Everett closed his eyes to pray but stopped midsentence, flashing back to the Christmas Eve dinner at Beau's Tavern and the loaded semiautomatic Glock he'd slipped into his coat pocket to take along—only to change his mind at the last minute.

What kind of believer considers taking a loaded gun into a restaurant?

Just as he had when he returned the gun to its hiding place that night, he wrestled with the depth of his faith.

Who are you to sing for almighty God?

He'd lost weight. Since Christmas Eve he had virtually no appetite. Even at the highly anticipated dinner with Karen, her folks, and Madison at Beau's Tavern, he'd only picked at his blackened grouper. Later that night, he couldn't even concentrate on the message at church; he was too busy scanning the auditorium for would-be assassins.

Look at you...

Wiping the sweat from his forehead with the thick white towel draped over his shoulder, Everett attempted once more to talk with God. But the phone conversation with the NYPD detective replayed itself, confirming what Eddie had prophesied: no body, no duffel bag, no evidence. Tony Badino was free.

There could be a contract on my life, right here—tonight.

And what about Karen and Sarah, alone at Twin Streams...

He'd become paranoid, plain and simple. This Christian life was all new to him. Soberness was new to him. As a millionaire superstar, everything had been handled for him. He hadn't learned to cope with real life, real people, fears, or problems. He'd never been the center of others' attention when he wasn't stoned out of his mind.

Now it was different. All eyes were on him.

Who am I?

Was he the new creation he claimed to be?

Or am I a fake?

His lack of concentration had gotten so bad on Christmas and the days that followed that Karen confronted him late one night. "Gray Harris is here, Lola and Oz...the whole band. They've come here for *you*, to stay at your home, to help you with this dream of yours. You owe it to them to get your mind on business—100 percent—and on to what God's called you to do. If you can't do that, maybe we need to call this thing off."

Those within Everett's inner circle understood the possibility that the Badinos may retaliate in some way, but no one seemed to be caving to the extent he was.

He writhed at Donald's desk. "I'm here for these people, Lord. You've put this desire in my heart. But I can barely move. It's like I'm paralyzed." He closed his eyes, still able to hear and almost feel the thundering anticipation of the boisterous crowd. "What's wrong with me?"

"Fear," God seemed to whisper.

"What do You expect? I'm worried. I'm self-conscious. I want a drink so bad..."

"I, I, I..."

"You're right; I'm so selfish!"

"Everett..."

Just remembering that God knew his name calmed him. "What's going on, Lord?"

"Am I your Shepherd?"

"Yesss." He squirmed, frustrated by the simple question.

"What can separate you from My love?"

"Nothing." He knew the answer. Why couldn't he live it?

"Tribulation?"

"No."

"Persecution?"

Everett shook his head.

"Death or a demon's powers?"

"No! None of that—ever. Nothing can separate me from You."

"But what about this valley of death?"

"I'm supposed to say I'll fear no evil."

"Can you?"

Hesitantly, Everett whispered, "Yes. I know You're with me. Your rod and staff comfort me."

"You are mine."

"Sometimes I forget, Lord."

The quiet settled in around him. He opened his eyes. The fluorescent lights seemed bright. He was to find a Bible. Scanning Donald's desk, he did—beneath a calculator. He knew just where to turn.

When he found it, he whispered the message God had revealed for the moment: "'There is no fear in love; but perfect love casts out fear, because fear involves punishment, and the one who fears is not perfected in love.'"

He read it again, drinking it in like water. Then he leaned his head on his arms on the desk and closed his eyes. "I'm Yours, Lord. I walk in the light. There's nothing to be afraid of, not even death. Everything's okay."

"It's exactly the way I want it to be."

The nervousness on their faces morphed into relieved grins when Gray and the band saw Everett round the corner of cell block A with a beat in his stride.

"Sorry about that, guys," he yelled against the backdrop of deafening noise. "Needed to get some things squared away." He raised a hand and waved them to follow. "Let's duck in here." He led them into a ten-foot by ten-foot cell, which was tucked into a small hallway about sixty feet from the stage. The small entourage of armed guards, including Donald Chambers, waited outside the cell.

Everett's bass player, Danny Dwyer, sat on the bunk. Jacob stood next to the sink, flanked by guitarist Randy White and violinist Lola Shepherd. Manager Gray Harris and drummer Oz Dublin leaned against the cold white concrete wall that Everett remembered so well.

"I owe you guys so much," Everett yelled above the stomping, which echoed in unison with the calls of "Les-ter, Les-ter." "Like we've discussed for months, this is God's day; it's His time." Everett dropped his head. "God, be glorified. Flood this place with Your Spirit…"

The dress code at the Miami-Dade detention center hadn't changed since Everett had been incarcerated during the Endora Crystal murder trial a year ago. Orange jumpsuits were everywhere, like fire ants on a dirt mound.

As dusk settled outside, its yellow haze filtered in through narrow window slits to reveal several hundred inmates sitting on the floor in front and behind the gray stage and on high stacks of amplifiers, while hundreds more lined the narrow aisles in front of the cells, which circled the facility four stories high. Guards in army-green uniforms were interspersed throughout, probably seventy in all.

As Everett and the band made their way down the hall and stopped some twenty feet from the stage to strap on their instruments, the lights were down, and the inmates were going ballistic.

Guided by a beam of light from Gray's flashlight, Everett was the last to bounce onstage, clutching his chest as he did. "Hey!" his low voice echoed strong throughout the cavernous room. "Good evening, Miami. Happy New Year!" It was mayhem. Everyone was on their feet, and the lights were still out. "It's good to be with you guys.

"As you know, I spent a good deal of time in this can a while back." He grasped the mike in one hand and the neck of his blue Les Paul in the other. "And when I did…I began to write some new music—to go along with the new life I've found in Jesus Christ."

The other band members were in place. Jacob and the rest of the crew stood in the wings.

"This first song is called 'Bailout'!"

Click, click, click, click… On the fourth crack of Oz's drumsticks flash pods went off, purple and yellow lights flooded the stage, and the band launched into a hard-driving rock 'n' roll number, with guitars and violin blazing, and Everett's penetrating voice taking command.

> How many roads have I traveled?
> Yet how much have I really learned?
> How many people have I befriended?
> Yet how many bridges have I burned?

> I'm deaf, dumb, and blind—in debt out of my mind.
> Drug habit climbin' higher—no end to the evil desire.

> Deeper and deeper I keep diggin',
> Worse and worse my sin grows.
> Farther and farther from Him I travel,
> Where they may find me, no one knows.

> I'm just a criminal at heart—a criminal,
> And now I'm hangin' here on death's tree.
> But aren't we all criminals? Criminals?
> Hey! Jesus shed His blood to set us free.

> Bailout, bailout!
> Bailout, bailout!

> All I did was fear my Maker,
> Asked Him to remember me—and suddenly…

> Bailout, bailout!
> Bailout, bailout!

> He said,
> "Today you'll be with Me in Paradise,
> 'Cause you believed in My sacrifice."

Bailout, bailout!
Bailout, bailout!

Everett was overcome with elation and laughter during the ovation, which was so loud that he noticed Gray squeezing earplugs in offstage. Everett switched to the acoustic guitar, took the stool a roadie set next to him, and slowed things down.

There were catcalls and cheers. Some inmates yelled the titles of Everett's new music, while others called out DeathStroke songs from a lifetime past, like "Souls On Fire."

"We don't do that one, anymore." He smiled and adjusted the mike with sweaty fingers. "You know, a number of things have happened in my life lately, in our lives," he waved an arm at the band and crew, "that have led me to believe, very distinctly, that Satan doesn't want us here tonight."

Thunderous applause sounded.

"But by God's grace, we *are* here—and so are you, each one of you. God wants us together tonight, on New Year's Eve. Why?" The one-word question echoed off of the walls, windows, bars, ceilings, and glossy linoleum floors. "Maybe it's because tonight will be the night you'll do something radical, something you've never done before, something that requires more guts than anything you've ever done—invite God into your life to take over and to give you a new beginning. Who knows, maybe this'll be the night you get born again…"

As Everett strummed hard and fast and the band broke into one of his latest releases, "Second Time Around," thousands of hands clapped, and the bodies of grown men—felonious criminals—swayed in unison. The hair on Everett's arms stood. Performing had never been like this before. There was clarity and unity and pleasure.

Everett, Gray, and the team of twenty volunteers who'd joined them to serve as counselors were overwhelmed by the scores of inmates who came forward after the concert. Even Donald Chambers filled in, greeting the men as they asked for prayer, sought counsel, and simply said, "Thank you for coming."

"What hit me was when you said we was all sinners, all in the same dang boat," one convict with leathery brown skin, a blond cowlick, and several missing teeth explained to Everett in a Southern drawl. "I never knew why Jesus died; now I know it was fur down-'n'-outers like me."

"And like me." Everett patted his bony shoulder.

"How could He love us that much?"

"I don't know." Everett laughed. "That's what's so amazing about grace. We just accept the gift. We believe. And we enjoy it."

"I accepted it tonight. I repented of all my sins—during that prayer you said. I wanted yous to know that."

Praise You, Father. "What's your name, bro?"

"Henry."

"If I don't see you again in this lifetime, Henry, I'll see you in Paradise."

They embraced, and Everett looked up to the next man in line—short and pale, with sad eyes and a pug nose. "Hey, Everett...Jimmy Blaylock. I saw you guys play in Port Charlotte couple years ago; that's where I'm from, Gulf Coast."

"Hey, Jimmy." Everett shook his soft hand. "I'm glad to get a chance to meet you."

"It's bad in here." He glanced around and stepped closer. "Well, you know. You were in here. 'Course, you had a cell to yourself."

"I know what you mean though." Everett was reminded of the brawls with Zane Bender. "It can be scary."

"I got a mental case from Oklahoma bunkin' with me. I mean, I go through hell, Everett, livin' hell." His sagging eyes filled with moisture. "Some days I don't think I can take it no more. I still got four years."

"Parole?"

He shook his head.

"Why don't we pray together. You want to?"

Jimmy sniffed and nodded nervously.

"Holy Spirit," Everett rested both hands on Jimmy's slight shoulders, "come now, Helper, and fill Jimmy. Give him the peace and protection only You can give. We pray he'll find hope in Your Word, gain strength in it, and come to rely on You for his every need, every comfort, and every protection. And may his life reflect Your transforming power—"

"God help me!" His eyes were shut tight, and his shoulders bounced with tears. "I'm scared as all get-out. I need things to change. Please protect me. They're all comin' against me. Usin' me." The tears turned to sobs. "I'll give my life to Ya. Please, just protect me…"

"Look at me, Jimmy." Everett gripped the sides of the man's arms. "God will protect you. He's got you at this scary place because He wants you to call out to Him, rely on Him for everything; not yourself anymore—"

"I know."

"I'm not talkin' about religion. And not just tonight, on this mountaintop. I'm talkin' about you starting a relationship with Christ. He's a High Tower, man, a Mighty Fortress. You're safe inside Him. But you need to trust God and have a partnership with Him. Do you have a Bible?"

"No."

"Get yourself one over there." Everett dipped his head in the direction of the table where Gray was handing out paperbacks. "And immerse yourself in that thing. Listen to me. It's not just a book, you hear? Jesus is the Word. He'll meet you in the Bible and can keep you from the evil ones."

Jimmy suddenly bear-hugged Everett, embracing him tightly—not caring what anyone thought. *Oh, Lord,* Everett nodded, *this is it. This is what You've been preparing me for. Thank You! Thank You for using me.*

Everett noticed several taps on his shoulder. He smiled and looked into Jimmy's eyes one last time. "Peace, brother," he said, and turned to face a solemn Gray Harris.

"It's Wesley." Gray rested his hands on Everett's shoulders. "He tried to commit suicide."

30

With an IV secured to his wrist and a white tube running into his mouth, Wesley lay asleep in a second-story room at Stamford Hospital on New Year's Day. Karen's head snapped away when her eyes found his neck, stained by a grotesque mixture of purple, yellow, and red bruises from where he'd secured the bedsheets and hung himself from a dismantled overhead light in his room at Horizons at Harbor View.

Karen and Everett stood over him holding hands, while Madison spoke in hushed tones to someone on the phone in the far corner of the room. Other than the bruises, Wesley actually looked better than he had the last time they'd seen him. Karen could tell his treatment had been working. His face was full, and his brown hair had grown out some.

Still on the phone, Madison stood, flipped on a standing lamp, doused the bright overhead light, and sat back in her chair.

The door opened slowly. "It's me." Sheila crept in, tried to adjust her eyes to the darkness, and flicked the overhead back on.

"Thank God he's going to make it." Everett rested a hand on Sheila's back. "We came as soon as we could."

Without a word, Sheila went to her boy and swiped her hand through his short hair. Her nose was bright red, and she reeked of whiskey or something equally strong.

"Madison says he's stable and improving," Karen said.

Sheila rested her tan hand on the side of Wesley's white face. There was a band of diamonds on her ring finger and a gold signet ring on her pinky.

"Sheila," Everett stepped toward her, "are you all right?"

She adjusted the tube in Wesley's mouth ever so slightly, then turned to face them. "That girl he met at Horizons—Cassidy." Sheila covered her lips with two fingers. "She died…the night she got out."

"Oh, no." Karen gasped. "How?"

"Meth." Sheila swallowed. "I talked to her mom. Cassidy went to a party she knew she shouldn't have. She was there for hours and had nothing, just seeing old friends. But the meth kept getting passed around the room; it was too much for her."

"What happened?" Karen asked. "Was it an overdose?"

"It started with an irregular heartbeat. Her heart got overstimulated. They said it actually burst. She was dead before the paramedics got there. Nineteen years old."

Everett's head shook in exasperation.

Madison was off the phone, and she approached her brother's bedside. "He liked her. One of the nurses—Veronica, the one who found him—said they'd gotten really close."

"Did Wesley know Cassidy had died…when he did this?" Everett asked.

"We're not sure yet," Madison said.

"What about Eddie?" Everett asked. "Where's he?"

Sheila and Madison looked at each other, then began speaking at the same time.

"Go ahead." Madison waved and turned away.

"He's in trouble." Sheila eyed them. "At least we think he is. He hasn't been home for two days. I've left messages on his cell, told him about Wes. We haven't heard back."

"Does he often do this?" Karen asked. "I mean, stay away from home?"

"I know he's hooked on gambling." Sheila closed her eyes and squeezed the back of her neck. "But he always comes home at night— even if it's late—unless he's on business."

"Wesley hasn't even asked for him." Madison had her back to them, staring out at the blowing trees. "Mom wasn't here either, when he first woke up." Her voice dropped. "Probably off filling up some-where…"

Karen shot Everett a glance and watched Sheila deflate. But she forced herself to shake off the blow as quickly as it had been dealt.

"A black car has been parked outside the house on and off all week." Sheila ran her fingers through her thick, dark hair. "I think someone may be after him."

"Who?" Karen wondered how much Sheila knew about Eddie's mob ties.

"I have no clue. Whoever he bets with. Probably the same crowd that beat him up at the racetrack. I haven't been able to get him at work. I don't even think he's been in this week; hardly anyone is, 'cause of the holidays."

When Madison's phone rang, she snatched it, glanced at the caller ID window, excused herself, and left the room.

"She told me about her…religious experience." Sheila rolled her eyes toward where Madison had exited, then meandered to the other side of Wesley's bed. "I can't say I've seen any difference in her. In fact, she seems to hate my guts all of a sudden."

Karen caught Everett's stare. He motioned with a nod and a wind-ing of his hand, as if to say, "Go ahead."

"Sheila." Karen hesitated. "Madison told us…she thinks you have a drinking problem. She's worried about you, and she needs you, especially now—"

"Oh, great." Sheila stuck her fists on her slender hips like pins going into a cushion. "So my drinking's the talk of the town. I suppose that gives Eddie the perfect excuse for all his shenanigans."

"No, it doesn't." Everett raised his hands. "Look, Sheila, we want to help your family—"

"It's over, okay? This 'family,' as you call it, lost its meaning a long time ago, long before you two came onto the scene. It's really none of your business, anyway."

"It *is* our business. Eddie's my brother. You *are* family."

"All you care about, Everett, is freeing your guilty conscience of David's death. Isn't that why you're here? Isn't that what this is about? Trying to get back in our good graces—and God's?"

Karen watched Everett take the direct hit, turn, and wander to the sink. He'd been struggling over those issues, and she prayed he would be able to receive God's counsel, no one else's.

"Sheila," Karen said, "Everett's here because he loves Eddie and his children and you, believe it or not. He's sacrificed—"

"If you love me, you should let me live my life." She stared at the sheets on Wesley's bed, straightening them repeatedly with her hand. "It's been over between Eddie and me for a long time. I'm ready for a divorce."

"But for Wesley's sake," Karen said, "and Madison's—"

"What good's it do if I stay in a washed-up marriage? That's not helping them—seeing us fight, watching us tear each other apart. What am I explaining it to you for? You're newlyweds. Just wait till you have kids."

The anguish of Karen's infertility reared its vexing head and ripped at her soul. She saw the consolation on Everett's face and closed her eyes.

"I'm sorry, Karen. That was…Madison told me. I didn't mean it. Please, forgive me." Sheila ran from the room.

Everett opened his arms and stepped toward Karen. She latched onto him and buried her face in his chest. They stayed like that for a minute or two, sharing the sorrow in the aftermath of Sheila's fiery darts.

But Karen chose to rise above, to forget herself and move on. "I'm going to check on Madison," she whispered, looking up into Everett's handsome face.

"It's okay, you know. We've got each other."

She squeezed him close again, with her head pressed against him. And she could hear his heart beating steadily. That's what she needed now—steadiness.

At the end of the hospital hallway next to the elevator, Karen saw Madison juggle her purse on one knee, searching through it almost frantically.

"Madison." Karen walked toward her. "What's going on?"

"I gotta go." She opened the purse wide with both hands, peering in at different angles.

"Is everything okay?"

Madison glanced at her then went back to searching the purse.

"What is it, honey?" Karen noticed the Down button was lit. "Can I help?"

"I can't find my keys." Her voice shook.

"What's the hurry? Where are you headed?"

"That was my dad. He's in trouble. I've got to go."

"Wait a minute. Let's go tell Ev. One of us can go with you—"

"No." She snatched the keys and pressed the lit button repeatedly. "There's no time. I told him I'd meet him. I'll be back. Don't worry."

The bell rang, and the elevator doors lurched open. Madison stepped in, and Karen's mind whirled. "Madi, please. Tell me where you're going."

"I can't! No one can know."

The heavy silver doors began to close, and Karen stiff-armed one, triggering them to reverse.

"Madison, the people your dad's dealing with are *dangerous*. You saw what happened to him and to Everett. Please, let me—"

"Stop!" She forced Karen's arm away. "I've got to do this alone. He needs me." The doors began to close again, and Madison reached a hand out toward her. "I love you, Aunt Karen. I'm sorry. It'll be okay. Just pray for us."

Karen ran back down the hallway to Wesley's room and swung the large door open. Everett was seated in a chair next to his bed, reading aloud from a Bible.

"Madison's leaving." Karen gasped. "You need to follow her! She got a call from Eddie, he's in trouble, and she's going to meet him somewhere!"

"She's in her Bug?" Everett patted his pockets for his keys and phone on the way to the door.

"Yeah, I assume. Light blue with a black top. You gotta catch her right now, or we'll lose her."

He was gone.

Everett scanned the oncoming cars as he hurried through the hospital crosswalk, then panned the surrounding city streets and parking deck all the way to the black Nissan loaner he'd been given—no sign of Madison's Volkswagen.

She's got to be headed back to New York.

All he could think to do was get to I-95 as fast as he could and head south.

Gunning the Nissan out of the parking garage, he searched for signs to the interstate but saw none. The streets were unfamiliar.

Show me the way, Lord.

He took a right on West Broad and immediately spotted signs for I-95.

Thank You.

Roaring through the gears, he flew down the city streets, hoping for no police and hunting for the light blue bug.

Within three minutes he was merging onto I-95, bound for New York City.

He opened it up, figuring if he didn't see Madison now, he might never see her again.

31

Karen picked up the open Bible on the chair next to Wesley's bed and sank into the seat herself. *Where did this come from?*

Examining the pages where it looked as if Everett had left off, Karen's eyes fell to some words that had been underlined in blue ink, and she read quietly: "'Mary took a jar of costly perfume…and anointed Jesus' feet with it—'"

Her phone rang, and she picked it up. "Ev?"

"Nope. Sorry. Gray."

"Oh…hi, Gray."

"Gee, Karen, don't sound so excited."

"Sorry about that." She snorted. "I thought it was gonna be Ev. Happy New Year! I understand you had quite a night in Miami."

"It was incredible," Gray said. "Wish you could've been there. One of the guards told me they counted more than 250 inmates who came forward afterward."

"Can you believe it?"

"If that's any indication of what's in store, we better hold on to our seats!"

She chuckled. "I know."

"Tell me about Wesley."

"Thankfully, he's going to make it." Karen looked at her nephew. "Right now he's sleeping. We haven't gotten to talk to him yet to find out why he did this, but we will."

"I'm praying for him, sweetie."

"Thank you, friend. We need that."

"Listen, I'm calling about SoundSystems…"

"Are they in?"

"They're in!"

Yes! Everett and Karen had been praying for one more big sponsor. "Oh, Gray," she turned away from Wesley, "that is *such* good news!"

"So, I'll see your husband tomorrow for practice?"

"Lord willing, Ev will be ready."

"Hey, one more thing," Gray said. "SoundSystems wants new artwork for the tour poster."

"This late? How are they going to pull that off?"

"They assured me they can make it happen."

"We weren't crazy about what we had anyway. What do they have in mind?"

"Nothing concrete. They want to play off the Living Water theme more. You got any ideas?"

Karen flashed back to Madison's house and her painting of the waterfall from the national forest in Oregon. "I've got a good idea. Who do I talk to?"

He gave her the name and number of the marketing coordinator handling the tour promotion for SoundSystems, then they hung up. After leaving a message for the coordinator, Karen opened the Bible and continued reading where she'd left off.

"'But Judas Iscariot…the one who would betray him, said, "That perfume was worth a fortune. It should have been sold and the money given to the poor.""'"

Karen rested the book in her lap and stared at Wesley for a few moments. *Did he just move?* She thought she'd seen his eyes flicker. *You haven't had enough sleep.*

She pondered what she'd just read. Judas had become outraged by a person who loved Christ enough to worship Him openly and boldly. Lifting the Bible again, she paged backward, searching for the same account told by Matthew. Oddly, it too had been underlined.

"'Jesus knew what they were thinking and said, "Why are you criticizing her? For she has done a good thing…" Then Judas…went to the chief priests, and asked, "How much will you pay me to get Jesus into your hands?" And they gave him thirty silver coins. From that time on, Judas watched for an opportunity to betray Jesus—'"

"Is that supposed to cheer me up?" Wesley's hoarse voice made Karen flinch.

"Wesley!" She popped up to the edge of the chair.

"It's me," he whispered, holding the white tube.

"I don't think you should take that out."

"It's okay." He finally opened his eyes fully, which were clearer and bluer than she'd remembered. "I did it before."

"How do you feel?" she asked.

"Sore."

There was an uncomfortable silence.

"That Bible." His eyes went to the book on her lap. "It was Cassidy's."

"Your friend from Harbor View?"

He closed his eyes and nodded.

Was Cassidy a Christian? Did her death lead you to attempt suicide?

"We were so sorry to hear about her…"

"How long do I have to stay here, do you know?"

Her mind shifted gears abruptly. She wanted to keep talking about Cassidy and the Bible.

"I'm not sure." She crossed her arms. "Your mom made it sound like it wouldn't be more than a day or two."

"Where is she, anyway?"

"She just stepped out for a minute." *Ran out, actually. Where is she?*

"What am I on?"

"Pardon?"

"What am I on—what meds?"

"Oh, I think some kind of strong pain reliever. Not sure what…"

Wesley turned his head toward the window. Karen suspected this would be one of the few moments she would have alone with him. *Give me the words, Lord.*

"Can you tell me what happened, Wesley?"

His head remained fixed as it was. He clasped his hands on his stomach. "What do you care? What difference does it make?"

"Tell me about Cassidy."

"She was good." Wesley turned to face her. "Life stinks."

"But it can be so much better—"

His hands pounded the mattress. "Don't give me that! Okay? You haven't lived my life. You have no idea what I'm feeling. So don't tell me how it can be."

Wesley's words came like gunfire. And he was right; Karen didn't understand. His feelings and experiences—his dark world—were foreign to her.

"I'll go check on your mom." As she stood, set the Bible in the chair, and trod softly toward the door, she wondered why she'd been placed there at all.

Everett was about to turn around and head back to the hospital when he spotted Madison's Beetle in the far left lane doing at least eighty. He dropped into the right lane and forced his stiff body to relax.

As he punched in the speed dial for Karen on the cell, a strong blast of wind nudged the Nissan. "Whoa."

"Hello."

"Hey, babe," he said, eyes glued to the VW. "I found her."

"Good boy! Where?"

"Going like a rocket down I-95, almost to the New York state line. I'm behind her a couple hundred yards."

"She's not gonna stop for anything," Karen said. "I'd stay back and just make sure everything's okay. She's not going to notice you in that loaner."

"Okay." He loosened his grip on the steering wheel. "What's going on at your end?"

"Wesley's awake."

"Really? How's he doing?"

"He's okay," she said. "I tried to talk to him about why he hung himself, but he shut me down."

"What do you mean?" His grip tightened on the wheel. "He didn't try to hurt you, did he?"

"No. He's just impossible to talk to."

"Kind of like I used to be?"

"Worse."

He sensed her discouragement. "Thanks for trying, babe."

After Karen shared the news about SoundSystems and her hopes for the new tour poster, they said good-bye.

"You have me here for a reason, Lord." Everett's gaze was fixed on Madison's Bug. "I don't know what it is, but I pray You'll protect Eddie and Madison and me. Give me wisdom if I have to get involved…"

Every now and then one of the minivans between Madison and him swerved slightly in the gusting wind. On a whim, Everett picked up his phone, found Eddie's number, and hit the speed dial. No answer.

Not long after the VW flew over the Connecticut state line into New York, Madison veered off, picking up Interstate 287 and heading straight for White Plains.

She's going home. Eddie will be there.

Question is, will the Mendazzos?

★ ★ ★

Sheila was flat-out drunk when she staggered back into Wesley's hospital room, plopped onto the bed, and tried to lie down on her back next to her son.

"How's my baby? You doin' okay, sugar?"

"Geez, Mom." The IV nearly ripped out of Wesley's wrist as he scowled and shoved her off the bed like a bag of smelly garbage. "You're plastered!"

She smacked the floor.

"Oh my goodness!" Karen shrieked. "Sheila, are you okay?"

Clinging to the white sheets and rising unsteadily back to her knees, Sheila's expression was one of shock and horror. "How dare you push me away!"

Karen reached to help her up, but Sheila knocked away her hands, nearly falling over as she did. "I don't need your help, little miss *saint*."

Wesley's face was distorted in anger.

Sheila grunted, out of breath and red-faced, as she rose to her feet. "I am so fed up with the whole bunch of you. I'm ready to walk out of this whole—"

"Go ahead!" The veins in Wesley's bruised neck protruded. "I wish you would! We're no *family*; never have been!"

"Well, maybe I would go, if you weren't such a child," her head wagged, "needin' to be coddled and watched every minute. When are you ever gonna grow up?" She was practically spitting as she strained to get the last words out without taking another breath.

Even though Karen believed in miracles, the ugly exchange unfolding before her seemed dreadful and hopeless. The heat from embarrassment and uncertainty filled her cheeks.

"People wonder why I'm so messed up." Wesley's head snapped the other way. "It's 'cause my world—my reality—*stinks*!"

"It's all about *you*, isn't it, Wesley? It's always all about you."

"Me? You're nuts. You and the old man are the selfish ones.

You've *never* had time for us. You're always off doin' your own thing."

"That is a lie, Wesley Lester! We've worked our tails off to provide for you—"

"I'm not talkin' about what you've provided for us!"

Karen's heart was pounding. She took a deep breath and tiptoed into the conversation. "Why don't you try to explain what you mean, Wesley, so your mom can understand—"

"Stay out of this!" Sheila snarled. "You don't have any idea what goes on in families."

"That's not true." He turned to his mom. "You dis Karen, but I've felt more love from her than I've ever felt from you or Dad."

That's when the room went silent. Sheila dropped into the closest chair. Her bloodshot blue eyes were half open and so was her mouth. She sat frozen in time, staring glassy-eyed out the window.

"Where's Dad right now? Huh?" Wesley shrugged. "Just forget it. Forget the whole dang thing."

In the drab light of the colorless day, Sheila bent forward, found her purse with patting hands, and brought out a glass flask with about a half-inch of gold liquid swishing in the bottom. Staring toward the light, she twisted off the silver cap and held both in her lap for what seemed like minutes. Then she closed her eyes, slowly brought the flask to her mouth, and tilted her head back—draining every last drop.

32

As New Year's Day travelers breezed about the streets of White Plains, Madison barreled through a traffic light that had just flicked from yellow to red. Four cars behind her, Everett slammed the steering wheel as he came to a stop.

Let her be going home; otherwise, I've lost her.

Twelve minutes later, he swerved the Nissan to the side of the road, about a hundred feet past the front of his brother's estate. *Thank God.* Madison's blue Beetle was parked just outside the front door, and no other cars were in sight. Turning off his cell phone, Everett hopped from the car and hurried toward his brother's residence.

Facing the fierce wind, he jogged up the wide, blacktop driveway, shivering as the tenseness of the situation and the cold, damp winter settled into his bones. Bounding up the steps, he found the front door ajar and pushed it open, stepping into the foyer.

"Madi?" He headed for the kitchen. "Eddie?"

Standing face-to-face, Eddie and Madison looked up at him simultaneously but said nothing.

"What's going on?" Everett stopped in his tracks. "I just wanted to make sure everything was okay."

Madison's hand was out. In it was Eddie's wedding band, a gold pocket watch their grandfather had given him, and several other pieces of jewelry Everett didn't recognize.

"I'm leaving the country." Eddie peered at him. "Madison's driving me to the airport. She may come, too."

"What? What are you saying?" Everett turned to Madison. "What's goin' on?"

"Hit another bad beat, brother. But there's no winning my way out of this one. Lost the Italian lottery. I'm into Badino way over my head."

Everett's mind exploded from the fallout. "How much?"

"A hundred and eighty-odd grand."

No way.

"Uncle Everett, will you tell him we'll help him?" Madison wrung her hands.

"Eddie," Everett approached his brother, "I'll pay it. Don't worry about that. We have the funds—"

"It's gone beyond that, Ev. Way beyond. I've heard Badino's furious. You're probably in danger, too." He made for the front door, pushed the sheer aside, and stuck his face up to the small window. "The lenders are all after me, repo men... I told Madison to have Sheila sell the house. There'll be some equity. Maybe she can move into town, like she wanted. A one-bedroom, maybe."

"So," Everett threw his hands in the air, "you're gonna leave your family high and dry, strapped with your debt?"

"Daddy, you just need God." She trembled. "Please, Uncle Everett, tell him..."

"Madison, no! Everett's been through that with me." Eddie waved. "It's not gonna work. I'm not a Christian, okay? I'm not going to become a Christian. I can't love a God who took my boy from me and let my marriage die—"

"Then I can't go with you, Daddy!" Tears jetted out the sides of Madi's brown eyes. "I can't go on without God. You can't either; you just don't know it yet."

Eddie turned away with a sickening frown.

"Why are you bringing her into this?" Everett thrust a finger toward his niece. "You want her to go down with you? What gives?"

"I needed her to drive me to the airport. That's all. I didn't want to ask you again."

"Why don't you drive yourself, you selfish... Why would you endanger your own daughter? And what about Wesley? He's lyin' up there in a hospital room!"

Eddie dropped his head and peered at Everett through the top half of his cold eyes. "I think the Amanti and the Yukon may be wired."

"What do you mean?" Everett stepped closer. "Bombs?"

Eddie nodded.

Everett's head pounded. And when Eddie spoke again, his voice sounded eerily distant. "The cars are in the garage, but I told Madison no one should go near them until the police check them out—after I'm gone."

Eddie pushed up his white cuff, checked his Rolex, and ducked into the family room, where he picked up his expensive overcoat from atop a large black suitcase.

"We gotta go." He faced Everett and Madison and began to put the coat on. "They're on my trail."

"Where are you going?" Everett asked.

"Not sure yet."

"Will you call me?"

"Yeah. You or Madison. I'll let someone know."

"What's with the jewelry?" Everett nodded toward Madison's closed fist.

"That's just in case..." Eddie headed for the door.

"Look, I'll drive you. There's no way Madi's going."

"Fine." At the front door, Eddie pushed the sheer aside. The suitcase he was carrying dropped to the floor. "Uh-oh."

Everett bolted for the other window and heard Madison's foot-steps behind him.

"That's Badino's thugs," Eddie said.

The long, black Lincoln glided in and crept up directly behind Madison's Beetle, stopping just inches from its bumper. Then one, two, three of its big black doors opened, ever so slowly.

"To the basement!" Eddie grabbed Madison's hand, rushed for the steps, and started down. Everett followed. "You guys need to stay down here or head for the woods out back," Eddie said. "I'm gonna have to deal with this."

He went straight for Wesley's apartment, back into the bedroom. Diving to his stomach, he reached beneath the waterbed and dragged out a heavy gray duffel bag while Everett called 911 on his cell phone.

"You're not callin' the cops." Eddie looked up from his knees, sweating.

Everett ignored him. "This is an emergency," he told the operator. "Armed men are entering this residence. Hurry!" He confirmed the address, hung up, and looked down to see Eddie loading several semi-automatic pistols.

"I've heard these guys only know how to shoot at close range." Eddie kept loading. "If I can keep my distance, who knows."

"Daddy, please, stay here with me." Madison squirmed. "The police will be here soon."

"You may need this." He tossed Everett a .45 he'd just loaded. "Madison, I want you to stay in this room and lock the door. Don't come out for anything." She tried to grasp his hands, but each con-tained a gun. He kissed her on the cheek instead. "I'm gonna protect you, honey. I have to do this. Now please, stay calm."

Everett stuffed the gun in the waist of his Levi's. "Pray, Madi." He tossed her his phone. "Call Karen. Tell her to pray, too." As he pulled the door closed, he heard it lock.

Eddie had already raced up the steps.

Everett stopped. He'd never seen Wesley's apartment. This was where Karen found the meth equipment and where Wesley had pulled the gun on her.

He touched the cold handle of the heavy pistol, which he knew how to use very well. And he remembered from his arms training that if you dare arm yourself against an intruder, you darn well better be ready to use the weapon.

But he didn't want to kill.

Crack!

The blast rang out from upstairs.

Crack! Crack!

It sounded unreal.

Heading outside and circling around to the front door seemed like a fair option, but Everett needed to be the roadblock between Madison and the enemy. He dashed up the steps. At the top, he grabbed the gun, chambered a round, and lay on the floor, with his knees on the top few steps.

"Eddie," he whispered loudly.

"I'm behind the couch," his brother said. "They tried to crowbar their way in."

"What were the shots?"

"I fired through the door to keep 'em back."

"Where are they now?"

"Not sure," Eddie called. "I see someone out there still. They may try to send someone in another way. You better go back downstairs. Watch Madi's door. I'll stay here."

Glass shattered from the direction of the basement.

"Madison!" Eddie darted in the crouched position toward Everett at the steps.

A blast of glass exploded at the front door, but the shot missed Eddie.

"Stay here," he barked at Everett. "Don't let 'em past that door!"

Eddie flew down the steps, and Everett crawled closer to the foyer. Chunks of glass covered the shiny wood floor. Through the gaping hole in the window, he could hear someone just outside the front door.

Madison's piercing scream rang out so loud and long, it chilled Everett to the core. He didn't even think but braced the .45 in front of him with two hands and blew four holes clean through the door. Then he whirled for the basement and plunged into the darkness three steps at a time.

Karen couldn't help it; she was repulsed by Sheila who, holding the empty flask in one hand, wiped the corners of her mouth with the middle finger of the other. "Your sister thinks I'm an alcoholic." Her head bobbed, she blinked slowly, and her words tumbled out in a slur.

"I don't want to talk about it, Mom," Wesley said. "You won't remember anyway."

"I want you to know why I drink, Wes." She leaned her elbows unsteadily on her knees. "There are reasons things have turned out the way they have."

"Why are we even talkin' about this?" Wesley shot out. "It's not gonna do any good."

"Because, honey, I want you to understand—"

"I understand plenty!" His head and shoulders pivoted away from her. "I understand that ever since David died you've given up; Dad too. We'd all be better off goin' our separate ways."

"Honey," she scooted the chair closer, "things were bad *before* David's accident."

"Just get out of my face, okay? You smell like a doggone distillery. Why don't you go home and sober up? I'll see you tomorrow."

Sheila reached for him, put a hand on his arm. He let it remain.

This was not her world; this was not her idea of family—so far from it. Karen was so out of place. She wanted to be gone from here.

What's my role in all of this?

She shuddered when she heard the muffled ring of the cell phone in her purse. Picking up the bag, she excused herself and made for the hall.

"Hello," she answered.

"Aunt Karen!"

"Madi? What's—?"

"I'm at my house—with Everett and my dad." She gasped for breath. "They're after us, Badino's men." She let out a cry. "Everett asked me to call. Please pray!"

Karen searched the room with her eyes. "Have you called the police?"

"Everett did. Oh. Oh my…ahhh! A window just broke!"

"Where are you in the house, sweetie?"

"Basement. Someone's outside the door. They're pounding…"

Karen could hear the bashing. Wood cracking and splintering. Madison whimpering.

Get out!

But before Karen could get the words out of her mouth, the line went dead.

33

The second Everett hit the bottom of the steps, hot weapon still locked in hand, he froze with his back to the left wall. The door to Wesley's apartment was open. He inched closer, wiped the sweat from his forehead with the back of his wrist, and concentrated on breathing inaudibly.

"Please, don't!" Madison cried.

"Let her go!" Eddie yelled. "I'm who you want. Take me. Let's go. Right now! Just leave her alone."

Everett eyed the top of the empty steps, then tiptoed to within several feet of the doorway. Extending his free left hand to balance himself against the trim around the door, he leaned into the path of the doorway ever so gradually, peering into the long room, then ducking back out of view.

The snapshot he took of the setting was dreamlike—Madison in the back bedroom, in the headlock of a tall goon with a revolver to her head. The man was one of the wiseguys from Pappano's restaurant.

Eddie's back was to Everett and his arms were outstretched, pointing two guns at Madison and her abductor.

"Put the guns down," came the intruder's low voice. "Or I kill her now and then finish you."

Silence.

"Your choice," the gunman said. "How many are gonna die here today? Don't make no difference to me. None. But I'm losin' my patience."

Eddie's guns clinked to the carpet.

"Facedown on the couch." The low voice was moving now. There was no backtalk from Eddie. A grunt from Madison sounded closer.

The gunman had kicked the weapons away, Everett was almost positive. His breathing got heavier, faster—and his ribs seemed to jump with each beat of his thumping heart. He strained to listen as sweat trickled down the side of his face, and he swiped at it with a rolling shoulder.

"I need rope or tape, Lester." The intruder's voice was coming closer. "Where is it?"

"In the kitchen drawer there's tape…I can get it—"

"Shut up! Stay put."

"Ouch!" Madison cried.

Everett was about to barrel in, but something held him back. Drawers were gliding open and banging shut.

"I don't know why I'm doin' this," the wiseguy said. "You don't know how lucky you are, lady. This ain't like me."

The instant Everett heard the shriek of the reeling duct tape, he made his move.

Karen burst through the door to Wesley's hospital room, making Sheila and him recoil.

"That was Madison! She and Everett and Eddie are in trouble at your house."

"Oh my word." Sheila wheeled around from Wesley's bedside. "What on earth—?"

"It's the mob family. They're after Eddie." She shook Sheila's shoulder. "Can I take your car?"

"Well, I'm coming too." She staggered to her feet.

"Keys, Sheila! Where're your keys?"

"Right here." She picked up her purse.

Karen grabbed it from her, took a last glance at Wesley, and booked for the door.

"Wait up!" Sheila called.

Karen made a beeline for the elevators, hit the down button, and sighed as Sheila lumbered toward her down the long hallway. Karen scanned the area for stairs but saw none. She took in an enormous breath, closed her eyes, and prayed for angels to guard her loved ones.

It seemed to take forever to get to the lobby and make for the exit.

"What are you driving?" Karen said, as the large double-glass doors parted.

"My green Lexus," Sheila said from four steps back.

"Where?"

"Straight across. First level. I'll show you."

The cold wind whipped beneath the huge concrete overhang, howling and buffeting them as they trudged across the drop-off lane, passing an assortment of people who were heading inside.

A heavy man in his fifties pushed a bony, blond woman bundled in a wheelchair; two nurses passed them with their arms crossed; behind them came a young man sucking every last carcinogen out of a glowing cigarette nub before flicking it to the ground.

Wait.

Karen did a double take.

Black trench coat.

But they had to hurry.

"It'll be straight ahead when we get in the deck," Sheila murmured. "I counted the rows when I parked. Let's see, was it nine?"

Gray ski cap.

"I can never remember…"

Dirty work boots.

"I think you better drive, Karen."

That was Tony Badino.

With his arms locked in front of him, the .45 bolted to his hands, and what felt like fifty thousand watts of electricity surging through his trembling body, Everett burst into the basement apartment, zeroing in on one thing—the wiseguy's hands. As he'd hoped, they clung to out-stretched duct tape and a clumsily held revolver.

"Drop everything *now*!"

The tape dropped. So did the weapon.

Everett was on the kneeling man as quick as a wasp, burying the nose of the pistol hard into his upper back. "Facedown. On your stomach! Hands behind you."

Eddie rolled off the couch onto the floor, where he scrambled to retrieve his guns.

"Tape his hands," Everett told him.

But his brother attacked instead, ramming both knees into the intruder's back, causing him to grunt as he bounced off the ground. Then Eddie smashed the barrel of one of the guns into the man's temple.

"I should kill you right now!" Eddie screamed. "You—"

"Get off him!" Everett slammed his brother to the ground. "Do what I say. Tape him. Now!"

Eddie's hair was glistening with sweat, and his brown eyes jumped wildly.

"Hurry!" Everett growled with gun drawn.

Hesitantly, Eddie set his weapons down and picked up the tape.

"Ahhh!" Madison's fingers shook at her mouth as her eyes enlarged and fixated on the door leading to the porch.

Before Everett could turn, he was being told not to move one single nerve, and to drop his gun. He did so. The second his weapon hit the carpet, his brother was in motion, rolling, grabbing one of the weapons on the floor, and firing.

An explosion of light blinded Everett. But seconds later, both men in the doorway were still standing, still coming.

In a blur, the hostage on the floor arose. His fat arm latched around Eddie's neck from behind and ratcheted tight. Madison squealed as Everett reached out for his brother, who was gasping for breath.

Then the sirens.

One of the men who'd just entered collected the guns while the other—a slender, pockmarked-faced man with black sunglasses—kept his weapon on Everett and Madison. "You two move and you're dead. No more games. Come on, Sonny." He wound his gun at the hench-man choking Eddie. "Bring him to the car. Quick."

"What about him?" Sonny grunted, nodding at Everett as he dragged Eddie across the room. "After what he's put us through…"

"No," the leader said. "Those aren't the orders. Come on."

"Oh, that's right," Sonny mocked, out of breath, "you're bein' saved for a higher purpose." Then his daffy smile morphed into a wicked scowl. "We'll be seein' you again real soon, little brother. This ain't no free pass."

As the three mobsters merged in the center of the room and backed their way to the stairs, Eddie reached out to Madison. His fin-gers spread like the spokes on a bike. "I love you, baby…"

Madison cried out and covered her quivering mouth with one hand.

"Tell Wesley I'm sorry," Eddie pleaded. "I wish I could have been a better dad."

As they started up the steps, Madison inched toward them. "I love you," she wailed. "Please, Daddy, believe in Jesus. Will you do that? Please! For me? I'm begging you, before it's too late—"

"Tell your mother," Eddie said, "I never stopped loving her."

Madison moved to the bottom of the steps, her whole body trembling.

"Stop there, missy," one of them said. "Don't you set one foot on those steps."

"Please, Daddy!" She bawled, with her outstretched hands shuddering. "I want to be with you in heaven. I'll see you there. Okay, Daddy? Okay?"

And with that, Eddie Lester was gone.

34

Early the next morning, Karen took solace in the stillness of the den and the ticking of the grandfather clock as she stared out the window at the many media vehicles that had converged on Twin Streams. Outside in the rain, reporters huddled with steaming coffee beneath umbrellas and with cigarettes in the back of TV trucks.

In somewhat of a fog, Karen repeated the verses she'd clung to of late: "Who can be compared with God enthroned on high?… He gives children to the childless wife, so that she becomes a happy mother."

She closed her eyes. Would they ever see Eddie again? And what would become of Wesley and Sheila? Such enormous hurdles stood in front of them. *And here you are, dwelling on your infertility.*

Then something told her not to be down on herself, that God wanted all of her cares, and that if she would petition Him, He would give her peace unsurpassed.

She desperately needed such peace as she faced the fact that, overnight, the news of Eddie's abduction had traveled across the nation at the speed of a tsunami. CNN reported that the brother of famed rocker Everett Lester may have been kidnapped from his White Plains estate by modern-day mobsters associated with Dominic "Machine Gun" Mendazzo and his infamous Mafia family, the same group suspected of a gangland-style murder in Canarsie several weeks earlier.

Karen walked into the family room and snuggled up next to Everett on the loveseat as CNN showed footage of Eddie's estate in the aftermath of his abduction.

Her parents were glued to the TV as well, coffees in hand. Cameras from the previous day had caught special tactics crews combing the Amanti and Yukon for bombs, and blurry, distant images of Everett and Madison inside the house speaking with detectives.

The station also broadcast a live, early morning feed from the Pelham Village home of Dominic Badino, who was being taken into custody for questioning by the NYPD. Wearing a grey Stetson, sunglasses, and a velour sweatsuit, Badino was escorted from his home by a tough-looking crew of plainclothes detectives.

Everett pointed out a frantic Margaret Badino, wearing a bathrobe and shuffling along behind her husband with her hands to her mouth in the prayer position, clutching a strand of rosary beads.

When the news update ended and Everett flicked off the TV, his thick brown eyebrows looked almost black against his ashen face. "I thought we were in trouble before." He paced. "We've got to do something. Eddie told me Badino owns half the NYPD. They're not gonna keep him; he's gonna walk."

"Okay, calm down," Jacob said. "We've been through tight spots like this before."

"Yeah, and I'm the one who always puts us here! This is nuts. These dudes are cold-blooded killers. We're all in danger—not just me!"

"Keep your voice down, babe," Karen said. "Sheila's still asleep."

"I just don't know if you realize how serious this is." Everett pleaded. "They wired both of Eddie's cars! I saw the look on those wiseguys' faces yesterday. These are not normal people; they kill with no conscience."

He turned to Dad and Mom. "Maybe I should go back to Badino…"

"And do what? There's no reasoning with him," Dad said. "You show up on his doorstep again, after accusing his son of murder, and—"

"Jacob…" Mom cut him off.

"All I'm saying is, there're certain people who are just hardened. It's like they're destined for evil. You can't talk sense to someone like that."

"Maybe we should cancel the tour." Everett marched toward the window.

Karen stood and threw her hands up. "That's exactly what Satan wants! If we cancel, we're not going through a door God wants us to go through—one He's thrown wide open!"

Everett crossed his arms and sighed as rain ticked against the windows.

"We can't stop living because of this," Karen whispered. "God's given us these fields—they're ripe for harvest."

"You know I don't want to cancel," Everett said. "That's the last thing I want. But I'm worried about your safety."

Thunder rumbled and shook the old house. Rosey came running in from the kitchen and plopped down at Dad's feet.

"I think you're going to be better off away from here," Mom said. "I mean, surely they're not going to follow us out on tour."

"Look, we can sit here all day and fret about all the things they may do." Her dad stood. "That Scripture kept coming to me all night: 'To live is Christ and to die is gain.' I just feel like God's saying, 'You can live flat-out for Me. Boldly. Even during this trial.' And if something should happen to us, we go to be with Him—"

"Call me immature or unspiritual," Everett paced, "but I guess I'm just not ready to die. And I don't want you guys to get hurt because of me! I've brought so much heavy stuff into your lives… You know, I can read the Word and talk spiritual, but this—this is tough. Sometimes this whole existence just overwhelms me."

Karen turned him slightly and rested her hands on his waist. "You're doing so well, Everett Lester."

Her father reached for Ev's neck with his big hand. "We're proud of you, son. A lot of people in your shoes would have folded by now. You keep pressin' on."

"I can't stop thinkin' about Eddie." Everett turned his face away from them toward the rain. "Madison pleaded with him to accept Christ. I mean, she begged him. Maybe he will—or did…"

"Maybe so." Karen hugged him. "And maybe you had something to do with it."

They stood there together, the four of them. As they did, Karen could almost feel the fire—the passion—burning inside Everett, to share what God had done in his life. Though all around her, she could sense the other fire, too, the one that was testing their faith so severely.

Suddenly, the rain came hard. Karen had never heard it pour so loudly.

At that moment she was sure that each of them was thinking the same thing: *God's here with us. Alive. Pouring down on us. Filling us. Letting us know—we can go through the flames.*

When Karen knocked softly and entered Wesley's hospital room—followed by Sheila and Everett—she found Madison asleep on a narrow rollaway next to her brother. He was awake, sitting up against two pillows, watching MTV with the volume low. The Bible Cassidy had given him was closed and sitting next to him on the bed.

Sheila made her way through the maze of furniture and hugged Wesley, with little response. "How'd you sleep?"

He shrugged.

"Better than me." Madison groaned and rolled over. "I watched him sleep most of the night. This thing," she pounded the cot, "should be outlawed."

"Listen," Karen said, "Ev and I can go down to the snack bar for a little while, if you guys need some time."

"No, that's okay." Madison yawned and stretched. "Anything new on Dad?"

"Not yet," Sheila said.

Madison sat up. "I've got to get freshened up."

"Well, Twin Streams is all yours," Everett said. "You have your key?"

"Yeah. I'll go get a hot shower and change."

"Help yourself to anything," Karen said. "There's plenty of food in the fridge and pantry."

Madison found her purse on the floor and ambled over to a large mirror above the sink. "How long's it going to take to get the house fixed, Mom?"

"They said two or three days." Sheila stood. "I still need one more cup of coffee. Haven't quite filled my tank yet. I'll walk down with you, honey."

Madison finished fluffing her hair, rinsing her mouth, and putting on some lipstick, then headed for the door with her mother in tow. "I'll be back in a couple of hours. Wes, see you later."

He looked over and raised a hand. "Thanks for staying."

"You're welcome. You need anything while I'm out?"

"How 'bout a Big Mac and fries? The food in here stinks."

Madi laughed. "We can arrange that."

Everett gathered up the blue blanket from the rollaway chair and handed it to Karen, who folded it while he lifted the cot and rolled it back into position within the chair. Then he found the cushion, put it in place, and offered Karen the seat.

Everett pulled another chair next to Karen and sat. "You doing okay, Wes?"

"Depends what your definition of 'okay' is."

Everett cleared his throat. "I know you've had your share of pain and troubles, but I think it's time we cleared the air, got things out in the open."

Reflex forced Karen's hand over her mouth. She was somewhat taken aback by Everett's timing but never by his boldness.

"What's there to get into the open?"

"We had some vandalism at our house." Everett stared directly into Wesley's eyes, which couldn't hold his gaze. "One of our dogs was killed. We saw a white Yukon. What do you know about it?"

Wesley's eyebrows arched, he shook his head, and smiled. "Nothin'," his voice cracked. "There're a lot of white Yukons out there, in case you haven't noticed."

Karen's stomach gurgled acidic. Everett glanced at her with his mouth shut tight, then looked back at Wesley.

"What about the meth lab in your basement?"

"What business is it of yours?"

"It became our business the night you killed our dog and drove over our manger scene!" Karen squeezed Everett's hand. He lowered his voice and slowed down. "It became our business when Karen found the lab in your basement, and you pulled a gun on her behind her back."

"I don't have to take this." Wesley gritted his teeth.

"We've been patient with you," Everett said. "We've tried to help. The least you can do is be honest—"

"So I tried to cook some meth." Wesley sneered. "What's the big deal? Shoot, you work your buns off to make enough for a couple bumps. It's not even worth it. I know a guy who deals the stuff in mass quantity, some big operation in Pennsylvania. I don't need to be cookin' the stuff myself. It was just an experiment."

"What about the gun you pointed at Karen?"

Karen looked down and waited, barely able to breathe.

"I don't know what you're talkin' about."

"That's lame."

You tell him!

"If I did that, it was because of the meth." Wesley scowled. "Stuff makes me insane."

"Okay, what about this Tony Badino?" Everett said. "He's your dealer friend, isn't he?"

"I figured you knew."

"Is he out to get me for some reason? Maybe you both are…"

Wesley's head was down, and he fidgeted with his hands, but his eyes eventually found Everett. "I think you may be paranoid."

Everett's face reddened. He stood and walked to the sink. Karen sat rigid on the edge of her seat.

Everett leaned back against the sink, crossed his arms, and glared at Wesley. "A brick came through the window of my home. Part of our manger scene reappeared with animal blood all over it. I don't call that paranoid; I call it ticked off at the cowards who did it!"

Wesley's eyes opened wide. "I didn't have anything to do with those things, I swear."

Oh, how I want to believe that.

"Okay." Everett threw his hands up and paced. "Let's just look ahead for a minute."

Don't let him off that easy, babe!

"What's gonna happen when you get out of Horizons? Tony Badino's gonna want to run with you again."

Wes looked out the window. "Gotta stay away from him."

"When's the last time you saw him?" Karen finally got up the gumption to speak.

He pursed his lips and shrugged. "Shoot, my memory's still fried."

"It's been a while, though?" Karen pictured Tony, sucking on his cigarette as he passed her on his way into the hospital. "Maybe back when you got shot in the wrist at the range?"

"That was it, probably. It's all pretty foggy."

Is it foggy? Or are you lying?

"Thing is, you need to have something to keep you occupied

when you get out." Everett leaned on the back of his chair. "A job or classes or something."

"That's what they preach at Horizons." Wesley shrugged. "Stay busy. Keep your mind on other things."

He needs to get a college education. But he'd never cut it socially.

"I got an idea," Everett blurted out. "How would you like to come on tour with us?"

Karen's head jerked toward him. She may have even let out a gasp as her mind reeled and her body stiffened.

"Thirty-six cities. You could work with the roadies or the sound crew. We could find something for you; pay you, of course." The enthusiasm on Everett's face dissolved the instant he made eye contact with Karen, who was too shell-shocked to let out the scream that was bridled in her throat.

"His doctors," Karen said. "We'd have to check with his doctors, and the staff at Horizons." She glared at Everett, her whole face on fire. "We don't know how much longer they'll want him to stay, or if he'd be up to all that travel. That's nothing to rush into."

"Actually," Wesley said, "the head honcho from Horizons was here this morning. She talked with my doc, and they agreed I'm good to go back later today. I'll be done in rehab in three to five days. So, maybe that would be a plan. It sounds cool."

"Hold on," Everett mumbled. "I may have spoken too soon…"

Ya think!

"Before I jump the gun, I better check with Gray first, see if there's even a spot—"

"You don't want me to go, do you?" Wesley raised his chin toward Karen.

"It's not that," she stammered, forcing a ceramic smile. "I…I just think we need to talk about it more first—Ev and I—and pray about it. That's a big commitment for all of us. I would feel responsible—"

"I am an adult, Aunt Karen."

"Wes, I jumped the gun." Everett nodded at him. "I'm sorry,

dude. My mind gets ahead of my mouth sometimes."

It's a little late now. You invited him, and I'm the one throwing a wet blanket on it.

Wesley's face went sour, and he stuck his hands in the air. "Hey, no worries. If you don't think you can trust me—"

"Wesley…" Her teeth gnashed and her head shook ever so slightly toward Everett. Taking a deep breath, she closed her eyes and contemplated before she spoke. "This tour means so much. It's going to have eternal consequences. We're all going to be working very hard, and not without opposition. For us, it's a mission. And someone's got to make sure we stay 100 percent focused on that mission. Part of that falls on me. I need to look out for Everett, make sure he's not overloaded—"

"And you think I'm gonna be the needy child."

This whole thing was out of hand! Satan was having a field day, and Karen had had enough. "Look, I don't know if this tour is the best place for you to learn to live again without meth, not to mention the fact that you…"

"Just tried to commit suicide." Wesley gazed at Karen with apathetic eyes.

"Okay, okay." Everett stood and walked between them. "This is my fault, Wes. I should have put more thought into this before opening my big mouth. Karen's right—"

"I mean, I understand Everett's intentions," Karen interjected, "and I want to help… But we have an obligation. If you come, Wes, I would feel divided, like I have an equally important obligation—"

"Forget it!" Wesley crossed his arms and forced a fake laugh. "I don't want to be your *obligation*. I've been that to Eddie and Sheila my entire life! I'm not about to become your ball and chain."

"Wesley, I didn't mean it like that," Karen said. "Please…"

Everett closed his eyes, shook his head, and turned away.

Karen crept to the edge of her seat. "Try to understand."

Wesley fumbled for the remote, lifted it toward the TV, and hit the power button, as if he were pulling the trigger on a gun.

35

Everett was allowed to make one visit to Horizons. That frigid Wednesday afternoon after the band had finished practicing, he picked up Wesley in the Nissan and drove him 120 miles north to Schenectady for the memorial service of his friend, Cassidy Hope Collins.

Scores of teenagers packed the local Presbyterian church; some of them recognized Everett. Of the people who spoke—from the young and old to the punk and paralyzed—each told of a girl who was selfless, who shone like the sun with a chronic smile and a habit of helping others.

With a steady flow of tears, tissues, and laughter, they said Cassidy loved God and people. She wasn't without her problems, having hit several months of hard times in the end; mixing with the wrong crowd and bad drugs; and ultimately, unable to pull out of the tailspin.

But they sang anyway. And they burned candles in shaky hands. And their faces glowed as they prayed and worshiped and celebrated into the night.

Wesley sat on the front of his seat most of the time, with his head craning over the balcony railing. The only time he glanced at Everett was when he sensed his uncle watching him, and then he did so without expression.

During the ride back to Horizons, Wesley's voice came out of the darkness. "The way those people talked, they made it sound like she was really into religion." He mentioned again that Cassidy had given him her Bible.

"Yeah." Everett kept his eyes on the road. "She sounded like quite a girl."

"I couldn't really tell that about her. I mean, I knew there was something different. We connected. She was interested in me, but she never preached."

Everett was pleased Wesley was opening up. "Did she mention God to you?"

"I guess so—once or twice."

They rolled on in silence for several moments.

"You doubt she was a Christian, don't you?" Wesley said.

"Not at all. I didn't know her. And that's not for me to say."

"If she believed in God, how could she die like that? OD, I mean?"

Whoa. Where did that come from? Everett's mind blanked out for a few seconds under the pressure. *Just be real. Talk to him like a friend.*

"Christians can get corrupted like anyone else," Everett said, "if they expose themselves to the wrong surroundings, the wrong people."

"That doesn't sound like a very powerful religion to me."

"Hey, all I can do is speak for myself. I was high every waking hour for what, like fifteen years? Rotten to the core. But thanks to Karen, I found out there was a loving God who wanted to have a relationship with me—"

"Oh, geez, here we go."

"You see the proof in me, Wesley. You're not blind. Maybe you just don't want to accept the fact that Christ has come inside and made me new and that He can do the same for you."

"Back to my original question: If Cassidy was a Christian, how could she be lured right back into the meth scene?"

"I can't answer for Cassidy—"

"Cop-out."

"Look. God's made me salt and light. He said the sick are the ones who need a doctor. So I interact with unbelievers and build relationships. But that doesn't mean I hang out at bars and overnight parties where there are drugs and booze and things that are going to tempt me."

"Are you still tempted?"

"Of course," Everett said. "I'm human. I still get tempted to sin, just like everybody else."

"How do you say no?"

"I try to let God fight my battles." Everett looked straight out into the night. "When I'm doin' well, I give up and He runs the show. But I definitely have my weak moments when it's not like that. Are you worried about being tempted when you get out?"

The Nissan hummed along quietly for about a mile.

"Have you ever heard voices," Wesley asked, "in your head?"

Now we may be getting somewhere.

"Back when I was doping, I thought I did. I opened myself up to that stuff. Why? Do you think you're hearing something?"

"Madison's a Christian now, isn't she?"

This is like ping-pong!

"Yeah. Yeah, she is," Everett said. "I'm happy for her… Have you heard voices?"

Wesley turned and stared out the partially foggy passenger window. "I've heard something."

"What?"

"I don't want to say."

"Is it bad? I mean, what's it saying? Is it telling you to do something?"

"I don't want to say!"

"Do you hear it when you're high or straight?"

"Mostly when I'm comin' down from a high or cravin' it."

"Is it something—?"

"It's real."

"It may seem real. It may be real. But Wes, if it's telling you to do something wrong, then it's a lie. That's how you can know."

"Do you think my old man's dead?"

Wesley was staring straight ahead when Everett peered over at him.

"He may be, Wes. I hate to say it, but he may be."

After getting Wesley checked back in for one of his last nights at Horizons, Everett began the fifteen-mile trek back to Bedford in the frozen blackness. What would his nephew think about when he laid his head on his pillow that night? What would become of him? Everett cringed when he admitted how easy it would be—how likely, even—for Wesley to slip back into the same drug-induced lifestyle as Cassidy had.

He reached for his ringing phone. It was Mary calling from Ohio. His sister had seen on CNN that Dominic Badino had been set free, following lengthy questioning by NYPD detectives. Everett also confirmed that there was still no sign of Eddie and no valid leads.

"How's Wesley coming along?" she asked.

"Physically, he's good. Mentally, he's up against it. There's a lot of baggage."

"Are Sheila and Madison still staying at Twin Streams?"

"Yeah, at least until all the damage is fixed at their place," Everett said. "It's been good for them. The band's been in and out practicing all week. Jacob and Sarah are there. All good distractions."

"Do you think Jerry and I should try to come?"

"Not now." He sighed. "There's nothing you can do. The tour's ready to kick off and we'll be gone. Madison's gonna join us as often as she can, at least on weekends. I'll tell you, I'm ready to get out of here for a while."

"Are the police doing all they can? I mean, are they on this thing?"

"Oh, yeah. I've been talking on and off with a couple detectives, even some FBI guys, feeding them info. They'll let me know the second anything turns up."

"What do you mean, 'feeding them info'?"

"I've been telling them as much as I know about this whole mob thing, Dominic Badino, his son, everything I've seen. They want the Mendazzo family, bad."

"Dangerous, Ev."

"No kidding!" A pressure valve was releasing just talking to her. "I thought Badino was gonna be satisfied letting Eddie keep betting and me paying his debts, but it went way past that. It got personal. These mob families put their honor above everything else, even money. And in their rulebook, I've dishonored them."

"Well, if you think they'll try to do something to you, where does that leave Eddie?"

"That's what worries me." As he maneuvered the backroads from Stamford to Bedford, Everett told her more about the continuing Wesley saga.

"Karen was so ticked at me for inviting him on the tour."

"Well, you should have asked her first, ding-a-ling!"

"Believe me, I know that! Can we drop it? The thing is, Wesley wants to come with us, but Karen's still getting red flags, big-time."

"And you're not?" Mary said.

"I have my doubts. I do. But I just keep thinking about what Karen did for me, just kept reaching out, loving me. I feel like maybe I'm supposed to be the one who does that for Wesley."

"She's concerned about the tour, about all of you, and your safety. It's understandable," Mary said. "She's probably having a hard time getting past having a gun pulled on her. I don't blame her!"

"I know…"

"Ev, here's the thing: If God wants Wesley to go on this tour with you guys, He'll have to change Karen's mind. That's all there is to it. But you guys definitely need to be in agreement."

"If Wes *isn't* supposed to come, I want Him to change *my* heart. Because right now, I still feel like he's supposed to be with us the night we open at Madison Square Garden."

"Well, then," Mary said, "we'll just have to see what God does, won't we?"

The lights were dim at Twin Streams, and the old house was silent as Everett entered the kitchen through the garage, thankful that Jacob was there to watch over things—two things in particular: Karen and Sarah.

There were no notes for him on the island. Rosey stretched and greeted him with a wagging tail. He gave her a small dog biscuit from her treat box in the pantry, turned off the few lamps that were still on, and sauntered back to the master bedroom.

"You still awake, babe?" he whispered toward the big bed.

"Yeah." Karen pulled the covers down, sat up, and turned on a small lamp next to her. "I've been waiting for you. How'd it go?"

"Great." He bent over, kissed her, then began unbuttoning his shirt and walking to his dresser. "The service was a tearjerker. Cassidy was something special."

"How'd Wesley do?"

"He was glued. He opened up on the way home. It was good."

She crawled across the bed in her red flannel pajamas, which were dotted with reindeer and snowmen, and patted the mattress. "Come here and sit down a minute."

"Uh-oh," he teased. "What's this about?"

Everett plopped down on the bed and Karen smiled and rubbed his shoulders.

"I've been thinking about Wesley and the tour."

He sighed and pretended to faint, flopping back on the bed with his arms over his head.

"Look at me." Karen leaned over him with a hand on his chest. "I talked to the folks about it, then Sheila and Madison. We all want Wesley to come on tour."

He could only lie there and stare at those gray-green eyes.

"Well? Are you happy?"

He grabbed her and brought her down in a bear hug, and her laughter came muffled against his chest.

"Are you sure, babe?"

"Yes."

"What changed your mind?"

"My old scrapbook, the one of you and DeathStroke. Madison wanted to see it. I looked at you, the way you were, and I figured if God could save one Lester who was so messed up…"

She lifted up to look at him, and he swept several lengths of blond hair behind her ear.

"I can't believe you," he said. "You're so unselfish."

"No, I'm not. I still have my reservations." She ran a hand through his hair. "But Mom and Dad thought it would be good for him, especially after the suicide attempt. And it's good for him to be away from Tony Badino during this critical recovery period, right?"

"That's right."

She smiled and bobbed her head. "So, we're on. Sign him up."

"Now, remember, I'm not promising anything," Everett said. "This could backfire."

"We'll just take our chances, won't we?"

On the last day of rehearsal at Twin Streams, the day before the Living Water tour was set to kick off at New York City's famed Madison Square Garden, Everett and Karen gathered everyone in the basement studio, including Gray, the whole band, Jacob and Sarah, Sheila, and Madison.

"Everybody just find a seat somewhere," Everett said, standing next to Karen at an easel covered by a navy sheet. "That's good…anywhere. Oz, pull up that stool from the kitchen. Gray, can you get Sarah that chair from the sound booth?"

As each person found a place, the lively chatter quieted. The people in the room looked tired but excited, like they do before a NASA launch.

"Well, we made it." Everett paused to enjoy the smiles and congratulations. "Tomorrow night's been a long time coming. How do you feel?"

"Yow!" shouted drummer Oz Dublin, as chatter and clapping broke out around the windowless room. Karen and Everett looked at each other and laughed heartily. "Living Water!" yelled guitarist Randy White.

Everett scanned the room, looking from face to face to face. "Guys, Jesus said if you drink the well water, the common water, you're gonna thirst again. And we know from Queens and Miami that many of the people who are gonna be coming to our shows have tried all the common things of this world but have found no contentment. Sound familiar?"

He reached out and took Karen's hand. "We have the chance—each of us—to help people drink *living water*, so they'll never thirst again. And that water will become like a well in them, springing up to eternal life."

When he squeezed Karen's hand and let go, her slender face turned slightly pink and she stepped forward, clasping her hands at her waist. "I just want to say how incredible the music is that you guys have created. Each song ministers to me, and I believe so much in what we're doing. May God be exalted on this tour."

Karen crossed her arms and looked down. "What I'm about to show you is such a God-thing…excuse me." She put a fist to her mouth, cleared her throat, and blinked back the tears. "Gray called me a while back. He told me when SoundSystems came on board, they wanted new artwork for the tour poster and asked if I had any ideas." She snickered. "All I could think of was this beautiful painting of a waterfall I had seen. It had Living Water written all over it."

She hoisted the navy cloth up into the air like a magician waving a piece of silk in a magic show. Madison let out a squeal before both of her hands muzzled her mouth, and she bent over weeping. Her mother gasped and draped her arms around her daughter, not taking her eyes off of the concert poster for one second.

"Everybody," Karen announced above the clamor, "my talented niece, Madison Lester, painted this picture, and as you can see, it is *the* brand-new, official poster for this year's Living Water tour!" Karen knelt to hug Madison, who was beaming. Others in the room arose, admired the poster, and congratulated the artist.

As Everett surveyed the lively room, it touched him as a most bittersweet moment. His heart rejoiced over the newfound faith of his beautiful niece, who had a full and promising life in front of her. Yet behind the mask, Everett was unable to shake the almost palpable fear that taunted him.

Someone's going to be in the crowd at a concert. Or in the dark hallway of a hotel. Tony Badino, the wiseguys, someone. They'll have guns, and they'll be there with a job to do. They won't think twice before ending my life.

Then Karen will be alone.

This must be how you felt, Lord—knowing the cross was coming...

It was, indeed, a bittersweet moment.

36

Dark was descending on New York City by four-thirty in the afternoon the first day of the Living Water tour. One of the digital clocks outside a bank on Thirty-fourth Street read thirty-one degrees. Snowflakes the size of quarters bombed the dingy city, cloaking it in a beautiful white blanket as people weighed down in heavy parkas rambled to and fro.

After the two black stretch limousines passed slowly through a security checkpoint and approached a ramp leading down to the belly of Madison Square Garden, they slowed and came to a halt.

"Mr. Lester," the driver of the first car looked straight ahead, "we got a situation."

Everett peered out the tinted windows. Blocking the ramp to the Garden's backstage auto entrance were dozens of people—a sea of long hair, tattoos, and soaked denim. Leaving several homemade fires, the revelers staggered toward the limos holding everything from beer cans and cigarettes to liquor bottles and pot pipes—and signs: Go Home Lester, TRAITOR, DeathStroke or Die! and others.

Gray was on his cell phone to security within seconds.

The interior of the car darkened as the mob engulfed it, beating on the windows—some so hard the glass was sure to shatter. Karen scooted close to Everett and squeezed his arm. "I feel like I'm suffocating," she whispered.

"Ahhh!" Sarah pointed to a gun that someone had pressed sideways against the window closest to her.

"Charlie, start driving!" Gray clapped his phone shut. "Security says they'll back down if we keep moving. Straight ahead. Down the ramp!"

As the car lurched forward, the crazed crowd began to rock the limo—up and down. Many of the faces outside were enraged. The people screamed obscenities while bashing the vehicle with their fists and flying feet. Others were howling with laughter and falling down drunk as the fancy car bounced even harder.

"Ma-an!" Wesley's voice broke with the bump of the car. "I guess the diehard DeathStrokers are alive and well!" He studied the faces and bodies pressed against the window twelve inches from his face. "I hope the clientele inside is a little bit more hospitable—"

"Would you be quiet." Madison scooted closer to Jacob.

As the limo pressed forward, some of the people outside moved along with it, some fell away, and others broke into fistfights.

"Lord, just get us inside," Karen mumbled.

Wesley pounded the flat of his hand against a bearded face smashed against the glass.

"Cut it out!" Madison yelled. "You wanna get us killed?"

"He's cussing at us!" He gave the guy a nasty look. "What losers."

"Cool it, Wes." Everett placed a hand on Wesley's shoulder. "We'll be fine."

"Check it out!" Wesley peered straight ahead as the mob parted, revealing twenty-five or so police officers who had lined the underground entrance, wearing helmets and riot gear and wielding shields and billy clubs. "You still got some clout, Uncle Everett."

The instant the front of the car tipped forward and descended, light filled the interior as the sea of clinging people began dropping away, some falling down on the slippery ramp.

The lead limo took one last hit—a blow to the hood from a flying Rolling Rock beer bottle—before it disappeared into the mouth of the famed arena.

Even with the blizzard, more than 11,250 people filed into Madison Square Garden for opening night. There were individuals of all colors, homeless walk-ins, church youth groups, middle-aged couples, DeathStroke diehards, tattooed teenagers, punks, believers, unbelievers, and everyone in between.

Throughout the evening, two or three fights broke out, and the band had to stop playing twice as security personnel stepped in to settle the disturbances. Everett had played the Garden a number of times in his DeathStroke days, but never sober—and never with the depth of meaning it had this night.

After the last song, "Blind/Faith," the dazzling stage faded to black. While Everett and the band wiped the sweat from their spent bodies backstage with large terrycloth towels, handed out by Wesley, the ovation climbed to a deafening roar. Everett peered out at the sea of blue cell phone lights and yellow flames that dotted the darkness like a hillside of lightning bugs. Squeezing Karen's hand, he felt twenty again, as if it were his first time playing a major venue.

Madison, Jacob, and Sarah were latched together, arm in arm, laughing their heads off. As he stared out at the throng, even Wesley appeared in awe of the Spirit consuming the place. The thunderous volume of the audience made speaking impossible, and Everett was glad for that; it helped him keep focused. Everything looked and felt so crystal clear to him. His purpose tonight was unmistakable.

Wesley approached him with a big white towel draped over his shoulder. His brown hair was about an inch long and starting to curl. He was still thin, but finally seemed to be getting some color in his plain face. He leaned close to Everett. "You want the black Fender?"

Everett rested a hand on Wesley's shoulder and bent toward him. "No," he yelled. "Gibson, acoustic." Wesley nodded and disappeared.

By the time roadies led the band back onstage by flashlight, roses and carnations were strewn everywhere, as were hats and T-shirts and even several old DeathStroke albums.

"Thanks for coming!" Everett's voice boomed into the blackness. "Whoa." He was temporarily blinded by a roving white spotlight. "Here I am." He chuckled, adjusting the mike stand in front of him.

"You guys are troopers for coming out on a night like this!" The crowd went haywire. "They tell me we got about eight inches of white stuff out there right now." Everett suspected it was the cocaine users in the crowd who went especially ballistic with that comment.

"This song we're about to do is special to me." The boisterous crowd grew quiet. "I wrote part of it a long, long time ago, and then I finished it just recently. If you'll listen to the words, I think most of you will be able to relate. This is called 'Deep Inside…'"

The crack of Oz Dublin's drumsticks sent the band strumming into a dramatic, melodious intro, which included deft harmonica work by Randy White and a blazing violin riff by Lola Shepherd. Everett's commanding voice rang out like a raspy storyteller of old.

> *Can anybody hear me? Hear me?*
> *Does anybody care how I feel?*
> *Those closest, they've abandoned me.*
> *My friends, they've proven they aren't real.*
>
> *And so begins the hatred, self-pity,*
> *Resenting anyone who says that they've found love.*
> *Inside I'm like a ticking time bomb,*
> *Knowin' my push will soon become a shove—*
> *It always does, it always does…*

So I strap on this here guitar,
I grab this mike in my shaking hand.
I cry out for your attention, I yell,
"I'll become famous—me and my rock 'n' roll band!"

And whaddya know, I'm a star now.
Whaddya know, I'm a wealthy man!
I finally made your heads turn, didn't I? Didn't I?
Now I'm the rock idol of every fan.

But what about deep inside, deep inside,
Beneath this gleaming armor?
What about deep inside, deep inside,
Behind this dark star you see onstage—
Where I'm all the rage, all the rage…

Let me confess, I've been a two-faced liar,
Yeah, what you see ain't always what you get.
Inside I'm just a frightened traveler.
Yeah, inside there's a man you've never met.

So I hit rock bottom and that's when I found Him.
Yeah, I was all curled up and a-waitin' there to die.
Then I realized, "Man, you're nothin', you're no one!"
I confessed my sins and reached toward the sky.
So high, so very high…

My friend, that's when He came to me,
Ridin' on the clouds He crafted.
Yeah, that was the day He filled my cup,
He filled it up, He filled it up!

I had never grasped such glory,
I had never seen the sacred fire by night,
I had never heard a voice like the waters,
I had never seen feet and eyes so bright.
Until that night, until that night…

When I invited Him deep inside, deep inside,
O Lord, look within, forgive my sin, fill my cup.

Come deep inside, deep inside,
Lord, make me new, tell me what is true, help me to follow You.

Live deep inside, deep inside,
Jesus, let me know, You overflow, I've nothing to fear,
'cause You are here…

Everett noticed it happening three-quarters of the way through the song. Like children playing some sort of game on a massive playground, one by one, people all over the arena began dropping out of sight. Near and far. High and low. Each one seemed to disappear in an eerie silence that rested somewhere above the rhythm of the music.

Looking closer, it began to dawn on Everett that people were kneeling, faces to the ground, some sprawled out prone in the aisles. And they were praying. They were repenting. Yes, they were inviting Christ to come deep inside, deep inside.

It was the same in Boston, Montreal, Philly, and Baltimore. As word spread about what the media was calling the Living Water "revival," several venues on the tour were proving too small. Half-mile lines were reported as much as twenty-four hours before some shows. By the time the tour reached Pittsburgh, it had become an international phenomenon.

"I'm keeping a scrapbook of everything, all the magazine and newspaper clippings I can get my hands on," Madison said after meeting up with Everett, Wesley, Karen, Jacob, and Sarah at Marriott City Center in downtown Pittsburgh. "The New York media is going absolutely nuts, Uncle Everett. You're going to be mobbed when you get back home. Did you see yesterday's *USA Today?* It said one to two thousand people are accepting Christ at *each show.* No one's seen anything like it since the old revival days."

"To you I suppose that means the ancient Billy Graham crusades," Everett teased.

"Very funny." Madison pretended to punch him.

"You're selling a lot of posters, aren't you?" Everett laughed.

"Oh, by the way," she said, "I've decided I want you to keep the money we make from the posters—"

"What?" Wesley broke in with a scowl. "Those things are gonna bring in a chunk of change."

"That's going to be my donation for the tour."

"You're crazy!" Wesley barked. "We're gonna need that money. You know we've got big-time debt—"

"Chill out!" she said. "What is your problem?"

"Wait a minute." Everett stepped in. "Madison, you don't have to do that. But if you're being led to, go for it. I think it's beautiful. And Wes, I promised Madi the proceeds from the posters. You do what you want with your pay."

"My pay isn't gonna compare to the stinkin' money those posters bring in!" He tramped to the window of Karen and Everett's room, put his hands on his waist, and stared across the street at sun-drenched Mellon Arena where the band was scheduled to perform that night, all the while mumbling something under his breath.

Ingrate. Everett was mentally scripting a verbal lashing but caught Karen's watchful eye and played the good boy.

Madison stepped in and changed the subject. "No recent news on Dad?"

"Nothing yet today," Sarah said.

Wesley fidgeted with the window locks, messed around with the heater controls, then made his way to the large entertainment center where he found the remote, flicked on the TV, and surfed till he stopped on *Judge Judy*.

"Nancy Grace did a show last night about Dad and the tour," Wesley said.

"We saw it," Sarah said.

"She thinks he's gone for good," Wesley said. "She was all over Mendazzo, Badino—the whole clan. Aren't you worried those mobsters might be after you?" Wesley looked over at Everett.

"It's crossed my mind." Everett tried to chuckle but was confronted once again by his very real fears.

"Nancy Grace made it sound like you've been leaking information to the FBI."

"I've told them all I know, because I want to find your dad," Everett said. "Besides, those scumbags from the Mendazzo family belong behind bars."

"On a brighter note." Madison crossed to Wesley, took the remote from him, zapped off the TV, and dropped the gadget on the couch. "I've got some good news." She looked at her brother to make sure he was listening. "Mom started AA on Monday."

"That is great news," Jacob said.

Wesley pursed his lips, shook his head, and wandered in the direction of the bathroom.

"She didn't miss a meeting all week. Some days she even went twice. They hooked her up with a sponsor she really likes—"

"Believe it when I see it." Wesley scooped a clear cup into a plastic bucket of ice.

"Hey, she's trying!" Madison yelled.

"That's right," Sarah said. "Poor thing has been through so much."

"She misses Daddy," Madison said. "She told me she wants to be ready for him."

Karen pulled Madison close as her eyes filled with tears.

For a moment, Wesley gazed at Karen and Madison. He seemed to be off in another world somewhere. Everett walked over and placed a hand on his shoulder.

"You okay?"

"No!" Wesley flinched, waking from his daydream with a start, and shaking Everett's hand away. He checked his watch. "I need to get going...Gonna go crash for a while before tonight."

"Wesley," Karen stepped toward him, "are you sure you don't want a Coke or some pretzels—?"

"No." He headed for the door, wiping his lips hard with the back of his wrist. "I'll meet up with you guys later. Call my room, would you, if there's any word on the old man?"

Everett and Karen looked at each other. After several seconds, she gave him a half smile, and he returned it. Nothing needed to be said. They knew this was the beginning of a long journey. Everett just hoped there wouldn't be too much turbulence from Wesley along the way.

37

Wesley writhed on his hotel bed like a fish out of water. Though he wore only baggy gray boxers, his head was soaked in sweat. The irresistible, cursed cravings were coming in waves—heat waves. They'd crept up on him and begun to take over his body, threatening to obliterate his soul.

Blinds drawn and sheets strewn, he sat up to the edge of the bed and slammed his head into his hands. Like a werewolf at full moon, he was morphing into another person, and there was nothing he could do about it. The drug called out to him like food to the starving.

Leave me alone!

Whacking things around on the nightstand, he found cigarettes. Lighting one, he flopped onto his back and exhaled straight up toward the ceiling.

"Vengeance," came the whisper.

He scampered to the bathroom sink. Cigarette in fingers, he examined himself. Skinny white boy. Eyes sunken. Ugly.

"Vengeance."

He jerked around, scanned the room, and ran to the far wall. Putting his ear up, he listened. But all he could hear were the hundreds of crawling creatures that seemed to invade his body. Scratching hard at his arms and scalp, he paced the room.

"Now he's brainwashin' Madison… That money's ours."

To the sink he went, throwing a small white towel in and turning on the cold water. Wringing it out, he smeared his face and ran it down his arms and legs. Ripping open a plastic cup, he slurped water, swished, and spit.

"Mr. Jesus Man. Out to save the world…" He stomped to his brown suitcase, unzipped the side pocket, and pulled out his little brother's journal. Yanking the curtain open a foot to let some light in, he crossed the room with the little book open. "Didn't save my little brother, though, did He?"

Ripping through the pages, he stopped, scanned with shaking fingers, then tore through some more. "Ahhh!" He fired the book across the room, watching it bash a lampshade, ricochet into the wall, and drop to the maroon carpet. Then he fell to the floor, too, chewing fretfully at his cuticles.

"I don't want to do this," he wailed. "I don't want to be this way. Stop! I'm better. I'm better. I'm better. I'm clean. I don't have to listen to you, *devil*. I'm good, now. I can make it—"

The voice came low and sweet. "Think about the high."

"No!" he cried with his face to the floor.

"One bump. That's all. Let it take you away."

Resting all his weight on his elbows and knees, Wesley looked up at the lampshade he'd just hit—it was askew. He got up and marched toward it. Unscrewing the top, he lifted the shade, dropped it in a chair, and stared at the bulb. Then he unscrewed it. "Seventy-five watts." He could convert that thing into a meth pipe so fast…

"You *are* going to get him back for what he did to David."

"No!" Wesley jerked. "You can't make me. Please…don't make me."

"I know you'll do whatever I say."

His head snapped toward the talking wall. Then to the tapping—at the door.

He tiptoed toward it. "Who is it? I'm just gettin' up from a nap. Not dressed yet."

Tap, tap, tap.

"Who is it?"

Tap, tap, tap.

He shut one eye and peered through the peephole.

Larger than life, there was the devilish face of Tony Badino, his right eye twitching.

Everyone was snacking, sipping sodas, and doing their own thing in Karen and Everett's hotel room to waste time before the afternoon sound check.

Jacob looked up from his crossword puzzle. "I think that's your phone, Ev."

He eased up from the bed, where Karen had dozed off, and moved quickly to grab the phone from the black leather shoulder bag in the corner.

"Hello," he whispered, heading for the bathroom.

"Mr. Lester?"

"Yes. Who's this?"

"Oh, I'm so glad I caught you." The woman's voice shook. "It's Margaret Badino."

A sudden hollowness hit Everett's gut. He closed himself in the bathroom and locked the door.

"Hello?" she said.

"I was just finding some privacy." Everett's breathing was labored. "What can I do for you?"

"It's my son, Tony. He's left; he's not here."

"Mrs. Badino—"

"I went up to his apartment early this morning. His garment bag's gone."

"Excuse me. I don't mean to be rude, but I don't understand why you're calling me."

"Where are you, Mr. Lester?"

"Why do you want to know?"

"I found a scrap of paper in his wastebasket. It was burned, but I made out several flight numbers. I checked them on the Internet. Then I checked your concert schedule. Are you in Pittsburgh?"

The word *Pittsburgh* seemed to zap half of Everett's energy, and he debated whether to trust her.

"I'm at a pay phone, and I have to hurry. Please…are you in Pittsburgh?"

"Tell me what else you know."

"Oh my goodness, my husband's due back any second. He thinks I'm in a bookstore."

"Please, Mrs. Badino…"

"Tony had written down flight information for Pittsburgh, Cincinnati, Detroit, and others I couldn't read. Your website said—"

"Those are the cities we're playing next."

"That's why I'm calling! You said to…if I suspected anything. He's very confused, Mr. Lester. He's just not right. Ever since Erica. I told you about his girlfriend, who died."

"She'd become a Christian."

"Yes, and he never has been able to live with the fact that God took her."

What are you trying to say? Everett waited.

"He's been meeting on and off with my husband lately. The police have been watching the house. I don't know. I'm thinking all kinds of crazy things. I thought I should warn you. I see the good you're doing—for God. It's all over the news."

"You're sure Tony's gone?"

"Yes. I even called the body shop where he works. They said he took some vacation time. They didn't say how much."

"Please, can you call me if you find out anything else?" Everett said. "If he comes home…"

"Of course. I've got to go now. Godspeed, Mr. Lester."

Click.

Everett kept Mrs. Badino's call to himself during the afternoon sound check on the sleek, silver stage inside Mellon Arena. But when he found himself taking a breather backstage next to Jacob on a black trunk during a break, he figured it was time to open up.

"What's it mean, Ev?"

"We watch our backs."

"Yeah, but there are tons of people each night." Jacob held up his arms and looked around the massive arena. "Badino could be any-where."

Everett bent over. "Tell me about it."

This is nuts. Other people are gonna be in danger…

"We need to let security know," Jacob said. "Can we get a picture of this guy to circulate?"

"Only way to do that is to call his mom."

"Let me meet with security first. They may be able to get one, if he has any kind of record."

"Listen." Everett sat up and grabbed Jacob's wrist, stopping him from standing. "If anything happens to me—"

"We're not going to let anything happen to you."

"But if it does—"

"Stop it, Ev." Jacob stood. "Just stop it. I'm going to find the head of security. You just rock on, man. Leave this to me. Okay?"

Everett nodded. He trusted Jacob. But more than that, he focused on giving himself to God. Just relinquishing control. Falling into His hands.

Jacob began to walk away, then turned around. "Hey, where do you want to go to dinner before the show? I need to book something. You know of any good places?"

Everett chuckled at how nonchalantly Jacob had shifted gears. "There used to be a place that did great cheesesteaks. I think it was called the Upper Room or the Upper Deck, overlooks PNC Park—where the Pirates play."

"Sounds good." Jacob walked around the corner. Everett lifted a bottle of spring water to his lips, drinking half of it. One of the arena workers—a tall, blond woman with red cheeks and freckles—approached him hesitantly.

After being in the limelight for more than a decade, Everett could detect autograph seekers by their body language alone. This woman held out her Living Water poster.

"I'll be glad to," he said. "What's your name?"

"Beverly. My friends just call me Bev. But this isn't for me; it's for my son."

"I bet you didn't know, Bev, that my niece did the watercolor on this poster. Her name is—"

"Madison," she interrupted, smiling. "I know. I read it on there, in the small print. Plus, my son already knew all about it. He knows everything about you. Chad's his name."

Everett chuckled.

"I just wanted you to know, too, that Chad was…well, he was a bad one. Oh, forgive me." Her face scrunched up and turned red from the sentiment. "You…your music…he just loves you. And he loves God, because of you and what you stand for."

Words like that kept him going. "That means so much to me, Bev. Thanks for sharing that. Will Chad be here tonight?"

"He sure will." She grinned. "He's meeting me down here later when he gets off work."

Just as Everett's cell phone rang, he signed: *"Dear Chad—thanks for your support. Together, let's keep pressin' on till Jesus comes. Your friend, Everett Lester. Matthew 11:28–30."*

He answered the phone. "This is Everett."

"Hey, little brother."

"Hey, Mary." He waved good-bye to Bev. "What goes on?"

"Jerry and I can come to the show in Cinci!"

"Very cool."

"Can we meet and break bread and get backstage?" She giggled.

"Love it. Let me have Jacob call you to let you know where we're staying. He'll get your passes and all that."

"You holding up?"

"Doin' okay." He decided not to tell her about the call from Margaret Badino. "Can't wait to get out there tonight. A lot of other chaos is swirlin' around, but when I'm playing and sharing, that's when I feel most in tune with God."

He stood and walked onstage, picturing the arena packed with people.

"Ev, I had a dream last night. I'm not going to tell you what it was about, so don't bother asking. But afterward, I got up and prayed. Then I couldn't sleep, so I read for a while. Can I just share something with you, real quick?"

"Sure. Let's hear it."

He envisioned a gunman in the front row, only five feet from the stage.

"Okay, now remember, you know it's not like me to go around plying people with Scripture and telling them, the Lord sayeth."

He offered a polite laugh. "I know. Come on. Give it to me."

"It's in Psalm 140. Do you mind if we kind of say it like a prayer?"

"That sounds good." Everett walked farther onto the stage, crossed one arm, and closed his eyes.

"'Lord, deliver me from evil men,'" Mary's voice was clear and strong. "'Preserve me from the violent, who plot and stir up trouble all day long… Keep me out of their power… Let their plots boomerang. Let them be destroyed by the very evil they have planned for me. Let burning coals fall down upon their heads, or throw them into the fire, or into deep pits from which they can't escape.'"

The phone call ended, and Everett looked up. The gunman from his imagination was gone, and so were his fears. At least for now, anyway.

"What the heck are you doin' here?" Wesley opened the door slightly, and Tony barged into the room with a small leather bag slung over his shoulder.

"Let's get this party started!"

"Dude," Wesley closed the door and followed him in, "we got a show tonight. I told you—"

"I know what you told me. And I also know what you *want*." He spread the bag open on the bedspread and pulled out a small baggie full of yellowish crystal. "You wanna induuuuulge."

"You flew with that?" Wesley found his white T-shirt, threw it on, and tried to figure out how to get rid of this maniac.

"In the bag I checked. Along with some other goodies."

"You're dang lucky." Pulling on his baggy cargo jeans, Wesley stepped closer to the bed, secretly admiring Tony's stash while being bombarded by the "warning triggers" they'd taught him about at Horizons. "You alone?"

"Yeah. That weasel Brubaker was supposed to come, but he wimped out. Mama's boy."

Within minutes, Tony's coat was on the chair, and he was seated on the floor leaning against the bed with his legs crossed in front of him. Holding a meth-packed silver pipe in one hand, he masterfully waved his flaming Zippo beneath the bowl, heating it until the crystal began to smoke.

"Ah. Smell that?" He snickered. "Been a while for you. I bet you're ab-so-lute-ly dy-ing."

There was no avoiding the familiar smell. Probably putrid to the unknowing onlooker, it hit Wesley like sheer seduction and sent him back to a thousand all-nighters.

"Come on, dude." Tony puffed and toked. "This thing is firin' on all cylinders."

Wesley turned his back and pulled a dark green sweater over his head, then moved slowly toward a chair to put his socks and boots on. "What are you doing here?"

Tony held the smoke in his lungs and talked quickly and quietly at the same time. "You sit down with me and take a hit and I'll tell ya."

The phone rang.

"Yeah?" Wesley welcomed the distraction.

"Hey, brother," Madison said. "How you doing?"

"Okay," He looked around, realizing he'd just lied. "What's up?"

"We're having dinner early. A place called the Upper Deck. Uncle Everett says you're gonna love the cheesesteak; they're famous for it. Meet us in the lobby at five?"

He looked at the clock by the bed. Ten to four. "Sure."

"You all right?"

"Yeah." He glanced at Tony and the smoking bowl. "Just wakin' up…"

"See you downstairs."

After hanging up, Wesley walked into the bathroom and splashed cold water on his face. "Tell me why you're here," he said, with his face in one of the big white towels. "I gotta get going soon."

When he looked in the mirror, Tony was right behind him. "I said, do a bump with me, then I'll tell you what I'm doing here." He waved the smoking bowl in circles beneath Wesley's nose.

"Get that outta my face." Wesley spun away.

Tony's eyebrows arched, and his face contorted with rage. "Don't tell me Lester's gotten to you." He swept the coffeemaker, glasses, and toiletries off the granite counter in one fell swoop, sending them shattering and bouncing to the tile floor. "He's taken David! Now, you?"

"Dude, look." Wesley gulped. "I need to try this—"

"You can't do it, Lester!" Tony's nasty, twitching, demon-face was three inches from his. "It's *not* gonna last. You know that? *You're one of us!*"

Wesley looked around, dazed. "Who's 'us'?"

Tony's head dropped back with a ghoulish laugh.

Standing amid the broken glass, Wesley felt reality slipping away.

He looked in the mirror. Tony was howling, while his own face wore a peaked scowl. His face and neck were covered with red splotches from where he'd itched. Now he knew how David must have felt. It had been a despicable existence. And like his brother, Wesley wanted to be set free. Whether that meant getting high or dying, he just didn't know anymore. He didn't care.

"Come in here and do what you really wanna do!" Tony marched back into the bedroom, and Wesley followed like a zombie.

"Gimme that." Wesley grabbed the hot pipe, took it to his mouth with trembling hands, hit it long, and held the lethal fumes deep in his chest. "Whoa." The room spun like a merry-go-round as he opened his mouth in the shape of an O and exhaled like a fire-breathing dragon.

"That's what I'm talkin' about." Tony cackled. "Go 'head. Load up. You deserve it."

Wesley plunked down on the bed.

"Where you headed?" Tony dropped into the chair next to him.

Wesley ignored him, savoring another enormous hit.

"I said, where're you off to?"

"Dinner, supposedly." Wesley smirked. "But now, I'm not so sure."

They both laughed, and Tony waved for Wesley to keep the pipe.

It must have been five minutes later, after Wesley had fired up the remainder of the bowl, that Tony leaned forward and rested his elbows on his knees. "I'm here to make a hit."

"A hit?" Wesley chuckled. "What're you talkin' about?"

Tony glared at him, that wicked eye twitching again. "What do you think I'm talkin' about?"

"Dude, take it easy." Wesley's stomach bottomed out, and his face ignited with a hot flash. "What's goin' on?"

"What's goin' on is, I'm here to do the deed on your uncle. And I'm gonna need your help."

38

After the sound check, Everett and Karen met back at the
hotel room, finished cleaning up, and eased down on the
king-size bed, lying on their sides, face-to-face.

"You okay?" She ran her fingers through his dark hair.

"Tired, for some reason."

"You sure that's all?" she asked, knowing it wasn't.

"I guess I'm just feeling a lot of pressure." He closed his eyes.

She squeezed the back of his neck, then massaged his shoulders.
"Whatcha thinkin' about?"

He pursed his lips and looked her in the eye. "I got a call from
Margaret Badino before the sound check."

Karen sat up. The massage stopped. "And…"

"She thinks Tony might be following us."

"What?" Karen shouted, then stared at him as the words seemed
to buzz through her bloodstream.

"She found some notes he wrote, about plane tickets and cities."

Everett sat up, too. "His suitcase is gone. He's gone. He had all of our tour cities written down."

Karen stood and whirled around. "I can't believe this! We are literally being tracked down by this…this Satanist!"

"I've already discussed it with your dad. He's telling security. They'll pass out a photo…"

Karen's hands covered her mouth and nose as she wandered about the room, trying to keep her composure.

"Honey, it's gonna be okay." Everett went to her. "God loves us." He turned her toward him and smiled. "Isn't that what you've been drilling into my head ever since you were a teenager? Look, I'm scared, but I'm also determined to leave this in His hands. It's up to Him to protect us."

Good! She wrapped her arms around him.

"God's put this thing in my heart, to sing and share Him. Remember what you wrote to me in prison? They overcame him by the blood of the Lamb and the word of their testimony? I know we're where He wants us."

Oh, how she needed to hear him take a stand and say those words. She'd grown so tired of being the spiritual leader in their house.

He looked into her eyes and held her cheek in the palm of his hand. "You're beautiful, you know that?"

She grasped his wrist. "I'm proud of you, Ev."

They kissed for several moments, then Karen combed his hair behind his ear with her fingers. "You'd make such a good daddy, you know that?"

She searched his face for an initial, unspoken response. "Why shouldn't we adopt, Ev?"

His striking brown eyes didn't flinch. They were steady and true. "I've been waiting for you…to talk about it. I wanna know what you think."

She took a deep breath and held his gaze. "I saw a little girl in the lobby, in a wheelchair—"

"I saw her, too."

"I think about all that's happened to us." She placed her hand on his chest. "And I think, life's too short. There are children out there, somewhere, who need a loving home, a godly home, and all the things we can provide." Karen reached for his hand, interlocking their fingers.

"I've said all along, you're going to make the world's greatest mom, babe."

She giggled. And then they laughed. It was a sweet release. Even though they both knew the enemy could be just beyond their hotel room door, suddenly it didn't matter. For the moment, everything was right again. Everything was good.

Karen looked into the mirror and brushed her long blond hair while Everett changed shirts. In the reflection, she noticed he'd thrown on one of his favorite old faded T-shirts and begun putting things in his shoulder bag, as if he was dressed for the show.

She turned around and eyed the shirt. "Are you wearing that onstage?"

"Yep." He continued stuffing things into his bag.

"What gives? I thought you didn't want the tattoos to show."

He came over and kissed her. "I am who God made me, and I'm gonna start livin' like it."

Karen's insides swelled with gladness.

He returned her smile. "You think that's good?"

"I think that rocks, honey!"

It was one of those moments when they were really clicking, enjoying the beauty, humor, and charm God had given each of them—and the fact that He'd joined them together as one flesh.

Karen applied some pink lipstick that matched her velour sweater. "I don't know why, but I keep thinking about that Bible Wesley had in his hospital room. You saw it, didn't you?"

"Yeah. It was Cassidy's." He was about ready to take off.

"I know. Did you see what was underlined in it?"

"I did, but I forget…"

"When Mary poured perfume on Jesus' feet."

"Oh, yeah, and the disciples got ticked."

"Judas." She turned to face him. "That's when he betrayed Jesus."

Everett tossed the black bag over his shoulder and finally stood still for a second. "What's bothering you about it?"

"I just thought it was weird that, in the whole Bible, that story was the only thing underlined."

"I wonder who underlined it."

"Cassidy, I guess."

Everett looked at the clock. "Whoa. I've got to catch your dad and Gray about security for tonight. You wanna just meet in the lobby at five?"

"Okay."

He put his hands on her shoulders and kissed her, long and sweet. "I'm stoked about tonight." His smile lit up the room.

"I am too." She held his gaze as long as she could before he marched confidently out of the room.

Walking to the bed, she flopped down and rested her head on the shirt Everett had just taken off. She closed her eyes, nestled up to the shirt, and breathed it in—never wanting that smell to go away, never wanting to be without him.

"You work for Mendazzo, don't you?" Wesley stared curiously at Tony, holding the hot pipe in his fingers.

"I get my orders from my old man."

"Your old man's Mendazzo's captain."

"*Maybe.*"

"Then where's my dad?"

Tony dropped back in his chair. "Don't know nothin' about that."

I think you do, you crazy psycho.

"You did the hit in Canarsie, didn't you?"

"Take another bump, Lester."

Wesley ignored him. "Didn't you?"

"Maybe."

"Why my uncle?"

"Dude came into our house." Tony jumped to the edge of his seat. "Interrogated my mom. Narked on me. Then my old man! Every one of those things gets death in the Mendazzo family."

Wesley hoisted his legs over the edge of the bed and handed Tony the pipe. "Yeah, but he's been paying my old man's debts. Why would you want to hurt him, unless my old man's not comin' back?"

"Look, the rock star dug his own grave, Lester. Has nothin' to do with your old man. I told you, I don't know nothin' about that."

Wesley didn't know what to believe anymore. He hated himself for being so weak. He was just a miserable little meth head who was easily coaxed from one bad situation to the next. "I just don't see why you think you have to hurt—"

"You are so blind!" Tony stood and fired the pipe across the room, a shower of orange embers exploding as it hit the mirror and chipped the glass. "Dude's spreadin' lies! Just like all those other fundamentalist big shots. Spouting their empty promises. Nothin' but spiritual pipe dreams for the insecure. We gotta stop them."

Tony marched over to the pipe and stomped out the burning embers. "Thing you don't know is, I had a girl once named Erica. You hear me? *Erica.* I was gonna marry her, until some self-righteous Jesus freak like your uncle got ahold of her—"

"Wait a minute." The words left Wesley's mouth at the same time he figured it out. "Did your old man put you up to this—or is this *your* idea?"

Tony smacked Wesley's cheek so fast, he felt the sting before he saw the flashing hand. "Don't you question me." The wide-eyed, wicked-faced, talk-spitting grease monkey was within inches now. "The big Jesus tour's over. It's crucifixion time. And you're bringin' the nails."

What have I gotten myself into? This is nuts.

The dude belonged in a rubber room. Wesley didn't dare speak.

"I'm makin' the hit and need you to set him up, so it's nice and clean." Tony's oil-stained finger was in his face. "Besides, you got no choice in the matter."

Wesley could only stare at the huffing monster, putting a hand to his hot cheek and trying desperately to come back down to reality.

Maybe I should run. Right now. Just take off.

"Think about your little brother. What about him?" Tony seethed. "You just gonna let that go? You forgot that already? What about the journal and the Other Side? Your uncle needs to pay! If we don't get him back, who will?"

Wesley's mind sucked backward like a vacuum. Everything seared white and distant. A thousand images of David and his family morphed together into one high-speed flashback.

Then he heard the voice again.

Vengeance, Lester.

"What'd you say?" Wesley staggered toward the wall.

"I said, I'm willing to pay you," Tony's voice came from behind.

Wesley turned to see the goon holding up a wad of bills. "I'll give you three thousand bucks to line him up for me. All you gotta do is call him, tell him to come meet you. That's it. Your part's done."

Tony stuffed the money in Wesley's hand. He looked down at it. *Blood money.*

Who really cared what kind of money it was? Nothing mattered anymore. *My life's garbage anyway.*

"I'm bein' very generous with you, Wes, because we're partners.

Besides, if you don't do it, I can't promise what may happen to that sexy sister of yours…"

Standing bewildered, Wesley squeezed the lump of bills in his fist. He took several steps and ran a hand along the wall.

Everything was way out of control.

He'd fallen again. Guilty.

I'll never make it without meth.

All the voices were speaking at once. Tony's. Everett's. Cassidy's. His dad's. And the one called Vengeance.

But loudest of them all was the voice that told him he must not let anything happen to his sister. She was innocent. And he couldn't be responsible for something like that…not again.

And then he heard one last voice.

But this time it was his own.

And it was saying, "What do you want me to do?"

On the thirty-fourth floor, atop the Pittsburgh Mutual Bank building, the Upper Deck restaurant was bustling with people. Jacob had arranged for a long table by the window overlooking the Allegheny River and, just beyond it, PNC Park. Everett counted twelve people at the dinner table; Wesley would have made thirteen. His absence ate at Everett's stomach but couldn't delude the afterglow he enjoyed from his time spent with Karen that afternoon.

"Well, it looks like everyone's here except Wesley," Everett announced as a wiry waiter with jet-black hair and an all-business blond waitress refilled drinks and delivered salads and soups.

"I can't find him." Madison arrived late, anxiously punching at her cell phone.

"When did you talk to him last?" Jacob asked.

"A little before four. He's not in his room; at least he's not answering. I can't think where he would've gone."

"Maybe he wasn't hungry and went over early," Sarah said.

"That has to be it." Madison nodded. "He must not be getting a signal in there."

"I've gotten a signal in there all day." Everett leaned over and whispered to Karen. "I'm going to run over to his room. Okay?"

Karen's shoulders slumped. "What about dinner?"

"You know I can't eat much before a concert."

She reached beneath the table for his hand. "Okay, just hurry up and get back here. You want me to order you anything?"

"The salad's good for now." Everett excused himself, grabbed his bag, and made for the elevators.

Once in the lobby, he threw his coat on, hustled through the circular doors, and trotted across the busy crosswalk leading back to the hotel. Buildings from the city skyline cast long, sharp shadows over the concrete landscape, and the winter sun was disappearing in the west.

His phone vibrated in the back pocket of his jeans. "Yeah." He waved to some gawking fans.

"Uncle Everett…"

He stopped just outside the entrance to the Marriott. "Wesley?"

"I…need your help."

This can't be good. Everett looked up at the tall buildings. "Where are you?"

"I need you to pick me up. I'm out of dough, or I'd take a cab."

Everett looked at his watch. "Where are you?"

"I'm not really sure," he muttered. "Downtown somewhere. I have the address."

"Wes, are you stoned?"

Nothing.

"Have you been getting high?" Everett repeated.

"I can't explain anything now. The address is…you got a pen?"

Darn it, Wes! Why are you doing this? "Wait." The cold shook

Everett's bones as he found a pen and the corner of a program to write on. "Go ahead."

"Seven five two, East Exchange Street."

"Seven five two East Exchange." He scribbled it down.

"The numbers are above the front door."

"Where is this, Wes? Tell me what's going on—"

Click.

39

Karen had only been able to nibble at the greasy potato skins cooling on the large yellow platter in front of her. Beyond the floor-to-ceiling restaurant window, night had fallen, and myriad lights dotted the metropolis that surrounded them and the glistening river below.

She couldn't wait any longer. "Excuse me, guys." She pushed her chair back. "I'm going to find a quiet place to call Ev. See if he's found Wesley."

Her mom and dad glanced at each other. "You need to eat something, honey," Dad said.

With the entire calamity that had transpired since Karen met Everett, she battled the notion that her parents might think she'd made a mistake in marrying him.

You're being ridiculous. She strode through the maze of chatting waiters, buzzing tables, and clattering dishes and headed past the hostess stand.

Just outside the restaurant, near a bank of elevators, she plopped down on an oversized leather bench overlooking the city and punched in Everett's number. A slow-moving elderly couple wearing fancy clothes and sparkling jewelry left the restaurant and got on the elevator. No one else was around.

"Yeah." Everett picked up.

"Hey, hon, it's me. Did you find Wesley?"

"No."

"Well, where are you? Why didn't you—?"

"Listen," he said. "I'm picking him up."

"What?"

"He called and said he was someplace downtown. Needed a ride back. Said he was out of money."

That's so lame. She checked her watch. "How are you getting there?"

"I'm in a cab."

"Where is he?" She shifted uncomfortably, feeling herself getting riled. "What did he say?"

"Not much. East Exchange Street is the address. Don't worry, I'll be back in plenty of time for the show."

"I'm not worried about the show! What's going on, Ev?"

"I asked him if he was high, but he didn't answer. I couldn't tell—"

"This isn't right." She pounded the seat. "Darn it, Ev! This whole thing with him is just weird."

"Hon, I couldn't leave him—"

"Why not?" She stood and glared out the window at the narrow streets below. "He's a big boy. Tell him to walk back! That wouldn't kill him."

"Karen, it's gonna be okay—"

"I want you to turn around and come back here, right now." She crossed her arms and paced within a three-foot circle. "I don't like the sound of this."

"Babe." He paused. "I need to help him."

She smacked her hand against the cold window, dropped her arm, and stood there wanting to scream. But she knew Everett too well. There were a hundred reasons he needed to do this. And by the tone of his voice, nothing was going to change his mind.

Sitting in the backseat of a warm, worn-out taxi in a dilapidated section of downtown Pittsburgh, Everett closed his phone and put it back in his coat pocket. Across the street was the run-down orange brick building at 752 East Exchange Street. A stocky man with a bushy black beard, hairy arms, and thick glasses stood shivering in front of the out-of-date, two-story facility—savoring a cigarette. He wore green pants, a camouflage T-shirt, and red high-top tennis shoes.

A dirty, salt-covered Mazda parallel parked out front, and then its young, gum-chewing, do-rag-wearing driver dashed through the old-fashioned double-glass doors.

"You want to stay?" The Middle Eastern driver leaned his head back.

"Yes," Everett finally spoke. "I may go inside. If I do, I want you to wait for me. You understand?"

The man nodded. "I wait for you."

"Good." Everett sat for a few more minutes, hoping Wesley would come out. A skinny black woman exited and tried to light a smoke. When the wind wouldn't let her, Camouflage Man handed her his cigarette butt before he ducked back into the building.

"I'm going inside." Everett got out of the orange and black cab and bent over to face the dark-skinned man with the beard stubble and protruding Adam's apple. "Wait here. Okay?"

By the time Everett crossed the street, the black woman had her cigarette glowing orange. She threw the butt to the pavement and glared at Everett as he pulled open the heavy door. Once through the yellow, linoleum-floored vestibule, he yanked open another glass door, and the blare of machinery rattled him.

His way was blocked by a heavy young man seated behind a gray metal desk. Wearing a black Steelers stocking cap and hooded sweatshirt, the young man stared at Everett, not bothering to remove his headphones.

"I'm here to pick up someone," Everett said loudly.

The man gazed at him, lifted his right headphone, and squinted.

Everett leaned closer and yelled, "I'm here to pick up Wesley."

"Who?"

"Wesley!"

The man eyed a clipboard in front of him, nodded, then pointed behind him, with rings on every finger. "Straight back through the wood door, down the steps, all the way to the end of the hall."

"Thanks."

As Everett ambled amid the large machinery, men and women wearing hard hats and goggles steered forklifts stacked with flyers and brochures. Others climbed on loud, churning printing presses, adjusting controls and watching huge white sheets of paper feed into the mouths of sophisticated equipment.

Looks innocent enough.

His nose burned from the smell of chemicals. It must have been more than a hundred yards to the old, varnished wooden door the kid had pointed to. As Everett reached for the black metal knob, he took one last glimpse behind him. The eyes of half the workers in the place were glued to him. *Do they recognize me or what?* He opened the door.

The stairwell was dim and musty. He took several steps down and shut the door, closing off the noise behind him. But his ears were ringing. One dingy lightbulb, covered in cobwebs, lit the way. The place smelled like urine.

Could I have taken the wrong door? No. There were no others.

He stared down at the concrete block walls. "Lord, protect me," he whispered, starting down the steps.

He got to the landing and faced a long hallway with doors along the left and right, all sealed up, dark, and quiet. *Never used.* Bulbs hung every ten feet overhead, but only two were lit. Everett took a deep breath and began the march.

The smell of rotten eggs engulfed him as he approached the end of the hall. There, a lone door was open. He peered in. It was an enormous rectangular room with low ceilings, flickering overhead lights, and a dark concrete floor.

He passed through the doorway. The portion of the room he stepped into was empty, except for several dozen propane tanks that sat precariously around the border. As he walked toward the massive jumble of equipment, ceiling-high windows, and people at the far end of the room, Everett's throat became irritated, as if something was caught in it. He coughed hard but couldn't dislodge anything. His eyes watered at the pungent odor. Removing a blue bandana from his pocket, he covered his nose and mouth and walked farther.

As the scene seventy yards away came into focus, a rush of heat swept over him.

This is trouble.

He stopped and turned around. His exit was still clear. He swiveled back to face the enormous operation at the other end of the cavernous room.

Seven men, wearing dark rubber aprons, miniature gas masks, and elbow-high elastic gloves, worked test tubes, hoses, vats, pressure gauges, stoves, and propane tanks like MIT grads conducting breakthrough scientific research.

Several glanced up at him but continued their intensive work.

On four long tables, Everett saw coffee filters—hundreds of them—some containing a white, pasty substance; others, a dark red sludge. Beyond the tables were six to eight wooden pallets, lined up side by side on the floor, each piled shoulder-high with dozens of shrink-wrapped squares—eight by eight inches each—containing what Everett assumed was methamphetamine.

A bright red light danced on the floor in front of him. It darted to his legs, shrinking to the size of a dime. Then to his stomach. Looking up, Everett was temporarily blinded by a blaze of red from the far end of the room. He covered his eyes with both hands, the bandana still in one.

"Quite an operation, ain't it?" A young voice yelled from inside the lab. "You're lookin' at the biggest meth operation in the eastern United States…"

But all Everett could see were flashes of red coming from the laser beam attached to Badino's gun and occasional glimpses of the backlit lab and its occupants at the far end of the room.

"These gentlemen are cookin' ammonium nitrate. Soon it'll be anhydrous ammonia. And with that, we make the best meth in the whole dang country." He cackled. "Don't suppose you'd like to try a sample…"

Why are you telling me that? Fact is, you wouldn't if you thought I was gonna live very long.

"Where's Wesley?" Everett yelled, hoisting his arms up in front of him to block the laser.

"I don't believe we've been formally introduced—"

"I know who you are, Badino. I said, where's Wesley?"

"He just so happens to be right here." Finally, Tony lowered the gun.

Everett made out Wesley's silhouette as he entered through a door near the meth lab. The workers stopped what they were doing and watched.

"Are you all right, Wes?" Everett took several more steps forward.

"You stay right there, Jesus Man!" Tony screamed. "You try anything and I'll rip you to shreds with this forty-five. You know what forty-five hollow points will do, don't you?"

"I'm here for Wesley—that's all." Everett could barely breathe, he was so overcome by the stench of the chemicals. He wiped his eyes again with the bandana, taking several steps forward. "Just let me take him, and we'll be out of your way—"

"You shut your face!" Tony snarled. "We play by *my* rules." He raised the red dot to Everett's stomach. "Here's how it's gonna work, rock star. I'm gonna ask you right here and now—in front of all these witnesses—if you believe in God," Tony mocked, "if you believe Jesus Christ died for everybody, to forgive their sins and save 'em from hell. If you say you believe—and you insist on coddling your meaningless spiritual pipe dreams—then you'll die right here and now." Tony racked the slide of the gun, locking it back.

Everett shot a glance at the men standing frozen in and around the meth equipment.

"This is nothin' they haven't seen!" Tony blazed. "You say yes to God right now and at least one of these fat police bullets is gonna rip your chest open. And then you're gonna see how wrong you were about sweet baby Jesus."

The laser found Everett's face again, and his eyes teared and stung. He cupped his hands at his face, trying to see his nephew. "Wes, listen to me—"

"No! You listen to me," Wesley shouted. "Ever since David died, I've hated you and Aunt Karen. He worshiped you, and you couldn't care less about him."

Tony dropped the arm with the gun. "You tell it, Lester."

"I hated Aunt Karen 'cause she changed you from David's hero to a Jesus freak. I resented her for it."

Tony took several steps toward Everett, laughing hideously. "See all the good you did? You be sure to enjoy these last few words of honor, rock star. They're probably gonna be the last words you ever hear."

"Wes, I'm sorry I let you down—"

"Not me! David!"

"It was both of you. And it's my fault. Maybe you can try to understand, knowing what the drugs do. I was a mess. I didn't think of anyone but me. And I didn't remember anything. I'd give anything to go back in time."

"Don't be so sure." Wesley swayed, waving his arms. "I was at Twin Steams the night your dog died—"

"Yeah, but I slit her fat throat!" Tony roared.

"I didn't turf the place, either." Wesley shook both hands in the air. "Badino jumped into the driver's seat—"

Tony clobbered Wesley with the fist that held the gun.

Whack.

Everett heard Wesley's head crack and watched his nephew crumple to the ground, hands to his head, rolling back and forth.

"Leave him alone!" Everett yelled.

"Before this party ends." Tony caught his breath. "You should know, Lester, I delivered the brick—and the bloody sign."

"You're goin' to hell, Badino. You know that? It may not be today—"

"Shut up!" Tony lifted the gun with both hands and locked its sights on Everett's face. "They should have called it the Farewell Tour, because your ride is over. And your life with your lovely little bride is finished, too, just like mine ended when my Erica died believing in your pitiful concept of a God!"

Wesley muttered something while on all fours, trying to get back on his feet.

"Shut up!" Tony screamed. "You're weak, Wesley! It's time for this martyr to fish or cut bait."

"Leave him alone." Wesley made it to his feet. "He hasn't done anything wrong. Here, take your money back!"

Wesley flung something at Tony. It was bills. They fluttered like confetti. Tony took a savage swing at Wesley, gun in hand. He missed, and the red light flashed across the room.

Everett was leaning toward Tony, a hairbreadth away from charging, but he was too far away.

"He's innocent!" Wesley cried, falling to his knees.

"What's that to me?" Tony booted him in the shoulder with a flying kick.

"Let him go," Wesley wailed.

"No! Since you think he's so innocent, let's make this more interesting." Tony spun around, letting out a chilling laugh.

He waved the piece at Everett, the red light zigzagging off the walls. "Here's what we're gonna do. You say you believe and you're dead meat, Lester. But here's the kicker. If you *deny* Christ, you get to live. Free pass. Your whole family lives. You go on with your little dog and pony show, happily ever after."

"Where is my brother?" Everett demanded.

"You don't want to go there, Mr. DeathStroke."

"Where?"

"You'll never see him again! That good enough for you? Now I'm not finished." He grabbed Wesley by the coat collar, dragging him five feet and glaring at Everett. "If you deny Christ to save yourself, there's one hitch." Tony mashed the barrel of the gun in the back of Wesley's skull. "Your nephew here takes two behind the ear…and you watch the whole thing."

Tony shoved Wesley to the floor and examined his watch. "You got one minute!"

Everett raised his arms, blocked the light, and tried to see his nephew for what he knew would be the last time. "Wes—"

"I'm sorry, Uncle Everett!"

"Wes, if he kills me now, I want us to be together—"

"Gimme a break!" Tony boiled, steadying the .45 in front of him.

"I love you, Wes! I'm sorry about David. I wanted to make it right…" He caught a glimpse of movement in the lab. Several workers were talking, beginning to argue.

"I set you up!" Wesley screamed.

"I know." Everett nodded. "It's okay. I'm going to be fine. You tell Karen and Madison and everyone, I'm fine. Tell them, at the last minute God came near and that, even now, I can praise Him—'cause I'm goin' home."

"Time's up!" Tony bellowed. "What's it gonna be?"

Everett took an enormous breath and closed his eyes. "Jesus Christ is alive. He is my Lord and Savior—"

"Nooo!" Wesley screamed. "How can you do this?"

Everett's arms were outstretched at his sides. "He's in heaven, preparing a place for me…" Chills engulfed him, as did the sensation that he was floating. "He's right here with me, walking through this fire with me! Comforting me. Giving me—"

Poof.

Everett flinched, thinking it was Tony's gun. He opened his eyes in time to see a small mushroom cloud rolling toward the ceiling.

Is that normal?

Murmuring in the lab.

Poof! A bright yellow flash.

Then yelling.

Something's wrong.

And a blue flame creeping…racing…

There's confusion. Maybe I can—

Whiteout.

BOOM!

The gust of heat blew Everett backward twenty feet, the seat of his pants burning from the friction of the slide.

A firestorm of metal and glass pelted him like a hurricane. His soul quaked at the horrifying shrieks.

Gotta find Wesley. He tried to lift himself. *No way.* He collapsed amid the carnage.

"*Heeeelp!*"

He rolled his throbbing head toward the terror-pierced screams.

On fire.

People were on fire!

40

Wherever he was, Everett felt like he could sleep forever. Eyes closed, he winced at the sharpness in his throat and the riveting pain that squeezed his neck and back like a vice. His elbows burned.

Cold water.

But not now…just sleep.

He drifted.

Wesley was screaming. Tony pulled the trigger. Everything exploded…

"Get out!" His eyes flicked open. His body was drenched, and he was panting. He felt a cool washcloth ease his forehead back down on the pillow and wipe the perspiration away.

"It's okay, baby." Karen. Lovely Karen. They were together again. "It's okay."

Thank God.

He let his eyes close and his body go limp.

"Rest, sweetheart," he heard her whisper. "I'll be here."

And he hoped it wasn't a dream.

The next time he awoke, he squirmed on the same warm, matted sheets. It felt much later. Was it? He opened his eyes, and Karen's lovely face came into focus. Her long, shiny hair was combed perfectly. She wore glossy lipstick and a gleaming smile.

"Hey, honey," she whispered. "How do you feel?"

In the low light, he took in the dark wood of the hospital room, then found his wife's smile again. "Okay, now that I see you." His voice cracked.

Sitting beside the bed, she lifted a drink to his mouth. He sipped, cringed a bit as the water ran over what felt like glass in his throat, then drank some more.

"You've been out for quite a while." She set the cup aside. "We're at Mercy Hospital in Pittsburgh. There was an explosion—"

"And a fire."

She nodded. "You've got a concussion and inhaled a lot of smoke, but you're going to be fine. No broken bones."

"Wesley…"

"He's going to be fine, too. He had surgery in the burn unit, and everything's looking real good."

"Are you sure?" He tried to lean forward, but she eased him back down. "It looked bad…"

"I've been over there. His leg got the worst of it, but he's had some incredible doctors working on him. God's good."

"What about Tony?"

Her head tilted and the smile faded. "He's dead."

Everett frowned, looked away, and shook his head.

Eternal torment. He tried to picture hell but couldn't.

She reached for his hands and brought them close. Their faces were within inches of each other, and he drank in the smell of her perfume. "I'm glad you're here."

She kissed him warmly on the cheek. "I talked to Wesley."

Everett raised his eyebrows.

"After his surgery, he asked for me." She smiled. "He was glad you made it."

Everett closed his eyes and relaxed.

"He admitted selling David meth before his accident. That's been his nightmare—it's why he tried the suicide. He said he was sorry."

Everett wanted to hear more but was too tired to ask. He stared into her eyes, and she knew.

"He told me about the night Millie died." Karen's hand covered her quivering lips. "Ev, he cried. He apologized..."

Everett managed a blink and a smile. Then he cleared his throat. "So...where are we playing tonight?"

Karen burst with laughter and tears and draped her arms around Everett. Then their lips touched, and the kiss lasted a very long time.

41

Summer was in full bloom at Twin Streams, and Karen relished the slower pace. After the last unforgettable Living Water show at Cleveland's Gund Arena on February 27—when an estimated 3,000 of the 13,900 in attendance gave their lives to Christ—Everett, Gray, and the band took some much-needed time off before regrouping for the next record and possible tour.

Seated at the kitchen table wearing denim shorts and a wispy, white linen top, Karen was coming to the last few pages of Madison's scrapbook, which detailed the events of the Living Water tour. The kettle whistled, and Karen stood and walked to the stove to pour two cups of tea for her and Madi. Turning off the burner, she stepped back and gazed out the open window.

Beautiful. The trees were full, the breeze was blowing the long grass on the hillside, and the locust trees running along both sides of the pebbled driveway were loaded with clusters of white flowers.

Everett and Wesley, both in ragged jeans, T-shirts, and work boots, bent over the hood of a big John Deere. Wesley was practically inside the engine.

"I can't believe your brother." Karen chuckled. "He's amazing. I mean, Everett's never fixed a tractor in his life."

"He's smart," Madison said. "It's been so good for him here."

"We've loved having him. He's like a different person without the meth. You told me he was sensitive; he really is."

Madison stepped to the window and peered out. The wind nudged her frizzy hair. "You can't even see the burns, can you?"

"Nope. He looks good as new."

"They'll never forget that day, will they?"

Vividly, Karen recalled the phone conversation with the Pittsburgh police officer who notified her about the explosion. It made her stomach turn again.

"Everett still wakes up at night sometimes. Says he sees Tony—burning. He can even smell it…"

"I'm glad he's dead," Madison said. "I mean, out of Wesley's life."

Karen swept some crumbs from the toaster into her hand and brushed them into the sink.

"Thank you for letting him stay in the farmhouse." Madison nodded toward Wesley. "The fresh air, the work…he's a different person."

"You're welcome, sweetie." Karen sighed. "We've enjoyed getting to know him. It's been a blessing."

"He's still not sure about God…"

"No." Karen smiled. "But he's comfortable around us. And he does ask questions, once in a while."

"And he gets to watch you and Uncle Everett up close and personal."

"Oh, don't remind me! We're far from perfect."

"Your lives will minister to him more than anything."

Karen reached for the cups. "How's your mom?"

Madison stared out the window. "I wish Daddy could see her. He'd be proud."

"She's still off the alcohol?"

"Oh yeah, and staying busy with a zillion things. If she didn't, she'd go stir-crazy. She misses him so much."

"Hmm." Karen shook her head and handed Madison her tea. "That must be incredibly tough."

Karen sat back down at the table with her tea and flipped through the last pages of the scrapbook. When she came to the end, she stared at the clipping from *Newsweek* magazine dated April 21.

The spread featured a two-page photograph of Everett, wearing a Cleveland Indians cap, black sweatshirt, boots, and faded jeans. He was leaning against the huge silo out back, with acres of tilled farmland blurry in the background. The tiny caption beneath the photo read: The former rock star at his 218-acre farm in Bedford, NY.

Karen's eyes drifted to the headline and then the story.

Lester's Harvest
by Howard Newcomb

Never before—even at the very pinnacle of the DeathStroke phenomenon—has Everett Lester's name been more at the forefront of the world's stage. Good or bad, this guy is apparently always going to make news or, at least, be there when it happens.

The explosion that rocked three city blocks in a poor section of downtown Pittsburgh last January brought an abrupt end to one of the United States' most prolific methamphetamine labs. And Lester was there.

But that blast was only the start of something even more extraordinary: what appears to be the long overdue dismantling of the Mendazzo mob, the East Coast's incredibly powerful Mafia family, headed by New York's Frank "Machine Gun" Mendazzo and Dominic "Brain Picker" Badino. Both men are awaiting trial on multiple charges, including murder, kidnapping, extortion, racketeering, loan-sharking, bookmaking, money laundering, and narcotics violations.

Lester's brother, Eddie, was abducted from his home last January by henchmen believed to have been part of the Mendazzo crime family; he has yet to be found. Again, Everett Lester was the flame that lit the fuse leading to the explosive trials that threaten to obliterate the Mendazzo empire.

Finally, there was last winter's little-hyped Living Water tour, a free Christian concert led by Lester's new band (which still has no name) and scheduled to be performed live in thirty-six cities around the globe. Sounded innocent enough. In fact, entertainment experts predicted the event wouldn't even be picked up on radar by top music and media sources. How wrong they were.

As it turns out, Lester still has the Midas touch. At the six-month mark, the *Living Water* CD has shattered both Christian and secular sales records, netting the star megamillions in proceeds.

What will he do with the money? "It'll be used to pay for all the concert venues we rented for the tour," Lester told *Newsweek*. "It's not cheap to rent Madison Square Garden."

Religious or not, here's an interesting and, I'd even venture to say, inspiring fact: Approximately 65,000 people from New York to LA, from France to Thailand, committed their lives to God for the first time as a result of attending the Living Water concerts. Before you scoff, consider the fact that many who claim they got "born again" at Lester's free shows admit they showed up at the concerts unemployed, alcoholic, homeless, involved in marital infidelity, guilty of criminal activity, or addicted to drugs. Many of those say they left the shows with new faith, hope, and love—as well as the determination to start over again. That's good news.

And speaking of "good news," Lester and company handed out more than 270,000 free Bibles during the 36-city tour.

So listen, the next time you see Everett Lester on the streets of New York or at a Christian rock 'n' roll show, tell him thanks—thanks for being there. I know I will. —HN

When Karen closed the scrapbook, Madison was gone.

Easing up from the chair, she strolled to the window. The tractor was still there, but the guys weren't.

"Madison," she called, heading for the back door. "Ev…"

Pushing the screen door open and wandering onto the porch in her bare feet, she noticed Rosey frolicking in the backyard. Then her eyes drifted to Everett, kneeling by a small box in the grass, and Madison and Wesley, sprawled out beside him. "What're you guys doing?"

"You need to come here, honey." Everett chuckled, then whispered something to the others. "We've got a problem."

"Everett Lester," she meandered down the steps, "why do I have a feeling you're going to embarrass me or something?"

"No, really." He laughed again. "We've got a problem here. Madi and Wes are no help at all. I think you're the only one who can deal with this. Hurry up!"

Rosey was dancing about, and Madison and Wesley were beaming.

"What have you done?" Karen stopped five feet short of the group. "I suppose you're going to have some engine part in there that needs fixing…"

"Kneel down here." Everett reached out his hand. "And close your eyes."

Karen shot a glance upward, took a deep breath, sighed, and knelt in the thick, cool grass.

"Close 'em!" Everett insisted.

Pursing her lips, Karen shook her head and reluctantly complied.

She heard the lid of the box open. And then a tiny whimper—a squeak so irresistible, it forced her eyes open.

"Millie's mom had puppies," Everett exclaimed. "We've got another girl!"

Karen moaned softly as she reached into the box and scooped up the little collie, a brown and white cotton ball.

So soft…and fragile.

Karen's tears came out of nowhere, and when she could, as she squeezed the puppy with all she had, she let out a squeal. "I love her, Ev." She glanced at each one of them through watery eyes. "This means so much, that you'd do this…"

Everett and Madison smiled enormously.

And Wesley…Wesley was crying.

Dear friend,

I hope you enjoyed *Full Tilt*, book two in the Rock Star Chronicles.

The Bible says that Christ Himself is kind to ungrateful and evil men. Think of that! How radical is His love? This novel really forced me—and the characters in *Full Tilt*—to deal with the question, and challenge, of loving the unlovable. I hope you'll be faced with similar thought-provoking issues because of this story.

One of the things that intrigued me most in creating this tale was the remarkable and often disturbing information I discovered in my research about methamphetamines.

One of our nation's top news magazines quoted a spokesman for the Drug Enforcement Administration as saying, "Meth is the number one rural drug in America—absolutely, positively, end of question." An Associated Press story painted the problem as even more widespread: "Already known as a rural scourge, methamphetamine is becoming a monstrous problem in U.S. cities… It's everywhere."

Meth can be smoked, swallowed, injected, or snorted. Its ingredients are common household items, and the labs that produce it can fit in the trunk of a car. This relatively inexpensive, highly addictive drug acts as a powerful stimulant that actually overwhelms the brain, spinal cord, and central nervous system by interfering with normal neurotransmission.

In other words, meth kills.

Not only is meth dangerous to the people who use it, but many of its users commit brutal, senseless, alarming acts of negligence and violence. That's because meth makes users feel euphoric and invincible. They do things they would never do sober, unspeakable things.

Please, watch for the symptoms in those you love and

others in your community. Meth users range from elementary-age children to adults. They span all races and economic levels. Meth users tend to be rail thin and suffer from various skin and health conditions, including chronic itching, nasal perforations and nosebleeds, muscle cramping, scabs, rashes, constipation, and dental problems. You can find out more on the Internet, including where to get help.

It has been my pleasure to hear from so many readers around the world. Thanks for your support, and I thank God for drawing us closer to Him through the power of story.

Stay tuned for my next novel. Until then, you may visit my website: crestonmapes.com. If you'd like to contact me, you may do so via e-mail at creston@crestonmapes.com or regular mail: Creston Mapes, c/o Multnomah Publishers, 601 N. Larch Street, Sisters, Oregon 97759.

Warm regards,
Creston Mapes
Galatians 2:20

Reader's Guide

1. In *Full Tilt*, Everett Lester is a relatively new Christian. He feels a great deal of pressure to live up to the expectations of a watching world and a watching church. As a result, he has some of his tattoos removed, gets his hair cut, and even changes the way he dresses. What are your thoughts about this? (Check out 1 Corinthians 6:12, 19–20; 10:23–24 as food for thought.)

2. The Bible says a Christian should make sure he is never a "stumbling block" in the life of another person. This suggests that it is possible to take the liberty that is ours in Christ and to actually wound the conscience of one who is weaker. Read 1 Corinthians 8 and discuss the principles of Christian liberty and the importance of being aware of our weaker brothers and sisters.

3. Karen dreamed of having children but was devastated to learn that she was infertile. Have you ever had a dream that was dashed? What was it, and how did you cope with the disappointment? Discuss specific Scriptures that helped you, and talk about how God has since used that circumstance for good.

4. Eddie Lester claimed he would not believe in a God who would allow his son David to die, his marriage to falter, and his family to disintegrate. How should we act toward people who will not surrender to God based on negative life circumstances? What, if anything, can we say or do to lead them to Him?

5. Everett's father was a sinful man, and for a good part of his life,

Everett himself lived a sinful existence. Even when he became a Christian, Everett often felt guilty about his past sins and that God might be punishing him for his rebellious years. Does this go against the New Covenant and everything for which Jesus died on the cross? Read and discuss Psalm 51; Jeremiah 31:34; 33:8; 50:20; Micah 7:18–20; and Acts 10:43; 13:39.

6. Everett found true forgiveness when he gave his life to Christ. As a result, God removed Everett's sins as far as the east is from the west and remembers them no more. God does the same for us— but does that mean we will not experience the consequences of our sin? Why or why not? What are some of the consequences you can experience from living your life outside of God's plan?

7. A person might say, "I want to believe in God, but sometimes I doubt. Am I a Christian?" What is the answer to this question? Does God sympathize with our weaknesses, our questions, and our humanity? Read Hebrews 4:14–16 and discuss how it relates to your life—and Everett's.

8. A person may also ask, "Who goes to hell?" What is the answer? Discuss the reality of hell and who is destined for this awful place. Is it people who want to believe in Jesus Christ but sometimes have doubts? Or is hell reserved for those who reject God and refuse to bow in humility before Him and believe in His Son? What was Eddie's position on all of this?

9. In the heat of Karen and Everett's troubles, Everett elected to strike out against Tony Badino. What was wrong with this decision, and what dangers did he open himself up to by doing so? Take a closer look at what the Bible says about vengeance in Romans 12:17–21 and Hebrews 10:30.

10. Throughout *Full Tilt*, it would have been easy for Everett and Karen to give up on sharing God's love with Eddie and his family, using the excuse that they didn't want to cast their pearls before swine (Matthew 7:6). But Jesus also instructed us to love our enemies and bless those who curse us (Matthew 5:43–45). Study these Scriptures in context and discuss why they do not contradict one another. (Hint: One passage governs our personal dealings with our enemies; the other governs how we defend the gospel in the face of those who hate the truth.)

11. Karen reached out to Madison at a time when she herself was hurting. What was it about Karen that appealed to Madison? What does this tell us about those days when we're hurting and when we're not perfect? Does God love us any less? Can He still use us during those trying times? Ask God if there's someone He wants you to come alongside and minister to, as Karen did for Madison.

12. Wesley Lester was one frustrated and miserable individual. If you knew a person like Wesley, what could you do to try to help him? Would you do it? Why or why not? If you had a child like Wesley, what would you do differently?

13. Karen grew up a Christian, worked with her church, and was close to her parents. But when she married Everett and moved to New York, her life became full of danger, trials, and persecution. It would be understandable if, at times, she wanted her old life back. But there's something special about taking pleasure right where God has us. Are you in the midst of a bad situation? Share about it with your friends. Examine it in light of God's Word. And discuss what He may be doing to glorify His name in your difficult time.

14. Discuss the similarities between Wesley's life in *Full Tilt* and Judas's life in the New Testament. Satan often attempts to use bitterness in our lives to turn us against the world and even the church. Talk about the role bitterness played in the lives of Wesley and Judas. If there's any bitterness in your life, confess it and repent before it becomes poison in your system (read Ephesians 4:30–32; Hebrews 12:14–15).

15. The Bible teaches us that nothing should have "mastery" over us. That was the problem in the lives of Eddie, Sheila, and Wesley— each was addicted to some habitual sin. Even Everett formerly lived a life as a slave to sin. Read Romans 6:1–14 and 1 Peter 2:24, and discuss the fact that "he who has died [with Christ] is freed from sin." Are you applying this powerful truth in your life?

16. By the end of *Full Tilt*, Everett learns that he does not have to be someone he isn't in order to please God. Quite the contrary—he realizes the Lord made him the creative individual he is and that God allowed him to go through the dark afflictions he did for the specific purpose of being able to relate to others, comfort them, and lead them to Christ. Read 2 Corinthians 1:3–7 and discuss how these verses relate to your life.

Dark Star Excerpt

My name is Everett Lester. I've been asked by a New York publishing house to pen these memoirs. The experiences and encounters you're about to read are true, I can assure you of that because I was there for all of it. And the story isn't finished yet.

I am presently seated in a rather sterile courtroom in Miami-Dade County, Florida, at a long-awaited murder trial, portions of which are being shown on major network television.

It's a media circus.

As I write this, mobs of press people with phones, recorders, shoulder bags, and bulky equipment flood courtroom B-3. Presiding judge Henry Sprockett, who resembles Dick Van Dyke, has had to settle the movement along the perimeter of the wood-paneled courtroom several times already. The hype is nothing unusual for me—I only wish it came under different circumstances.

The prosecutor was having a field day with former DeathStroke drummer David Dibbs, who had occupied the witness stand for the past fifty minutes and was nervous as a cat.

Dibbs looked old now. White beard stubble showed distinctly on his tan face, and he repeatedly threw his stringy brown hair off his face, back behind his right ear.

No wonder Dibbs was antsy. The bulldog, county prosecutor Frank Dooley, had led witnesses to reveal incriminating evidence from the past about Dibbs himself. The drummer had been forced to confess that all of us in the band, except Ricky, used drugs in excess during the heyday of DeathStroke—including marijuana, Valium, hash, cocaine, and heroin.

In reality, however, Dibbs had nothing to worry about. After all, he wasn't the one on trial here.

I was.

The prosecutor was a piece of work. Thick, dark brown hair, not one out of place. Dark blue suit with a white hankie sticking up out of the breast pocket. His Southern drawl was as thick as Coca-Cola syrup; every word had at least two syllables.

"Your Honor," he said in response to an objection from my attorney. "It is my intention to make it crystal clear to you what kind of individual we are dealing with here. Everett Lester has been a troubled soul since the day he was born, and I am simply asking the witness, who has been a lifelong friend, to answer some specific questions about Mr. Lester's youth."

Judge Sprockett pinched at his protruding Adam's apple and overruled the objection.

"So then, Mr. Dibbs, is it true that the defendant, Everett Lester, was excessively violent as a boy?"

"I don't know if you would call it excessive. Boys are—"

"Mr. Dibbs," Dooley interrupted, "is it true that Everett Lester smashed mailboxes, shot guns at street signs and picture windows, set roads on fire, and tipped over cars with the help of friends?"

"Pellet guns. He used pellet guns, not real ones."

"That is not the question, Mr. Dibbs. Did Everett Lester destroy mailboxes, shoot at homes, set fires, and roll automobiles?"

"Well…yes."

"And is it true that when you and Everett Lester were boys, he was known to sell drugs?"

"At times, yes, but his family—"

"Steal cars?"

"Yes, but you need to—"

"Sleep around?"

"Yes."

"And beat the living tar out of other boys for even looking at him wrong?"

Shaking his head and looking down, as if he were being disciplined, my old best friend managed one more yes, and Dooley was done with him.

My attorney, Brian Boone, was a Harvard Law School graduate. He knew how to listen, and when he spoke, it counted. He stood in front of the witness stand, shirtsleeves rolled up.

"A great deal has been said about Everett Lester's character during this trial, and over the years in the media," Boone explained in his cross-examination. "Mr. Dibbs, you have known Everett since the two of you were children, growing up in the shadows of the smokestacks and refineries in Cleveland, Ohio. How would you describe him as a youth?"

Dibbs straightened his slight posture. "Everett was the best friend anyone could have. I…I was a nobody growing up. Unpopular. Unnoticed. But Everett didn't care what other people thought. He was real. He would do anything for me, back then and now. Deep inside, there's always been a big heart."

"What was his home life like?" Boone strolled in front of the jury box with his hand on the wood rail and his back to Dibbs.

"Tough." Dibbs shook his head. "Everett's old man, Vince, was a maniac. Heavy drinker. Hardly ever around. Disappeared for weeks, staying with other women. And he was strict. He would…hurt Everett. But his mother, Doris, worshiped his father. She didn't put a lot into the four kids, just lived for Vince."

"You used the word *maniac* to describe Vince Lester," Brian said. "That's a pretty strong word. What exactly made him a maniac in your eyes?"

"Everett's dad played head games. That's the best way I can describe it."

"What do you mean by that?"

"Everett could never measure up. Never. Every once in a while he would do something good, maybe score well on a test or help out around the house. Like he was reaching out to his parents, testing them to see what their response would be. I believe he tried to love his dad. But Vince would just tear him up."

"Can you give an example?"

"Yeah, for one, Vince would actually slap Everett, kind of jokingly. He would just slap his face again and again real quickly, laughing, egging him on. It would humiliate Everett, because Vince didn't care who was watching. In fact, sometimes I think he did stuff like that on purpose when others were watching, just to embarrass him. I know it frustrated Everett."

"How do you know?"

"He would turn red and hold back the tears. Sometimes it would outrage him, and he would be on the verge of striking his dad, but I never saw him do that. I think Vince would have killed him."

"To your knowledge," pressed Boone, "did Everett's father abuse him physically, beyond what you've told the court today?"

"Objection, Your Honor." Dooley groaned, standing up. "Does this really have relevance in the case we are here to deliberate?"

"I think it does. Overruled. Answer the question, Mr. Dibbs."

"I saw the slapping sessions quite often. And Everett would show up with bruises on his face and arms all the time. We all just assumed Vince was beating him, but I never discussed it with Everett. That's something I regret. He kept it all inside."

Dibbs was right. I felt like I was hemorrhaging inside back then. There was no such thing as love in my world, and I began to hate its concept. So I covered my bruised heart with a ready-to-fight exterior, and I covered the bruises on my arms with my first tattoos.

When former lead guitarist John Scoogs was called to the witness stand, Frank Dooley tugged at his cuffs and licked his chops.

Scoogs looked good. His black hair was still long and in a ponytail, and he was clean-shaven. He had put on a much-needed few pounds since I last saw him.

Dooley's questions covered much of the same ground he'd already been over with other key witnesses. But the next series of questions began to hit a nerve with me, Scoogs, and, I was sure, the jury.

"Mr. Scoogs." Dooley took his time, scanning his notes. "How well did you know Madam Endora Crystal—Everett Lester's personal psychic?"

"Fairly well," Scoogs said quietly. "She often traveled with the band, so she became a friend."

"I see." Dooley approached the witness stand. "Do you recall a stay at the Four Seasons Hotel in Charleston, West Virginia, in 1995 when a discussion ensued between Madam Endora and Everett when Endora attempted to convince Mr. Lester that she was hearing from his dead father?"

Closing his eyes as if searching the past, Scoogs said, "I…may recall something like that."

"Well, Mr. Scoogs, why don't you stretch your mind a bit and tell the court what you can recall, precisely, about that conversation." Dooley tugged at his sleeves.

Scoogs cleared his throat and looked squarely at the prosecutor. "When Endora caught up with us at our hotel in Charleston, I remember her saying to Everett something like, 'I've been walking around all week long with this energy.' After jockeying around for a long time, she finally got around to telling Everett that the spirit of his dead father had been trying to communicate with her."

Instead of a loud uproar, I heard a great deal of movement all at once in courtroom B-3. People shifting positions in their seats. Papers ruffling. Equipment moving.

"Was this good news or bad news, in Mr. Lester's opinion?" questioned Dooley.

"Bad. Everett's old man was taboo. Vince didn't want much to do with Everett when he was alive, and Everett definitely didn't want to communicate with Vince from the dead."

"So, what happened?" Dooley strolled toward the jury.

"Endora told Everett, 'I tried and tried to block Vince's spirit from coming through, but he persisted.' Finally, she gave in. She said Vince's spirit talked to her and made it completely clear that he was okay on the Other Side, and that he apologized to Everett."

"How did Everett Lester respond to this?"

Scoogs shrugged. "He was ticked."

"How ticked?"

Silence.

"I must remind you, Mr. Scoogs, that you are under oath, and perjury is a felony offense punishable up to—"

"You've got to understand: Endora had problems. She had some totally weird beliefs. I felt like she took advantage of Everett's drug addiction, trying to use him to accomplish her own agenda. She would—"

"Mr. Scoogs." Dooley stood on his toes. "Can you please just answer my question? Did he or did he not threaten Madam Endora Crystal's life?"

"He did, but he was bombed out of his mind at the time."

"What did he say to her? 'I'm going to stab you'? 'I'm going to shoot you'? What exactly was his threat?"

"He said something like, 'Endora, if you ever mention my father again…I'm gonna kill you…'" His voice trailed off with the last words.

Dooley raised both eyebrows and nodded a pompous "I told you so" to the jury. "I have no further questions for this witness."